Murder Outside the Lines

KRISTA DAVIS

KENSINGTON PUBLISHING CORP.

www.kensingtonbooks.com

KENSINGTON BOOKS are published by

Kensington Publishing Corp.
119 West 40th Street
New York, NY 10018

Special book excerpts or customized printings can also be created to fit specific needs. For details, write or phone the office of the Kensington Sales Manager: Kensington Publishing Corp., 119 West 40th Street, New York, NY 10018. Attn. Sales Department. Phone: 1-800-221-2647.

The K logo is a trademark of Kensington Publishing Corp.

ISBN-13: 978-1-4967-2464-9 (ebook)

ISBN-13: 978-1-4967-2463-2
First Kensington Trade Paperback Printing: October 2021

10 9 8 7 6 5 4 3 2 1

Printed in the United States of America

Praise for Krista Davis's Pen & Ink mysteries

"Clearly this book was written by a genius." —*Buzzfeed*

"The mystery is pleasantly twisty . . . [an] appealing cast of characters—whose backstories lend themselves nicely to future plots for this carefully crafted cozy series."—*Publishers Weekly*

"The theme was unique and new, the characters were relatable and entertaining, the mystery was unpredictable, and the writing was excellent." —*Night Owl Reviews*

"I love a book that immediately grabs my attention and this new debut series does that. This was a well-written and fast-paced whodunit that was delightfully entertaining. The author did a good job in presenting a murder mystery that had me immersed in all that was happening." —*Dru's Book Musings*

Praise for Krista Davis's *New York Times* Bestselling Domestic Diva series

"This satisfying entry in the series will appeal to readers who enjoy cozies with a cooking frame, like Diane Mott Davidson's Goldy Schulz mysteries." —*Booklist*

"Reader alert: Tasty descriptions may spark intense cupcake cravings." —*The Washington Post*

"Davis . . . again combines food and felonies in this tasty whodunit." —*Richmond Times-Dispatch*

"Loaded with atmosphere and charm." —*Library Journal*

"A mouthwatering mix of murder, mirth, and mayhem." —Mary Jane Maffini, author of *The Busy Woman's Guide to Murder*

"Raucous humor, affectionate characters, and delectable recipes highlight this unpredictable mystery that entertains during any season." —*Kings River Life* magazine

Krista Davis is the author of:

The Domestic Diva Mysteries

The Diva Cooks Up a Storm
The Diva Sweetens the Pie
The Diva Spices It Up
The Diva Serves Forbidden Fruit

The Pen & Ink Mysteries

Color Me Murder
The Coloring Crook
Murder Outside the Lines

To Anne Chamberlain,
who left us too soon but still lives in our hearts

ACKNOWLEDGMENTS

I am not a writer of historical mysteries, but this book was great fun to research. Some of you will be familiar with details of life in the 1800s, but many of the spooky facts were new to me. The details about duels, grave robbers, and President Lincoln are all reportedly true, if curious and somewhat gruesome. Any errors are, of course, my own. While there was a Russian ambassador residing in Washington at that time, the Sokolov family, O'Malley, and Bosworth are figments of my imagination, and to the best of my knowledge no such people ever lived. The story associated with them is pure fiction.

While the quote that begins this book is often attributed to Albert Einstein, the Albert Einstein Archives have informed me that he did not say it. Nevertheless, it's a great quote and is clever, no matter who thought of it.

Ghosts have been a personal interest of mine in recent years and I continue to research them. The Division of Perceptual Studies at the University of Virginia does exist and was founded in 1967. They collect and investigate data on the survival of consciousness after death. If you have an interest in that subject, you may be intrigued by the researchers' panel discussions, which can be found on YouTube.

You have to color outside the lines once in a while if you want to make your life a masterpiece.
—Unknown

CAST OF CHARACTERS

Florrie Fox—manager of Color Me Read and adult coloring book artist
  Peaches—her tabby cat with peach spots
  Frodo—her parents' golden retriever
Bob Turpin—employee of Color Me Read
John Maxwell—owner of Color Me Read
Jacquie Liebhaber—romance writer, a former Mrs. Maxwell
Harry—the skull
Roxie Oldfield Brimble—Jacquie's personal assistant
  Finley Brimble—Roxie's husband
  Cyril Oldfield—Roxie's father
Ellis Willoughby IV—private detective and friend of John Maxwell
Hilda Rattenhorst—psychic, author of ghost book
Coralue Throckmorton—neighbor
  Hayes Throckmorton—Coralue's son
  Gene Germain—Coralue's next-door neighbor
Manny Menz—bakery employee
  Kaya—Manny's girlfriend
Nola and Steve Boyle—owners of the Curiosities shop
The Sokolov family
  Irina—the mom
  Ivan—the son
  Natalia—the daughter
    O'Malley—Natalia's husband
    Henry Bosworth—killed in a duel by O'Malley

Chapter 1

The crate was delivered to Color Me Read around noon on Thursday. Most of our deliveries came to the bookstore from publishing companies and looked quite ordinary, compared with this box. Our regular delivery guy, Glen, plunked it on the checkout desk and wiped his hands against each other as if they were dirty.

"Glad to be done with this one," he said.

It was a busy morning and we were swamped. I was doing three things at once, and Bob Turpin, a fellow employee, was waiting behind me to ring up a sale. I didn't want to be rude to anyone. I hunched my shoulder up to hold the phone between my shoulder and my ear, thereby freeing up a hand. I counted out change for Coralue Throckmorton, who had bought a dozen of the Halloween coloring books I had drawn, and I was nodding to a woman who was asking if we carried birthday cards and wrapping paper.

Suddenly a scream screeched through the phone. It was so loud that everyone looked at me in shock. The line went dead.

"My word!" exclaimed Coralue. "Who were you talking to?"

"A salesperson. I hope she's okay." I thanked Coralue for her purchases. As she exited the store, I directed the other lady to the stationery display all the way down the hall near the back.

Then I called the salesperson who had been checking on an order we placed. A recording came on, telling me the hours of the business and to leave a message. "Hi. This is Florrie Fox at Color Me Read. I was abruptly disconnected after someone screamed. I just want to be sure everything is okay." I hung up.

Bob was examining the box. "This is so cool. It looks like something Indiana Jones would receive."

Frodo, my parents' golden retriever, who was staying with me while they were on a Rhine River cruise, sniffed the box. He growled at it and backed away.

Studying the square box, I realized that it was actually a wooden crate made of rough planks. It was about three feet wide on both sides and just over a foot high. It was addressed to Professor John Maxwell, who had sometimes been called a real-life Indiana Jones. Professor Maxwell owned Color Me Read but was far better known for his daring adventures in search of historical artifacts.

"Must be something exotic!" Bob turned it around, examining it. "But Frodo doesn't like it."

Glen held out an electronic tablet for me to sign. "I'm just glad I'm not hauling that thing around anymore."

I signed for the package. "I don't get it. It's just a box. Is it heavy?"

He looked at me coyly. "I'll check back with you when I bring your next delivery. Then we'll talk." Glen hurried out the door.

"Bwahahaha," sang Bob, holding up his hands and wiggling his fingers. "Everybody is into Halloween. What do you bet he's saying that to everyone to freak them out?"

"Probably. I'll take it up to the professor if you'll check on the lady looking for wrapping paper."

"Deal."

The phone rang. It was the salesperson to whom I'd been speaking on the phone when she screamed. "Florrie! Is everything all right there? That shriek was the most horrible thing I've ever heard. I was afraid someone was attacking you."

I laughed. "There must have been some kind of glitch on the line. I was afraid something terrible had happened to *you!*"

"That's too funny. I'm glad you're okay. Anyway, I tracked down your order and we're going to expedite it. Sorry about the delay."

I thanked her and hung up. What a crazy day.

I lifted the crate. Although it was made of wood, the package wasn't very heavy.

My sister, Veronica, had found removable vinyl stickers at a local store called Curiosities that we had applied to the stair risers. From the checkout area and the front door, it looked as if you were going to walk into another dimension. Bare limbs hung at the top of a bluish-green mist and odd glowing eyes made us feel they were watching us. Veronica and I had always loved Halloween, and the store showed it. We had placed pumpkins, lanterns, and faux candles among the books throughout the store. The candles and lanterns operated on batteries for safety but the wicks flickered and looked remarkably real.

Frodo followed me as I walked up to the third floor of the bookstore, where the professor kept an office. It was decorated with artifacts he had brought back from his many travels. Cyril Oldfield was seated comfortably across from Professor Maxwell.

"I hope I'm not interrupting," I said as I marched into the office carrying the crate.

The professor was a distinguished man with a well-trimmed graying beard. As an artist, I was fascinated by the shades of his beard. It was snow white along his sideburns and at the bottom of his chin, but his hair changed to black pepper on top of his head and along his jawline.

Heir to the Maxwell fortune, the professor was a member of one of the oldest families in Washington, DC. His roots ran deep in the community.

Cyril Oldfield had been one of the professor's students, and they remained good friends. Unlike the professor, Cyril was balding. A ring of fluffy white hair circled the back of his head. He wore a gray circle beard that was little more than a mustache and a chin patch. A loyal customer of Color Me Read, he visited the store quite often. He had been widowed for many years but had never remarried, which surprised me because he was quite charming. I put him close to fifty. He adjusted his wire-rimmed glasses and smiled at me. "Hi, Florrie."

"Good morning." I handed the box to the professor, who tilted his head. "What have we here? I wasn't expecting anything." He studied the exterior labels. "Most intriguing."

Cyril leaned forward for a better look. "Unexpected packages are always the most interesting."

The professor pulled out an ornate knife, which had surely come from one of his adventures, and used it to turn the screws that held the wood together. When he lifted the lid, I saw nothing but shredded newspaper. Someone had made certain the contents wouldn't shift or break in transit. The professor lifted the mass out of the box and gently separated the shreds to reveal a skull.

Chapter 2

I recoiled at the sight of the deep empty eye sockets and the eternal grin where his teeth clamped together. "Ugh."

"Well, well. Who might you be?" asked the professor. He gingerly set the skull on his desk.

Frodo yelped and galloped down the stairs.

Cyril chuckled, "That was quite a reaction. I thought dogs liked bones."

Undeterred, the professor pawed through the remaining shreds of newspaper. "Aha. A note and, what's this?" He blew at the bits of paper. They flew aside to reveal a dark mirror. He flapped open a small sheet of paper and read aloud.

> *My dearest Maxwell,*
>
> *I find myself in a dire situation, and I don't know if I shall manage to wangle my way out of this one. If I could, I would wrap myself up and crawl into this box to be posted along with Harry's skull. I apologize for burdening you with Harry, but you were the only person I could think of who would treasure him the way I would. I plan to collect him in the near future, should I survive this nightmare, and at that time we*

*shall share a drink to life and return Harry to his right-
ful place. If news of my demise should reach you, then
have that drink for me and follow your heart. I hope
Harry won't be too much trouble.*

Ellis Willoughby IV

To be honest, I was glad I didn't have friends who would
send me a human skull. I frowned at it.

The professor, on the other hand, beamed. He smiled
broadly. "I do hope Ellis makes it. He's a delightful fellow but
inclined to take too many risks." He picked up the packaging.
"Looks like it was posted right here in town."

Cyril frowned. "I don't like the sound of that. Ellis had
better be careful. Maybe I should give him a call to see if he
needs our assistance."

The professor picked up Harry, the skull, and held it in the
air. "What do you suppose Harry's surname is? And just what
makes him so special?"

I didn't want to be rude, but, after all, that skull had been
someone! Presumably someone named Harry. "Um, is it even
legal to have a human skull? Shouldn't it, er, he be buried?"

"The last time I checked, only three states had laws regarding the possession of human skulls. I imagine Ellis intends
to bury or inter Harry's skull. After all, he mentions something about returning him to his rightful place. Or perhaps he
was stolen from a museum," he mused.

"Why would anyone steal a skull?"

The professor looked at me in surprise. "Many famous
people have been buried in unmarked spots so people won't
dig them up. It depends on who Harry was. He may have had
political enemies. Or he might have been a famous actor or
musician." He eyed the skull.

In a teasing tone, Cyril added, "Or he could have been in-
famous, a murderer, possibly."

I shivered. "I hope not! Poor Harry. I wonder what happened to him. Can you tell the age of a skull? Is it ancient or"—I sought a nice way to say it—"of recent vintage?"

"You can't say by looking at them, but archeologists have been radiocarbon dating them for some time. However, if Ellis knew Harry, then one could assume he is a contemporary of ours."

Now I was thoroughly grossed out. I shuddered. I couldn't imagine having to retrieve the skull of a friend. Ick! I left the professor and Cyril to their musings. I was far too timid to join the professor on one of his adventures, let alone procure a skull and ship it to someone. As I headed downstairs, Professor Goldblum, a short man with a shiny balding head and a winning grin, passed me. "You're in for a surprise," I said to him.

His small eyes widened with excitement and he picked up his pace.

I continued down the stairs but paused on the landing, where Frodo had taken refuge. As I reassured him, Cyril's son-in-law, Finley Brimble, caught my eye.

A dedicated bibliophile who made a living dealing in rare books, Finley haunted bookstores. We had a room on the second floor devoted to used books, and we also kept a section of rare books in the historical and philosophical book room.

Finley was exceedingly cordial and had made friends with our employees. True, his wife had a connection to Color Me Read, which might account for his friendliness, but I'd heard other people rave about his genial character as well.

His wife, Roxie Oldfield Brimble, came down the stairs behind me. She bent to stroke Frodo, and said sotto voce, "Florrie, don't ever marry anyone who is drop-dead handsome."

She watched as a young woman moved through the store with her eyes glued to Finley. You would have thought he was a rock star from the way she shadowed him.

"Did you know your dad is upstairs with the professor?" I asked.

She nodded. "We had breakfast with him and walked over here after."

Roxie was what my mother called pleasingly plump. She had a curvy figure and always seemed to be going on a new diet. While she worried about her weight, I didn't think anyone else did. Roxie was always smiling. She was one of those lovely people who could be counted on to pitch in and lend a hand. Without doubt, she was one of the most fun people I knew. It seemed as though a laugh perched on her lips, ready to bubble out at any time. Except for now. I could feel her annoyance with the woman.

If Finley noticed that he was being watched, he didn't show it in any way. In fact, he didn't even turn to look at the woman.

Finley was handsome in a glamorous way that reminded me of movie stars in the 1950s. He dressed impeccably, even when he was being casual, like today. He wore lush trousers the color of burnt caramel. His cable-knit sweater was a shade lighter but in the same family. He wasn't wearing a shirt underneath. A tan-and-chocolate-brown–plaid scarf with a fine line of cranberry mixed in hung around his neck, adding a smart twist. He could have walked straight out of a Ralph Lauren advertisement. The color of his hair reminded me of pecans. He wore it short and parted on the right. And when he smiled, as he did at that very moment, long dimples appeared.

The woman smiled, too, at the mere sight of them. She had a slight frame and a long face. If I had to guess, I would have said she was a bottle blonde.

"Honestly!" Roxie whispered. "She's an adult. You'd think she would know better than to follow a man around. A married man at that! And the nerve of fawning over him in front of me!"

"She seems fixated on him. Maybe she doesn't know that he's married."

"He's wearing a wedding band, for heaven's sake." Roxie trotted down the stairs, marched directly toward the woman, and dropped a pen at her feet.

The woman bent to pick it up and handed it to Roxie with a smile. I suspected that meant the woman didn't know Finley was married. Or at least she didn't realize that Roxie was his wife. It would have taken some real grit to smile at Roxie if she knew.

I reached the main floor, picked up a box of new books, and got to work arranging a table display of books about ghosts.

Finley thumbed through one of my Halloween coloring books. He looked up and gazed at the bookstore ceiling. In an oh-so-romantic English accent, he asked, "Did you just see something, Florrie?"

I hadn't noticed anything unusual.

"There was a disturbance in the air, as though something flew through overhead," he said, still looking up.

Bob was right. It was the season of ghosts, vampires, and pranks. I thought Finley might be joking. I didn't know him very well. Finley ran with an elite and moneyed crowd. If he hadn't been married to Roxie or wasn't a bibliophile who lingered in the store, our paths probably wouldn't have crossed.

"I'll take this one, please," he said, clutching my coloring book.

As an adult coloring book artist, I always found it a thrill when someone selected one of my books. Even though I managed the Color Me Read bookstore by day, I made a concerted effort not to steer people to *my* coloring books. It would be entirely too self-serving. There was also the fact that I was unquestionably introverted. Promoting myself and my coloring books was as unappealing to me as jumping off a cliff attached to a bungee cord. I was a "curl up by the fire with a good mystery" kind of person.

"Do you also sell pencils for coloring?" he asked.

"We do." I led him to the coloring book section of the store. "Let me know if you need any help."

I returned to my task arranging books. Moments later, out of the corner of my eye, I watched as Bob rang up Finley's sale. They laughed together about something. As far as I could tell, Finley remained oblivious to the woman who was following him.

She did an excellent job of darting behind him so that he wouldn't notice her. She quickly made a pretense of examining an audio book display, thus neatly hiding from his line of vision while still watching him.

Finley took his purchase and smiled sweetly at Roxie. "Ready to go?" he asked.

Roxie threw me a can-you-believe-her glance, and the two of them walked out together.

The woman watched them leave.

"May I help you?" I asked her.

She blushed as though she'd been caught ogling Finley. "No, thank you. I'm enjoying browsing."

There was no obligation to make a purchase, of course. We had plenty of browsers. How else would people find things they wanted or didn't know they needed? I nodded at her. "Let us know if we can be of assistance."

Bob ambled over to me and sighed. "I wish I had Finley's style. Maybe I should buy some new clothes. Would that make me more dashing?"

His drab stone-gray T-shirt bore the words *Book Nerd* across an ample pizza belly. His dark brown hair was adequately cut but did nothing to enhance his looks. It lay flat and limp on his round head, making me think of Charlie Brown. "You're wonderful just the way you are," I assured him. I was being honest. Bob was genuinely nice and he looked it.

"Good grief, Florrie. You sound like my mother." He mimicked her in a high pitch: "Some nice girl will come along and appreciate you one day." His mouth twisted in a dissatisfied grimace. "I'd rather not wait until I'm Professor Maxwell's age."

In exceedingly poor timing, Professor Maxwell happened to be walking down the stairs. "Wait for what?" he asked.

Poor Bob's eyes widened in panic.

I tried to rescue him. "To meet a girl."

The professor gazed at him. "I quite agree, Bob. I was married and divorced by the time I was your age."

The professor had been kind enough to let me live in the carriage house behind the Maxwell mansion. Due to the unfortunate and untimely death of his only nephew, I had learned a good bit about the professor and his family.

He had been married quite young to a woman of whom his parents did not approve. They divorced after a year. He subsequently married Jacquie Liebhaber, a well-known romance novelist. They had one child, Caroline, who was kidnapped from a birthday party and never seen again. The stress and horror of the kidnapping had devastated them and led to their divorce. Caroline had never been found. The professor married a third time, but rumor had it that his wife considered herself European royalty and had departed in short order.

In the strange way that the world works, Jacquie found herself in a personal crisis and sought out the professor, whom she knew she could trust. Their relationship blossomed again. Or, perhaps, as some suggested, it had never really died.

In any event, the professor had a good deal of personal knowledge about women and marriage.

"Finley Brimble was just here," I explained to the professor.

"Ah. Now I understand. He's rather dapper." The professor eyed Bob. "Jacquie enjoys matchmaking. Perhaps you should speak with her. I believe she'll be here this afternoon."

Scowling, he picked up a copy of a book about ghosts. "Such nonsense," he said. "Do you expect to sell a lot of these?"

"Of course. People love ghost stories. Besides, it's the season!"

The professor shot me a sideways look. "Surely you don't believe in ghosts?"

To be honest, I had never given them much thought. "I can't say that I've ever met a ghost. But I do enjoy reading about them."

"Mmm," the professor murmured. "People enjoy the momentary fright because they know all will turn out well in the end"—he smiled at me—"because we all know ghosts are not real. Florrie, I have placed Harry on a shelf in my office and closed the door. I trust no one will even realize that he's here."

He left the store without inquiring about the reading scheduled later that day. It amused me that Professor Maxwell loved books and took pride in owning a bookstore but was completely oblivious to the business of running one. He used the room on the third floor as his office, but usually spent his time perusing old maps and going through obscure ancient documents in his quest to find relics of historic importance, leaving me to do everything from ordering stock to signing paychecks. A few times a year he packed up and headed for exotic, off-the-beaten-path locations to search for items of significance while the rest of us kept everything on track at home.

I checked my watch. "We probably ought to start bringing up the chairs for Hilda Rattenhorst's reading."

Bob nodded and headed down the hallway toward the basement, with Frodo tagging along. Meanwhile, I fetched two extra boxes of Hilda's book, *Spooktacular Ghost Stories*, opened them, and stacked the books behind the checkout counter. There had been a good bit of interest in the books we had set up on a table near the entrance, so with any luck, we would sell out.

In between helping customers, I arranged the folding chairs that Bob carried into the parlor, where most readings were held. Color Me Read was located in a building that had once been someone's home. The large parlor was surely where a family had entertained guests, and it remained well suited to that task.

It featured a lovely old fireplace, which we used on snowy winter days. Newspapers from all over the world hung on a custom-built rack that filled one wall. To make room for readings, we shoved back the cushy leather furniture that was reminiscent of a fine home library. When we didn't have a reading planned, regular patrons often met in the parlor. Many of them were retired professors who helped themselves to coffee and held fascinating discussions with their cronies.

At four in the afternoon, I headed down the street to a bakery, which had prepared goodies for the reading.

In spite of the sunny day, the crisp air of fall chilled me to the core as I left for the bakery. Sweater weather had definitely arrived. A strong wind blew, sending red and gold leaves fluttering past me. The scent of smoke from a fireplace lingered in the air.

Manny Menz, an employee of the bakery, had my order ready. A small man in his early twenties, he had masses of chestnut brown hair, which spilled onto his forehead and swept to each side as though it were parted in the middle intentionally. He hadn't shaved in a day or two, a popular look that only succeeded in making him appear scruffy. He handed me bags loaded with goodies. "I guess you heard about Glen?"

"Glen? The delivery guy?"

"Apparently, on his route this morning, a snake appeared in his truck and bit him!"

Chapter 3

I was horrified. Wait a minute, a snake in October? Wasn't it getting too cold for snakes? "Ha, ha," I said drolly.

"For real, Florrie." Manny gazed at me earnestly. "They think the snake was being shipped or had crawled into a package and somehow managed to get loose inside his truck."

"Is he okay?"

"Last I heard he was in the hospital and they had quarantined his truck in a warehouse to see if they could find the snake. We have a delivery on board that truck but they're not delivering anything that's in it until they've caught the snake."

I wished the story didn't sound plausible. "I'm so sorry to hear that. It must have been very scary for him. I'd have had heart failure on the spot."

"Not me." Manny puffed up his scrawny chest. "I'd have grabbed that snake and let him know who was boss. I ain't afraid of a snake."

"Keep us posted. If he's still in the hospital tomorrow, I'd like to go by to see him." Loaded down with doughnuts decorated as jack-o'-lanterns, cookies in the shapes of ghosts, and spice cupcakes with orange frosting with squiggly ghosts arising from each, I left the store and walked past Federal-style buildings with show windows on the first floors. Stores not only had display windows packed with spooky merchandise but had decorated their exteriors as well.

Located in the popular Georgetown section of Washington, DC, the bookstore was in a perfect location for spooky tales. Founded in 1751, Georgetown was the oldest neighborhood in Washington. The red brick sidewalks and old streets had seen a lot of joy and misery. Color Me Read occupied a three-story building with a balcony across the second floor. A sandwich board on the sidewalk advertised Hilda Rattenhorst's reading today. Faux cobwebs hung on the front stairs, books about ghosts were clustered in the show windows around grimacing pumpkins, and on our balcony, two life-size glow-in-the-dark skeletons leered at passersby.

My sister, Veronica, saw me through the glass door and hurried to open it for me. "Florrie! How many doughnuts did you buy?"

The scent of hot cider wafted out to me. If you asked me, as much as I liked the other seasons, fall had the best smells and flavors. While I was gone, Veronica and Bob had started a fire, which crackled softly in the parlor fireplace.

"I thought I'd better stock up. *Whooooo* knows how many people might attend?"

Veronica sighed at my poor imitation of an owl. She loved Halloween and was always willing to dress up but she readily dismissed ghosts as "supernatural nonsense."

"What are you doing here on your day off?" I asked.

She gave me a sheepish look. "I wanted to hear Hilda. It's so interesting that she's a psychic. Do you think she can really communicate with the dead?"

I shrugged. "I know I can't." Our laid-back parents had raised us to be open to all possibilities, with the exception of the supernatural. They were adamant that ghosts were fun but imaginary.

"I saw Harry the skull." Veronica wrinkled her nose. "I hope the professor finds a new home for him soon. It's so creepy having him in the store."

Veronica and I got along fairly well for sisters who were exact opposites. While I was happy to stay home curled up with my cat and draw my coloring books, Veronica loved to go out and was usually the life of the party. She was positively willowy, with blond hair and athletic ability. I was five feet two inches if I cheated and stretched, had mousy brown hair, and looked nothing like her at all. Still, when she needed a job, I had offered her one at the bookstore. She had never been a big reader, but it turned out she had a gift for social media and had done wonders for the store's popularity. It had become a true neighborhood hub.

When I entered the parlor where the reading would take place, Roxie, Jacquie's personal assistant, was arranging silver tea and coffee samovars, a definite step up from our usual modern dispensers.

"Aren't they beautiful?" she asked. "Jacquie insisted that we use these. They're Maxwell family antiques."

She helped me arrange the cupcakes, doughnuts, and cookies on ornate silver platters lined with elegant, yet slightly creepy, black lace doilies.

Frodo eyed the goodies on the table. "This is why I don't believe in levitation," I said to Roxie. "If the power of the mind could lift things, then cupcakes would be floating through the air and into Frodo's mouth right this minute."

Roxie laughed and blew her bangs out of her face. It didn't help much. Her thick baby blond hair was cut in layers that I assumed were intended to give her a tousled look. It fell below her shoulders in loose curls. If I could have looked like someone else, I would have chosen Roxie. Her blue eyes were kind, and when she smiled, her prominent cheekbones were adorable.

Roxie whispered, "I'm not sure fancy silver samovars are the right thing for a psychic, but Jacquie loves using them."

"Maybe they're the kind of antiques that will summon someone from the past," I teased.

Jacquie Liebhaber heard me as she whipped into the room with boxes of more cupcakes. "We can hope that's the case. Wouldn't it be wonderful if that happened?" She looked at the doughnuts and laughed. "Good thing I didn't get cupcakes with jack-o'-lanterns on them!"

Like most authors, Jacquie loved bookstores and often recommended we invite her friends to speak about their books. I hadn't known her personally until she turned up unexpectedly about six months before and rekindled her relationship with the professor.

They suited each other. John was an explorer, fascinated by history and its mysteries. Jacquie was as romantic as the books she wrote. A graying blonde, Jacquie favored crisp white shirts with upturned collars and amazing bold jewelry hanging against her décolleté.

She checked her watch. "Is everything ready? Have we forgotten anything?"

"We're ready to roll," I said.

Jacquie frowned. "Shouldn't Hilda be here by now?"

"Maybe something delayed her." Roxie headed for the checkout desk. Jacquie and I followed.

"Veronica, has Hilda called?" I asked.

"No." She glanced over at the answering machine. "No messages. Is something wrong?"

I shook my head. "I'm sure she'll be along shortly, Jacquie. It's still early. We have plenty of time."

"I hope she didn't forget. She was supposed to meet me here before the reading so we would have time . . . to talk." Jacquie pulled out her phone. "Maybe I'd better check." She tapped the screen several times and held the phone up to her ear. "It rolled over to voice mail."

Roxie blurted, "The gift! The gift you wanted to give Hilda is upstairs in the professor's office."

"I'll run up and get it." Jacquie started up the stairs.

When she was out of earshot, I glanced at Roxie. "Did you do that on purpose?"

"Sort of. Don't get me wrong. Jacquie's great! I love being her assistant. But after everything she's been through, she panics easily when things don't happen according to schedule."

"Why did she want Hilda to be here so early?"

Roxie sighed. "Don't tell the professor. Jacquie wants to see if Hilda can reach Caroline. She's hoping for a private session before everything gets started."

My heart broke for Jacquie. "I won't say a thing." I stepped outside on the stair landing and gazed up and down the street. Darkness had fallen and the wonderful ghastly, ghostly, ghoulish symbols of the season had lit up in store windows.

A woman wrapped in a shawl caught my attention. She weaved and almost stumbled in her hurry. As she drew closer, I realized that the woman was Hilda Rattenhorst.

I rushed down the steps, worried that she was ill or possibly intoxicated. I hoped that wasn't the case! "Hilda? Are you all right?"

"Florrie!" She grabbed hold of me like her fingers were talons. Her breath came hard. "I saw a murder."

Chapter 4

"A murder?" I screeched. I was certain I had heard her correctly. "Come inside. Have you called the police?"

She kept her head down. "No, no. Off the street. I have to get off the street. Quickly, now!"

Maybe I was too jaded, but I wondered if she was putting on some kind of act to promote her book. It was a little premature, since I was the only audience at this point.

I followed her up the stairs and into the bookstore.

"Jacquie!" she cried, holding her arms out. "You won't believe what I've been through."

Jacquie, who was at least a head taller than Hilda, wrapped an arm around her. In a calm and reassuring tone, she said, "You must sit down and catch your breath."

Hilda had worn a dress that was the ominously dark red of dried blood. Her shawl was crocheted of black yarn dotted with threads of silver. I did a double take when I realized that the crochet pattern consisted of hundreds of lacy skulls.

"Hilda said she saw a murder," I whispered softly.

Jacquie's eyes went wide and she gazed at me in shock. "Is that true?" she asked Hilda.

"I did!"

"Right out on the street? Did you call the police?" asked Roxie.

Hilda's eyes seemed to seek answers in the ceiling. "I think I saw the murder in my head."

Huh? Maybe there wasn't a murder at all?

"It was like watching it on a TV show, except I was the only one who could see it."

Jacquie's eyes met mine. I wondered if she was having the same sort of doubts that I had.

"I shouldn't have gone down that street," said Hilda. "But I was compelled to do it. I was drawn there, like I didn't have any options. I'm not sure I could have turned around if I had wanted to."

"What street?" asked Jacquie.

"You see, it wasn't so much the murder itself as the body. I saw a foot."

"A foot?" squawked Veronica. "Just a hacked-off foot?"

"No," breathed Hilda. She stared at Veronica as though she didn't see her. "Well, I don't really know. It was in a rug."

Bob brought Hilda a cup of hot cider and handed it to her.

"Thank you, dear. Oh my! I must pull myself together. It was just so unexpected."

"Maybe it was a Halloween decoration," Jacquie said very kindly.

"Most certainly not," Hilda snapped, sounding offended by the suggestion.

I tried to phrase my question as kindly as I could. She was our guest and I didn't want to insult her. "Was the foot in the rug something you saw in a vision or was it actually a physical foot in a physical rug?"

"What's the difference?" she asked. "I saw it. Some person's foot is rolled up in a rug!"

"You said you saw the murder in your head. Can you identify the killer?" I asked.

Hilda gazed at me briefly. She closed her eyes and shook her head. "No. It all happened so fast. It was as though there was a filmy curtain. I just could see it."

"I'm calling the police," said Veronica.

Jacquie shook her head ever so slightly. "Florrie, do you think Sergeant Jonquille might come over?"

I stepped behind the checkout counter and phoned my boyfriend, Sergeant Eric Jonquille. If I recalled correctly, he was working in Georgetown anyway, so he was probably available to pay us a visit.

Happily, he was close by. I had met Eric by chance when he responded to a 911 call. To this day I couldn't believe my good fortune. I knew I was out of his league the moment I first saw him. Guys with gently billowing honey-colored curls and startling blue eyes dated people like my sister, not me. But for some extraordinarily lucky reason, he had been just as smitten with me as I was with him. I smiled just thinking about it. It must be that mysterious chemistry everyone talked about.

In a matter of minutes, he walked through the door. We had been dating for almost six months but my heart still beat a little bit faster whenever Eric walked into a room.

He planted a quick kiss on my cheek. "What's up?"

I led him to Hilda. "Ms. Rattenhorst thinks she saw"—I wasn't quite sure what she had actually seen—"something unusual."

Eric was all business. "Sergeant Jonquille, Ms. Rattenhorst. What exactly did you see?"

"A foot. It was definitely a foot."

To his credit, Eric didn't treat her like she was foolish. He was polite and serious. "Where was this foot?"

"It was sticking out of the end of a rolled-up carpet."

Eric's expression became more serious. "Only one foot?"

"Oh! I see what you mean. They usually come in twos." She thought for a moment. "No, no. I only saw one foot."

"When you say foot, do you mean a naked foot? No sock or shoe on it?"

"Yes, precisely. That's it!" She whispered to Jacquie, "He's marvelous. It's like he saw it himself."

"Did it appear to be a man's foot or a woman's foot?"

"Honey, I was so taken aback that I ran. Like the wind, I ran! All I know is that it was a foot with toes."

"Hilda, it must have been a huge shock." Jacquie spoke in a comforting tone.

"If you don't mind, I have just one more question for now," said Eric. "Where exactly did you see this foot in the rolled-up carpet?"

"It was in a recessed doorway, on the block where Annie Metcalf gives massages."

Eric remained remarkably calm in the face of such an ambiguous response. "And that would be on which street?"

Hilda gazed at him with a completely bewildered expression. "How should I know that?"

Not the most impressive answer. "I know where it is," I said.

"You get massages?" asked Veronica.

"No, but I've delivered books to Annie." In an effort to remain competitive in the face of home deliveries by big companies, we offered same-day delivery within the Georgetown neighborhood.

"Would you mind showing me?" asked Eric.

I tried to suppress a grin. It would be nice to take a walk with him.

Jacquie piped up. "You two go. We have well over an hour before the reading is supposed to start. Assuming Hilda is still up for it?"

"Oh my, yes." Hilda smoothed back masses of curly dark chocolate hair that bushed around her shoulders. "What is it they say? The show must go on. A cup of coffee and I'll be on my game again. I hope. Would the professor have a splash of bourbon in his office?" she inquired.

As Eric and I left Color Me Read, it felt as though we were going the wrong way. Most people were walking into the bookstore.

"Looks like you'll have a good turnout tonight." Eric slipped his hand into mine.

We reached the end of the block and turned left. "'Tis the season for things that go bump in the night. Hilda's stories are usually based in the greater Washington, DC, area, so locals love to read them. They're early. But that means more sales for us if they browse before Hilda begins."

"I was planning to poke my head in."

"You're into ghosts?" I asked.

"It's not like I'm obsessed with ghosts, but I like a good ghost story. And there is something intriguing about the dichotomy between the lack of any scientific proof and the remarkable number of people around the world who claim to have seen them."

"Have you seen one?" I asked. We walked at a good pace under the streetlights. I glanced up at him.

"Maybe. I'll tell you about it sometime."

We turned right and walked one more block. "This is it. The house with the plaque on the door is where Annie lives."

"Thanks for showing me. I want you to head back to the store now for your own safety."

"I hardly think a fake foot is going to be dangerous."

"I wouldn't have brought you along if I thought there was anything to Hilda's story, but I can't take that chance. I'll see you later, okay?"

I understood, but I was curious and not a bit afraid. Hilda

had been so scattered in the way she described it all that I figured it was something silly. But it was probably breaking every police rule for me to be there. I watched him while I took a few steps backward.

He produced a strong flashlight and walked calmly along the street. He stopped at one point and directed the flashlight into what I assumed was a recessed entryway to a house. He continued walking and then returned to the recessed area.

I dared to sneak toward him. The alcove was unremarkable. The house was built of red brick. A concrete extension of the sidewalk ran about fifteen feet to a dark walnut door. There was no sign of a rug or a foot.

"You're not very good at taking directions," Eric muttered.

"You hadn't noticed that before?" I teased.

Eric aimed the flashlight at the dove-gray concrete sidewalk. "No sign of blood. Fresh blood—or dried blood, for that matter—would show up on this concrete. If anyone tried to scrub it off, it would be smeared and wet."

"What do you think she saw?"

"It's hard to tell. I'll have to investigate further, but there's certainly no outward sign of anything untoward."

"Jacquie probably had the right idea. I bet it was a Halloween decoration," I said.

"Possibly. Or part of a costume or other Halloween gag. Some of those pliable masks and body parts look amazingly real. Still, I'll look into it and make sure we patrol around here just in case anything is going on. Now if you'll excuse me, I really should knock on this door."

"Okay, okay. I'm leaving." I walked away but looked back when I reached the end of the block. I couldn't see him, but I could hear him knocking on the door.

The truth was that Georgetown had seen agony, turbulence, bliss, and elegance over the centuries. Countless people had died there, probably some on the very street where I now walked. By any measure, if ghosts were real, they surely abounded here. I wondered what they might think about the mock wraiths and skeletons.

Georgetown embraced Halloween with fervor. At one of my least favorite houses, a light had been trained at the gargoyles on the roof, and three life-size wraiths with doll-like faces and haunting eyes seemed to watch me as I walked by.

Across the street, in the shadows, I made out a man leaning against the side of a house as though he didn't want to be seen. I couldn't make out much about him but was totally creeped out.

I looked back just as oncoming car headlights shone on him. He was surprisingly attractive in a benign sort of way. Prominent cheeks created angled brackets on each side of his mouth. He had a broad forehead and a full head of neatly trimmed hair.

Nevertheless, he had spoiled my stroll back to the bookstore. How many other people were lingering in the shadows?

On the next block, a spotlight illuminated a skeleton lounging against the wall of the house at the corner of the block. He wore a top hat and a black scarf around his neck. His bony hand held a leash attached to the rhinestone collar of a dog skeleton. Despite the fact that they were nothing but bones, the two of them were surprisingly dashing.

As I studied them, a man's face slammed against a front window of the house. It smashed against the glass, pushing in his nose and distorting his face.

Chapter 5

I screamed in shock. The spotlight and the light in the house illuminated the face enough for me to recognize agony in the man's expression.

Was it a gag? Had I tripped a motion detector that caused a dummy to slam against the window?

I sucked in shallow breaths. But then I heard banging inside the house. This wasn't a Halloween joke.

I dialed 911 on my phone and reported what I had seen. I gave the dispatcher the address of the house. She calmly asked questions while I wondered what I could do to stop the mayhem inside. I glanced back in Eric's direction, but he was blocks away and would never hear me yelling.

Still talking to the dispatcher, I tried the front door. It was locked. She kept asking questions, but I didn't hear sirens yet. Meanwhile, someone inside could be in mortal danger.

At that very moment, I heard muffled sounds from inside the house.

I had no weapons. And I certainly wasn't the kind of person who might intimidate or tackle someone committing an act of violence. But maybe I could frighten the assailant. He didn't know if I was big or small or had a gun.

In desperation, I looked around. A red brick lay on the ground. I picked it up and, with all the might I could muster from my unathletic self, I threw it at a first-floor window.

The sound of the glass breaking was far louder than I expected, followed by a shower of shards hitting the floor inside.

The stillness that followed shook me to the core. It was as though I were the only person left on the planet. Not even a car cruised by.

I peeked around the corner of the house. A dark figure ran along the sidewalk away from me, into the night. I spewed a breath of relief. My plan had worked.

I hurried toward the back of the house. A door hung open and the lights were off. I debated waiting for the emergency medical technicians. But what if there wasn't any time? I glanced around. Hadn't any of the neighbors heard the sound of the window breaking?

Proceeding cautiously, I stepped just across the threshold and peered inside. The light from another room glowed dimly through a doorway, providing just enough of a hazy glow for me to see the light switch. I pulled my sleeve over my hand and knocked the light switch. Suddenly lights blazed. I was standing on the threshold of a kitchen.

A bloody knife lay on the floor.

Leaving the door open behind me, I crept forward. With any luck, that had been the assailant I saw running down the street.

From the doorway that led to the dining room, I spotted a man on the floor bleeding. I turned around and searched for kitchen towels. Armed with a few, I rushed toward him.

I never dreamed it would be Cyril.

He tried to speak but his neck was bleeding and I thought talking would be a bad idea. "Hush. Don't say anything. Help is on the way." I wrapped a towel around his neck, but it wasn't enough. I needed to add pressure to stop the bleeding.

I rushed back to the kitchen and tore open drawers in search of plastic wrap. Relieved when I found a box, I grabbed it, returned to Cyril, and as gently as I could, wrapped the plastic firmly over the now bloody towels covering his throat. I could only hope I was doing something helpful and not harmful. To my mind, I had to stop the bleeding while not choking him.

That accomplished, I clutched Cyril's hand. "Can you breathe okay?"

He looked scared. His fingers tightened on my hand.

It seemed like an eternity, but I felt certain I sat there with him for only a matter of minutes before the welcome sound of EMT sirens broke the silence. Someone knocked on the front door.

I ran to the foyer off the dining room and threw the door open. "In here!" I motioned to them to follow me and led them to Cyril.

Two of them attended to Cyril at once. One of them asked me questions. All I could do was tell them who he was and give them Roxie's name. I knew nothing about Cyril's medical history.

Suddenly Eric arrived. He took one look at me and his eyes widened. "Didn't you just leave me minutes ago?" he asked.

It felt as if hours had passed.

I went through a long explanation about the face hitting the window and throwing a brick through the glass, and then seeing someone running away. And then I showed him to the knife.

He knelt on the floor for a closer look. "Did you touch this?" he asked.

"No! That's exactly where it was when I walked in."

He gazed around the kitchen at the pristine white drawers marred with bloody fingerprints.

Only then did I realize my hands had Cyril's blood on them. "That was me," I blurted. "I was looking for something to stop the bleeding."

Eric blew air out of the left side of his mouth. "They'll be asking for your fingerprints."

"That's fine. They'll be on the brick, too. I don't know if the surface of a brick is too rough to retain a fingerprint but I readily admit that I'm the one who threw it and broke the window. I was trying to scare the person who was attacking Cyril."

Eric appeared pained. "Yes. The lab will be able to get fingerprints off the brick." He winced. "Are you all right?"

"I will be if Cyril is." I inched over to the doorway and watched as they rolled Cyril out on a stretcher.

I couldn't see much, but from the way they were acting, I gathered he was still alive.

I started to reach for my phone to call Roxie but was grossed out by the blood on my hands. I looked over to Eric. "May I wash my hands? I need to phone Roxie."

He nodded his head, then abruptly said, "No. The perpetrator might have washed his hands. I don't want to contaminate the scene."

At that moment, additional officers arrived. One took photographs of my hands and clothes. Another peppered me with questions. If Eric hadn't been there, they probably would have taken me to the police station. But when the photographer was through, Eric quickly whisked me out of there and drove me home to the carriage house.

He returned to the scene of the crime while I hopped in the shower. Rushing back to the store, I called Roxie and explained what had happened.

Naturally, she was horrified. Before she disconnected the call, I could hear her telling Jacquie that she had to rush to the hospital.

I arrived fifteen minutes after Hilda was scheduled to begin but they hadn't started yet.

Hilda and Jacquie hurried toward me. "Well?" Hilda asked breathlessly.

"I don't know much," I said. "I saw someone attacking Cyril. I hope he'll be all right. He was bleeding profusely."

Hilda stared at me in confusion. "Was there a foot in a rug?"

I had forgotten all about that. "Eric is looking into it. But when we got to the place you described, there was no sign of a foot or a rug, Hilda."

"Of course not," said Jacquie. "The only reason you would wrap a person in a rug would be to transport him. In the time it took for Hilda to walk here and for you to go back there, the killer must have removed the body."

If there had ever *been* a foot, that probably would have been true.

"Or it could have been a vision," mused Hilda.

Jacquie looked put out. "A prognostication? You really could have told us that sooner, Hilda, before everyone went off searching for it."

Hilda seemed hurt, which must have bothered Jacquie because she patted Hilda's shoulder.

"At least the police have been notified." Hilda tugged at her dress and adjusted her shawl. "I feel like a spirit has been trying to get through to me. I hope he'll be polite and won't bother me while I speak to all these lovely people."

Jacquie and I exchanged a look. Was she going to pull some stunt to publicize her book? I hoped not.

Veronica was chatting with a tall man whom I recognized as a customer. His blond hair verged on peach. With them were the owners of the shop called Curiosities, Nola and Steve Boyle.

Nola was on the pudgy side and wore a fussy black dress, complete with a ruffled scarf around her neckline and a peplum at her waist. It looked expensive, like something an exuberant designer had thrown together. She wore high-heeled black suede boots with it, and as she waved her hand around, I noticed that she was wearing black nail polish as well. While I knew perfectly well that many people had natural hair that was a deep, dark black, there was a vague hint of midnight blue in hers that made me think she had colored her hair black.

Her husband, Steve, kept his dark hair extremely short. Their clothes coordinated as if they had discussed what to wear. His black shirt was open at the throat, the sleeves rolled up informally. His black jeans were unremarkable except for the fact that both of them were dressed in black from head to toe.

I wasn't surprised to see them. Curiosities carried a good bit of ghostly and paranormal merchandise.

I grabbed a cup of cider and a doughnut and watched from the doorway to the parlor as Jacquie introduced Hilda.

"Ladies and gentlemen, welcome to Color Me Read for an evening with world-renowned psychic, Hilda Rattenhorst. I'm sure you all know that she is the author of this fascinating book." Jacquie held up a copy. "*Spooktacular Ghost Stories*. I had the honor of reading an advance copy and I can assure you that it will keep you up at night." She motioned toward Hilda. "Ladies and gentlemen, Hilda Rattenhorst!"

Applause broke out as Hilda took over. "I am delighted to be with you tonight. The first thing I want you to know about my book is that all the stories are true. They may seem like fiction, but they're not. I didn't invent them. People actually had these experiences. You have the great honor of living in a city that buzzes with ghosts. Some of them quite famous! Did you know that several first ladies have reported seeing President Lincoln's ghost in the White House? But there are other, lesser-known ghosts in Georgetown whose stories I have related in the book."

She smiled at a gentleman in the first row. "The second thing you should know is that I speak with the dead."

Chapter 6

"Some people call that being a medium," said Hilda. "Spirits come to me because they know I can relay information to you, their dear loved ones. I am a channel through which they can make contact with those of us still in the earthly realm. Let me tell you, there are quite a few asking for my attention right now. But tonight, I didn't come to do that kind of reading, I'm here to talk about my book and to hear about your experiences with ghosts."

She held up a copy of her book. "I have been called in on many cases by private individuals as well as the police. It can be frustrating at times because, like many of you, I sometimes sense and perceive things that others cannot see or hear. On one occasion, I met with police at the home of a woman who was missing and presumed dead. I instantly smelled cigar smoke although no one was smoking. I mentioned it to the police but no one else in the room could smell it. Of course, they thought I was daft. It turned out that the man who abducted her was a cigar smoker. It was a huge clue to his identity. The smell wasn't actually present, but through my psychic abilities, I was able to smell his scent."

She held up a small fancy bottle. The glass stopper was

shaped like a multidimensional star and had flecks of gold in it. Hilda pulled off the top and handed it to the man closest to her. "Tell me what you smell."

He sniffed the bottle. "Nothing. Is it supposed to smell like something?"

She smiled at him and asked him to pass it on. In total, five more people smelled the bottle. One identified it as patchouli oil, one as lavender, one as pine, and the last person claimed it smelled rancid, like spoiled food.

"Which is it?" asked a woman.

Hilda waved her arms dramatically. "With the exception of the first gentleman, you were each picking up a scent through your own innate psychic abilities. You can do what I do but you need to hone your skills. Instead of pushing away things like a scent that no one else can smell, you need to embrace them."

The bottle was passed toward the back, with various people sniffing it as she spoke. When it reached me, I was positive that I smelled mint.

"Ms. Rattenhorst?" A portly man raised his hand. "If you have a ghost"—his face flushed a ruddy red—"I mean, if you happen to encounter one, what should you do?"

"You can enjoy meeting the ghost and treasure the moment."

The audience tittered.

"But if you'd rather the ghost go away, legend holds that the cure is to circle the ghost nine times. Or you can pull out your pockets to show the ghost that they are empty, and the ghost will not be able to harm you."

Without warning, Hilda looked directly at me. Her eyes locked on mine. "Oh! This has never happened to me before. A spirit is trying to convey . . . Oh dear! There's a killer in the building!"

I had never heard it so quiet in Color Me Read. Everyone

stared at her in shock. And then a moaning wail echoed through the bookstore. Loud and unmistakable. I almost expected to hear chains rattling. Frodo bounded toward me and wedged his nose between my legs as if he wanted to hide. People looked around wide-eyed and wriggled in their chairs uncomfortably.

Hilda's eyes rolled upward, and she collapsed into a heap on the floor.

I ran toward her. All around me people gasped.

"Hilda!" I picked up her hand and patted it. "Hilda?"

Jacquie rushed over and knelt next to me. "Good heavens. She fainted dead away!" she exclaimed.

As gently as I could, I tapped Hilda's cheeks. She opened her eyes and grasped Jacquie's arm. "There's evil here. Earthly evil."

Chapter 7

"I don't know who it is," said Hilda. She whispered, "I've never experienced such a cold heart." She sat up suddenly. "I have to go. He knows I'm here." Color drained from Hilda's face, leaving her ashen.

I could see fear in her eyes. "I don't understand. Are you talking about a ghost?"

"No," she whispered. "This person is very much alive."

I was shocked and puzzled. Was this an act? Could she really know that someone intended evil? I could hear a small tussle going on behind me. I glanced in that direction. Bob and Veronica were involved. Part of me wanted to go check that out, but I felt obligated to make sure Hilda was okay first.

Hilda gazed around, wild-eyed. "I should go! I have to get out of here!" She scanned the ceiling in fear, as if she were looking for a ghost floating above her.

"No!" cried Jacquie. "We'll protect you. You're far better off surrounded by so many people. No one would dare harm you here."

Hilda shrank away, as if she didn't know whom to trust.

Honestly, I was a little bit confused. I tried to muster a

gentle, low voice. "You're saying that someone here intends to harm you?"

"A real person," said Jacquie. "Not a ghost?"

"Don't be silly. A spirit wouldn't hurt me. They need me as their voice! Well"—she appeared to reconsider—"perhaps an evil spirit would do me harm."

"She said 'earthly evil,' didn't she?" Jacquie whispered to me. "I heard her say 'earthly.'"

Uh-oh. Who knew what she meant? This was turning into a mess and a half. I asked as gently as I could, "Do you have the strength to sign some books before you go? You have so many fans here."

"I won't know which one is harboring malicious thoughts," she protested. Looking at Jacquie, she added, "But I think you're right. I'm far safer in the company of others."

I was still having some trouble understanding the precise nature of the problem. "What exactly happened?"

"A spirit warned me of malevolence in the building. And then it was like I was inside someone else's head. I could hear him thinking." Hilda gazed at the people milling around. "There's going to be a death."

Jacquie gasped and covered her mouth with her hand.

"You're saying '*him*.' So it's a man?" I asked just to be clear.

Hilda looked at me as though I had said something astonishing. "I don't know. Maybe. Do you hear yourself think in a female voice?" She cocked her head from side to side. "Yes. I believe I do sound like a woman in my own head."

I looked at Jacquie, wondering if she was thinking what I was—Hilda had either lost her marbles or she was putting on a grand show.

But Jacquie focused on Hilda. "Honey, I thought you only communicated with the deceased."

Hilda's hand trembled. "I'm a sensitive. An empath. I can

predict things. For instance, I can hold your hand or an item of yours and pick up on your energy. I'm afraid this thought came from a living being."

"Do you think you're ready to stand?" asked Jacquie.

Hilda brushed her hair back off her shoulders. "Do you think they'll ever forgive me?"

"Of course, we will! Not that there's anything to forgive." It was a small voice, which came, not surprisingly, from a tiny woman who clutched a copy of Hilda's book in her hands.

Hilda rose to her feet and the flush of health began to return to her cheeks. "How lovely of you. I must sign your book. Please come to the signing table with me." Hilda straightened the shawl of skulls and with her head held high swept toward the signing table.

She paused abruptly and stared at Bob and Veronica.

Jacquie grabbed my arm and breathed, "Not again."

But Hilda squared her shoulders and continued to the signing table.

Jacquie watched her. "I'll keep an eye on her. I don't think she should be alone." She joined Hilda at the signing table.

I hurried over to Bob and Veronica. As I walked toward them, I caught sight of Finley near the door.

He flashed those enchanting dimples and a winning smile. "Florrie! Have you seen Roxie? I can't find her anywhere."

Oh no! He didn't know yet. "She's at the hospital with Cyril. He was attacked earlier this evening."

Finley gazed at me. "Are you serious? Why didn't she text me?" He pulled out his phone. "Blast it! This awful thing is always turning itself off." He flicked a button on the phone. "There it is. She's wondering where I am. Thanks, Florrie."

I finally turned to Veronica and Bob to see what was going on with them. Veronica crooked her forefinger at me to join them. I knew the expression she wore. She was mad.

Manny Menz, who worked at the bakery, sat in a chair in front of them, acting cocky. "Hey, you guys know me," he was saying. "I see you at the bakery all the time."

I had bought our goodies from him only a few hours ago. "What's going on?"

"Florrie!" He grinned at me. "There's been a mistake."

Bob pointed at the skull, which sat on the checkout desk. "Manny was stealing Harry."

"Why would you want Harry?" I asked.

Manny brushed his hair off his forehead but it fell back into place. "I wasn't taking him anywhere. I wanted to buy him." *Eww.* "Why?" I asked.

"Best Halloween prank ever. It looks so real," said Manny as he eyed the skull.

"It *is* real," muttered Bob. "And I think we ought to treat Harry with some respect."

"Now you see? I did *not* know that." Manny looked around. "So is the woo-woo lady gonna talk more or what?"

"She's signing books," I said.

"In that case"—Manny stood up and stretched—"I believe I'll be going home. See ya at the bakery." He strolled out of the store with the brashness and swagger of the supremely self-confident. He certainly could lie with aplomb.

Veronica's arms were crossed over her chest. "I always thought he was a nice guy."

Bob looked at me. "That was a bald-faced lie. He had Harry tucked under his jacket. I knew he had something. I walked in front of him and said, " 'Let's see what you've got there, Manny.' I can't believe he would steal from us."

It surprised me, too. I had thought he was a decent kind of fellow. I wondered if it was a full moon. Why were people acting so weird?

"Well, I'm not going back to *that* bakery," said Veronica. "He'll spit on our food for sure."

"Let's keep an eye on him when he comes into the store from now on," I said.

Bob scowled. "Has he ever been in here before? I don't remember selling him anything."

"Me, neither," I said. "Maybe he's into ghosts and only came to hear Hilda."

"She looks much better now. The color has returned to her face," Veronica observed.

Hilda showed no sign of distress as she signed a book for Zsazsa Rosca.

One of my favorite customers, Zsazsa was a retired professor who had become a friend. She always wore a good bit of makeup, applied very precisely, if with a heavy hand. Her fiery-colored hair fluffed high on her head and matched her lively and determined temperament. Of Hungarian heritage, her mother had named her after the movie star, Zsa Zsa Gabor. The name suited her flamboyant personality.

She had recently coupled up with Professor Goldblum, who was now engaging Hilda in an animated discussion.

I cupped Harry carefully in my hands and placed him in the show window where he would be out of the way while throngs of people browsed through the store.

The checkout desk was swamped and I hurried over to help. Whether people bought books because of the ghostly tales or as a result of Hilda's odd performance, I wasn't sure. When the line of buyers dwindled, I collected Harry and carried him upstairs to safety in the professor's office.

By the time Eric showed up, most of the attendees had begun to clear out.

"We have some leftover doughnuts," Bob joked.

"Very funny." But that didn't stop Eric from helping himself to a doughnut and a cupcake.

"Well? What happened?" Veronica asked. "Did you locate the foot?"

I quickly told Eric that Hilda had changed her tune and was now calling the foot in a rug a vision and that she hadn't actually seen it.

Eric didn't seem upset. "Interesting," was all he said. "The house she sent us to is rented by a Mr. Balthus de Gama."

Veronica's eyes widened. "Balthus?"

"You know someone named Balthus?" I asked.

Veronica sighed. "You would, too, if you got out more. He's very wealthy. The heir to a pharmaceutical fortune, I think."

"Mr. de Gama was not home," said Eric. "How well do you know him, Veronica? Any chance that he's out of town?"

"He was here," she said.

"In the store?" I blurted.

"Yes. We had a nice conversation before Hilda started speaking."

"The tall man with reddish blond hair?" I asked.

"So you do know him."

"Not really. I've seen him in the store a few times."

Veronica held up her hands helplessly and spoke to Eric. "I didn't realize you were looking for him or I would have texted you."

Jacquie emerged from the parlor with Hilda.

"Sergeant Jonquille!" cried Hilda. "Did you find the foot?"

"I'm afraid not." Eric spoke with calm graciousness that I would not have been able to muster now that we knew she hadn't actually seen it.

A shiver ran through Hilda with such strength that I saw her body twitch. For a moment I feared she might pass out.

"Why, Hilda!" said Jacquie. "Did it happen again?"

"I'm sorry. I don't know why I'm having these moments. Someone is in terrible danger, but I can't see who it is." Hilda's breath was so labored, I could see her chest heaving.

"Why don't you come home with me tonight?" asked Jacquie. "We have a ton of guest rooms and Mr. DuBois will fuss over you. That way you won't be alone."

"Normally I would decline, but in this instance, I believe I would prefer to be in the safety and company of other people. Thank you for your kind offer, Jacquie."

The two of them left the store, and I quickly explained Hilda's sinister premonition of a death to Eric. He gazed at the front door in silence for a moment.

Bob laughed, "Come on! Don't tell me you believe in psychics."

Eric grimaced. "Police records are replete with instances of psychics leading the police to bodies and crime scenes. I prefer good detective work, but I'm open to the possibility that psychics can be helpful. I don't understand how or why they sometimes know things for no apparent reason. They usually don't even have a connection to the deceased. But I figure there are a lot of things in this world that I don't fully understand. That doesn't mean they don't exist or that they're not valid."

I beamed. He was so logical. No wonder I was goofy over the guy. "I hate to say it, but I thought the whole thing might be a show. Seriously, we only know about it because she told us. The only thing I can't figure out is that wail. I don't know how she pulled that off."

"Wail?" asked Eric.

"It was horrible!" Veronica shuddered. "I hope I never hear that again."

Eric's radio crackled unintelligibly. I had no idea how he could understand it.

"I have to go. See you tomorrow, Florrie." He leaned in to kiss my cheek and was out the door in a flash.

Veronica departed to meet friends for drinks, leaving Bob and me to lock up the store.

I was checking the basement door when I heard Bob call me. I walked upstairs. "Where are you?"

"Up here. Third floor." His voice was loud enough to hear but he sounded somewhat unsure, like something might be wrong.

Frodo sprang up the stairs ahead of me. I continued to make my way up and found them about five stairs down from the third floor. Frodo was growling. The lights were still on and I could see very clearly what had stopped Bob in his tracks.

The skull.

Chapter 8

The skull named Harry sat atop the newel post next to the landing. It leered at us with a deadly grin.

Frodo growled at it again and Bob stood frozen beside him. It wasn't like Bob to be creeped out by a Halloween joke.

"That's odd. I'm certain I put him back in the professor's office."

"I'm not picking it up," said Bob. "Even Frodo thinks there's something scary about it."

"You don't believe in psychics but you're afraid of a skull?" I teased.

"It's a human skull! Not some plastic piece of junk."

"Okay, I admit I'm somewhat grossed out by it, too. We could leave it there, I suppose. Chances are good that the professor will be the first one to arrive in the morning."

"I vote for that. Let's get out of here."

It was silly of us. We weren't kids. The skull had sadly been someone, but that didn't mean we shouldn't touch it. In fact, because it had been a person, we should have reverence for it and put it back on the shelf, where it belonged for the time being.

I sucked in a deep breath, slid my hands underneath it to cradle it gently, and carried it back to the professor's office. The space he had made for it was apparent. I deposited it on the shelf, turned off the light, and said, "Good night, Harry," closing the door behind me.

"You've got some guts, Florrie," said Bob.

"No, I don't. It's an inanimate object. It can't hurt you. I respect that it was a living person, but it's not like a live snake. Now, if you'll excuse me, I have an overwhelming desire to scrub my hands."

After washing up thoroughly, I met Bob and Frodo at the checkout desk. "Ready to call it a night?"

I set the alarm and we left together, making sure the front door was locked. Bob headed off to buy pizza for his dinner, while Frodo and I walked home. I was enjoying the orange and purple lights that twinkled in windows and on bushes. Ghosts appeared to be all the rage in Halloween decorating. They peeped out windows, floated on porches, and gathered in trees. I saw only one vampire glaring at me from a porch.

"Florrie! What do you think?"

I peered through the darkness. Coralue Throckmorton waved at me from across the street. Her grand home appeared positively sinister. Masses of tiny orange lights dangled from oak trees and foggy mists drifted past, giving me the shivers. She stood next to a hunched butler who held a lighted candelabra in one hand. The lights on the candles flickered, illuminating a tapered coffin at his feet.

Coralue Throckmorton, who wore her hair in a short bob and was the queen of ladylike sweater sets, had never struck me as the type to go overboard for Halloween. She was a woman who would undoubtedly be trusted by most people simply by virtue of her sweet appearance. However, now that I thought about it, she often bought scary books for her grandchildren. I didn't know much about her, except that she was widowed and a dedicated volunteer at the children's hospital where her husband had been a physician.

Frodo and I crossed the quiet road. "Hi, Mrs. Throckmorton. Who's your friend?" I asked.

"Hi, Frodo, sweetheart." Coralue reached out to pet Frodo, but he was warily concentrating on the butler. He approached it from behind and appeared somewhat reassured when the butler had no worrisome scent.

Coralue giggled. "Isn't he darling? Don't tell the real Mr. DuBois, but I'm calling him my Mr. DuBois."

He did resemble the professor's butler, Mr. DuBois. I had to chuckle with her.

"I hired the nicest carpenter to make this coffin for me. It looks so authentic, don't you think?"

"He did a great job." It resembled the old-timey coffins used in the Wild West, broad at the shoulders and narrow at the feet.

"Gosh, you even roughed up the soil to make it look like he's going to bury it."

She laughed. "That's actually laziness on my part. It's a garden plot. I usually plant mums there but Gene Germain, next door, is trying to beat me at my own game. I had to step up my décor this year to compete! Instead of planting something pretty, I planted a coffin! I love Halloween," Cora confessed dreamily. "It's the one time of year we all get to act like silly children. My grandchildren are coming to stay with me on Halloween Eve. I always throw a party. I hope you'll come by. It will be a spooky event! The city has agreed to close our street to traffic on Halloween." Her forehead furrowed. She shot me a mischievous glance. "I trust someone has told you about my house?"

"No," I said slowly, wondering what I was supposed to

know. I didn't want to offend her. "It's certainly beautiful." And it was. The massive Georgian-style home stood out on a street of similarly impressive houses.

"Thank you, but that wasn't what I meant. Your reaction tells me you haven't heard the tale of the Sokolov family. Do you have a minute? Come inside for a cup of hot cider?"

It was late and it had been a long day, but I was curious about the house. "That's very kind of you."

She seemed delighted, which made me wonder if she was lonely. Coralue led Frodo and me through a large, well-appointed foyer into a modern white kitchen. She heated two mugs of cider and plopped cinnamon sticks into them, then loaded them onto a tray. We followed her to a charming conservatory, where she set the tray down on an ornate metal table with a decoratively scrolled bottom. The top was simply glass. She struck a match and lit candles around the conservatory. With the flick of a switch, she turned off the electric lights, and I realized that a spotlight was trained on a circle of witches dancing in the backyard. Ghosts hanging from nearby tree branches glowed eerily.

Coralue took a seat at the table. "Do you think my grandchildren will like it?" she asked.

"It's amazing." I hoped they wouldn't have nightmares.

"This house is quite old. In the early 1800s, it was the residence of the Russian ambassador to the United States. He had a daughter named Natalia, who had everything she could have wanted. Her life was gracious and genteel. Meaning well, Natalia's father arranged for her marriage to Andrew O'Malley, a man of means thirty years her senior. Natalia was distraught. Her father thought she would be well off and live a refined life, but Natalia found her new husband repugnant."

"Are you serious? You mean Natalia and her father may have sat right here where we are now?"

"I knew you'd like hearing the story. The conservatory was

built some years later, but they undoubtedly strolled around the grounds where we're sitting. Natalia's wedding was the talk of Washington. Her father threw a lavish party and everyone of any importance in Washington was present. Well, don't you know, Natalia's instincts were correct. It turned out that her new husband was a lush of the worst sort. The money he had inherited was nearly gone and his primary interest in young Natalia was her family's wealth. Not to mention that he had done a good bit of damage to his own status and reputation during drunken escapades. Marrying the daughter of the ambassador elevated him once again in polite society."

Coralue paused to sip her cider. "On a particularly drunken evening, during a concert at the Maxwell mansion, her husband, O'Malley, stumbled upon Natasha alone in the library with Henry Bosworth."

I grinned at her. I'd never heard a story from the 1800s that took place in a private home that I knew so well. "I've been in that library! It's gorgeous. All the walls are paneled and lined with bookshelves. Do you suppose it was the same back then?"

"Probably. Most of these old mansions have handcrafted libraries that are worth preserving. They're not like the kitchens that desperately need to be updated to stay with the times. It would cost a fortune to reproduce most of the libraries. Unfortunately, on that night, O'Malley jumped to incorrect conclusions about Bosworth's intentions toward Natalia and challenged Bosworth to a duel. Natalia was horrified and embarrassed. She rushed her husband home, insisting nothing untoward had happened.

"But O'Malley did not believe her. He was convinced that his lovely young wife who spurned his attentions had found another man. O'Malley insisted that Natalia had brought shame upon his name.

"On the appointed day, the two men met in a park not far

from here. Determined to stop the duel, Natalia defied everyone and went to the park. Bosworth's wife, Clara, was there as well. Natalia pleaded with her husband, but, scum that he was, he fired upon Bosworth prematurely. As Bosworth dropped to the ground, Clara fell to her knees and O'Malley feared he had shot the wife. They say Clara was so close when her husband was shot that droplets of blood splattered on her dress. Of course, Bosworth died from the gunshot wound. Making matters worse, Clara was pregnant at the time, and was now a widow with seven children and another one on the way. All because of a jealousy that had no foundation."

"What a terrible story. Is this true? I've never heard of it."

"It's a tale that has been passed down over the ages. The people involved weren't widely known. Duels were such a stupid practice. With his last breath, Bosworth was heard by several people to mutter, 'A pox on the O'Malleys. Your children will have faces like withered apples, and money will run through your fingers like rainwater. Look for me, for you are not done with me yet. Neither you nor your descendants will live in peace, for I will bring misery to your doors.'"

"How awful! Even if O'Malley was scum and deserved it. Have you heard Bosworth here in the house?" I asked teasingly.

"Alas, I have not. People put a lot of stock in curses back in the day. The family was already devastated by O'Malley's behavior. You can imagine how awful it was for them to be cursed as well."

"What happened to Natalia? Did she ever get rid of her horrible husband?"

"The ambassador felt terrible about arranging Natalia's disastrous marriage to O'Malley and was extremely concerned about his daughter's welfare. He returned to Russia on business, leaving his son, Ivan, to manage matters here. While in Russia, the father died in a freak accident. They say his horse reared up and threw him when frightened by a ghost. Ivan meanwhile had developed a gambling habit and did a fine job of running through the Sokolov money. Natalia and O'Malley lost their home and moved into this house with Natalia's widowed mother. Natalia was desperate to escape the marriage and was reportedly relieved when her dreadful husband was run over by his own carriage. But you see what's happening here?"

I sipped my cider and nodded. "The father dies in a freak accident. Then poor Natalia is widowed in another strange incident."

"Exactly. The curse was at work. Natalia and her mother were left destitute. All they had was this house. Natalia divided it into apartments and rented them out. Her mother took the top floor."

Coralue lifted her arm and motioned gracefully toward the looming mansion behind us. "Here, in this very house. In the vast room at the top of the house. The one with the beautiful arched window in the center overlooking the front lawn. Ivan was certain his mother was deranged because of Bosworth's curse. He brought in doctors to examine Irina. They chalked up the voices she heard to madness. The family kept her at home and tried to play down Irina's eccentricities. Natalia's poor mother spent the remainder of her days speaking with her dead husband. I have seen records and letters from tenants complaining about the person who *lived* on the top floor. They heard footsteps at night. And when the moon was full, they always heard voices coming from her quarters."

I was reeling. I couldn't imagine going through anything so horrible. "That's so sad." I gazed into her eyes. "Do you really think all this happened?"

"There's no question. It was a tragic story all the way around. I never knew a thing about it until we bought the house. My first clue, of course, was the stairway that led to a wall. There are other houses with odd stairways that don't go anywhere. For some reason, people believed that spirits would be confused if there were doors and stairways that didn't have a purpose. It was a most curious time. Imagine thinking that! Someone had bricked up the windows on the top floor. From the outside, it looked like a two-story house with a tall second floor. One day I made a hole in the wall and realized there was a lovely third floor."

"The seller didn't tell you what had happened?"

"He had passed on. But not because of a curse. He was one hundred six, which most certainly defies any curse. But we hear voices when the moon is full. And we hear Irina's footsteps."

"You say that so cheerily."

She flapped her hand. "Oh, well. At worst, it's Irina's ghost, looking for her husband. She was never malicious."

"What do the other members of your family think?"

"The children grew up with Irina, and they seem to enjoy sharing the story with their own children."

If Coralue wasn't so adorably sweet and motherly looking, I would have leaped from my chair and run out of the house. What she was telling me couldn't be true. Yet she reveled in it. "You're not afraid living in this big place by yourself?"

"Don't be silly. I'm not from O'Malley's bloodline." She leaned toward me. "I'm currently researching Natalia's genealogy. After all, I would assume that either Ivan or Natalia would have had a child."

I thanked her for the cider and the story. "Let me know what you find out in your research."

"Oh, I will! And don't forget my Halloween party. Do you think you could talk the professor into decorating this year? The Maxwell mansion is so beautiful, but it's always drab and boring on Halloween."

I had a hunch that Professor Maxwell might not be a fan of Halloween. But I suspected Jacquie might be. "I'll see what I can do. We should be part of the street party."

"That's the idea, sweetheart. I'd like to get Maxwell involved." I guessed Coralue to be in her fifties. She always looked so proper and put together. Who would have imagined that she believed in ghosts?

I hurried down the brick walkway with Frodo and stopped at the street. I looked back at the house with some trepidation. I didn't believe that ghosts lingered in these old mansions. They certainly couldn't swoop down at me or anything. I was being ridiculous. Yet even though I found myself a little bit anxious, something inside compelled me to look back at the house.

It was gorgeous. Bright lights on either side of the front door beamed in the night. Dimmer lights showed through the first-floor windows, probably from the kitchen, where Coralue was cleaning up. The beautiful arched window at the very top of the house should have been dark. But a candle was glimmering on the sill, and in its glow, there was no mistaking the face of a woman.

Chapter 9

The woman gazing out the window vanished inside the house with the candle. The window was black as pitch.

I shuddered. Goose bumps covered my arms. I'm ashamed to say that I actually took off running for home. I wasn't much of a runner, so it was really more of a jerky fast walk. But Frodo and I didn't stop until we reached the Maxwell mansion.

I laughed at myself. How silly of me to have let Coralue put Irina in my head. I must have imagined the candle and the face. I took a deep breath and relaxed as I viewed the Maxwell home from the sidewalk. Warm, golden lights shone through the windows. A lot had happened in that house over the last century. Mr. DuBois insisted the mansion had a ghost but I had never heard or seen it.

I strode across the street and along the driveway to my own little home in the back.

The Maxwell mansion wasn't far from the bookstore. It was tucked away on a quiet street with other fancy homes. I had searched long and hard for an affordable apartment in

Georgetown. I didn't have the heart to live in a drab, run-down home the size of a closet, so I had commuted each day for years. I had given up hope of ever finding an apartment when the professor offered me the carriage house behind the mansion. It was once a real carriage house for horses and buggies. When Jacquie was Mrs. Maxwell number two, she had renovated it to be her writing studio. She had fabulous taste, and now that she was back in the professor's life, I worried a bit that she might want it again. She assured me that wasn't the case, so until that day came, I was more than happy to live in the little house in the back.

As I approached my home, the professor stormed out of the back door of the mansion.

Jacquie was right behind him, shouting, "John Maxwell! Stop! You cannot run away when something displeases you."

It was terrible timing on my part. I considered turning around and darting back to the sidewalk but Frodo yipped and tugged me in their direction. I froze in place and held his leash firmly. Should I hurry by them to the carriage house or stay put?

The professor stopped under a light and faced Jacquie. "You do realize why you cannot win with that charlatan, don't you?"

Jacquie swallowed hard. "I'm hoping we may learn that Caroline is alive."

The professor ran a hand over his face. "C'mon, Jacquie. It doesn't matter to Madame Hilda. As long as she thinks you'll pay her to try to reach Caroline, she won't be able to. If you give up and the money dries up, she will miraculously make contact with Caroline, just to keep you on the hook. Can't you see that? She's using you."

Jacquie couldn't have looked more shocked if he had slapped her. Her voice was gentle, if hurt. "John, I don't make fun of you when you take off on an expedition to find the

Holy Grail, even though I don't think you'll ever locate it. Don't you dare ever question what I do in my search for Caroline."

Jacquie turned on her heel and marched back to the mansion, letting the door slam behind her.

The professor hung his head and I could hear a big sigh. He turned slightly and caught sight of me.

"Don't tell me you're joining the insanity, too," he grumbled.

I had to think he was talking about Hilda. I let Frodo go to him. "Um, no. I don't think so."

He swallowed hard and petted Frodo. "Don't let me spoil your fun. If you want to join them, go right ahead."

"I'm just getting home from the bookstore. I guess I wasn't invited."

"I'm sorry, Florrie. I didn't mean to take it out on you. Jacquie brought that crazed psychic home. Of course, DuBois is a firm believer in the supernatural, so now the three of them are having a séance. I thought you might be participating."

"Does that sound like something I would want to do?"

He bellowed a laugh. "No. It does not. Enjoy your evening."

It probably wasn't the best time to ask if he knew anything about Coralue's home and the story about Irina. "Would you like to come in?"

"Thank you, Florrie. I think I'd rather take a walk and clear my head of their nonsense." He strode along the driveway toward the street.

I unlocked the door and was greeted by the plaintive mews of my cat, Peaches. Although she was a brown-and-cream tabby, spots of peach showed up in random places on her fur. Peaches was a talker. She didn't hesitate to let me know what she wanted. Right now, I was fairly sure that she was telling me it was dinnertime.

The carriage house had few windows facing the mansion. That wall was covered with bookshelves from end to end. Along with my books, they housed my clock collection and my artwork. The kitchen was to the left and the living room, with a fireplace, was farther inside on the right. Together they formed one large living space. Straight ahead, a wall of French doors led out to a wonderfully private walled garden. A gently curving staircase soared upstairs to a bedroom and a full bath. A tiny bathroom was tucked away behind the stairs on the main floor.

The original carriage house had once been part of the Underground Railroad, through which slaves escaped to the North. When Jacquie renovated, she left the original tunnel that existed between the carriage house and the mansion. The entrance to the passage was well hidden in one of the massive columns that flanked the fireplace.

We had reached the time of year when it was beginning to be nippy at night, but it wasn't quite time to turn on the heat yet. With Peaches and Frodo springing along ahead of me, I padded upstairs and changed into a cozy loungewear set. Orange pumpkins dotted the cream-colored top, and cream-colored pumpkins dotted the orange pants. My sister, Veronica, who possessed a closet filled with fifty shades of black, had long claimed my clothes were too drab. I admit that I lived in muted colors for many years but the truth was that I loved colors. All colors! Only recently had I dared to try bolder shades and now I was hooked.

My home reflected that fondness, too. It was a gorgeous place to begin with, but now that I had lived there awhile, I was beginning to put my own slightly eclectic stamp on it. My favorite piece by far was a nightstand, which I had snagged at a yard sale. It had lovely twisted legs and an open shelf for books at the bottom. After I painted it turquoise, umber, and rosy red, with light touches of gold, it had definitely become a focal point in the bedroom and inspired me to try painting more furniture.

Peaches and I ate tuna for dinner. Hers was flaked in a bowl, but mine was between two slices of bread, nicely blended with a squeeze of fresh lemon and a dollop of mayonnaise. Frodo happily devoured the liver dog food my parents had left for him. When we finished eating, I took my mug of hot tea, well diluted with milk and a touch of sugar, to the sofa and sat down with my sketch pad.

So much had happened today. I loved to draw and doodle, so instead of writing a journal, I often drew things that had caught my attention during the day. I thought of them as doodles, but Eric always called them my sketches, which I thought was very sweet of him, because it seemed to elevate their importance.

Harry the skull emerged first. Doodling a human skull was somewhat easier than I had expected. The hollow eyes and deathly grin creeped me out and I flipped the page.

I sketched Finley's face, focusing on those endearing dimples. He had bright eyes, a prominent chin, and high cheekbones. I smiled as his image took shape and added the fashionable plaid scarf hanging open around his neck.

I flipped the page and moved on to the rug with a bare foot sticking out of it. It probably hadn't really existed or maybe it was a Halloween gag. Still, I doodled a rolled carpet from the far end, having fun creating the circular rolls. What colors had the carpet been? Not that it mattered. Had the foot been pointed? Was it flexed at the ankle? Probably somewhat flexed, I decided, and drew a foot that looked rather masculine.

With a start, I remembered Cyril. I glanced at my clock collection. It was too late to phone Roxie now. I checked my texts in the hope she had sent me a message. No such luck. I hoped he was okay.

Against my better judgment, I found myself doodling the woman in Coralue's window. Her hair appeared to have been pulled back. In the front, it lay flat on her head. She had a remarkably oval face. Although I had seen her from a distance and in a dim light, her eyes were what I remembered most clearly. I didn't understand how that could be. The power of suggestion, I decided. She had been sad, as if she were resigned to a life of tragedy. The ruffled collar of a blouse covered her throat. When I was finished, I thought she looked like someone from another era. How could I have seen so many details from the street? Was I embellishing? But that was nonsense. It was all ridiculous. Coralue obviously loved Halloween. Her mother or sister was probably visiting and had been upstairs gazing out the window. Or maybe she had some kind of gadget that lighted every few minutes, then went dark. That would be spooky!

I moved on to Hilda, who at that very moment was probably conjuring up dead spirits next door in the mansion. Her hair, which began flat at the top of her head, grew like a pyramid until it bushed out at her shoulders. Her round face was really quite sweet and grandmotherly. She had marionette lines along the sides of her mouth and a slight sagging under her chin. I realized suddenly that if I replaced the bushy hair with white curls, she might resemble Mrs. Santa Claus.

Could she really have read someone's evil thoughts at the bookstore? How and why would that happen? Fortunately, in spite of the dire warning, no one had been murdered at the bookstore before we closed for the night. So maybe it had all been a show, after all.

Hilda wouldn't be the first author to do something unexpected to attract attention to herself or her book. I had trouble understanding that. But just because I wouldn't do something didn't mean another person felt the same way. I didn't like standing out, yet many people wanted to be the center of attention.

And then I remembered the man I had seen just before the attack on Cyril. I drew him as I recalled, leaning against the side of a house. I hadn't gotten a close look at his face, but it was amiable, with those very distinctive angles bracketing his mouth.

I went to bed hoping there wouldn't be a body in Color Me Read in the morning.

Chapter 10

If Hilda had summoned any ghosts during the séance the night before, they hadn't come to visit me. Peaches, Frodo, and I slept quite well. I checked my phone for updates from Roxie but there weren't any. I hoped her dad was okay.

Even though I had a decent blanket on my bed, I woke up a little bit chilly. It was time to bring out the down comforter. Outside my bedroom window, the sun shone brightly in a beautiful autumn blue sky. It was cruelly misleading about the temperature.

Happily, it was my day off. I longed to stretch and stay in bed but the crisp air had forced me awake.

After a hot shower, I pulled on an aqua sweater and faded blue jeans, then double-wrapped a long scarf around my neck. One of my favorites, it consisted of a cream background with large abstract patches in several shades of blue. I slid my feet into teal sneakers and poked around in the storage room upstairs. In two minutes, I found my favorite Halloween wreath.

A witch's face with a playful expression was on the upper right of the wreath. She wore a traditional pointy hat with stars hanging off the tip. On the lower left, her black cat was peering at something. The cat's tail followed the curve of the wreath up to the witch's face. A spider on the upper left watched them warily.

I carried it downstairs and hung it on my front door.

Apologizing to Peaches for the delay in serving breakfast, I dressed Frodo in his halter and leash and hurried outside, tucking a doggy-poo bag into my back pocket.

We strolled around the neighborhood, taking our time and enjoying the leaves that were turning shades of pineapple and butterscotch. Mission accomplished, we headed for home and breakfast.

I had barely closed the door behind us when there was a timid knock at my door and the telephone rang. I glanced at the phone briefly, intending not to answer because I needed to deal with the person at the door.

But it was Professor Maxwell.

I answered the call and opened the front door at the same time. Mr. DuBois, the Maxwell's butler, rushed into the carriage house as though he was running from someone. A small elderly man who insisted on wearing a butler's uniform, DuBois had very firm opinions about everything. He was addicted to true-crime shows on television, and I had wondered if that addiction hadn't led to a degree of agoraphobia. He seldom left the Maxwell estate.

"Hi, I'm just on the phone with the professor."

Maxwell skipped the formalities and calmly asked, "Florrie, why are there masses of people outside the bookstore? Are we having an event that I don't know about?"

"How peculiar. No, we don't have anything special planned. I'll go over right away."

I hung up the phone and told Mr. DuBois what the professor had said.

"I apologize for barging in on you, Miss Florrie." He stared uneasily out the window at the mansion. "May I clean your quarters today?"

Even though I was beginning to feel rushed, I stopped in my tracks. In the few months I had lived there, Mr. DuBois had never cleaned the carriage house. Nor had he ever offered to. In fact, I had been cleaning it myself all along and assumed that was the norm. I glanced around. Did it appear particularly messy? Had I overlooked washing the floors or missed spider-webs?

But when my gaze returned to his face, I suspected that something else had prompted his offer. I tested him. Mr. DuBois disliked cats. "Peaches will be here all day."

"I can't help that. You're the one who insists on housing a feline. The cleaning must be done."

The crowd at the bookstore would have to wait a few minutes longer. "Do you want to tell me what's going on?"

"I can't imagine what you mean."

I took a guess. "Mr. DuBois, what happened at the séance last night?"

He stiffened. "Ms. Rattenhorst summoned a ghost."

"Uh-huh."

"And she's still in the mansion."

I tried to judge his expression. Did that mean there were now two ghosts? "If I'm not mistaken, you have long believed that ghosts haunt the mansion."

"Not this one."

In my mind's eye I could envision hordes of people breaking down the door at Color Me Read and pillaging the store. I would have to talk with Mr. DuBois about the new ghost in more detail at another time. "You are welcome to clean anything you like as long as you are kind to Peaches. You may even cook here if you like." In light of the situation at the bookstore, I thought it wise to leave Frodo at home with Mr. DuBois.

"Would you feel better if Frodo stayed here with you?"

He brightened considerably. "Thank you. I would enjoy

his company. When you come home tonight, your quarters will shine."

I wondered if he had considered that the new ghost could probably waft itself through the tunnel connecting the buildings and emerge on the carriage house side. But I wasn't going to plant that idea in his head.

I hurried out the door and took off down the street in my awkward half run. I finally decided that I actually made better time at a brisk walk. When I rounded the corner to the store, I discovered masses of people gathered on the sidewalk. My first thought was that there must have been a bomb threat or a fire in an adjoining building.

Repeating "excuse me" over and over, I wedged past enough people to see that the stairs leading to the store were packed.

A guy had climbed on his friend's shoulders in an attempt to reach the second-floor balcony. Thankfully, they weren't tall enough to accomplish that feat.

I asked a friendly-looking woman, "What's going on?"

"The bookstore is haunted."

What? Of all the silly things. What had possessed people? Why were they all imagining ghosts? Was there a full moon or was it just Halloween that was causing this mayhem? "Why is everyone here?"

She looked at me as if I were from another planet. "Aren't you on Twitter? The ghost attacked someone inside last night."

Not too long ago I had actually found a body in the bookstore. I was fairly confident that no one had been assaulted by a ghost, but after Hilda's bizarre pronouncements, I had to admit there was just a tiny bit of doubt in my mind.

Fearing I might be overrun if I unlocked the front door, I quickly turned and made my way back through the crowd. As

I had hoped, the alley behind the store was quiet. Save for a man getting out of a plumbing truck, there wasn't a person in sight. I unlocked the back door, shut it quickly behind me, and made absolutely certain that I locked it.

The bookstore was peaceful. There wasn't a sound inside. Not even a mouse scampered past me as I walked up the stairs to the main floor. But as I switched on the lights and walked toward the checkout desk to turn off the alarm, I became uneasy.

Harry's skull rested on the checkout desk, facing the door.

If that wasn't bad enough, people banged on the glass door and peered inside, frighteningly reminiscent of the angry villagers in old Frankenstein movies.

I turned off the alarm so it wouldn't notify the police that the door had been opened. And then I turned it on again—just in case someone broke the door.

"Professor Maxwell?" I called.

There was no response. Knowing him, he was already deep in some kind of research and had forgotten all about the people outside. Once again, I cradled Harry's skull in my hands. I headed upstairs, hoping I wouldn't trip and send it flying.

"Now, Harry," I joked, "you really have to stop wandering about the bookstore." I wondered why the professor had carried him down to the checkout desk.

I managed to reach the professor's office without any skull mishaps. Sure enough, he sat at his desk laying one map over another as if comparing them. I deposited Harry on his desk.

"Good morning, Florrie. A colleague of mine has sent me the most intriguing map purporting to show the lost city of Atlantis. I fear he has fallen prey to an elaborate hoax, yet these things are always intriguing. Would you care to see?"

"I would. However, I feel I should take care of the people

at the door first. I'm not sure what to do other than alert the police and make an announcement that there are no injured people or ghosts in the bookstore today."

"Ghosts?" The professor stroked his beard. "DuBois and I have gone around in circles about apparitions. He insists the mansion is haunted."

There wasn't time for dallying, yet I dared to ask, "What do you think?"

"Bah! There are many lost artifacts in the world that I have never seen but all are well documented. Ghosts have never been scientifically proven to exist. Alas, to the chagrin of Jacquie, DuBois, and their questionable friend, Hilda Rattenhorst, there simply are no such things."

I longed to stay and ask him more questions, but the crowd at the door had to be handled first. I picked up the phone on his desk and called the police station to ask for assistance in crowd control. I wasn't sure that was necessary, but unlocking the door and being overrun by people did not appeal to me.

The professor was focused on the map when I left his office. As I walked down the stairs, it dawned on me that instead of opening the front door, I could make an announcement from the second-floor balcony. I walked through the room of philosophical and religious books to the French doors that opened onto the balcony.

I stepped outside into the chilly morning air and stood beside a faux skeleton. Raising my voice, I said, "May I have your attention? Please be advised that there is no ghost in the bookstore, and no one has been injured. We appreciate your interest, but I'm afraid there is simply no truth to the story that is being spread through social media."

It was partly a lie, of course. I hadn't searched through all the rooms of the bookstore. But I had to admit that I sided with the professor and doubted the presence of a ghost, much less that anyone had been attacked by one.

Someone in the crowd yelled, "I want to see for myself."

"We welcome you to come back at a later time and shop in the bookstore. But I am here almost every day and I can assure you that no ghosts dwell in this building. I hear the Old Stone House on M Street is home to several ghosts. You'll probably fare better there."

I could hear a few people muttering, "Old Stone House?"

While some seemed determined to enter the store, the majority began to drift away. Several looked at their watches, and I had a feeling they would probably head to coffee shops to determine what other mischief might be fun.

A uniformed officer arrived about then, so I wasn't sure whether it was my announcement or his appearance that prompted them to leave. I stepped inside and locked the French doors behind me before rushing down the stairs to unlock the front door. Veronica and Bob showed up for work as I was turning the sign around to *Open* and unlocking the door.

The police officer entered behind them and very kindly introduced himself. He hung out at the checkout desk in the front, where anyone walking through the door would see him.

"What's going on out there?" asked Bob.

"Someone posted about a ghost murdering people in the bookstore. It was crazy this morning. Why do they believe every stupid thing they read on the Internet? Even if it's implausible?"

The officer shook his head. "It's not implausible. Well, maybe the murder part, but I can tell you from experience that I've seen a few things that can't be explained."

Chapter 11

"Like what?" Veronica asked dubiously.

"Like dead people who yell for help."

Veronica gasped and took a step backward.

I snickered. "He's pulling your leg, Veronica."

The cop didn't even smile. "I'm serious as a heartbeat. I arrived once at a traffic accident. I could hear someone calling for help clear as day. No one else was around. The car had careened down an embankment. My partner and I climbed down there because we could hear a woman shouting. When we got to the car, all the adult passengers were dead. Looked like they had been deceased for some time already. The only live person in the vehicle was a baby boy who was too young to speak."

I studied his face, expecting him to break into laughter.

"You ask other cops who have been around for a while. I guarantee weird and inexplicable things have happened to them." He nodded. "Mark my words and ask a cop."

I assumed he didn't know that I would be able to do just that!

His radio crackled. "I'd bet anything I'll be called to the Old Stone House next."

"Thank you so much," I said to the police officer. "I wasn't sure what to do."

"No problem."

"I'm sorry about the Old Stone House. I didn't mean to make more work for you."

He waved his hand. "No worries. It's that time of year. Just give us a call if they return." He walked slowly and stood on the stoop outside the door briefly as if he meant to be seen there.

Undeterred by his presence, a lady entered the store and spent some time perusing Hilda's book. She presented it to Veronica and pulled out her wallet. "I wish I had been here last night. Is it true that she connected with a spirit?"

"We don't really know," I said hastily.

"She was overwhelmed by something," Veronica gushed.

I shot her a look. She didn't need to encourage the notion that a spirit had been present.

"I'd like to see if she could channel my husband," said the woman.

As luck would have it, just as the woman spoke, Jacquie walked through the door and made a beeline to her. "Hilda would *love* to do that." Jacquie looked at me. "Hilda didn't get to do much channeling last night. Maybe we could re-book her."

I'm sorry to admit that my first reaction was horror. Not another evening like that! "If you would like to leave your name and phone number, I would be happy to pass them on to Hilda." I handed the lady a sheet of paper and tried to divert Jacquie's attention. "Do you know Coralue Throckmorton?"

"Of course. She's so sweet."

The customer slid the paper with her name toward me. "I hope she will call me. I'm very eager to contact him."

I smiled at her. "I'll let her know."

As the customer left, Jacquie snatched up her name and

number. "I'm seeing Hilda later on today. I'll pass this along to her."

"Coralue says our street is going to be blocked off for Halloween this year."

"What a brilliant idea! I noticed her wonderful decorations last night when we walked home. That coffin is marvelous! I'm writing a book right now that is tentatively titled *The Midnight Spell*. Decorating would put me in the spirit." Jacquie paused. "I don't know if we have any Halloween décor at the mansion. Is John here?"

"In his office."

"Perfect. I'll go up and talk to him about it."

I took that opportunity to make my escape before I became embroiled in something else at the store. It had a way of sucking me in and keeping me there. With a quick wave to Veronica and Bob, I headed to Rose and Violet, a local flower shop run by none other than a woman named Rose and another named Violet.

When I browsed bouquets, Rose greeted me and asked, "Are these by any chance for Cyril?"

"How did you know?"

"Everyone is talking about him. Frankly," she said, while selecting golden sunflowers, "I think everyone is on guard. It's a miracle that you interrupted the attack. Is it true that his assailant was already in the house when you arrived?"

"Yes. I don't know how he managed to get in."

"We're all a little bit uneasy." She selected roses that matched the golden hues of the sunflowers, but each rose petal was outlined with orange. To that she added bright orange gerbera daisies. She assembled them in a vase and plunked thin black wires into it. Bats attached to the wires seemed to fly in the air. Instead of a ribbon, she inserted a stick that held a faux skull. "Cyril will love this. Please give him my best."

"Could you whip up another one for Glen?" I asked.

"I'd love to. We miss seeing him. That was something, huh? A snake in the delivery truck. I'd have crashed, too!" Rose gathered flowers and made another bat-and-skull arrangement.

I paid Rose for the bouquets. "You must know Cyril pretty well."

"He's a good customer. I have standing orders for his wife's grave. Every major holiday, her birthday, and the day she died."

"That's so sad."

"He sends flowers to Roxie a lot, too. He's a doting daddy."

I thanked her and walked to the hospital. I found Cyril's room easily and peeked inside the open door. I set one vase outside the room by the door.

Cyril stood by the window, gazing out. Fortunately, his hospital gown was completely closed in the back. He was attached to an IV drip on a pole with wheels.

"Cyril?" I said.

He turned around. "Florrie! My guardian angel!" He opened his arms wide to embrace me. After a hug, he held on to my upper arms. "I was just thinking of you. How can I ever repay you?"

His voice sounded different. A little quieter and strained. "Don't be silly. I'm just glad that I happened along when I did. You're the one in the hospital! How are you doing?" I set the vase of flowers on a bedside tray.

His fingers touched a large white bandage on his neck. "Better. But I'm worried about Roxie."

"Roxie is fine."

"No. She's not." He sat down in a chair near the window. "Those are beautiful. I love the skull. It reminds me of Harry!" He pointed to a plastic chair. "Close the door and have a seat, Florrie."

I shut the door, perched on the chair, and faced him. "I take it they haven't caught the perpetrator?"

"No. The police say it wasn't personal. They think I interrupted a robbery. I own a Chinese ormolu clock from the 1700s that was passed down to me from my grandfather. It's worth a considerable amount of money. Interestingly, they discovered it leaning against the outside of the house near a basement window."

"Then it had to be someone who knew you," I blurted. "And someone who knew the value of the clock."

Cyril shrugged. "Maybe. It could have been someone who heard about the clock but was never in the house. Word gets around sometimes. Roxie or Finley might have mentioned it to a friend, who told someone else about it. Who knows? But it's very disturbing."

Cyril gazed at me, grim. "I know you care about Roxie. But I share this with you in the strictest confidence. Do I have your word that you won't tell anyone?"

Chapter 12

How was I supposed to answer that? Roxie was a friend. What if Cyril was dying? What if he was going to tell me something earthshaking, like he wasn't her dad?

"I need your help, Florrie. Please."

I relented. He was a nice man and he looked so desperate. "May I use my judgment about whether to tell Roxie?"

"No." He took off his glasses and cleaned them. "Roxie cannot know this."

It wasn't sounding any better. But I could see his despair. "All right." I held my breath.

He gazed at me without his glasses. I hadn't noticed before that his eyes were a beautiful, clear sky blue.

"After my wife died, I thought I would never meet anyone else. Roxie was the focus of my life," he said. "And then a couple of years later, I met a woman who changed everything. I actually thought I might have that very rare thing, two incredible loves in one lifetime. But her ex-husband killed her."

"Because of your relationship?" I gasped.

"The police said it had nothing to do with me. He was a very troubled man. The intellectual part of me could accept that. But the rest of me was tormented by the notion that I may have influenced the thinking of her former husband. I couldn't shake the possibility that our relationship had driven him to the brink."

"I'm sorry, Cyril." I didn't see why Roxie shouldn't know about that, though.

He nodded. "I had won and lost at love twice. I was done. You've heard of helicopter moms? I was the drone dad. I threw myself into everything and anything that interested Roxie. Ballet and soccer, then we went through a long period of riding and horse shows. I refused to allow other parents to drive Roxie and her friends. Please understand, it wasn't an obsession or anything weird. I was so afraid I would lose her, too."

I felt terrible for him. But how had Roxie felt? Smothered?

"She went to college as far away from me as she could get." Cyril smiled wryly. "I can't blame her. She wanted freedom. What she doesn't know and would never forgive is that while she was there, I paid someone to check up on her now and then. She still talks about the night she was mugged outside of a bar and a man swooped in and saved her. She never knew who he was, but I did."

Good heavens! I would have been furious with my dad had he done something like that. It turned out well, of course, but it would have angered *me* if my father had done such a thing. "Didn't you trust Roxie?"

"You'll be happy to know that I went to a therapist who helped me understand that I wasn't evil or unhinged. It wasn't even that I was trying to protect Roxie. I was protecting myself from losing the only person I had left in my life." He held up both palms as if to prevent me from jumping to conclusions.

"I won't say that I never worried about her anymore, but I threw myself into charities and focused on helping people for whom I could make a difference. When Roxie graduated and came back to Washington, she made me promise that my drone dad days were over. And they were. In spite of me, not because of me, Roxie is a wonderful person. I'm very proud of my little girl."

He swallowed hard. I had a feeling more was coming. "When Roxie married Finley a couple of years ago, I didn't want to be the third wheel. I didn't want Roxie to feel like she always had to include her old dad or worry that I was alone."

Oh no, now what had he done?

"I'm not the type to meet women online. That strikes me as odd. How do you know if they are who they claim to be? So I signed up for a ballroom dance class."

"A dance class?"

"Think about it. What could be better than meeting women who like to dance? Plus there's no pressure or obligation. If you're not interested in someone, you don't have to make excuses. There's no implication of a commitment. You don't know anything about them and they don't know anything about you. It's all very casual. Unfortunately, I met Hilda Rattenhorst."

"You did say ballroom dance?" Hilda didn't strike me as the ballroom-dancing type.

"I did. Hilda took a liking to me. I think she was drawn to me because of my background."

"Is that a nice way of saying she wanted to contact your lost loved ones?"

"Something like that. It began so innocently. I saw her at our class and that was it. I never asked her out. Never phoned her. Never had any outside contact with her at all. And then, suddenly, it seemed as if I saw her everywhere I went. I realized that she must be following me or tracking me in some way. Fortunately, the class came to an end, and I stupidly thought that would solve the problem. That her infatuation, if that's what it was, would come to an abrupt end. But that wasn't the case. She hounded me as if she knew my every step."

His voice rose as he grew more agitated.

The door opened and a nurse peered in. "Everything okay in here?"

Cyril waved at her to go away. "Fine."

In a low voice she said, "You're supposed to stay calm, Mr. Oldfield. Perhaps your visitor should leave."

I could take a hint. I stood up but Cyril reached out and grabbed my hand. "Just a moment more, Nurse Ratched."

I turned to look at her. She grimaced and closed the door.

Cyril released my hand and whispered, "I'm worried about Roxie. I've had a lot of time to think. The truth is that there's no reason for anyone to want to kill me."

"I thought it was a burglary gone wrong."

"Nonsense. The clock had already been removed from its place on the mantel and was found outside the house in the backyard near a window where the burglar presumably gained entry." Cyril leaned toward me.

"With all respect to the police, if the burglar had already removed the valuable clock from the house, why would he or she return inside to kill me? The logical thing to do would have been to flee and grab the clock on the way out."

Cyril sat back in his chair. "No, Florrie. Even an armchair detective like myself can see the giant flaw in that theory. He or she had the goods. Yet the burglar returned. He didn't smash me over the head with something and leave me unconscious. He intentionally slit my throat. I hadn't seen him or her. I couldn't identify the person. There was no reason to take such a drastic measure."

I was reeling. Cyril's argument made sense. A common thief might go back to retrieve more valuables, but a *common* thief probably wouldn't have known the value of the clock. He wasn't running through the house with a pillowcase, throwing silver into it. No, he had come for the clock and had already achieved his goal. Even if Cyril surprised him or her by coming home early, he could have easily slipped out the window, grabbed the clock, and been off before Cyril even realized that it was missing.

"Do you want me to talk to Eric about this?"

"That wouldn't be a bad idea. But I have a bigger problem. I don't know who would want to kill me or why."

"Is that why you told me about Hilda?"

"Yes. I understand that Hilda was with Roxie at the time. It couldn't have been her."

"I'm not sure she could have overpowered you, either. Even unexpected and from behind."

"Quite so. I can't shake the notion that Hilda had a hand in this, though. Now I'm worried about Roxie's safety. I have spoken with Finley, who has agreed to make excuses to walk her to work and back home. It's a blessing that Roxie's job as Jacquie's assistant keeps her at the mansion most of the time. I know she's safe there because Mr. DuBois almost never leaves the premises. Can you help me? Keep an eye on her? Dissuade her from traipsing around unaccompanied? Watch who is following her?"

"You're asking me to spy on Roxie?"

"I was trying to avoid that word."

Roxie would hate me. On the other hand, maybe she would be relieved that we were all looking out for her. In any event, given Cyril's situation, I could hardly say no, even if it was only to calm his mind and I didn't spy on Roxie.

"Cyril, I don't understand. That person attacked you, not Roxie. Why do you think she's in danger?"

"That person meant to kill me. I won't allow him or her to hurt Roxie. I have a call in to Ellis Willoughby."

"The guy who sent the skull?"

"The very same. I'm hoping he can set up around-the-clock protection for Roxie. And maybe I can help him out of whatever mess he has found himself in."

"I'll see what I can do." I was about to say that I couldn't make promises, but decided it was wiser to change the subject quickly so his blood pressure wouldn't spike. "You seem to be doing well, except for that bandage and a croak in your voice. Will you be going home soon?"

"I hope so. Now they're worried about my heart, if you can believe that. To be honest, as much as I want to go, I don't know that I'll ever be comfortable there anymore. I had no idea that guy was in my house. How can I ever close my eyes and sleep peacefully in my own home again? I'll always be listening for him."

His heart? That didn't sound good.

"He tried to kill me." He touched the bandage on his throat briefly. Cyril reached for my hand. "Don't let anyone hurt Roxie."

It wasn't as though I would be glued to her or able to defend her if the need arose. But to make him feel better, I said, "I'll look after her. You just get well."

Cyril closed his eyes. I figured that was an opportunity to leave. Suspecting that he needed a nap, I slipped out the door and picked up the other bouquet.

A quick inquiry at the nursing station revealed that Glen was on a lower floor. I found his room, knocked, and peeked in.

Glen's left leg was propped up on a pillow. Even from a distance I could see how swollen it was.

"Florrie!" Glen waved for me to come in. He smiled when he saw the flower arrangement. "At least it doesn't have any snakes in it."

"How do you feel?"

"A little better today. Yesterday I was dizzy, nauseous, and in incredible pain. But the swelling seems to have stopped, so the docs are hopeful."

"I can't even imagine. I heard it happened in your delivery truck?"

Glen shook his head as if he could hardly believe it. "Isn't that the strangest thing? I've heard those stories about snakes wrapping themselves around plants and being transported across the country to a store, but I never imagined one would end up in my truck. The company is researching my load yesterday. Either someone shipped a snake that got loose or it hitched a ride in a package."

I couldn't help shuddering. "People ship snakes?"

"Yeah. They're not supposed to but it happens. Usually they give them a tranquilizer or something so they'll sleep in transit. I guess this one didn't get enough of the snoozy juice."

"You're being very upbeat about it. I think I'd be bitter."

Glen crooked his finger at me to come closer. "Have any weird things happened at Color Me Read?"

I was saying no when I realized that lots of odd things had happened. "Like what?" I asked.

"You know that package I delivered to you yesterday? The crate?"

I nodded. I knew perfectly well which box he meant. The one Harry came in.

"I tell you, Florrie, I heard sounds coming from that package. Sort of a moaning."

Chills ran through me. Was Harry the source of the horrible wailing we had heard? That couldn't be.

I must have looked skeptical because Glen said, "I stopped the truck and looked for the source but it never happened when I was watching the package. I know it sounds crazy, but after I delivered it to you, the wailing didn't happen anymore. It was coming from your box. What was inside it?"

I was hesitant to tell him the truth. Would he freak out? "I promise you that there were no snakes or anything else inside that was alive."

"Uh-huh," Glen said in a tone that conveyed his disbelief. "What was it? Come on, now. I'm laid up here in the hospital. The least you can do is tell me what was in your package."

I sighed. "A skull and a scrying mirror."

Horrified, Glen shrieked, "It's possessed! I knew it. That's why the snake bit me. Get rid of it, Florrie. That skull is bad mojo. Devilry, I tell you! You have to burn it!"

He was screaming so loud that a nurse rushed into the room.

I could feel my face flushing. I seemed to be upsetting everyone I visited. And I had meant well!

"I'm sorry," I said. "I didn't intend to upset him."

The nurse calmly assured me, "It's not you. It's the venom. It happens. They seem okay, and then they're delusional. Perhaps you should go."

I hurried out the door before I could agitate Glen further. I was glad to leave the hospital but Glen's screaming stayed with me. As I walked and took in the real world around me, I relaxed. Cyril had something—or, more precisely, *someone*— to fear. Glen was delusional. At least, that was what I wanted to believe.

Because of the ghost marauders, I had hurried to the bookstore and hadn't eaten breakfast. As I recalled, Auntie Amy's Doughnuts was on the way to Roxie's house. The scent wafted out to the street as I approached the shop and it almost pulled me inside. How could anyone walk by without buying a doughnut? Minutes later, I was armed with lattes and the fresh-from-the-fryer cinnamon doughnuts that were Roxie's favorite. I continued to her house at a brisk walk so the doughnuts would still be warm when I arrived.

Roxie and Finley lived in a gorgeous two-story white brick home that had to be at least one hundred years old. Forest-green shutters flanked the tall windows. The door was painted to match them.

A tree on the tiny lawn bore leaves that I stopped to admire. The stems were bright red and ran through the spiky round leaves like veins. In the middle, the leaves were still green, but their spiky edges had turned a brilliant red.

When I clanked the door knocker, a gracious lion with a ring in his mouth, I heard someone inside the house move. "Roxie?" I called.

There was no response. "Roxie? It's Florrie!"

I heard shuffling on the other side of the door. "Roxie! Are you all right?"

The door opened one inch. She peered at me. "Hurry inside," she hissed.

I stepped into a small foyer. She slammed the door and locked it. "Did you see her?" asked Roxie breathlessly.

"Who?"

"The woman who was following Finley in the bookstore."

"She was here?" I asked. "I didn't notice her outside."

"She's been lurking around the house."

Roxie was thoroughly disheveled. Her beautiful blond hair hung in a ratty ponytail that had migrated toward the right side of her head. The buttons on her blouse were in the wrong holes. But it was her eyes that worried me. They were large with fear and her pupils were dilated.

I reached for the doorknob to look outside.

Roxie slammed her hand down on mine. "No!" she howled. "What are you doing?"

"Looking for her."

"Please don't." She glanced around as if she didn't know what to do.

I had been to Roxie's house before but hadn't ventured upstairs or into the kitchen. "You look like you could use some coffee. Where's the kitchen?"

Roxie led me through a classic living room and dining

room that had been decorated in soothing tones of cream, beige, and pink. They were feminine and extremely elegant.

"This is such a beautiful home," I said.

"Thank you. It's very special to me. Florrie, I can never thank you enough for saving my dad."

"I didn't save him. All I did was make a racket to scare away the intruder. I just came from the hospital. He looks pretty good except for that bandage on his throat."

"They're keeping him a little bit longer." Roxie winced. "I can't even imagine how horrible it must have been when that guy tried to cut his throat. What a barbaric thing to do. What kind of sicko does that? It's just . . . horrific!"

"Has he told you how it happened?"

She nodded. "He came home and walked straight into the dining room to pour himself a drink. Suddenly someone grabbed him from behind and slit his throat. I can't imagine how afraid Dad must have been."

Chapter 13

"The knife was from his kitchen." Roxie pressed her fingers against her temples. "I can hardly bear to think of it."

"That's horrible."

Roxie shuddered. "Thank heaven you were there to interrupt or Dad would be dead. The doctor said he's very lucky to be alive."

Chills ran through me. It was horrifying to imagine what he went through. No wonder he was concerned about Roxie's safety. "Have they said whether he will make a full recovery?"

She nodded. "The doctor says the prognosis is good, so I'm very hopeful."

We reached the kitchen, which appeared to be in an addition. A charming round table by a giant Palladian window looked out on the fenced backyard. I set the lattes down on the table and found small dishes in the kitchen.

When we were seated, I asked, "Is Finley around?"

"Mmm. These are still warm! Thanks, Florrie." Roxie drank some of her latte. "Finley isn't home at the moment."

I frowned. Hadn't he promised Cyril that he would walk

Roxie to work? Or maybe, like me, he had only said that to calm Cyril.

"Have the doctors indicated when Cyril can go home?" I asked.

Roxie set her doughnut on the table. "Apparently, he has an irregular heart rhythm, and they want to put him on Coumadin, but it's too soon, given the nature of his injury. So they're going to watch him for a couple of days before they release him. Frankly, I hope they keep Dad as long as possible. I don't want him to go home. I've called a couple of security companies to give us estimates on beefing up the alarm system."

"The intruder managed to get in despite an alarm?" I asked.

"Dad and I have never used it. We didn't think we had to. The alarm system is ancient. I don't know if it works anymore. We need to be sure the house will be safe for him. It breaks my heart. That house has been in my family for over a century. And now all the wonderful memories and happy events have been tainted by the actions of one sick creep."

"I'm so sorry." What else could I say?

She sighed. "I'm grateful that Dad is alive. It could have been so much worse!" She forced a smile. "Thank you for bringing the doughnuts and lattes. Everyone has been so kind. Jacquie said to take all the time I needed. I think it would do me good to work, though. You know, take my mind off things for a while. If you wait while I dress, I'll walk over there with you."

When she disappeared upstairs, I walked to the front door and opened it as quietly as I could. The street was amazingly still. Not a single person, dog, or squirrel was to be seen. I heard Roxie upstairs and closed the door quickly. There was no point in agitating her further.

Roxie looked better when she reappeared, but she still

wasn't quite her usual self. She seemed worried. I gave her a hug. "Your dad will be okay and home before you know it."

"I hope you're right." She sucked in a deep breath. "Now, if I can get that woman to leave Finley alone, maybe life will get back to normal."

While we were walking back to the Maxwell mansion, I said, "Finley has that charming British accent we Americans love. Maybe she's smitten with his accent. Did he grow up in England?"

"His background is so sad that just thinking about it makes me want to embrace him and hold him tight. He lived in London with his parents, a brother, and a sister. But his parents and siblings were killed in an airplane crash when he was five. He was the only member of the family not on the plane. They had left Finley at home with the nanny because he had chicken pox. I lost my mom when I was young, but I can't fathom what it must be like to lose your whole family. How can anyone learn to cope with that?"

"I can't imagine. Who raised him?"

"An uncle took him in—well, technically. He had nannies until he was seven, at which point he was shipped off to boarding school. Just between the two of us, I think his loneliness and lack of family are the reasons he came to the United States. Even though he doesn't really have much family in England, he doesn't feel it as keenly here because that life is an ocean away."

"Does he go back to visit?" I asked.

"He never mentions it. I don't think he wants to go back. Maybe it's too painful for him."

"And he has a new family here now," I said.

We had reached the paved area between the mansion and the carriage house. Roxie shot me a dazzling smile. "I think he's very grateful for that."

She entered the mansion through the back door. I was

greeted by Frodo and Peaches at my place. Mr. DuBois was nowhere to be seen but my kitchen sink sparkled. I took Frodo out for a quick walk. On our return, Peaches crunched on salmon cat food, Frodo chewed a tooth-cleaning faux bone, and I munched on crackers and hummus.

That afternoon I baked pumpkin cupcakes and had fun decorating them with cream cheese frosting that stood up to look like ghosts. I added chocolate-chip eyes and was very pleased with the results. When I was finished, I retreated to the sofa with a mug of tea and pulled out my sketchbook.

I doodled Roxie's beautiful, round face first. I drew her baby blond hair and kind eyes of better days. She'd been completely traumatized by the attack on Cyril and certainly wasn't herself at the moment.

Cyril's face was easier to draw than his daughter's. The rectangular wire-rimmed glasses that largely hid his honest eyes were a snap, as were his mustache and chin patch. I hoped he was doing better and could go home soon. He was so worried about Roxie, but when I thought about it, he hadn't actually said why he thought someone might harm her. To hurt him, perhaps?

I hadn't known that Finley had lost his parents. He was so young. He never really had a family. I couldn't imagine growing up that way.

I drifted off on the sofa. At six o'clock, Frodo and Peaches joined forces to wake me. They pawed me gently. Peaches sat on my chest and Frodo finally let out a soft woof. I laughed at their efforts and took their hint. After a walk with Frodo, I fed them dinner. I spent the rest of the evening curled up with a good mystery.

But just after two in the morning, my telephone rang, awakening me from deep sleep. A man on the other end informed me that the police needed access to Color Me Read.

Chapter 14

What now? The officer who called didn't give me much information. I hung up the phone and pulled on jeans, a long-sleeved T-shirt, and a warm, fuzzy scarlet vest.

Frodo was ecstatic that something was afoot. I was less enthused. I suited him up in his halter and leash. Peaches, with the serene confidence of a cat, remained curled up on the bed. No silly midnight phone calls would disturb her!

The streets in my neighborhood were calm and quiet. It was actually a lovely time to walk. Few cars passed us. I could tell where night owls lived by their windows that still glowed warm from the lights within.

Everything changed abruptly when we reached the bookstore. Four police vehicles were parked on the street. A few people, presumably some who lived close by as well as university students who had been out partying at local bars, stood around in small groups, watching what was going on.

Six officers waited at the front door of Color Me Read.

"Hi. I'm Florrie Fox, the manager," I said.

"Sorry to have to bother you, ma'am, but it appears someone was locked up in your store tonight."

"I beg your pardon? Are you saying someone is inside?"

How could that possibly have happened? Veronica and Bob knew they were supposed to do a walk-through before leaving the store for the day.

"Yes, ma'am. We received a 911 call from someone claiming to be stuck inside the building."

I was stunned. "You'd better be careful when you go inside," I said. "Not only do we check the entire building before we close, but for fire-safety reasons, both the front and back doors can still be opened from the inside after we lock up. It sounds to me like someone might be trying to draw you inside."

A couple of the cops exchanged looks of concern.

"I'll have to turn off the alarm," I said. "I can only do that inside the store."

"Ma'am, it would be safer for you to remain out here until we give you the all-clear," said one of them. That was fine by me. I unlocked the front door and the police officers rushed in.

They flicked on lights and spread through the store, shouting to the person who was allegedly locked inside. Naturally, the alarm went off at that point, attracting even more attention from people on the street.

One of the officers returned and asked, "Can you turn that thing off?"

Frodo and I dashed inside. I punched in the code, which silenced the alarm and then quickly called the alarm company to assure them that the police were on the premises.

Chicken that I am, I hurried back outside and observed anxiously through the front door while Frodo made friends with people who were hanging around, watching the excitement.

I'm not much for woo-woo sensing of things, but a creepy feeling came over me, as if someone were watching me. I turned my head to the right. Harry was in the display window. A battery-operated candle flickered behind his eye sockets. For just a moment, I could have sworn he was grinning at me.

I shook it off and focused on the police officers. Two of them were coming down the stairs. The one who had spoken to me walked over, shaking his head. "I don't get it. The call originated from inside the store but there's no one in here."

"Maybe the person let himself out?" I suggested feebly. I killed my own theory by adding, "But that would have set off the alarm and I didn't receive a notification that a door had been opened."

"We know the alarm was working," observed one of the officers wryly.

"It was my day off," I said, "so I wasn't here when they closed last night. The only thing I can imagine is that someone was waiting by the back door and let himself out at the exact moment that the alarm went off a few minutes ago."

The officers gazed at one another doubtfully.

"Exactly what did the caller say?" I asked. "Is it possible that it was a gag?"

One of them said angrily, "A false or fictitious report of a crime is punishable by a fine and jail time. If we find out who did this . . ."

That wasn't helpful. Why yell at me? It wasn't as though *I* made the phony call. "You're certain the call came from inside the store?"

"That's our understanding."

"Wouldn't most people stuck inside a store call from their cell phones?" I mused.

"You'd think so. We'll go back through one more time. Man, Halloween is starting early this year. Strange things always happen." The officers disappeared inside again.

After another thorough search, the cops gave up. The people gathered on the sidewalk drifted away. I set the alarm and locked the front door.

A wild wind blew along the street when I left the bookstore. Leaves fluttered through the air, and a cat yowled somewhere in the distance.

It was too bad it wasn't Halloween yet. The moon was almost full and it shone in the sky like a huge flashlight casting the earth in a bluish light. For a change, Frodo and I strolled along the opposite sidewalk for a better view of the Halloween decorations on the south side of the street. Many of the decorative lights were off, but some people kept them on all night. Jack-o'-lanterns grimaced at us from porches and ghosts swayed in the wind.

Ancient trees lined the street. The moon gleamed through the trees with nearly bare branches. Leaves that had been loosened by the blasts of wind floated down in the night.

As I approached Coralue's house, three thin boys cackled and ran around, darting back and forth in front of her Halloween display. As I drew closer, I could hear them daring one another to lie down inside the coffin.

They quieted with suspense when one of them lifted the top. When the hinges creaked, he screamed like he was in a horror movie and let the top drop back in place.

One of them called him a sissy. I watched as he boldly raised the lid of the coffin again. He peered inside, yelped, and took off running with the other two on his heels.

I chuckled and wondered what Coralue had placed inside. It was having the desired spooky effect—whatever it was.

Frodo tugged at his leash and eagerly sniffed Coralue's display.

She was a master of Halloween pranks. I found myself hesitant to look up at the window where I had seen the woman with the candle. It was ridiculous, of course. I was letting myself be spooked by her story about the poor woman who had lived there confined to the top floor. If I had seen anything, it was fake and had been arranged by Coralue.

I forced myself to look up at the beautiful window where I thought I had seen the woman. It was completely dark. I felt a little bit better. No ghostly apparitions looked back at me.

Frodo sniffed around the coffin.

I stared at the faux butler holding a candelabra with glimmering plastic flames on the candles. There was something different about him. A scarf! Coralue had added a long scarf around his neck. My gaze fell upon the coffin at his feet, and curiosity got the better of me.

What clever thing had Coralue stashed in the coffin to scare kids?

Grinning, I lifted the lid to see for myself.

Chapter 15

The dim glow from the butler's candelabra illuminated a woman's face in the coffin. I screamed and jumped back. The coffin lid banged shut with a loud thud, which only made me scream again. No wonder those kids had taken off. It looked so animated and lifelike. And, worse, the face seemed familiar.

The front door of the Throckmorton house opened. Coralue shouted, "Who's out there? Leave my Halloween decorations alone!"

"It's . . . it's me, Florrie, Mrs. Throckmorton."

Coralue marched toward me wrapped in a quilted bathrobe. "Florrie! What in heaven's name is happening out here?"

"The body you placed in the coffin spooked some kids. It scared me, too!"

The faint rays of the faux candle quivered across her face. She stared at me for a long moment. Then she burst into laughter. "That's very good, Florrie! Oh! We should set up a haunted house. You're so convincing."

I was going to be a lot more convincing in about a second. I gulped hard. "Are you saying there isn't anything in the coffin?"

"Well, of course there is. Look again, honey." She lifted the coffin lid and I hesitantly peered inside.

The light from the candelabra didn't help much. Frodo placed his front paws on the side of the coffin and the dark image suddenly became clear to me. I burst out laughing. I was looking at an image of Frodo and me.

"How devilishly clever of you to place a mirror inside. No matter who looks in, the last person he will expect to see will be himself."

"I'm so glad you approve! There's nothing like spooking people by having them find themselves inside the coffin." She cackled with glee.

"No wonder those kids took off running." Frodo tugged at his leash. I had slipped the end over my hand and held on tight. I glanced at him to see why he was pulling. He was digging! Not in Coralue's perfect lawn!

"Frodo, stop that," I hissed.

"What's he after?" asked Coralue.

"I have no idea. Frodo!" I pulled on the leash but he used every ounce of muscle to stay put.

"Look at this," said Coralue. "One of those kids must have smashed my pumpkin."

I turned on the flashlight in my phone. The pumpkin had broken open. Seeds and pumpkin guts were strewn in the grass. I walked toward Frodo. "Did you find a ball or a toy?"

Coralue edged close to me and we peered at the soil in her garden bed that Frodo had churned up.

For a long moment, neither of us spoke.

"Is that a foot?" whispered Coralue.

"Looks like it," I murmured in response. Surely it couldn't be the foot in the rug of which Hilda had spoken.

"Pull on it and see if it's a gag," she said.

"No way. It looks real. It's your display. You pull on it!"

It dawned on me that she was acting as if she hadn't placed it there. A woman who would put a mirror inside a coffin wouldn't hesitate to add a lifelike foot sticking out of the ground.

"Ha, ha, ha," I said drolly.

"Florrie," Coralue spoke in a frightened tone. "I did not add a foot to my display. It's actually a good idea, but I didn't put it there."

I wasn't sure whether to believe her or not. "Are you saying the foot isn't part of your decorations?"

"That's exactly what I'm saying."

We peered at it again.

Coralue released an unladylike snort. "The foot is too pale. It has to be latex. I know who did this—my neighbor, Gene Germain. Well! Two can play his game. Tomorrow morning I'll check out his yard and add a few touches of my own."

"That makes no sense whatsoever. Why would a neighbor add a foot sticking out from under the coffin?"

"That's the only possible explanation," she said indignantly.

"Maybe it's pale because the owner is dead."

"Nonsense . . . Go ahead and yank it out of the ground."

I pulled out my phone to call the police but thought better of it. What if it was a prop? Coralue loved Halloween frights. Chances were good that she had planted it there in the flower bed where she had placed the coffin and was trying to pull a fast one on me.

Frodo reached one paw toward the foot for a last dig. "No!" I yelped. But it was too late. He had exposed a bony ankle. It looked entirely too real. Either someone was buried in Coralue's flower bed or she was having a great time scaring me. "Coralue," I said in the firmest no-nonsense voice I could muster, "is this one of your props?"

"No!" Her voice was a little louder in protest.

"You're not trying to trick me?"

"One of us really ought to touch it," she suggested.

"Not me. I'm calling 911." I turned off the flashlight and dialed.

"Nine-one-one. What is the nature of your emergency?"

"I believe we have discovered a corpse. Well, a foot anyway."

"What is the address?"

"Mrs. Throckmorton, what's your address?" I asked. I repeated it to the dispatcher.

"Is he breathing?" asked the dispatcher.

"I doubt it." Did she not hear me say *corpse*?

"Can you check?"

"Ma'am, I'm not touching it." It totally grossed me out to tell her, "The body, if one is attached, is mostly buried."

"It would be helpful if you could tell me. If he's breathing you could assist by performing CPR."

I was going to have to come right out and say it. "It's a completely pale and dirty foot. I don't know if it's attached to a person or not but I can assure you that I'm not touching it, okay?"

At that moment, Coralue took it upon herself to reach out in the dark and feel it. She screamed, scaring Frodo.

"Are you under attack?" asked the dispatcher.

"No."

"Are you in a position where you cannot speak freely?"

"No. It's just that there may be a dead person."

"Officers have been dispatched to your location. Stay on the line with me until they have arrived."

I could see a squad car approaching. "They're here." I disconnected the call, ran to the edge of the street with Frodo, and waved my arms above my head. The vehicle parked in front of the Throckmorton house.

Two officers stepped out. The older one sniffled and blew his nose. "Where's the body?" he grumbled.

"It's under the coffin." I pointed toward Coralue, who stood beside it.

The older cop looked at me like an angry bulldog. "Very funny. Dead body in a coffin. You two are old enough to know better. I can charge you with a crime for this."

Coralue blabbered hysterically. "No, no, no. You don't understand. This isn't a joke. I know my decorations are pretty good but—"

He's not *in* the coffin," I explained.

The younger cop flipped open the coffin long enough to see his own reflection and slammed the lid down.

I turned the light in my phone back on and aimed it directly at the foot, "Right there."

The younger cop swayed a bit on seeing it. I wondered if it was the first time he had seen a death on his beat.

The older cop went back to the car and returned with a small jar. He rubbed some on his mustache and handed the container to the younger cop. "Vicks VapoRub. Smear it under your nose." He walked toward the coffin and squatted to examine the foot. "Either of you know who he is?"

He had to be kidding. I presumed that some feet might be readily identifiable through scars, tattoos, or jewelry but that wasn't the case here. "No."

For someone who loved frightening other people at Halloween, Coralue surprised me. She appeared to be in shock. "Coralue?" I clasped her hand. It was freezing. "Are you all right?"

She didn't say a word, but she shook her head ever so slowly.

While the older cop called the foot in on his radio, the younger cop asked, "When did you find him . . . er . . . it?"

"Just a few minutes ago." I was glad I was there. Coralue

might not have been able to handle it all by herself. "My dog, Frodo, found it."

The younger police officer moved Coralue and me to the sidewalk. He pulled out a pen and pad to write down our names and addresses. "How did you come to be here?"

Coralue had the best reason, of course. She lived there.

"I work at Color Me Read and was called because the police thought someone was locked inside the store. When I was walking home, some kids were opening the coffin and screaming. I thought Coralue had put something grisly inside as a joke, so I opened the coffin to have a look. Frodo was sniffing around and found the foot." I hastened to say, "But I saw a lot of people all day long, so no matter what time anything happened, I have alibi witnesses." Except, of course, for the entire afternoon and evening. Why had I said that?

The young cop stared at me. "What do you think happened?"

"I don't know but it can't be good. I seriously doubt that a person is walking around out there without his foot."

He glared at me.

Make a mental note, Florrie. Never suggest anything about a crime scene or a victim. You'll only appear guilty if you do.

"It's not like I buried the foot." The words were out of my mouth before I realized how obnoxious they sounded. No sooner had I realized that I shouldn't suggest anything than I went and did it again.

Thankfully a couple of police cars arrived just in time to distract the cop. Coralue looked sick. I wrapped an arm around her and gave her a little squeeze, which I hoped reassured her even though I was feeling very uneasy myself.

"How could this happen?" she whispered. "If I had thought someone might bury a body in my flower bed, I would have poured concrete over the entire yard."

"Coralue, I have a feeling that whatever happened here

would have happened anyway. I seriously doubt that the presence of a flower bed or your decorations had anything to do with the buried foot."

"Oh, Florrie! I'll never forgive myself. I was having fun, thinking about spooky things. I never expected anyone to get hurt. Do you think I need a lawyer?"

I held my breath. Coralue was the last person on the planet I would have pegged as a killer. But she was already worried about hiring a lawyer. Was that a natural reaction? Or did she have more to worry about because the body was on her lawn? Had I been too hasty to imagine that Coralue had nothing to do with the foot?

We watched in silence as the police set up spotlights around the coffin. The fake butler standing over it looked perfectly ludicrous. While we watched, an officer asked us to move back. He strung yellow police tape in a wide swath across the front of Coralue's house.

Still, we had a close view of what they were doing. Only Frodo appeared to be taking it in stride. He sat down beside me as though he was bored. We watched as they removed the dirt and uncovered a rolled-up rug. The foot jutted out of the end.

Chapter 16

It took some time for them to unroll the rug. When they did, the older cop walked toward us and lifted the crime scene tape. "Would you come with me, please?"

We followed him to the corpse.

"Now do you recognize him?"

Coralue and I peered at the body of a man. He did look familiar.

Coralue gasped.

In that moment, it came to me. "Manny Menz," I said.

Coralue moaned like he was her very best friend. She leaned forward for a closer look. "Yes. I believe you're right. It's Manny. The kid from the bakery."

But why would he be in a rug in her yard? That was definitely odd. However, a bigger question loomed. *Why was Manny dead?*

I honestly didn't think that Coralue had murdered Manny, and if she had, she was savvy enough not to bury his body in her own yard where someone would surely notice it. But why was she already thinking about calling a lawyer?

"When was the last time you saw him?" asked the older cop.

I hoped my panic wouldn't show. I had nothing to do

with whatever had happened to Manny. But he had tried to steal Harry. Would that be considered an argument? A confrontation? It wasn't like I had anything to hide. Still I tried to choose my words wisely and accurately. It was after midnight. Was it accurate to say night before last? He glared at me like I was taking too long to answer. "The night before last a psychic read from her book at Color Me Read. Manny came to hear her. I saw him there."

"What time was that?"

"Must have been around seven thirty or eight o'clock."

"Did you see him today?"

"No." I breathed a little easier.

"You're sure about that?"

What was he getting at? "Positive." I wasn't about to admit it to this cop, but everyone who worked in the store would have been on the alert for him, especially today *because* Manny had tried to steal Harry. I hadn't been there, but surely Bob or Veronica would have phoned me if Manny had come to the store again. I reconsidered my stance. Maybe I *should* tell the cop that Manny tried to steal the skull. If he found out from someone else, he might think I was keeping something important from him intentionally.

Coralue tugged me and Frodo into a dark, shadowy corner of her yard. From where we stood, the orange lights twinkling from her trees only made the scene surrounding the coffin more surreal. Silhouettes of people, probably neighbors, began to appear on the sidewalk, their murmuring a haunting sound in the night.

Coralue still clutched my arm when she said in a whisper, "It's my son."

"Manny is your son?"

"No. Manny had a run-in with my son. It was over a judo competition. My son, Hayes, says Manny cheated. They've been arguing ever since." Her grip on my arm tightened.

"Maybe you do need to consult a lawyer. Is your son in town?"

"Yes, of course. He lives in a house over on O Street."

"Surely their tiff wouldn't have ended in murder?" I asked with hope.

Coralue took a deep breath. "I believe I'll step inside to call our lawyer. He usually handles wills and such, but maybe he'll know where to send me for advice."

I watched as her small figure receded and disappeared inside her house. I looked back at the police milling around the spotlights. Poor Manny. What a horrible end to his life.

Eager to avoid anyone chatty who had lined up on the sidewalk to see what was going on, I steered Frodo through a couple of bushes to the neighboring property that belonged to Gene Germain.

Frodo and I jumped when someone screamed. As far as I could tell, we had set off a talking skeleton that appeared to be trapped in the bushes. Frodo wasn't sticking around for it. He tugged at his leash, desperate to get away.

Gene's yard was like walking into a horror movie. A face with deranged eyes peered out at us from a window. A giant spider guarded the front door. Trick-or-treaters would have to walk between its legs to collect candy. Even worse, the spider had captured a desperate zombie in his web. On the other side of the lawn, a clown was begging to be let out of a jail cell. A glow-in-the-dark sign hung on it that said, *Do not feed the clown.*

We must have triggered something in the clown because his begging turned into a deep, scary voice that issued threats. We ran to the sidewalk and walked home.

In the morning, my alarm clock went off far too early for my taste. It had been a late night and I longed to stay in bed.

Frodo poked my face with his cold nose a couple of times. Apparently, he wasn't as pooped as I was.

After a shower, I dressed in a black-and-white houndstooth skirt with black tights and a tomato-red turtleneck sweater. My long hair air-drying, I hurried to the kitchen for a cup of coffee.

Somewhat caffeine-fortified, I took Frodo for his morning walk. Naturally, we ambled in the direction of Coralue's home. A couple of police officers were still working there, ignoring the passersby.

Traffic slowed as drivers craned their necks to get a better look.

Gene Germain, a portly fellow whom I judged to be in his sixties, watched with great interest. According to Mr. DuBois, who knew all the neighborhood gossip, Germain was a semi-retired lawyer who courted the neighborhood widows in hopes of home-cooked meals.

Frodo greeted Gene's bulldog, excited to see another canine.

"Good morning." Gene held his hand out to me to shake. "Florrie Fox, if I'm not mistaken?"

"Yes. And this is Frodo."

"He's a good-looking fellow. Liberty always enjoys meeting other dogs. Would you by any chance know what happened here?"

Ugh. I skipped over my own involvement in the matter. "Manny Menz from the bakery was buried in Coralue's flower bed."

"Is Coralue all right?" he asked.

"She's quite shaken."

"I can imagine. I was ready to make jokes about going to extremes with her Halloween decorations, but this is truly disturbing. Manny . . . little guy? Lots of dark hair?"

"I'm afraid so."

His eyebrows rose. "I figured his boorish ways would catch up to him. I've seen it too many times. Bad eggs never end up well."

That was interesting. Maybe his behavior with the skull was the kind of thing he did all the time. "Was he in trouble with the law?"

"Not that I know of. But he associated with reprehensible people. I warned him to clean up his act. You know how kids are, though. They never take good advice. Nice meeting you and Frodo." He and Liberty drifted away on their morning walk.

Frodo and I went home for breakfast.

Peaches's meal of pumpkin and chicken smelled more enticing than the cold yogurt I had opened for myself. It was worrisome to me that the canned cat food was more attractive than my own breakfast, which I turned my nose up at.

Keeping an eye on my clock collection, so I wouldn't be late opening the store, I fed Frodo and packed a dozen cupcakes in a bag to take to work with me. I was putting the rest in the fridge when someone knocked on the door.

I peered out the window. Mr. DuBois again.

"Good morning," I said, opening the door.

He marched inside carrying a tray, which he deposited on my coffee table. He lifted the cover off a plate. "English breakfast tea just the way you like it and cinnamon-apple pancakes with maple syrup."

Except for the time when Eric was staying with me while he healed from an accident, Mr. DuBois had never done this. I was immediately suspicious.

"To what do I owe this luxury?"

"You were very kind to allow me to stay, er, clean here yesterday. And I've heard via the domestic grapevine that you might have been involved in the chaos in Coralue's front yard?"

I had to love the nosy guy. "No one will be at the mansion today?" I guessed.

He whipped out a napkin and held it up. "Please eat before your food gets cold."

He didn't have to ask me twice. I took a bite of the pancakes. They were redolent of autumn flavors and I could see apples inside them. I turned my head to see where he had gone.

Peaches was rubbing against his legs! My instinct was to leap up and remove her so she wouldn't bother him, but then I realized that he was whispering to her. I could hear her purring.

I tried not to chuckle and ate my breakfast.

Mr. DuBois sat down opposite me. "Is it true that Manny Menz is dead?"

"I'm afraid so." I filled him in on the phone call from the bookstore and the discovery of Manny's corpse.

He sat quietly for a moment, musing. "It had to be a ghost. Possibly even Manny's ghost."

I finished the last bite of pancake. "I don't understand."

"The phone call from the bookstore. I've heard of such things before. Deceased husbands calling from the wife's home when she needed help. That sort of thing. It happens."

I doubted that. But I questioned the wisdom of arguing about it with him. I would have to get someone in to have a look at the phone system in the store.

Mr. DuBois made a tent with his fingers. "Miss Florrie, I fear we have a problem. Maxwell and Jacqueline are having a tiff over Hilda Rattenhorst."

"I'm not surprised."

"Maxwell believes that Hilda is a charlatan, intent on taking advantage of Jacquie. Jacquie, on the other hand, hopes that Hilda will be able to lead her to Caroline."

"That's very sad. Poor Jacquie. If a child of mine had gone missing, I think I might feel the same way."

"I can see how easy it would be to trick a bereaved parent," said Mr. DuBois. "I come to this dilemma from a different point of view than Maxwell. I fully believe in ghosts and that some people have the ability to contact them."

I sipped my tea. "The professor says there is no scientific evidence of ghosts."

"Once upon a time, we thought the world was flat. And that atoms were the smallest unit of matter. Imagine all the things we may not yet have figured out. Just because current science proclaims that ghosts are preposterous does not mean they aren't here. Just ask anyone who has encountered one."

He had a point. "Mr. DuBois, it was very kind of you to bring me breakfast. It was delicious. However, I sense that you are here to request something of me."

The left side of Mr. DuBois's mouth twitched. "It would have been less complicated had Maxwell rented the carriage house to someone I could manipulate more easily."

I laughed at his droll humor. "You don't have to bribe me. What is it that you want?"

"Maxwell and Jacquie had been getting along so well. She's the only one of his wives who was tolerable. I fear that if we don't take some sort of action, they will separate once again. Jacquie will end up with a loser and Maxwell will brood and go off on dangerous adventures."

"And you will worry yourself sick about them."

"They're far better together. They're *meant* to be together. I don't say that lightly. There are far too many mismatched marriages. But the professor and Jacquie are like bread and butter. He's a little crusty, and she's a mellow softy."

Though Veronica might claim differently, because I had warned her about dating questionable men, I wasn't in the habit of interfering with people's love lives. But I agreed with Mr. DuBois. The professor had been much happier since Jacquie came back into his life. "What do you have in mind?"

"I thought perhaps we might introduce Jacquie to a gentleman who would take an interest in her. A little bit of jealousy could convince Maxwell that life with Jacquie is worth indulging her interest in the paranormal."

"Ohhh, Mr. DuBois. I see your point, but interfering with their relationship that way could lead to disaster. What if Maxwell doesn't react as you hope? I'm not so sure about that."

"Or we could arrange for Maxwell to see a ghost."

He said it so simply, so airily, as if it would be easy to accomplish. "Mr. DuBois, if we did that, he would throw us both out."

"Nonsense. He needs us."

"Not that much! He would lose all faith in us."

"What if a male ghost were interested in Jacquie?" asked Mr. DuBois.

I nearly spewed my tea. "Then the professor would definitely break up with Jacquie and think we had all lost our marbles!"

"I shall ponder this. Halloween might be an excellent opportunity to help Maxwell reconsider his position."

I tried to discourage him delicately. "I'm not sure, Mr. DuBois. Your heart is in the right place, but in my experience, trying to trick people always backfires."

"I shall take your advice under consideration. In the meantime, I should like to wash your windows today."

"You are more than welcome to simply enjoy yourself without cleaning."

"Thank you, Miss Florrie." He collected the tray and set it beside the sink. "I do love your garden. The mansion garden is grand and formal. It's lovely, but there's something very

Zen and calming about the small world of the carriage house garden."

It sounded silly but I understood what he meant. An avid gardener had planted it with great forethought. It was an amazing place to lounge. Almost like a magical forest. Even though we were in the nation's capital, where life proceeded at a frenzied pace, that tiny garden felt removed from it all.

I brushed my teeth and said good-bye to Peaches and Mr. DuBois. Grabbing my jean jacket and Frodo's leash, I set off for the store.

Between regular business and everyone talking about Manny and the foot in the rug, the morning passed quickly. The social media news about Hilda and her premonition of a foot in a rug and murder brought more people into the store. We were ridiculously busy, even with all three of us working. There were those who seemed intent on finding a ghost or a dead man, but a lot of them were immediately intrigued by books.

As soon as I had a chance, I called the company that had installed our phone system. It seemed to be working fine at the moment, but after the false call the night before and the strange scream, I thought we'd better have it checked out.

"Maybe we should have Hilda come back again," suggested Bob. "This is crazy. Business is booming!"

I hated to admit it, but maybe I would have to relent and invite Hilda back before Halloween.

At ten minutes past one in the afternoon I was momentarily distracted by Roxie running into the store and dashing to the parlor with uncharacteristic speed.

Chapter 17

Roxie stopped abruptly in the entrance to the parlor.

Her beautiful hair was a mess again, as though she hadn't brushed it. It looked like she had pulled it back in a ponytail and spent a restless night tugging it every which way.

I left the checkout counter and walked over to her. Bags under her eyes suggested she hadn't slept. Her plump face, usually calm and serene, was flushed bright pink.

"Roxie? Are you all right?" I asked.

Her eyes were large. "Um, Jacquie sent me over for some copies of her books." She nervously fingered her earring.

Roxie knew perfectly well where we kept Jacquie's books. "Is something wrong?" I asked.

"No!" She said it too soon and too fast. "I'm just going to get a cup of coffee to warm up."

I returned to the checkout desk to help a customer but I saw her walk into the parlor, clutching a mug with both hands. When the customer left, I peeked inside the parlor.

Roxie stood at the display window, looking out at the street.

I walked up to her.

"Is it true that Manny was rolled up in a rug just like Hilda said?" she asked.

"His foot was even sticking out."

She swallowed hard and coughed. "How could she have known that? Jacquie says he was still alive when she told us about the foot in the rug."

Roxie was right. Hilda had announced the existence of a rug with a foot in it as soon as she arrived. Yet I had seen Manny later on in the evening when he tried to steal Harry.

I gazed at the display window. Harry wasn't there. Why was someone moving him around?

I could hear Veronica calling my name. I excused myself for a moment. Both Bob and Veronica were at the checkout desk with a guy from the company that had installed our phone system.

"Hi, Florrie. What kind of problem are you having?"

Veronica and Bob scooted out of our way.

I explained about the odd scream and, more important, that a call had been made from our phone to 911 but no one was in the building.

He tested the line and then the phone. "I hate to tell you this, but there are apps that enable people to make it appear they are calling from a different number."

"You mean like the spammers?" I asked.

"I mean you could do it if you wanted to. Kids do it all the time. It's a rotten trick, but it's not all that difficult."

"You're saying that someone intentionally arranged to have it look like he was calling the police from the bookstore?"

"Yup. It could have been a fluke. He might have made up a number and it happened to be yours."

"I don't think it was accidental. He told 911 that he was locked inside the building."

The phone guy laughed. "I haven't heard that one before. Of course, tying up 911 with that kind of stunt is probably illegal. So he created a fuss for no reason. I bet he was across the street watching. Kids do all kinds of crazy things."

"What about the scream?" I asked.

"There's nothing wrong with your phone or your connection. Maybe it originated on the other end. Hard to say what it was. Sometimes the weather causes problems. We've also seen a lot of issues with other electronic equipment interfering. That's annoying because you have to unplug everything and reconnect it all one at a time to find out which item is causing a problem. It was most likely a onetime thing." He grinned. "It's the time of year when ghosts and witches cause problems, too."

"Very funny."

"Call me if it happens again. From what I can see, you're in fine shape."

I thanked him and he walked out the door.

"I've heard static on a phone, Florrie," said Bob, "and that scream was not static."

"While we're on the subject of odd things happening, did one of you remove Harry from the display window?" I asked.

They looked ever so innocent when they chimed, "No."

Bob even managed to appear surprised. I thought that might have been a true reaction. After all, he had refused to touch Harry.

"The professor usually comes in early, maybe he moved Harry for some reason." Veronica did a convincing job of seeming disinterested.

At that moment, Jacquie walked down the stairs carrying the mirror the professor had received with the skull. "Did you see this? It's marvelous!"

"It's a black mirror," Bob said with all the enthusiasm of one who didn't care about interior decorating.

"Oh, sweetheart! It's not just a mirror. It's a scrying mirror." She turned around. "I think we should hang it somewhere."

"Crying mirror? What's that?" asked Bob.

"Ssssscrying," hissed Jacquie. "You can see the future or the past when you look into it."

"Like in Harry Potter!" exclaimed Bob.

"Honestly!" Jacquie let out a big sigh. "You do know that stories were written before Harry Potter, don't you? For instance, there was a scrying mirror in *Snow White*. They've been around a long time. Where shall we hang this? Ah, right here behind the checkout desk. I'll bring a black feather boa to dress it up a little bit."

"So, if I look into it, will I see the past?" asked Bob.

"You might" said Jacquie. "Or you might see the woman you will marry. Now on that subject, John tells me you don't have a girlfriend."

I was eager to leave that conversation and scurried into the parlor, where Roxie was chatting with Goldblum, who was making her laugh. I wasn't about to interrupt that. It was a relief to see her smile again.

I refilled the coffee and, using the need for goodies as an excuse, headed to the bakery where Manny had worked.

A line of people waiting for takeout coffee wound outside the door. But inside the bakery, it was nearly silent. Few people made use of the tables and chairs available for enjoying a treat with a cup of coffee. Mostly I was surprised that I didn't see anything about Manny. If it had been Bob who died, wouldn't we have closed the store for the day? Or at the very least, wouldn't people have been coming by to say lovely things about him? Nothing of that sort appeared to be happening here.

A gentleman with a very short, well-trimmed beard, whom

I suspected might be the manager, sat at one of the tables, making out what looked like a work schedule for employees.

I took a deep breath, hoping to gain courage to approach him. "Hi. Are you the manager?"

"Owner. Rami Kuchar." He looked up at me with interest. "Are you here for the job?"

"Job?" I repeated stupidly before I realized he probably meant Manny's job.

He pointed at the glass window in front of the shop. "Yeah. The *Help Wanted* sign?"

I sat down opposite him. "Are you filling Manny's position?"

He eyed me warily. "You don't look like one of his friends."

"Oh? How do they look?" I asked.

"Rough-and-tumble hooligans. He was my neighbor's nephew. I was trying to do him a favor by hiring the kid, but I regretted that from day one."

"Why was that?"

"Are you a cop?"

Seriously? I looked like a cop to him? It was sort of flattering. "No! I run Color Me Read just up the street. In fact, I ordered cupcakes and pumpkin cookies from you a couple of days ago."

Rami's lean face opened up. "Oh, yeah. I appreciate your business."

"They were great. And adorable."

"Yeah?" He brightened, as if I had given him a wonderful gift. "I love to bake but I don't usually hear what people think unless there's a problem, ya know? I'm back in the kitchen most of the morning so I depend on my employees to keep things running out here. I guess the bookstore is the same way."

"It is. I understand completely. As soon as there's a complaint, everyone comes looking for me."

We both laughed. I was surprised that we'd found something in common. It lightened the mood.

"So, I guess you heard about Manny," he said.

"Heard about him? I'm the one who called 911. I can't imagine why anyone would have wanted to hurt him."

Rami huffed. "Somewhere deep down I thought he was a good kid. But he was always bluffing and trying to make himself sound important. He ran into some trouble in a judo competition. I did my best to explain to him that he had to straighten up and fly right, but as you see, it did no good."

"A lot of people were angry with him?"

"Not so much angry as distrustful. Manny was a big talker. You know the kind? Claimed he was the son of a mafia boss in New York. He told stories about learning judo to fend off the people who were after him because he was a police informant. That kind of rubbish. Not a word of it was true."

"You're sure about that?"

"His uncle assures me the family has no connection to the mob. And his parents live right out here in Adams Morgan. He was basically a local kid. And the cops would have to be idiots to use him as a police informant. He'd have blabbed everything. He just wanted to paint himself as a big guy who was important. I bet most of the stories he told came straight from movies."

"That's sort of sad."

"Kids like to build themselves up that way, I guess." Rami leaned toward me. "He was running his mouth about coming into a lot of money. I thought it was another one of his elaborate lies. But maybe someone believed him and killed him for it."

"Did he say why he was getting the money? Did a relative leave it to him?"

"Hey, Arnie!" Rami gestured to an employee with his hand.

A slender young man hurried over to us.

"What story did Manny tell you?" asked Rami.

"You mean about not needing to work here? He'd found a new lucrative line of work and he wouldn't be rubbing elbows with guys like me anymore."

"Did he say what it was?" I asked.

"He gave me some smart-guy answer like, 'If I told you, I'd have to kill you.' I blew him off. He also said he was gonna win the lottery because he figured out a system. And he was going to buy a racehorse and win the Triple Crown." Arnie looked bored and shrugged. "I'm sorry he's dead, but Manny was a phony and a bigmouth."

"That's not much of a reason to kill someone," I observed.

One side of Arnie's mouth twisted upward. "It all depends on what he might have said to the wrong guy."

Chapter 18

Arnie sauntered back to his work and Rami nodded. "Even if most of what he said was a lie, Manny talked too much."

I thanked Rami and bought a box of oatmeal-raisin cookies for the store. Rami went back to his work but I felt sad that people waited to buy cupcakes and pastries and Manny's coworkers went about their business. It was as if Manny had never been there. I hoped there had been some sadness when they came to work in the morning and learned of his demise.

On my way back to the store, I took a detour and swung by the carriage house to check on Mr. DuBois.

I found him sitting outside on the patio, enjoying a cup of tea. Peaches lay in the sun, lazily watching goldfish in the pond.

"Miss Florrie! I wasn't expecting you to return so soon. I finished cleaning the windows some time ago. Do you have any silver in need of polishing?"

"I'm afraid not." I offered him some of the cookies. "Mr. DuBois, I was wondering if the grapevine offered any"—I chose my words carefully—"insights on who might have killed Manny."

"As you can imagine, the hot topic was how accurate

Hilda's prognostication was. Except for the location, she nailed it!"

"You mean because he wasn't found in a doorway?"

"Precisely. But everything else about the foot and the rug was dead-on. Hilda has remarkable abilities. Rumor has it that Coralue's son had some kind of beef with Manny. I also heard that Manny worked on the side for a private investigator. He may not have been the silly boy most people thought he was."

"Thank you. Keep me posted if you hear anything else?"

"Most certainly. Miss Florrie, I've spoken to Jacquie. Apparently, I was not the only person who noticed the ghost left behind after the séance. We have arranged for Hilda to return this evening in an attempt to send him away."

The professor wasn't going to like that!

As if reading my mind, Mr. DuBois added, "Jacquie has arranged for Maxwell to have dinner with an old friend who is known for keeping him out late at a club they like. Perhaps you would care to join us?"

I had to admit to some degree of curiosity. Would Hilda be overwhelmed and claim she sensed other people's thoughts again? Or was that something she reserved for larger audiences? "I have to work tonight, but if I return before Hilda leaves, maybe I'll come by."

I headed back to the store, stopping to buy pizzas for a late lunch. Bob could eat one all by himself and some of the regular patrons would probably want a nosh, too.

Business had picked up as it usually did in the afternoon. I set the pizzas and cookies next to the coffee maker and got right to work showing a woman where the history books were.

The professor passed me on the stairs. "I'm going home and don't plan to return today, unless that woman is still there."

I knew which woman he meant—Hilda. "Professor Maxwell, I don't completely trust Hilda, either. But yesterday, Eric told us that he didn't understand psychics but that there are countless examples of them leading the police to crime scenes and victims."

Professor Maxwell stopped in his tracks and stared at me thoughtfully. "How many times have I told others that one must keep an open mind?" He inhaled deeply and smiled at me. "Thank you, Florrie. You continue to be a fresh breeze to my old brain." He went on his way down the stairs.

When I returned to the checkout desk, a box of pizza lay open. Bob stood in front of the scrying mirror eating a slice of pizza. Frodo sat patiently at his feet, waiting for a piece of the crust.

During my absence, Jacquie had dressed up the mirror for Halloween by draping a black feather boa across the top, as she had promised. A fake bat hung on it upside down.

Bob swallowed a bite and said, "I don't get it. All I see is a dark reflection."

"I've never looked into a scrying mirror. But I think you're supposed to go into a trance or meditate or something."

"Customers have been asking about it all day. One guy was so creeped out that he refused to stand where he would have to look into it."

"I wonder what he was afraid of seeing." I picked up a slice of pizza with a napkin.

"The grim reaper."

"Eww! That's awful."

The door swung open and Zsazsa Rosca swept in. "A scrying mirror! Here? In the store? This must be the work of Jacqueline."

"A friend of the professor shipped it to him with a skull," I told her.

Zsazsa's carefully drawn eyebrows arched. "How very curious." She tilted her head and peered into the mirror. "My grandmother in Hungary had one of these. In America, they say if you look into such a mirror on Halloween, you will see the face of the man you shall marry." She laughed aloud. "I never saw one! Perhaps the mirror knew it was my fate to remain single."

"That's a nice fable. Far better than expecting to see the face of death," I grumbled.

"There is always that danger," she cautioned, waving her forefinger. "One doesn't know what will appear. Where is the skull?"

"I don't honestly know. In the professor's office, I guess."

"What an interesting chum he must have. None of my friends would send me a skull and a scrying mirror. I must cultivate more exotic friends!" She headed up the stairs, undoubtedly to get a look at the skull.

The rest of the afternoon passed quickly. People continued to gossip about Hilda and the fact that she had *seen* a foot in a rug before the murder happened. Hilda was getting a lot of publicity out of Manny's death. It saddened me that Hilda was the topic of conversation and not Manny. That didn't seem right to me.

It also made me wonder if Hilda could have had anything to do with Manny's death. After all, it would be much easier to make a prediction of that kind if you had a hand in making it happen.

During a lull, I poured myself a cup of coffee and took a little break at the checkout desk. I scrounged for a pencil or a pen. How did they always manage to disappear? I used a crayon to doodle Manny's face but it didn't look much like him.

Holding my cup, I turned around and studied the scrying mirror. It was really too dark to see much. But as I gazed at it, a face appeared in the murky glass.

Chapter 19

I froze. A chill ran through me until the face became clear and smiled. It was my own Sergeant Eric Jonquille. Although he appeared friendly, I couldn't move. Was this how these mirrors worked? I had thought they were nonsense.

"Florrie?"

I whipped around. At the sight of Eric standing across the desk from me, I broke into hysterical laughter. No wonder his face was in the mirror. "It's the power of suggestion," I said to him. I explained about the mirror. "You're supposed to be able to divine things from what you see, so I was shocked when I saw your face. I didn't think I would see anything!"

He laughed along with me. "You might be right about the power of suggestion. Sort of like looking into a crystal ball. Some of us will never see anything, yet others seem to have some kind of ability to foretell the future."

"You mean it's something that might be in their subconscious?"

"Could be. Or it could be something that dawns on them simply because they focus. It was always in their minds, but they hadn't concentrated on putting the details together. Don't we all do that? We're distracted by so many things in

our lives. Sometimes just shutting everything else out and focusing helps us realize something important." He reached out
and touched my arm. "I heard about last night. How are you
doing?"

"I'm okay. The phone guy came in today and said someone probably faked the bookstore number when they called
911. Any news on Manny?"

"I haven't heard anything definitive yet. But I don't like
the sound of some jerk making fake calls to 911." He scowled
at the thought. "Is Hilda here?"

"Not today. But everyone is talking about her."

Veronica waltzed up to the desk. "I hope Hilda comes
back. That was fascinating!"

"If she comes in," said Eric, "tell her that I met Mr. Balthus
de Gama's landlord. It seems Mr. de Gama is behind on his
rent and vacated without notice. The furniture belongs to the
landlord and is all still there, but the closets and drawers have
nothing in them. The place is so empty that voices echo inside. Neighbors claim de Gama kept odd hours, but no one
noticed him loading a rug into a car."

"So he's in the clear," I said.

"Maybe. I'm trying to get a forensics team in there to
check the place out. It's complicated because, other than
Hilda, there's no evidence linking Manny to de Gama. If they
found carpet fibers in the apartment matching the ones on the
rug Manny was in, then we'd have something. I'm wrestling
with the folks in power, trying to get the place checked out
forensically."

I could understand that. I hoped they would hurry. When
a new tenant moved in, evidence might be destroyed or de-
graded. "Did the landlord say a rug was missing?"

"No. According to him, he rents it furnished and the place
has nice hardwood floors. He said he no longer furnishes his

rentals with rugs because people leave them in such bad shape. If they want rugs, they should buy their own. There's not a rug to be seen in the house. It was a very nice place, though. Chandeliers, decent furniture, gourmet kitchen. Definitely not geared to the college student market."

"You're much more open-minded about the ability of psychics than I am, but isn't there a chance that Hilda imagined the foot in the rug at de Gama's house but it was never there?"

Eric tilted his head. "That's certainly a possibility. All I know is that no one on that street saw a rug or a foot. Or, at least, no one is admitting it. I'd like to locate de Gama."

Veronica, who had stood by silently listening to Eric, said calmly, "I didn't know that Balthus moved. But I can put out some feelers. Don't worry, I won't tell anyone I'm asking for the police."

"Thanks, Veronica. Do you know where he works?"

"He doesn't. Balthus comes from big money like Finley. I think the de Gamas are in the pharmaceutical industry. It's something kind of boring like that. Balthus is a big spender, prone to buying champagne for all his friends and generally living the high life."

My eyes met Eric's. If Balthus was wealthy, then why was he behind on his rent?

Bob walked up. He must have heard Veronica because he muttered under his breath, "Must be nice."

"That's the kind of people you run around with?" I asked.

"You're a snob, Florrie Fox!" Veronica threw back at me. "What's wrong with being obscenely wealthy?"

"I write your paycheck," I said. "I know *you're* not flying off to ski in Vail and summer in the south of France."

"Excuse me? You live in the Maxwell mansion," Veronica said drolly.

"Correction. I live in the carriage house like the hired help. I *am* the hired help!"

"Well, Balthus and his kind aren't as snooty as you are. They would welcome you, too."

I doubted that. But we had done enough sisterly sniping.

Eric pointedly addressed Veronica. "Since I also work for a living, perhaps you can fill me in. Where does Balthus spend his days?"

"I hear the Starlight Café is popular," suggested Veronica.

"The one that's two blocks away from the bookstore? Thanks."

"What if I went down there for a latte and fabricated a reason for him to come back here with me?" Veronica suggested. "You could just happen to be here."

"That's not necessary," said Eric. "But I appreciate the offer."

"It would be fun. Florrie isn't the only Fox sister who likes a good mystery."

I wanted to point out that she didn't read much, but I knew what she meant. We both liked sleuthing and putting facts together.

Eric gave us a brief wave. "See you later. This working stiff has to get back on the job."

And then Bob and I, who also did not have trust funds, got back to work.

Less than fifteen minutes later, I walked into the parlor and found Veronica speaking with the strawberry-blond man. The same one she had been chatting with the night Hilda spoke.

"Florrie," said Veronica, "you remember Balthus, don't you?"

Veronica was right. I did know Balthus de Gama. I just hadn't known his name. He was a large man, not overly heavy, but tall with hefty hands. Big-boned, my mother would have said. His hair looked as if it had been kissed by a setting sun.

His skin was burn-to-a-crisp-in-a-minute fair. He wasn't a regular at Color Me Red, but he browsed in the store often enough for me to recognize him. As far as I could recall, he was a quiet man, probably in his early thirties, and he usually paid with cash.

I gazed at him now with fresh eyes. Could he have murdered Manny? Had this big man rolled little Manny up in a rug and buried him in Coralue's yard?

I didn't think so. There was something gentle about him. Even his hands appeared soft and pale.

I smiled at him. "Of course, I do. I believe you were here the night of Hilda's reading."

He nodded. "She didn't do much reading that night. Have you heard from her? Is she feeling better?"

"I understand she's conducting a séance tonight. I guess that means she has made a full recovery."

"A séance!" Veronica exclaimed. "I would love to go! Why don't we have a séance here at the store on Halloween?"

Balthus asked in a very serious tone, "Is there someone you want to contact, Veronica?"

"Is that how it works?" asked Veronica. "You have to ask for a particular deceased person?"

"I've never been to a séance, but I was under that impression. Maybe I've watched too many movies that got it all wrong," said Balthus.

"Did you hear about Manny?" asked Veronica.

I was astonished by my sister's moxie. What was she thinking?

But Balthus didn't seem uncomfortable. In fact, he appeared appropriately sad. "He was just a kid. His family must be devastated."

In a cheery voice, Veronica said, "I hear you've moved to new digs. Where are you living now?"

"I'm staying with a friend until I find a house to buy."

"In Georgetown?" I asked.

"That's the plan. I enjoy the atmosphere here. It's not easy to find the right place, though. I don't know if I'm up for massive renovations. Some of the houses need a lot of work. The real estate agents make it sound so easy. I wouldn't mind picking out my own light fixtures and kitchen cabinets, but rewiring and ripping out plumbing? I don't think that's for me. If you hear of anything, let me know. Hey, what's the news on Cyril?"

"I saw him yesterday," I said. "He's doing fairly well."

"I have to stop by to see Roxie. She must be distraught. She and Cyril are so close."

I could hear voices at the checkout desk. "I need to get back to work. Nice seeing you, Balthus."

"Likewise, Florrie." He turned his attention to Veronica, and as I left the parlor, I could hear her asking, "Are you coming to the ghost walk?"

Around dinnertime I discovered Professor Goldblum browsing through books in our Halloween display. He saw the bookstore as his hangout, not unlike Balthus and friends in the coffee shop.

"You've lived here for a long time, Professor. Have you ever heard of Ambassador Sokolov?" I asked.

His eyes widened. It was as though my question had awakened him. "I have indeed. What a story. His son-in-law, O'Malley, and his son, Ivan, made quite a mess of things for their family."

"So it's true? I thought Coralue Throckmorton was making it up, or at least embellishing."

"It was a big scandal at the time. I suppose it's still somewhat scandalous today when men of wealth lose their money through gambling and bad habits. Back in the day, though, one's reputation rode on such things. People were very aware of the family name and the need to avoid bringing shame on their families."

"The duel really took place?" I asked.

"In those days, it would have been considered honorable. They weren't always deadly. Some duelers talked it out and came to a gentlemen's agreement. And others agreed to only aim below the torso, or to try to avoid hitting each other entirely."

"I think I would have chosen that option. I had no idea people made deals like that. It seems reasonable. Although it would have been wiser not to duel at all."

"No doubt. But then there would be the shame of backing out. Apparently, O'Malley and Bosworth didn't understand that they could strike a bargain. What a disaster. Of course, the duel was only the beginning of the story. You see, at that time, the eldest son inherited the family fortune. By all rights, Ivan expected to receive everything. But his father, Ambassador Sokolov, was concerned about his daughter's welfare. He gave her two dozen solid gold coins and cautioned her to hide them from her husband, O'Malley, who would surely have frittered them away. Ivan was outraged because he thought the coins were part of his birthright.

"It was somewhat comical, at least in retrospect, though probably not to the players involved at the time. In the belief that O'Malley had gained possession of the coins, Ivan embarked on a series of stunts. He stalked O'Malley and spooked his horses. He even broke into the family home to search for the coins. Meanwhile, O'Malley thought this series of misfortunes was the result of the curse Bosworth had uttered upon him as he lay dying from his wounds in the duel!"

"Oh no! O'Malley believed the curse?"

"It sounds odd to us today, but hundreds of years ago,

people explained a lot of things they didn't understand by attributing them to the supernatural. At the time, grave robbing was quite commonplace."

"Eww."

"Oh, it's very interesting. A bit unsavory, I'll admit, but they weren't after jewels, as one might think."

I looked at him skeptically. "Why else would they rob graves?"

"For the bodies! They were body snatchers."

Chapter 20

Professor Goldblum grinned at me. "You see, the medical schools needed fresh cadavers for their students and they paid handsomely for fresh corpses."

"You're making this up."

"Fascinating, isn't it? It was a bit of a moral dilemma, because the young doctors needed the bodies to learn. But no one wanted *their* friends or relatives to end up in a medical school being dissected! Embalming and refrigeration weren't what they are today, so freshness was crucial. It must have been an interesting time. Apparently, grave robbers followed funeral processions to know where the bodies were being buried so they could dig them up while they were fresh. Of course, eventually families had to stop processing for that reason."

"Here? In Washington?"

"Yes, indeed! Wealthy families hired guards to watch the graves so their loved ones wouldn't be stolen. Cemeteries hired guards, too, but in at least one case that I heard of, the guards were also grave robbers! Many families chose to bury their loved ones quietly in their own private plots so grave robbers wouldn't know about it. But I digress. I do that all too often when a subject fascinates me."

I smiled at him. He was a font of knowledge on many subjects yet he kept on learning.

"O'Malley, believing he would be rid of the curse, paid grave robbers to dig up Bosworth. There were all sorts of superstitions at the time and O'Malley thought he would be rid of the curse if the body snatchers removed him from his proper grave and took the body elsewhere. From what I understand, the belief was that Bosworth's ghost would be confused and unable to find his way back to continue the curse on O'Malley."

I sat back in my chair. "How strange that people would think something so silly."

Goldblum's eyes widened in fascination. "That's the least of it. There was a very serious fear of vampires in New England that led to outrageous behavior as well."

"Poor Mrs. Bosworth. What happened to her?" I asked.

"I don't know. Perhaps I'll find out."

I smiled at the inquisitive little man. "Let me know?"

"Absolutely. Are any of those cookies left?" he asked as we returned to the coffee urn.

Just then Veronica joined us. "Bob went home."

"Did you learn anything from Balthus?" I asked.

"It was boring. He knows nothing. He moved out two weeks ago and hasn't been back."

"I guess that brings an end to the foot-in-the-rug drama." If we knew who killed Manny and if Cyril would be released from the hospital, we'd almost be back to normal. The story about O'Malley and the duel based on nothing made me think of Roxie.

"Veronica, is Finley having an affair with anyone?"

She shot me a sad look. Whispering, she said, "Probably. I don't know for sure, but women flock to him. He's quite the flirt. It's like he always knows what to say to flatter women. Poor Roxie. She deserves better."

"I thought you liked Finley," I whispered.

Veronica stopped whispering. "I like a lot of people. It doesn't mean I admire every facet of their personalities."

Professor Goldblum applauded her. "Wise words, Veronica. All people have flaws."

"Thank you, Professor." Veronica looked immensely pleased with herself.

"You do realize that forgiving attitude is the reason she ends up with crummy boyfriends," I said to Professor Goldblum.

"It's also what makes people like her." Goldblum poured himself a cup of coffee and wandered into the parlor.

He was right. And it made me feel crabby and judgmental. Why was I suspicious of people when Veronica accepted them the way they were? In high school I had attributed her popularity to a dozen different things. It never occurred to me that people were drawn to her because she had a forgiving nature. Nevertheless, that lack of discretion sometimes led her down the wrong path with questionable people.

After the craziness of the last two days, closing time couldn't come soon enough. I looked forward to changing into my jammies, settling in with Peaches and Frodo, and sketching. It was just after nine o'clock when Veronica and I locked up and left.

Frodo snapped at leaves that tumbled along the sidewalk. I made it a point to walk on the side of the street opposite Coralue's house. Still, I couldn't help myself and paused briefly to stare at it. The police had left. Under the glow of streetlights, I could see the crime scene tape fluttering in the breeze. But it appeared that Coralue wasn't home. None of the Halloween lights glowed. I didn't even see any lights on inside of the house. It was like a vast empty hole on the street. Had Coralue done that on purpose? Out of respect for the dead?

We walked on and I almost didn't recognize the Maxwell mansion. Jacquie had been hard at work. Pumpkins spilled from the landing at the front door all the way out to the street. A witch with a long nose hunched over a cauldron. She wore a glamorous witch hat that sparkled. A fine mist arose from her black vessel and wafted through the air. Next to the witch, the green eyes of a faux black cat gleamed in the night, watching all who dared enter.

In the mist, a lady ghost glowed in a diaphanous gown. I could only imagine that Jacquie had somehow arranged lights inside her long dress. I knew she was a prop, but she truly looked how I imagined a ghost would appear. Not that I believed in them, of course.

From inside a second-floor window, three fake skulls peered out on a diagonal, each one a little higher than the previous one. Faux flames from dark candles on the windowsill illuminated them.

A thick black garland surrounded the front door and orange lights twinkled on it.

It was a masterpiece that rivaled Coralue's decorations.

Mr. DuBois opened the front door. "What do you think?"

"It's very impressive. Did you help Jacquie?"

"It was a team effort. I fear Ms. Rattenhorst was a bit put off by the ghost, but I thought it quite authentic."

"Maybe she did, too."

Mr. Dubois chortled. "In that case, I would call it a job well done. Would you care to come in and join the séance?"

I walked to the front stoop, where he was standing. I was exhausted. But I trudged into the mansion with Frodo. Maybe it would be interesting.

Mr. DuBois rushed me to the kitchen, where Jacquie and Hilda sat at the table.

While putting on the kettle he said, "Hilda was correct. Right down to the foot sticking out of the rug."

Hilda was sitting right there, so I didn't point out that she had the location wrong.

Hilda blurted in a monotone, "The second murder."

"What do you mean?" asked Jacquie. "Has someone else been killed?"

"You don't remember? At the bookstore reading I was overcome by an evil presence. Manny was the first victim."

Chapter 21

Mr. DuBois set a cup of tea before me and handed a dog cookie to Frodo. "Am I to understand that the killer has now murdered two individuals? Who is the second one?"

"I'm not sure," said Hilda. "He said there would be a murder. He wasn't thinking about the foot in the rug. So that would imply two."

Mr. DuBois seemed to shrink before my eyes. "It could be any one of us!"

Jacquie spoke reassuringly, "Now, DuBois. Perhaps the police will be able to prevent the second murder."

Hilda held her hands to her face. "I don't think so. The foot in the rug, that was definitely the first victim."

I watched Jacquie's expression. Wrinkles formed between her eyes. Was she as skeptical as I was? After all, the foot in the rug had not been where Hilda claimed. Eric had looked for it. He had even questioned neighbors. No one had seen the alleged foot in the rug. Unless . . . Hilda had committed the murder to bolster her claim.

Jacquie's eyes met mine. I wished I knew what she was thinking. As much as I wanted to be open-minded about Hilda and her remarkable abilities, she seemed a little bit melodramatic with her pronouncements. Was that why she didn't seem credible to me? Or was I just a born skeptic?

Was it remotely possible that Manny had been rolled in a rug as a coincidence? I wondered if there were statistics about how often a murderer rolled a corpse in a rug. Maybe it happened more frequently than one would think. After all, a body had to be hard to move. A rug seemed like an easy solution. It disguised the body, assuming a foot wasn't sticking out, and it was probably easier to drag a body in a rug than just a body.

Mr. DuBois appeared to be reveling in Hilda's every word. "Can you make contact with that person again? If you're in his head, perhaps you could assist the police."

Hilda considered his suggestion. "I don't know. I didn't mean to make contact with him at the bookstore. I . . . I'm not sure how I would reach him. It all happened so spontaneously that night." She pulled her lips into her mouth as if she were afraid. Whispering, she said, "I'm not sure I want to hear from him again. It was horrifying. I have been able to channel a lot of dead people but they're usually pretty nice. Some are grumpy, but I always assume that's how they were when they were alive. The person whose thoughts I picked up at the bookstore was frightening. Pure evil."

Most murderers were.

"Perhaps if you returned to the bookstore," suggested Mr. DuBois.

"That's right," said Jacquie. "You could do a relaxed reading in the parlor or come just to chat. We'll provide some snacks and let people know you're available to talk."

At that point, all I wanted was to go home, shower, and do something comforting, like sketch. The thought of another night of Hilda's drama at the store drained me even more. I wished I knew whether she was for real or not. I didn't want to be unfair to her. And it really wasn't like me to be so closed-minded. I wasn't a genius. I didn't know everything. Far from it. But if someone as smart as the professor didn't believe in ghosts, maybe Hilda *was* a big fraud.

Or maybe not. The professor didn't know everything, either.

Hilda appeared uncomfortable and averted her gaze. "I would like to come back to the bookstore. Even though I fear channeling that man's thoughts again, perhaps"—she forced a smile—"perhaps that would help the police. I should do whatever I can to assist them."

I nodded reluctantly. As graciously as I could, I said, "We would welcome another visit from you. If you don't mind, I was up most of the night and it has been a long day. Plus, I think I'd better check on Peaches."

"She's fine," said Mr. DuBois. "She had a rather good day and ate all her salmon."

Had I heard correctly? Were those words actually coming out of the mouth of someone with an intense dislike of cats? I tried to hide my smile. "Thank you for the tea. I hope you'll forgive me for heading home but I'm exhausted. Good night."

Frodo and I left through the back door and quickly crossed the paved area to my home. Peaches yawned and stretched when I entered. I picked her up. "Good job with Mr. DuBois. I have a feeling he likes you!"

She purred but kept her secrets about Mr. DuBois to herself. After a long, hot shower, I dressed in an oversize crimson T-shirt that reached my knees. Veronica had given it to me. It said *Color Outside the Lines*.

The thing was, even though I was home and relaxed, I didn't really feel any better. Whether Hilda thought someone had communicated an intent to commit murder didn't matter. The reality was that Manny was dead.

Peaches and Frodo leaped down the stairs ahead of me. Peaches zoomed to her dish and yowled repeatedly.

"I get it. Time for dinner." I opened a pouch of shredded beef in broth and poured it into her bowl. She purred while she ate. Frodo contently snarfed turkey dog food.

I didn't have much appetite. I scrounged in the fridge and found some cheese, which I folded into an omelet and ate at the counter. I warmed apple cider and took it over to the couch. I felt better just picking up my sketchbook.

The first thing I doodled was Manny's face. I hadn't been able to do him justice with a crayon. He was only a few years younger than me, I guessed, but, according to his boss and coworker, his attitude and demeanor had been that of an immature person.

The hair that parted in the middle and fell into his forehead was easy. But as I drew, I saw that he had a narrower jawline than I had realized. It ended in a pointy chin. His eyes reminded me of almonds but they drooped slightly in the middle of the bottom lid, giving him a somewhat petulant appearance. For no good reason, I felt compelled to draw the coffin with the wide shoulders and narrow end. The soil had been loose around it. I added Manny's foot sticking up out of the ground.

Why had his killer buried him there? Granted, it was a flower bed, so the soil wasn't packed hard. And the coffin was empty, so it would have been easy to move aside. Had the foot sticking up been a mistake? An oversight in the dark?

Why hadn't anyone noticed the killer burying the rug? It stood to reason that it must have been done at night and quickly, which, unfortunately, pointed to Coralue.

Poor Coralue. I hoped she would be okay. And I fervently hoped her son wasn't involved in Manny's demise. Coralue was far easier to sketch. Her face and hair style were so round.

She always had a kindly expression, as though she was confident about herself and her life. I drew a small mouth with full lips and the ladylike bob that always seemed to be in place.

I got up to fetch a throw and snuggled underneath it. When I picked up my sketchbook, it fell open to Harry. Where was he? We had been so busy that I hadn't checked to be sure he was back in the professor's office, where he belonged.

I started to draw Roxie, but my eyelids grew heavy. I checked to be sure the front door was locked and headed up to bed.

I woke early, thinking of Manny. And of Coralue's son. If Mr. DuBois didn't make another appearance, I might have time to visit Coralue before work. She had been in distress the last time I saw her. Maybe I should have been concerned about all her lights being off. Why hadn't I checked on her last night?

I showered quickly and slid on gray slacks and a white shirt. Drab, drab, drab. I searched my closet for a violet pullover. Much better. I added two long chains and turned the cuffs of the shirt sleeves back over the violet sweater. I drank a quick cup of java while I fed shrimp in aspic to Peaches. I packed Frodo's breakfast and stashed it in my purse, planning to buy something to nosh on for myself.

I promised Peaches that she could come to the store the next day, and dressed Frodo in his halter. We were off in the brisk morning air and headed for Coralue's house.

Police tape still hung in front of the mansion but the coffin and the butler had disappeared. No one was around, so I ducked under the police tape but took care to make a wide swath between myself and the actual scene of the murder.

I stopped in my tracks and looked over at the spot where the coffin had been. Was it the site of the murder? Probably not. If there had been an argument on the street, Coralue might have heard it. And the killer happened to have a rug. That was unlikely unless he was some kind of rug dealer. No, Manny must have been killed elsewhere and brought here in the rug.

Would Coralue's son be stupid enough to kill Manny and hide the corpse in his own mother's yard?

I held Frodo's leash short so he wouldn't disturb anything, and tiptoed at the edge of the flower bed to reach the front door.

It opened before I had a chance to ring the doorbell. Coralue wore a black sweater set with a black skirt. She looked like a ladies-who-lunch version of Morticia Adams. She had taken time with her hair and makeup. They were flawless. "Come in, Florrie. I've been expecting you."

That frightened me a little bit. "Why?"

She showed us to the lovely conservatory in the back of the house. "Because the two of us went through a trauma together. I don't think anyone else would understand the horror we experienced. That kind of ghastly event bonds people."

She wasn't kidding about expecting me. She had set out a tray with cobalt-blue-and-white teacups adorned with gold. She poured an amber liquid into them from a matching teapot. "Russian tea," she said. "It's not actually Russian. I don't know how it got that name. But hot tea blended with orange juice is always comforting to me."

Next to the tea was a matching platter overflowing with chocolate croissants and blueberry Danish. "You have to try the pastries. I baked them myself."

"I didn't know you liked to bake." I sat down on the soft cushion of a wicker armchair.

"I've attended some classes. I bake when I'm stressed. It takes my mind off the things that trouble me."

"You must be tired," I said. "The nightmare continued long into the night for you."

"I hope I never go through anything like that again. I was up all night. I kept peeking out the window to see what they were doing."

"Did they remove the coffin or did you?"

Coralue picked up her teacup. "The police took it. They're hoping they can get some DNA off it. I removed the butler with their permission. He's in the basement for now. I can hardly bear to look at him."

"Have you contacted your son?" I asked.

"I have. The police wasted no time interviewing Hayes. They hauled him into the police station early yesterday morning. Apparently, the animosity between Hayes and Manny was widely known in the judo community. Some sided with Manny and some with Hayes. I knew about it but I didn't realize that it had become such a big deal."

She tore off a bit of chocolate croissant. "They interviewed me, too. Of course"—she flicked her hand carelessly, as though it didn't matter—"I don't have an alibi. Neither Hayes nor I have one."

"But what motive would you have for killing Manny?"

She stared at me in disbelief. "For my son! Naturally, it's preposterous. I didn't murder Manny. The thought never even entered my head. It's a sport. Sometimes someone cheats. You learn from that and move on. The one who cheats is always watched very carefully once there's an allegation in the air. Manny would have been marked by that questionable episode forever. He never could have gotten away with it again. To my way of thinking, that's the appropriate punishment. It would be absurd to murder someone for something like that. His own judo community would have seen to it that he never did it again."

"Have the police said how he was killed?" I asked.

"Hayes said their questions led him to believe that someone used a judo maneuver on him. They didn't ask me anything of the sort."

When I didn't say anything right away, Coralue asked what I was thinking.

"Two things, actually. It's probably a coincidence that someone attacked Cyril Oldfield. That person used a knife, though."

"Cyril? I had no idea. Is he all right?" asked Coralue.

"He's still in the hospital. He survived the attack but I have to think it was a close call if they're keeping him there."

"Surely there couldn't be a connection. Unless . . . could Manny be the one who attacked Cyril?" asked Coralue.

"I don't think so." But no sooner were the words out of my mouth than I remembered Manny claimed he was getting into a more lucrative line of work. Had he planned to steal Cyril's clock? After all, he had intended to steal Harry.

"I'll have to pay him a visit," she said. "I haven't seen Cyril in years. I remember when his wife died in that boating accident. Cyril was broken. I mean physically and emotionally, he was just devastated. Poor little Roxie was only three. The cutest bubbly little girl you can imagine. I doubt that she remembers her mother. Why would anyone attack Cyril?"

"That's what we're all wondering."

"What was your other thought about Manny's death?" She picked up her teacup and cradled it in her hands.

"If Manny was into judo, wouldn't he have known how to defend himself? Aren't there tricks they learn to resist attacks?"

"One would think so. Isn't that the point of martial arts? I'll have to ask my son. It's quite obvious to me that it wasn't Hayes. It's not in his character. And one would think the killer would be bruised if there had been a confrontation. Unless the killer attacked him from behind. That poor young man. I don't care how much he cheated, he didn't deserve to have his life end at such a young age."

My phone buzzed, letting me know I had a text message. I ignored it.

"Maybe you should get that, sweetheart. We all need to be alert right now."

Reluctantly, I pulled the phone out of my purse and glanced at it. Professor Maxwell had sent me a text.

Florrie! Where are you? Come to the store quickly!

Chapter 22

"I hope you won't think me rude, Coralue, but something is awry at the bookstore."

She smiled at me. "Yes, I know."

I gazed at her for a moment. "How could you know that? And how did you know I was coming?"

Coralue tilted her head. "My family says I shouldn't tell people this. They're embarrassed by my sixth sense. I think it's just logic. Expecting to see you today is a good example. I had a hunch you would be coming by. Unless you had something very pressing to do, like a trip out of town, how could you not come back to the scene of the crime? Especially when it's so close to where you live? You see what I mean? I figure things out. I assume other people don't give as much thought to those little details."

"But how could you know they would need me at the bookstore?"

"I'm on social media, Florrie. Hilda made quite an impression. People are still talking about it. Plus it's almost Halloween. Anything involving ghosts is a big deal."

I was afraid to ask her more. But I did in spite of my misgivings. "Is there anything I should know?"

"I'm not a fortune-teller, Florrie. My kids sometimes claim I am. I just deduce things, that's all. I think most people can do it. Haven't you ever picked up the phone to call someone and found out they were just phoning you?" She shrugged like it was no big deal.

I felt fairly confident that her children told her that she was unique and other people didn't sense things the way she did. But I did know one thing: I needed to get going and find out what kind of chaos was in progress at the bookstore.

I thanked Coralue for breakfast and gave her a hug. Frodo and I left through the rear and walked along the alley to the next street. As I rounded the corner, I nearly bumped into Balthus. He was walking rapidly but looking over his shoulder. Frodo and I dodged him. "Good morning!" I said.

Balthus choked in surprise. "Morning." He smiled at me but kept going. I didn't have time to chat but I stopped and looked back at him. He scanned the street nervously and ducked into the alley from which we had come.

At the bookstore, I unlocked the door and rushed in to turn off the alarm before it blared. Professor Maxwell often arrived early in the morning, but he usually turned the alarm on again before going up to his office to work. I glanced around. The store was quiet and peaceful. No marauders were waiting outside. I took a minute to start the coffee and switch on lights.

As I turned the sign on the door to *Open*, Veronica, Bob, Zsazsa, and Professor Goldblum arrived. They gathered at the checkout desk, exchanging pleasantries and I headed for the stairs to check on Professor Maxwell.

And then it happened. The same wail we had heard the night of Hilda's reading resounded through the building and drowned out their voices.

The silence that followed was nearly as frightening. The

sound of footsteps on the stairs drew our attention as Professor Maxwell ambled down them.

"You're here. What in the devil is that, Florrie?"

I found it somewhat amusing that the most intelligent person I knew thought *I* should be able to explain what that sound was.

"It's the skull," declared Goldblum with a tinge of delight in his voice. He smiled broadly and his eyes opened wide with excitement.

"Nonsense," protested Professor Maxwell. "The skull is nothing but an inanimate remnant. It has no ability to produce sound or feel anything."

"Maxwell! No less than the prestigious institute of the University of Virginia is home to the Division of Perceptual Studies, which engages in the examination of postmortem existence."

Bob's forehead wrinkled. "What does that mean?"

"Life after death," said Goldblum. "Inanimate objects with far less significant ties to a human being than a skull have been known to be imprinted on by a person who once lived. Such varied items as lockets, music boxes, even walking sticks may be tied to ghosts. Most certainly the fellow, presumably Harry, whose brain once functioned inside the skull, might have an interest in that skull."

"Goldblum, with the greatest admiration for your accomplishments and your intellect, I say rubbish." Professor Maxwell tsked at us. "There are no such things as ghosts. Your beloved Ms. Rattenhorst has tapped into a human weakness, the desire for life after death. And you are all following her like lemmings. She has put utter nonsense into your brains. Whoever Harry *was* is long gone. And to imagine that somehow the person he once was might be here in some form is the height of ridiculous mysticism."

"Maxwell, I'm surprised at you." Goldblum waved a forefinger at Professor Maxwell. "How can you close yourself off to the possibility? Science is finally beginning to move in that direction. There are a lot of eminent scientists who have begun to reconsider their stance on this subject. You know why? They have had entirely too many experiences themselves that cannot be anything else. They don't speak about them publicly out of fear of being ridiculed but talk to them privately, and they admit that there is much we do not know or understand. It is far more dangerous to insist something cannot be than to open yourself to the possibility that it might exist."

Professor Maxwell smiled at his friend. "Ah, but my dear Goldblum, the small group gathered here is perfect evidence of why these things cannot be considered seriously by the scientific establishment." He gazed at us. "Who here believes that the source of the wailing sound is something paranormal?"

Bob's hand shot up. He was quickly joined by Goldblum and Zsazsa.

Professor Maxwell rubbed his beard. "You see, Goldblum? Everyone except the eminently sensible Fox sisters is willing to jump to a conclusion that the source of the sound is somehow otherworldly, when the truth is that no one has so much as tried to figure out from whence or why the wail has come to be. Florrie, that is your job. We shall show everyone that what they believe to be from a skull"—he chuckled—"originates from a very ordinary source. You only need find it."

Oh, swell. I had mixed feelings. I was flattered by the professor's confidence in me, but how on earth was I supposed to find the source of the wail? I didn't have the first notion where to look.

"Is that the urgent matter you needed to discuss with me?" I asked.

"Yes," said Professor Maxwell.

I heard Bob snicker.

As our little group broke up, Professor Maxwell passed behind me and whispered, "Don't let me down."

I watched as he retreated to the parlor with Zsazsa and Goldblum. I suspected the discussion about the afterlife would continue.

Ugh. How in the world was I supposed to come up with a plausible explanation for that horrible moan?

"Hey, Florrie," said Bob. "Hilda is leading a Georgetown ghost tour tonight. Wanna come?"

"I'm going!" Veronica nodded in my direction, as if she were coaxing me. "It'll be fun."

"Okay. What time?"

"It starts at eleven thirty, just before midnight. Meet us out front at eleven fifteen."

"I'll be here." I picked up a box of books and almost collided with Eric.

He caught me with one arm and planted a lingering kiss on my lips. "I haven't seen much of you lately."

"I miss you, too. Any developments on Manny's murder?"

"We don't have a handle on what happened to Manny yet."

"I heard he was killed by some martial art move."

Eric's eyebrows rose. "That's not supposed to be public knowledge. Where did you hear that?"

"Coralue."

"I see. I trust that will stay between the two of you?"

"I can't speak for Coralue but I won't blab."

He took a deep breath. "The real reason I stopped by was to tell you that I'm off tonight. I thought we might spend some time together."

"I was planning to go on Hilda's ghost tour of Georgetown, but I'd rather do something with you."

His cornflower-blue eyes widened with interest. "That sounds like fun. I'll try to catch a few winks this afternoon."

We worked out the details and he was off. Business was brisk at the bookstore, with Halloween and ghost books topping the sales. When we had a brief lull, I let Veronica and Bob handle customers while I ordered books, cut paychecks, and paid bills.

Professor Goldblum found me in the office on the third floor, next to the professor's office.

"May I interrupt your work?" he asked.

"Always. What can I do for you?"

"I've done a little bit of research. It appears there is some anecdotal folklore about screaming skulls. Unfortunately, most of the stories have little or no evidentiary basis. But then they hail from previous centuries, so that's hardly surprising."

I honestly did not know what to say. Was he trying to tell me that Harry *could* be the source of the terrible wails? "Thank you."

"My point is that Harry is not happy. Most of the screaming skulls were murdered or killed unjustly, and then left in a place where they did not wish to be. In an effort to placate them, some of them were given places of honor in their rightful homes, and the screaming and mayhem ceased," explained Goldblum.

I couldn't help thinking of Glen, the delivery driver who claimed the package containing Harry was causing strange sounds and wails. I didn't like where this was going at all. I took a deep breath and tried to help Goldblum realize how ridiculous that sounded without insulting him.

"As Harry's origins are unknown," I said, "how do you propose we figure out where he would like to be?"

"A decade ago, it might have been futile. As luck has it, a former colleague of mine is the chairperson of the department of evolutionary anthropology at a local university. I propose that we allow him to take a DNA sample from Harry. Perhaps we can glean something from that."

It wasn't the worst suggestion. Of course, it would be far easier to ask Ellis Willoughby, the man who had sent Harry to the professor in the first place, about Harry's origins. "It's okay with me, but, technically, he was sent to Professor Maxwell. It's not my place to make that decision. And perhaps it would be easier to ask Ellis where Harry came from."

"Funny you should mention that. It would indeed be much easier if I could reach Ellis. I've been calling him for days but there's simply no answer. I'll take the subject of DNA up with Maxwell. Even if he doesn't believe in screaming skulls, he may be interested in learning more about Harry."

Goldblum left in a hurry, excited about his plans, and I got back to work.

When we closed for the night, I took Frodo for a much-needed walk and noted that Coralue's house had lights on inside but her decorations were not lighted.

At ten thirty Peaches and Frodo had been fed and were ready to snooze.

Eric arrived at the carriage house, looking refreshed. He picked up Peaches and stroked her. She purred contentedly. "I'm eager to hear Hilda's ghost stories. Is it true that we'll be walking in a cemetery?"

I tried not to make a sour face. "At least she won't be overcome by a murderer in a cemetery. Even Hilda wouldn't want to collapse there."

"Do I detect a note of disbelief?" he asked.

"You detect a whole song of disbelief. I guess that's not fair of me. She was just so melodramatic about everything the other night."

"How do you think a person should act when hearing the voice of a killer in her head?"

I burst out laughing. "I'm fairly certain I would be hysterical. I get your point. It would be quite a shock. However, I am not in the habit of hearing ghosts speak. If you're used to hearing ghosts in your head, maybe it's not such a frightening leap to hear a killer?"

I locked the door and we set off for the bookstore.

The moon cast the earth in a bluish silver light. "A perfect night for ghost hunting," teased Eric.

Veronica and Bob were already at the bookstore when we arrived.

They chattered eagerly about the ghost tour, but when I looked up at the store, I stopped cold. Harry was in a show window of the bookstore again. A short candle must have been behind him because his eye sockets glimmered a golden orange as though he were magical and watching us.

Chapter 23

"Florrie?" Eric touched my arm.

I stumbled forward, still looking over my shoulder at Harry. Had I imagined it? Except for the professor, I would be the first person in the store tomorrow. I would take a good look at him. I was sure of one thing: he wasn't moving around the bookstore on his own power.

We walked over to a local cemetery, where everyone was to meet Hilda.

She swept down the street toward us in a black cape, which billowed around her. As she neared, I realized that she had used glitter eye shadow and ruby-red lipstick.

Zsazsa, Professor Goldblum, and Jacquie hurried to join the group.

Jacquie sidled up to us. "Can you believe it? Neither Maxwell nor Roxie would come along. They're just no fun at all." She changed her focus. "Julie! Over here, honey."

A smiling blonde hurried toward us, promptly dropping her purse. Everything spilled out of it.

Eric and I bent to gather makeup, hard candy in wrappers, and glasses from the sidewalk.

"I'm so embarrassed." Julie shot a winning smile at us. "Thank you." She straightened up. "I'm a hopeless klutz."

"Bob! Veronica!" called Jacquie. "I want you all to meet Julie. She's coming along with us tonight."

We all introduced ourselves.

Eric gazed at her. "You look so familiar. Where would I know you from?"

"Oh! I work at Nonno's Pizza up Wisconsin Avenue. You've probably seen me there."

"Sure," said Bob, "I've been there a million times. Great pizza! The elderly gentleman who works there is always hysterically funny."

"That's my grandfather, Nonno. It's his place. He started it from scratch, and we can't talk him into retiring."

"I don't blame him," said Bob. "I'd hang around just to smell the air!"

Hilda began speaking in a singsong way and gestured for us to follow her.

Jacquie leaned over and whispered, "What do you think of Julie? A good match for Bob?"

"This is a setup?" I was stunned. I knew Jacquie had talked to Bob about introducing him to someone but I hadn't thought it would happen.

"*Shh.*" She held a finger across her lips. "They don't know. I think it works better that way. No pressure or expectations." She crossed her fingers and hurried off to spy on her love match.

Eric slid his hand into mine. It was a simple gesture, but one I still wasn't used to. I was glad it was dark because I knew I was grinning like a smitten schoolgirl.

The cemetery, which housed many famous occupants, had made an exception to its usual closing hours. An employee handed out lanterns to us as we entered the sprawling lawns. "It's twenty-two acres, folks," he cautioned. "Stay with your group and don't get lost. There are ghosts wandering about."

At night, with only the lanterns and the cold light of the moon to show the way, it was positively chilling. I shivered, but not from the cold. The roots of ancient trees stretched toward us like giant gnarled witch fingers. Historic mausoleums loomed, their entrances blocked by locked wrought-iron gates. Simple headstones lay among the fancier ones topped with angels and ornate crosses. In some sections, the headstones weren't lined up in neat rows. They appeared to have been haphazardly placed and many of the very old ones tilted.

Hilda pointed out the graves of the rich and famous as she walked. She paused at a mausoleum. "In 1862, Willie Lincoln, the eleven-year-old son of President Abraham Lincoln, tragically died from what was most likely typhoid fever. The Lincolns were bereft and couldn't bear the thought of burying little Willie in Illinois while the rest of the family remained in Washington. William Carroll, the clerk of the Supreme Court, offered the use of his family vault. This is where Willie was interred. Mr. Lincoln himself walked exactly where you are standing right now."

I felt silly looking down at my feet, but was glad to see I wasn't the only one who had that reaction.

"After Willie's death, President Lincoln often visited, and on at least two occasions, opened the casket to view him again. Fortunately, a Dr. Charles Brown had been called upon to embalm the boy, which was unusual for the time. As was opening the casket. When President Lincoln was assassinated, the president's body was loaded onto a funeral train to be carried to Illinois. Willie's casket was removed from the vault and placed on the same train to be transported to Oak Ridge

Cemetery in Springfield, Illinois. That, however, did not prevent the ghost of President Lincoln from continuing to visit this cemetery. People who live in nearby houses report seeing a tall, slender man in a top hat right here where we stand."

I was having a little trouble with the fact that the casket was opened twice after Willie was deceased. "Eww. Do you think that's true?" I whispered to Eric.

"I've heard it before. Kind of gruesome, huh? Apparently, the Lincolns had an exceptionally hard time accepting Willie's death."

We followed Hilda through the cemetery again. She pointed out graves of famous people but I was more interested in the fact that Bob and Julie appeared to have paired up during the walk. Maybe the professor was right. Jacquie was an incurable romantic and she had a talent for making matches.

The cemetery was probably beautiful and peaceful in daylight. But in the light of the moon, hearing murmuring voices and seeing the lights of lanterns in the distance as other groups walked through the graveyard, I had to admit that it was very spooky.

We followed Hilda to a section where the cemetery abutted Rock Creek Park. The gentle tinkle of water in Rock Creek made me pause. The woods on the other side were pitch-black. I could hear only whispers of city sounds. It was mind-bending to think that a real park still existed in the middle of Washington, DC. I held up my lantern for a better look.

Eric raised his, too. "What are you searching for?"

"Nothing in particular. It just seems so out of place. Lovely, but isolated."

"We'd better catch up to our group. Do you think Hilda will manage to talk to any of the dead people here?"

I giggled and stopped abruptly. My lantern had caught a flash of something. I backed up a step, trying to catch the glimmer again.

"What is that?" I asked. I stepped off the path and into the wooded area.

Eric watched me. "Probably just a stone. Be careful, Florrie."

The moment he said that, my foot hit something and I went sprawling onto the ground.

"Florrie!" Eric shouted.

The scent of moss and leaves mingled with the stench of something vile. I could hear crunching leaves as Eric bounded after me. In a matter of seconds, he fell next to me.

"Ugh." Eric pulled himself up. "What is that?"

I scrambled to my knees. "We're on top of something. A fallen tree trunk, maybe?"

"Not with that smell. Hold up your lantern."

"It went out."

"Rats. So did mine. Bob!" he yelled.

I turned around. The lanterns were already a good distance away. "I doubt that he can hear you."

I stood up and gently kicked the mound with my toe. "Uh-oh."

"What?"

"It's kind of soft." I prodded it with the toe of my sneaker again.

Eric pulled out his phone and switched on the flashlight in it. The two of us brushed away leaves, revealing a body lying facedown.

I shrieked and clapped a hand over my mouth. Goose bumps stood up on my arms and a shudder rolled through my entire body.

It must have been only a matter of seconds, but the two of us stared at it for what seemed a long time.

"It's unlikely that he's still alive." Eric kneeled next to the body and reached under his jacket collar in search of a pulse.

I dreaded whom we would see if we rolled him over. Stepping carefully, I used the light on my phone to see where I was going and I rounded his head. I aimed the light at his face and gasped. I had seen him somewhere before.

Chapter 24

"Do you know him?" asked Eric.

He rose to his feet and joined me on the other side. Kneeling on the leaves, he peered at the man's face. "He's not familiar to me."

"I'm trying to remember where I saw him. There's something about him, his mouth maybe." The most distinguishing feature of his face was the angled bracket on each side of his mouth. I had drawn them recently in my sketchbook. And then it came to me. "You know the weird house with the gargoyles?"

"Sure."

"I saw him across the street in the dark, leaning against the side of a house like he was watching it."

"This guy? Are you certain?"

"I wouldn't want to swear to it in court, but I'm pretty sure he's the one I saw right before Cyril was attacked."

Eric slowly turned his head to look at me. His voice was soft and level. "Was there enough time for him to break into Cyril's house and attack him?"

I considered his question with a certain degree of horror.

Had I seen Cyril's attacker only moments before he tried to kill Cyril? Was that possible? "Maybe. I was ambling back to the bookstore, looking at the Halloween decorations. I guess it's possible if he was fast and knew his way into the house." I shivered.

Eric remained calm. "Well, he's definitely dead, and since it's likely a crime scene, then we've already contaminated the site by being here. Maybe we shouldn't turn him over. Let's just leave him as is." He was on his phone in an instant. "Hi, Dolly. Eric Jonquille. I've got a body on the edge of Rock Creek Park where it backs up to the cemetery."

So many thoughts ran through my head.

Maybe it was the creepy light that the moon cast on the world. Maybe it was because we were in a cemetery. Maybe it was the shock of finding a second corpse. But the thought that kept coming back to me was that Hilda had been correct. I had no idea how long the body had been there, but Hilda's prognostications seemed to be coming true. The only thing she got wrong was that the rug had been in a doorway.

Was I reading too much into it? This corpse might not be the second murder that she predicted. And maybe Manny's murder wasn't the one she told us about, either.

Just because there happened to be two murders didn't mean either one of them had any relation to what Hilda had predicted.

Eric ended the call.

We stood alone in the dark next to a dead person.

He flicked on the flashlight in his phone again and aimed it at the feet. The corpse was wearing high-quality black leather shoes. "Hilda said there would be a second body."

"Do you think she was right?" I asked.

Eric ran the light all the way along the body from one end to the other. Without moving, he aimed the light at the ground on both sides.

"It's peculiar, that's for sure," said Eric.

"You don't believe her?" I was surprised. "You're the one who tries to keep an open mind."

"I don't like to jump to conclusions."

That made sense. Eric was right.

I was the one thinking that Hilda might have killed two people. She could have done it just to promote her abilities. Or she could have made up that story as a cover for murders that she had planned. But in that case, wouldn't it have been smarter not to say anything? And would she have been stupid enough to lead us here to the second body?

I heard voices, and a painfully bright beam focused on us.

As they neared, the shadowy forms of three people took shape in the dark. One called out, "Jonquille?"

"Right here."

They joined us and I recognized a couple of the cops.

"Florrie and I saw something reflect in the light of our lanterns. She took a step off the path to see what it was and we both fell over this guy."

They trained their flashlights on the body. He wore pressed trousers that looked to be a heathered gray, and a black bomber-style jacket. He had a full head of graying hair. I couldn't see his face at all, but the pressed pants and the good cut of his hair suggested that he was a professional of some kind.

I overheard one of the cops call for homicide detectives.

"We'd better catch up to the others before they think we're lost," said Eric.

"If you want to stay here, I can use the light on my phone to find them."

"Not a chance. What kind of gentleman would let his best girl wander through a dark graveyard at night by herself?"

One of his buddies chuckled, but said, "You better go with her."

We didn't say much as we left the crime scene. Eric took my free hand into his. "I'm sorry you had to see that, Florrie."

"Don't worry about me. Are you going back there tonight?"

"Maybe. I'd like to follow up on this case."

"Because of Hilda?"

"Partly. Mostly because I was looking for a body rolled up in a rug with a foot sticking out. And then it appeared."

"You think this corpse might be related to Manny's death?" I asked.

"Hard to tell at this point, but it could be."

"Hilda is up to her eyeballs in this whole thing."

He squeezed my hand. "Let's keep this under wraps for now. Okay?"

"You don't want me to say we found a body?"

"I think we have to tell them that much. They're going to wonder what happened to us. But let's not mention the part about a connection to Hilda just yet. It will be in the news soon enough anyway."

I could see lanterns ahead. It wasn't long before Veronica was shouting my name.

"It's us! We're okay!" I responded.

The group gathered around us.

"We thought a ghost nabbed you!" joked Bob.

"You might say that," said Eric. "Florrie stumbled over a body."

I looked up at Eric. Unless I missed my guess, he was studying Hilda's reaction. As far as I could tell, it wasn't significantly different than anyone else's. Most of the faces displayed horror and shock, but a few seemed doubtful.

"We had to wait for the police to come," I explained.

Veronica hugged me. "You poor thing!" She held me at arm's length. "Why do you keep finding bodies?"

"She really did fall over this one," said Eric. "It's probably a good thing that kids playing in Rock Creek Park didn't happen upon him."

In the glow of the lanterns, we all looked creepy, but Hilda, with her flaring cape and wild hair, would have frightened small children. She walked toward me and clasped my hand.

I wanted to blurt out that we had found the second body of which she had spoken. But maybe we hadn't. Maybe it was a different murder.

"You have a power within you," Hilda stated. "I can feel it. Florrie, the spirits say you have to let it grow and develop. You're trying to suppress your natural abilities."

I . . . was . . . appalled. I shivered all over and snatched my hand away from Hilda.

"Are you sure you're okay, Florrie?" asked Eric.

I pulled my shoulders back and took a deep breath. "Sure. Go on back and do your thing. I'll stay with the group."

"Thanks for understanding, Florrie." Eric kissed me on the cheek.

I grabbed his hand as he turned to leave. "Find out what caught the light of our lanterns."

"Will do." He handed me his lantern and walked away, using the flashlight in his phone to light the path.

I watched him until he became one with the darkness.

"Maybe I should take you home," said Veronica. "You've had a shock three times in the last few days."

What I wanted was to be a fly on Eric's collar to find out what was going on. "I'm fine," I said. But when I heard my voice quaver, I didn't even convince myself.

Our group moved off quickly. I spied the cemetery entrance not too far away. I whispered to Veronica that I was going to head home and insisted that she continue.

They walked on. I was watching them when I saw a slender man walking alone without a lantern. Had he come here at night to visit a grave in secret? For one long moment, I feared he might be President Lincoln, but he wasn't wearing a top hat. That was when I realized that he didn't have a head at all.

I was fairly sure that I stopped breathing.

And then, right before my eyes, he walked smack into the wall of a mausoleum and disappeared. I blinked several times. How was that possible?

My hands trembled. Surely, I hadn't seen a ghost. Part of me wanted to run over and examine the mausoleum wall. But the greater part of me wanted to get out of there as fast as possible.

Breathing somewhat erratically, I rushed toward the entrance and handed the two lanterns to the gentleman who had given them to us.

He smiled knowingly. "Did you see the headless ghost?"

I was taken aback. "You know about him?"

"Oh, sure. He's a regular here. We don't know who he is, but we think he's looking for someone. We joke about the fact that he can't find who he's looking for because he doesn't have a head."

A quiver ran through my entire body. "I hope he's not looking for me, because I'm out of here."

The man laughed. "Your first ghost sighting?"

My heart pounded in my chest. "Yes. May I ask you a question?"

"Sure."

"Does the headless ghost walk through walls?" I felt incredibly stupid.

"On a regular basis," he assured me.

I thanked him and gladly returned to the more earthly surroundings of Georgetown. It was late and the streets had grown less busy. I wasn't far from the bookstore. I walked the few blocks, trying to shake the image of the headless ghost. But then I couldn't help thinking about the man in the leaves. What a horrible ending for someone. He had surely been murdered. There was no other way or reason for a dead person to be in an offbeat location like that. Eric may not have wanted to concede that the new body and Manny were the same ones Hilda had seen or imagined, but I couldn't help wondering if they were exactly the same. Could there be a connection between the two deaths? And I was seriously spooked by Hilda's suggestion that I was finding dead bodies for a reason. That it was some sort of mystical power. I shook all over. What nonsense!

Lights were still on in the Maxwell mansion when I returned home. To be honest, I was in no mood for company. All I wanted was to curl up with a cup of hot tea.

Peaches and Frodo met me at the door of the carriage house. I interpreted Peaches's demand for attention to mean that she had missed me. Frodo was happy I had returned but all he really wanted was a cookie.

I took care to lock my front door. While I didn't think I had anything to fear, someone or two someones were murdering people in my part of town. There was no reason to keep the front door unlocked anyway. I paused in the kitchen to put on the kettle for tea and headed up the stairs.

Peaches and Frodo followed me to the bedroom, where I changed into a Christmas-red plaid nightshirt. It was probably silly of me, but red plaid always made me feel warm and cozy.

The teakettle whistled and the three of us returned to the kitchen. I stroked both Peaches and Frodo, glad I wasn't alone. I plunked an English breakfast teabag into a mug, poured the boiling water over it, and added plenty of milk. I didn't let it steep long, though. I didn't want to be up all night and would have a hard enough time sleeping as it was.

I fed Peaches a cat treat that reeked of fish. Frodo received a special dog chew for his teeth. I preferred a gingersnap cookie. I carried my tea to the sofa and curled up with my sketchpad.

So much had happened that I hardly knew where to start. I doodled idly while I thought about the fact that my entire perspective on ghosts had just changed. I had lived quite happily believing them to be myths and scary tales. But there was simply no denying what I had seen. No wonder other people who had seen ghosts were afraid to admit it for fear of ridicule.

As my doodle developed, the tall headless ghost I had seen took shape. His collar had been crisply folded. I hadn't seen a neck at all. Just a body. But it was finely detailed. It wasn't like a big blob or an amorphous figure. I had read about people who claimed to have seen lights moving or a fog. I hadn't seen him long enough to make decisions about his attire, but something about him screamed 1800s to me. It had to have been his clothing.

I wanted to tell myself that I hadn't seen him. That it had been the power of suggestion. That I imagined him because of Hilda and Jacquie's incessant talk of ghosts. But the truth was that I knew what I had seen. He had been completely clear to me. And, even worse, the man at the gate had confirmed it. He hadn't said something that was so universal that it would have applied to every gust of dust and fireplace smoke tendril. The man at the gate knew. He knew the ghost didn't have a head. Chill bumps rose on my arms again.

I flipped the page to start fresh. I had drawn a foot in a carpet recently. This time the corpse hadn't been covered by anything except leaves. I drew the man's body as I remembered it, lying on the ground with dried leaves on top of it.

I went to the next page quickly and sketched the skull again. If there were such things as ghosts, could there also be such things as screaming skulls? I would have to ask Bob and

Veronica which one of them had placed the skull in the window. In a way, it had been a brilliant, if frightening, idea. I drew the eye sockets with streams of white shooting out of them. Taking my time, I blurred the area along the beams, and used a variety of shade values on the skull.

I was studying my results when someone pounded on my door.

Chapter 25

I recognized Veronica's voice shouting, "Florrie! Let us in!"

When I opened the door, Veronica and Jacquie shot inside, chattering nonstop. I closed the door and Jacquie reached over and locked it.

"We saw a ghost," Veronica blurted, completely out of breath.

"Everyone did," added Jacquie. "The whole group of us!"

Why did I find that immensely comforting? I held my breath. "Was it a headless man?"

They stared at me in shock.

"How could you know that?" asked Jacquie.

Strangely enough, the fact that other people had seen the same ghost calmed my nerves considerably. I felt so much better! "I saw him, too. Now I'm beginning to wonder if it was a setup. Maybe the cemetery arranged it."

"No way," Veronica headed straight to my liquor cabinet. "It was real. I will never pooh-pooh anyone else's ghost visions again."

"What did Hilda say about it? Could she tell who he was?" I asked.

Veronica poured two glasses of Grand Marnier and

handed one to Jacquie. "Hilda took it in stride. I guess ghosts are a big part of her life. It's not like he was the first one *she* encountered."

Jacquie sipped from her glass. "But Hilda couldn't get him to talk with her."

Veronica laughed hysterically. "Maybe you need a head to be able to communicate! Oh gosh. I'm sorry. I'm a little shaken. Florrie, would you mind if I slept over tonight?"

"Of course not. Are you afraid he might follow you home?" I was teasing, but Veronica wasn't a wuss. She had to be very frightened to sleep over.

"No. At least I don't think so. Where do ghosts go? Do you think he hangs out at the cemetery all the time? Are they like vampires? Do they only come out at night?"

It was a ridiculous conversation. Ghosts didn't roam the streets looking for people to pursue, did they?

"Wait a minute," I said. "If ghosts roam the streets looking for people, why is this the first ghost Veronica and I have ever seen? No, no, no. I think there's something fishy about this ghost."

"We have one in the mansion, you know," said Jacquie, taking a seat and elegantly crossing her legs. "Maxwell won't talk about it. He's funny that way. And he doesn't want DuBois to know who it is."

Veronica nestled in a chair, her shoes off and her legs drawn up under her. "Why not?"

I took the sofa. Peaches vaulted onto my lap and Frodo jumped up beside me.

"Because the ghost was once a butler for the Maxwells. It's very sad, but a wonderful story. Well, to me it is. You know how I love a romance. Of course, we all know about upstairs and downstairs in England, where the domestics didn't mingle with the people for whom they worked. It wasn't all that different here. The butler was the head of the domestic staff.

However, even though he was at the top, he didn't socialize with the family. In the 1800s, the Maxwells' butler was a gentleman named Grover Throop. He fell in love with a society lady who lived in this neighborhood, a Natalia O'Malley."

I choked on my tea. "Natalia? The daughter of the ambassador?"

Jacquie looked at me in surprise. "I've never heard that but I suppose it's possible. By all accounts, Natalia was just as smitten with Grover. The lovers met secretly in garden nooks and private spots. You can imagine what a scandal it would have been if their love for each other became public. Poor Natalia was reportedly married to a vile man. Even a rumor of her interest in a butler would have ruined her and likely gotten her thrown out of the house!"

"This is so sad," said Veronica. "They were star-crossed lovers. There was no way out for them."

"Not in those times," said Jacquie. "Can't you see them sneaking around the mansion? For all we know, they might have met out here in the carriage house!"

"I don't get it," I said. "Why would that upset Mr. DuBois?"

"DuBois is a stickler for formality and proper behavior. He would be aghast at the thought. But there's more. Natalia's father was worried about her welfare. He gave his daughter a number of gold coins in case she fell on desperate times. He warned her to hide them from her husband. She knew she couldn't keep them in her own home because her husband would surely find them. So she gave them to the one man she trusted—Grover Throop. Grover was a decent and honest man. Unfortunately, Natalia's brother, Ivan, got wind of what their father had done. He had a terrible gambling habit and was broke. He wanted those coins! He figured that Natalia's husband, O'Malley, had taken them from her. So he spied on her husband, O'Malley, intending to demand or steal the gold coins. Unfortunately, O'Malley was a superstitious man with a bad drinking habit. One of the chambermaids, wishing to endear herself to O'Malley, told him about Grover and Natalia. On a misty evening, O'Malley and Ivan confronted the hapless butler on the doorstep and shot him on the spot. But in their haste, they didn't realize that they had killed the only person who knew where the gold coins were hidden."

I longed to hear a happier ending. "That's it? They murdered the poor butler?"

"Now you know why Maxwell doesn't want DuBois to know about it," Jacquie explained.

"I hope O'Malley and Ivan rotted in a filthy, cold jail for that," said Veronica.

"I don't honestly know what happened to the two of them," said Jacquie. "Perhaps Maxwell knows. He grew up hearing relatives talk about Grover the butler, who was murdered because of his affair with a society lady and that he now walks the grounds, continuing his job."

"Coralue told me O'Malley was run over by his own coach," I offered.

Jacquie cringed. "Sometimes when the wind blows through the trees at night, I could swear I hear someone calling, *Natalia!*" She sang the name.

Veronica frowned. "Maybe I should sleep at home. I don't think I have a ghost in my apartment."

Jacquie glanced at her watch. "Oof! I'd better head back before Mr. DuBois wonders what happened to me."

But when Jacquie opened the door, she screamed.

Frodo barked and ran to Jacquie's side. Veronica and I were right behind him.

Frodo wagged his tail, which made me feel a little bit better.

I opened the door wide. It was Roxie. She barely looked like herself. Her beautiful face was haggard, her skin sallow. Her baby blond hair was snagged and ratty, as if she hadn't brushed it in days. "I'm sorry! I didn't mean to shock you. I was just getting ready to knock on the door. Since the lights were on, I figured Florrie was still up."

Jacquie sagged and heaved a sigh of relief. She reached out for Roxie's arm. "I'm sorry I screamed, sugar, I didn't expect to see anyone."

"I apologize for coming here so late. I . . ."

Jacquie pulled her inside, and I closed the door.

In a whisper she asked, "I heard someone found a body." She swallowed hard. "Is it Finley?"

Chapter 26

Veronica gasped. "Finley?"

Jacquie shrieked and covered her mouth with her hand.

I reached for Roxie's hand and clasped it tight. "Why on earth would it be Finley? I was there. I don't think anyone knows yet who he is, but I can assure you that he didn't look like Finley."

"I'm so worried that something terrible happened to Finley. I don't know if he's dead or off with that woman."

Jacquie locked the door behind Roxie, and Veronica led her to the sofa.

I filled my kettle, a fancy black-and-white harlequin model that had been a gift from Professor Maxwell, and put on water for tea. I was pretty sure I'd read that black tea calms the nerves, so I went with that. I pulled out four mugs in an array of colors, all of which had white polka dots on them. I plunked tea bags in the four mugs, poured boiling water in them, and brought them to the living room with spoons, napkins, sugar, and milk.

Jacquie added hefty doses of sugar and milk to a mug and handed it to Roxie, whose pale skin now bore cherry-red blotches.

Roxie's fingers trembled.

Frodo laid his head on her knees as if he knew she needed comforting.

"Why would you think Finley was dead?" I asked.

Roxie heaved a great sigh and massaged her forehead. "Someone tried to kill my father. How do I know that Finley isn't next? My mind sometimes gets the better of me. I worry about everything. The truth is that he's probably with that woman."

"What woman?" asked Jacquie.

"Florrie saw her. She was at the bookstore the other day, stalking him." Almost as an afterthought, Roxie added, "She's quite attractive."

Veronica tilted her head like a puppy. "You're afraid she's having an affair with him or that she killed him?"

"I don't want to think either of those things happened. He hasn't come home tonight. That woman was standing outside our house the other day," said Roxie.

"That's quite brazen." Jacquie frowned. "What did she say?"

"Oh, she didn't knock on the door. She hung around on the street like she was spying on us or she wanted to see where Finley lived."

Poor Roxie. I longed to think that her imagination was running wild, but Veronica had been fairly sure about Finley's infidelity. I needed to get Roxie focused on reality. "When did you last see Finley?"

"This afternoon. He said he was joining some friends for a poker game tonight."

Jacquie shot her a sad look. "Has he lied to you before?"

"I'm sorry. I shouldn't have come here." Roxie massaged her forehead.

"Of course you should," I protested. "We're your friends."

She gazed around at us. "You are. I'm so embarrassed about this. I wish I had never seen that woman. I feel my marriage slipping away and I don't know what to do."

I wanted to be nice and reassure her despite my misgivings. Wasn't that what a friend would do? "I trust you have called him. He's not answering his phone?"

She shook her head. "I have called, texted, and emailed. No response to anything."

"Have you called the police?" asked Jacquie.

Roxie gazed into her tea. "No," she said in a timid tone. "He'd be so angry if I involved the police."

For the first time I wondered if she was afraid of him. "Is he often angry?"

She shot me a look that I had seen before on women who were determined to defend someone dear to them. "We all get upset sometimes. And Finley lost his family at such a young age. Really, he's had more than his share of terrible tragedy."

I wasn't sure that was a valid reason to be angry with Roxie. But who was I to judge? After all, it wasn't like I had had a lot of successful relationships.

"That doesn't make sense," Veronica said. "If he has been spending time with that woman, what was she doing in your neighborhood?"

"I think she's obsessed with him."

"It would serve him right if you called the police," I blurted. "There's no good reason for him not to stay in contact with you. Even if he is seeing another woman."

Roxie almost spilled the tea. "I hadn't thought of that. Oh no! Florrie, it's worse than I thought. I assumed he was probably living it up with her, but you're right. He would at least answer his phone to lie to me. Wouldn't he?"

He would, unless he planned to make a clean break and

walk away. But if there was one thing I had learned, it was that people often didn't act the way we expected of them. "Has he ever stayed out all night before?"

Roxie shook her head. "He's been out very late without me, but he always comes home."

"Where does he go when he's out late?" asked Jacquie.

Roxie took a deep breath. "He parties. He runs with that fancy crowd. I call them the trust-fund babies because they're all rolling in money. They don't have to work, so they sleep late, shop, and then stay out until the wee hours. You know, the ones who go to all the chic galas and such."

"You don't go with him?"

"Not usually. I find it boring. They're nice enough to me. I'm acceptable in their crowd because my dad has connections, but I was never really into all that socializing."

I was confused. Cyril lived in a fancy house and owned a priceless vase. "I thought Cyril was a professor."

"He is. But he was born to money, so I'm considered to be one of them by virtue of birth. That's how I met Finley."

"Is there someone in that group you might call?" suggested Jacquie. "Maybe they would know where Finley is or where he was last seen, anyway."

A moment passed in silence before Roxie admitted, "The thing is that this isn't like any other time. I'm terrified. I have never been so afraid in my life. What's going on in my family? Why would anyone want to murder my dad? And what if they're after Finley? Am I next? Will someone find *me* in my own home with my throat slit?"

I hadn't thought about it that way. "I would be scared, too. I don't blame you at all."

Jacquie piped up. "Honey, you can bunk with us at the mansion until we figure out what's going on. Mr. DuBois loves to have someone to fuss over."

"I don't want to impose . . ."

"Oh, sweetheart!" said Jacquie. "It would not be an imposition at all. We have lovely guest rooms and I, for one, would feel so much better if you were staying with us. Come on. We'll go to your house right now. You can pack what you need and we'll help you carry everything."

Roxie was so upset that I could see her chest heaving with each breath she took. "Okay. That's very nice of you. I would feel safer with other people around."

I ran upstairs and changed into jeans and a warm sweater. I took Frodo with us for whatever small degree of comfort he might give Roxie.

We walked quietly to Roxie's house. Georgetown rarely slept. Even now, in the wee hours of the morning, we could see lights on in some houses and hear distant voices. An occasional car drove by.

Roxie's house stood out from the rest. Lights beamed from every single window, as if she were having a party.

"Roxie, why are all the lights on?" asked Veronica.

"I don't want anyone hiding inside. I'm terrified every time I come home. The guy who tried to kill Dad was waiting inside his kitchen. How do I know there's not someone upstairs in a closet watching for me?"

She unlocked the front door. When we stepped inside, Roxie held a finger up against her lips. We were all silent for a moment.

"I don't hear anyone," whispered Veronica.

"Maybe we should stay in teams," I suggested.

"I'll go upstairs with you and help you pack, Roxie." Jacquie started up the steps, followed by Roxie.

At that moment, the front door swung open and all four of us screamed.

Finley stared at us blankly. "I know it's Halloween but I didn't think I was that scary."

Roxie gripped the banister. She laughed too heartily. "We had a wee bit too much to drink," she said cheerily.

The three of us followed her lead.

"We were making sure Roxie got home okay," Veronica fibbed.

Finley held the door open for us. "Thank you kind ladies for looking after my darling wife."

On another day I might have thought he was sweet. But I was beginning to wonder if Roxie was hiding something about their relationship. He was a little bit cloying. It was as though he was trying too hard.

We said good night and stepped outside. Jacquie and Veronica started down the street, but I hung back for a moment and listened. I didn't really think I would hear screaming but who knew what went on behind closed doors?

Veronica looked back at me. "Florrie, come on!"

I caught up to them. While Veronica and Jacquie chatted about Roxie's marriage, I was a little creeped out by the Halloween decorations. Fun and scary under other circumstances, tonight they were hitting a little bit too close to home. The leering skeletons and evil-faced ghosts served to remind me that two people were now dead.

"Roxie's house is to die for. The next time I go out with a penniless guy, remind me about Roxie's house. I guess there are benefits to marrying wealthy," said Veronica.

Jacquie chuckled. "Finley didn't pay for that house. It was a wedding gift to her from Cyril."

"Wow! Nice gift. They must have been thrilled," I said.

Jacquie nodded. "But Cyril had thought that gift through. He always felt guilty about Roxie losing her mom at such a tender age. He was mother and father to her. He put his own life aside to raise her. For years, he didn't date, he barely socialized. Roxie was his world. I think he hoped that if she had a nice house, she might not move away from him."

"That's so sad. Cyril seems like a very nice man," I said.

"He is. But a gift like that often comes with a hefty obligation attached to it."

Veronica was probably trying to lighten the mood when she said to Jacquie, "The professor is going to wonder what happened to you."

Jacquie snorted. "I doubt it. He'll think I'm off somewhere in a snit. We've been arguing quite a bit lately. Maxwell thinks Hilda is a charlatan, intent on making money off people's grief. More specifically, my grief. He doesn't believe that she can speak to the dead or prognosticate. The trouble, of course, is that neither one of us can prove our side. He can't prove that ghosts don't exist, and I can't prove that they do."

Veronica looked at me with a worried expression. "I'm sure that won't come between you," she said. "It's such an unimportant thing to differ on. Besides, now that there *was* a foot in a rug and a second body, it looks like Hilda was right."

"It runs deeper than that. Maxwell is actually disappointed in himself. He has traveled the world and found priceless treasures, but the one thing he can't get over is that he has never been able to find our daughter, Caroline, right here at home."

I winced. She was completely right. Caroline's disappearance was the worst thing that had ever happened to either one of them. Not knowing what happened to Caroline might even be worse than believing that she had died.

As it turned out, Jacquie was wrong about the professor. He and Mr. DuBois greeted us at the back door of the mansion with cries of "Where have you been?"

The two of them had waited up and were as exhausted as the rest of us. Veronica and I peeled off as fast as we could.

When we were in the carriage house and getting ready for bed, Veronica said, "Thank heaven it's Sunday tomorrow and I can sleep all day."

It was her day off. I was so exhausted that I envied her.

We opened at noon on Sundays, so at least I could catch a decent nap before opening the bookstore.

"Veronica," I said, in what I hoped was a nonjudgmental voice, "don't you think there's something suspicious about the fact that we all saw the same headless ghost? I left at least an hour before you did. If ghosts exist, there must be tons of them in a graveyard. Why would we all see the same one? Maybe it was some kind of projection designed to spook people for Halloween."

"If it was, they certainly did a good job of it. I don't think that was the case, Florrie. It was so real! Tell me he didn't scare you!"

"Of course he did. Seeing him throws everything I believed into question. Veronica, do you believe in ghosts?"

She hesitated. "I thought I didn't before. It's fun to pretend and joke around as though they exist. But there's no doubt in my mind now. I mean, I had never actually seen one. Some pictures had made me wonder, but in the back of my mind, I knew photos could be manipulated. It's not like seeing one with your own eyes. The headless ghost at the cemetery tonight sealed it for me. There was no other logical explanation for his presence. Face it, Florrie, a real person cannot walk around without his head."

"But aren't there headless costumes?" I argued.

"I guess so. Did that look like a costume to you?"

She had a point. "No," I said with great regret. "It didn't. It looked kind of misty."

I brought a blanket and pillows for Veronica, who was going to bunk on the tufted daybed with a trundle I had bought for overnight visitors.

"Do you think Manny was murdered over a woman?" Veronica asked.

I hadn't expected that! "Anything is possible, I guess. Do you know something?"

"No. I was just thinking about the poor butler and his sad love triangle. Have you heard anything yet about who might have killed Manny?" she asked.

"Nope. But no one where he worked seemed very sad about his death. It sounds like he was universally disliked."

"That's so sad! Tomorrow I shall do something nice for someone. Something unexpected."

"We should all do the same." I hoped that thought would cheer her up and clear her dreams of murdered butlers.

Chapter 27

I was still yawning when I unlocked Color Me Read. I had left Frodo with Veronica and Peaches.

Minutes later, Bob arrived full of energy and wearing a big grin. It was the happiest I had ever seen him.

"I've got a date tonight!" he blurted. His cheeks blazed as crimson as the maple leaves blowing in the breeze.

"With Julie? The girl who went on the cemetery tour last night?"

"Can you believe it? I'm psyched! We have so much in common."

"Besides pizza?" I asked drily.

"Very funny. She's into *The Hobbit*, and Minecraft, and *Star Wars*."

I smiled at him. "I'm really happy for you. She seems nice."

The door opened and an exhausted Eric joined us.

"Have you been up all night?" I asked.

"Unfortunately. I used to think I'd like to be in the homicide branch, but I don't know. It's pretty brutal."

"Have you identified the body?" I held my breath.

"Yes. He was a local private investigator named Ellis Willoughby the Fourth."

I let out a little squeal. *"Noooo!"*

"You know him?" asked Eric.

"I never met him. Follow me." I raced up the staircase to the professor's office and barged inside. I spotted what I was looking for. The professor had pinned the note from Willoughby on a board next to his desk. I removed it carefully and handed it to Eric. "This came with the skull and the scrying mirror."

Eric scanned the letter. "Does Professor Maxwell know what Ellis's dire situation was?"

"If he does, he hasn't told me. Cyril knew him, too."

"Cyril?" Eric's eyebrows shot up. "Now this is getting interesting. We were working under the presumption that Ellis's death was related to his job. But it never occurred to me that the job might involve Cyril or Maxwell. There's a curious connection."

"Eric, did you find the thing that flashed? The item that drew us closer to Ellis's body?"

"We think it was a steel cylinder. About four inches long and a third of an inch in diameter. Open on both ends but there were two holes piercing one end."

"Something from a car engine, maybe?" I suggested.

"Possibly." Eric wrapped his arms around me and rested his head on mine. When he pulled away, he didn't seem so tired anymore. We returned to the main floor. He pecked me on the cheek, ran out the door, and was gone in a flash.

Although we had a steady stream of browsers in the store, it seemed empty without the professor, Veronica, Zsazsa, or Goldblum.

I did notice that we heard no wailing. When I was upstairs, I looked in Professor Maxwell's office. Harry wasn't on the shelf.

I took a minute to gaze around. The professor had a lot of artifacts on his shelves. But Harry wasn't among them.

At that point I wasn't too worried. I had seen him in the show window the night before. But he wasn't there, either.

"Bob?" I called. "Have you seen Harry?"

"I am very pleased to say I have not. That thing creeps me out."

A customer needed my assistance, forcing me to put off my search for Harry. At least temporarily.

I was relieved when five o'clock rolled around and it was almost time to close for the day. I took my time walking through every room looking for Harry. I didn't see him anywhere. That was odd. I hoped Professor Maxwell took him home for safekeeping.

I set the alarm and locked the front door.

Bob had an overabundance of energy and rushed down the street to meet Julie.

Meanwhile, I was thinking about what Eric had said. Could Ellis's death have something to do with the attack on Cyril? Roxie was terrified. I couldn't help wondering if she knew something more than she was revealing. Why had she jumped to the notion that Finley might have been murdered last night?

I walked home slowly, mulling over the possibilities. As I neared the mansion, the front door opened. The light from the foyer shone on Balthus and Roxie. Balthus gave her a long hug and a familiar kiss. I was too far away to hear what they were saying.

Roxie closed the door and Balthus looked up and down the street. I dodged behind an old oak tree. When I dared to peer around it at Balthus, I could see that he was uneasy. He walked away from me and I followed, trying to stay in the shadows.

Balthus hurried for two blocks, all the while gazing around. Then he turned left. I followed him into a neighborhood of smaller homes. Even they cost astronomical amounts. I knew that for certain after searching for a place for years.

He slowed and looked around again. In a flash, he disappeared down stairs. From where I stood, I guessed they led to a basement apartment. I crossed the street. There wasn't a reason in the world that I shouldn't be there. If he noticed me, I would pretend to be making a book delivery to a nearby address.

I kept my eye on the spot where he had presumably entered. When I passed it and rounded the corner, a light gleamed through a tiny window with bars on it. I knew that basement apartment. About two years earlier I had been inside and looked at it, considering it for myself.

While some basement apartments were gorgeous and well thought out, this place was a dungeon. One room and a bath. As I recalled, the kitchen consisted of a tiny refrigerator and a hot plate. The horrid little window was the only window in the entire apartment. In fact, calling it an apartment was a wild overstatement. It was a room with a shower and toilet.

Balthus had mentioned staying with a friend. I hoped he was visiting someone and that this wasn't his new digs. I had run from it because it was too depressing, even if the rent was cheap.

I walked home wondering what the deal was with Balthus. Was he worried that people might realize that he was living in that horrid little place? Was he trying to keep up appearances? Or was he visiting someone there? Someone he didn't want to be associated with?

The moment I unlocked the carriage house door, Peaches

mewed and demanded my full attention. I swung her into my arms and listened to her happy purrs.

Veronica had left a note on the kitchen island. *Hope it's okay that I took Frodo home to Mom and Dad for you. Thought I'd bring them dinner because it's their first night back. Sorry you're missing it.* She signed it with a heart.

"It's just us again, Peaches."

She rubbed her head against my chin. I took that as sign that she didn't mind too much.

After I changed clothes and we ate dinner, I gladly curled up on the sofa with my sketchbook. I examined the sketch I had drawn of the headless ghost first. I wondered if the long coat I had drawn was what he wore or something my mind had embellished. It was decidedly tailored, not ratty or shabby. The collar stood up, hiding his neck. He had struck me as being tall, with long arms. I had sketched him about to disappear through the wall of the mausoleum he had walked into.

Suddenly, I was overwhelmed by the desire to see whose mausoleum it was.

There wasn't much to draw of poor Ellis Willoughby IV. But I drew the funny little cylinder with two holes on one end. It was rudimentary at best but it didn't look like anything that I could readily identify. I presumed that it was possible the item had somehow landed in that pile of leaves and had nothing to do with Ellis.

Peaches leaped into my lap, and the sketchpad slid to the floor. We snuggled for a short time. Then, as cats are wont to do, she abruptly departed and embarked on a major cat bath.

I picked up my sketchpad. It fell open to Manny. I tried to set emotions aside and look at the drawings factually.

Hilda with the bushy hair had started everything by telling us about the foot in the rug. I had been doubtful about her all along and had to suspect she could have murdered Manny and Ellis to prove her ability to predict the future. People would flock to her if they thought she was accurate. I hated to think that way, but people had done stranger things for fame and fortune.

Manny had told coworkers at the bakery that he had a new and lucrative job or deal. Next to his face I wrote *new job?*

Of course, the skull had preceded everything. But even if Goldblum had found stories of screaming skulls, I knew for a fact that Harry could not murder anyone.

I smiled at Coralue's pretty face. I thought I had done a fairly good job of capturing her likeness. Could she have murdered Manny to avenge her son, Hayes? Would she have been stupid enough to bury her victim in her own yard?

Or was that smart? She didn't have to find a place for the body. She wouldn't have to drive him anywhere. And no one would give a second thought to sweet Coralue outside working in her yard. Had she planned to murder Manny and ordered the coffin in advance for that purpose? That was a chilling thought!

Or had her son, Hayes, killed Manny in revenge? Had he called his mom for help? Or had he known there was a nice, soft flower bed in her yard where he could deposit Manny's body?

I flipped the page and sketched Balthus. He was tall and hefty, yet there was something soft about him, almost flaccid. Still, he would have had no problem subduing someone as small as Manny. But why? Was there a connection between the two of them? Hilda had claimed the rug with the foot was in Balthus's doorway. Of course, no one lived there when she made that statement. Balthus had already moved out. And there was no evidence that a rug with a foot had ever been there.

As I drew Balthus's face, a wary expression emerged. He had scanned the street in fear when I followed him.

What was he afraid of?

Roxie seemed to know Balthus fairly well. Maybe she knew more about a relationship between Balthus and Manny.

And I had almost forgotten that Cyril was attacked. Maybe the cops were right about that and it had been a botched burglary attempt. Or maybe not.

I flipped to a fresh page and drew quick sketches of Cyril, Balthus, and Manny in a triangle. I longed to draw some lines linking them but didn't know of any connections between them that might lead to murder.

I woke early on Monday. Still in my nightshirt, I fed Peaches a kitty version of beef stew and made myself a mug of coffee and a piece of cinnamon toast for breakfast. Peaches watched me eat, then followed me upstairs to the shower. I pulled on a pumpkin-colored sweater and a plaid skirt of chocolate and honey with a line of pumpkin running through it. Wearing flats, I trotted down the stairs. I dressed Peaches in her halter and struck out for Color Me Read.

Peaches had become used to the walk to the store and no longer dawdled as much as she had in the beginning. She balked, though, at the Halloween decorations that moved with the breeze.

The ghosts along the street weren't as menacing in the daylight. In fact, they appeared quite harmless, more reminiscent of Casper than Freddy Krueger.

I stopped for a moment in front of Coralue's house. The ancient butler and faux coffin had been the best décor on the street. I was sorry they were gone. But I couldn't help looking up at the huge arched window. It was beautiful. If I were a ghost I wouldn't mind hanging out in digs like that. Happily, no faces appeared in the window. Maybe it had been my imagination, fertilized by Coralue's story of Irina.

On arriving at the shop, I paused for a moment to assess one of our show windows. Veronica had done an excellent job. A realistic-looking cobweb hung in the upper right corner. Fall leaves in shades of orange and red from a real tree looked like they were part of the plan. Books on mystical subjects crowded the window with suns, moons, and stars. I was pleased to see that the battery-operated candles I had bought looked genuine from the street. Their flames flickered as though a breeze were wafting by them inside, and the faux drips down the candles seemed authentic, too. A lone pumpkin sat on the window box in honor of the season.

I unlocked the door and turned off the alarm before releasing Peaches from her halter. She disappeared up the stairs while I started coffee and turned on the classical music that played softly in the background while shoppers browsed.

I had a hunch that Professor Maxwell was in his office. That would account for Peaches's haste to run up the stairs. I switched on lights and made sure all the battery-operated candles in our ghostly displays were working. I poured coffee in a mug for the professor and walked up to the third floor.

The door to his office was open and Peaches was already on his desk.

"Thank you, Florrie," said the professor. "Now that Ellis is dead, it is incumbent upon us to find out what we can about Harry. Goldblum and I have been researching records. I'll be seeing Ellis's family at the funeral, of course, but it's too early to bother them with this sort of matter. He was a delightful person. I'm sorry you didn't know him."

The bell rang downstairs, indicating someone had entered the store. I ran down to find Bob and a weary-looking man at the entrance.

His face was gaunt, with practically no cheekbones. A fat gray mustache hung over his upper lip and wire-rimmed glasses framed tired eyes. "I'm looking for Florrie Fox." He flipped a badge at me far too fast for me to see exactly what it was.

"I'm Florrie. How can I help you?"

"Detective Brannigan. Is there someplace we can talk?"

Bob nodded at me. "I'll watch the store."

I showed the detective to the parlor. "Would you like a cup of coffee?"

His eyes met mine and I had a feeling I had accidentally just changed everything.

"Yes, please."

"I'm on it!" yelled Bob.

I tried not to grin but even Detective Brannigan managed a smile, even if it was brief.

He accepted the mug of java from Bob and thanked him. Even though Bob could most likely hear everything from the hallway, Brannigan waited until he left before proceeding. "I'm investigating the murder of Manny Menz. Could you tell me what happened that night?"

I began with the call from the police that woke me and finished with my own call to 911.

"Could you identify the boys you saw playing with the fake casket?"

"No. It was dark outside, and they took off running before I reached the casket. I didn't get a good look at any of their faces. They struck me as kids who were clowning around, maybe fourteen or so."

"Who saw Manny first?" he asked.

I had just told him it was Frodo. Was this an effort to trip me up? Did he want to see if I could stick to my story? I wished Veronica hadn't taken Frodo home. Brannigan might be the kind of guy who softened around big, friendly dogs. "Frodo was the first to find Manny's foot. If he hadn't been with me, I might not have noticed it in the dark."

"How long had you known Manny?"

"A year or so, I guess. I didn't know him well. It wasn't like we hung out together. I only knew him from the bakery."

Brannigan nodded.

I weighed whether to mention the episode with Manny on the night of Hilda's reading. Was it better to bring it out in the open before someone else told him or was it safer to only answer his questions? I decided it would be best for me if I said something now. "The evening before, a couple of our employees caught Manny trying to steal a skull from the store. We were all surprised by that."

"A skull? Like a Halloween decoration?"

I could feel my face flushing and knew the tops of my ears were flaming. I hadn't done anything wrong. Why was I turning red? "A human skull that Professor Maxwell was keeping in his office upstairs."

His voice was stern. "A human skull."

"That's correct." I tried hard to sound matter-of-fact. Like everyone had a human skull lying around.

Brannigan stared at me. "I have heard of Professor Maxwell. Is this skull something he brought back from one of his expeditions?"

"A friend sent it to him. One Ellis Willoughby the Fourth."

Brannigan almost dropped his coffee cup. "Is it valuable?"

"Not that I'm aware. It's not inlaid with gold or anything like that. It's just bone." I shrugged. "A regular skull."

"Why would Manny want it?" he asked.

"We wondered the same thing."

Bob leaned against the doorway. "I caught him with it under his jacket. He said he thought it would be a good Halloween prank or something along those lines."

Brannigan didn't turn around to look at Bob. "Did anyone else witness this?"

"My sister, Veronica."

"Of course," he said sarcastically. "Was this witnessed by someone who doesn't work here and isn't related to you?"

"The store was packed that evening. It's entirely possible

that someone else noticed. Although I suspect most of the attention was on Hilda Rattenhorst."

"What did you do?" asked Brannigan.

I shrugged again. "We let him go."

Bob piped up. "We decided to keep an eye on him if he came into the store again. I don't think he was much of a reader. I don't recall seeing him here before."

Again, Brannigan didn't bother to look at Bob.

I could hear the front door open. A male voice said, "I'm looking for Florrie Fox."

Brannigan rose to his feet. He walked over to the opening that led to the checkout desk.

"Well, well," he said. "All the yellow jackets do return to the nest."

I had no idea what he was talking about. I jumped to my feet and peered at the man who had asked for me. I had never seen him before in my life.

Chapter 28

"Hello, Brannigan. Upsetting ladies again, are you?" asked the man I didn't know.

He was of medium height with a long face and thick cinnamon hair that he wore short. His blue eyes were mischievous, almost laughing. He crossed his arms over a Carolina blue sweater like he was daring Brannigan.

Brannigan's lower jaw turned ruddy. To me he said, "I'd like to see the skull."

Uh-oh. "I wasn't able to locate it last night before we closed." I couldn't exactly tell him that Harry seemed to move around the store on his own volition. "He's supposed to be in the professor's office. I would be happy to accompany you there."

Brannigan nodded.

I started up the stairs.

The man I didn't know asked, "Are you Florrie?"

Brannigan snorted. "Don't dig yourself any deeper, Hayes."

Hayes? Coralue's son? I turned and smiled at him. That seemed to aggravate Brannigan.

I continued up the stairs. Poor Brannigan was huffing by

the time we reached the third floor. He followed me to the professor's office.

Naturally, Harry wasn't there. And neither was the professor.

I threw my hands in the air. "I'm sorry. I don't know where the skull has gone."

"You read a lot?" he asked.

"Yes."

"Mysteries?"

"Yes."

"I don't know what you cooked up with the Throckmortons but I will get to the bottom of this. Manny deserved better."

"I didn't cook up anything with anyone. I hope you do figure out who murdered Manny. He might not have been the greatest guy ever, but you are quite right. He did not deserve to be murdered."

Brannigan walked down the stairs with me right behind him. He headed straight for the door.

"Detective Brannigan?" I called. "Ellis sent this mirror with the skull."

Brannigan turned around and walked closer, staring into it. His eyes widened in horror and he fled out the door.

"Wow," said Bob. "What do you guess he saw? I never see anything interesting."

Hayes held out his hand to me. "Hayes Throckmorton."

I shook his hand. "You don't look like your mother."

"I favor my father. I just wanted to come by to thank you for indulging my mom and being so nice to her."

"I love your mom!"

"That's nice of you to say. She's a little obsessed with ghosts. That scares a lot of people away."

"I think she's fascinating. She told me all about the house you grew up in and the Sokolov family."

Hayes moaned. "Her favorite topic."

"Did you hear ghosts when you were growing up?" I asked.

Hayes nodded somewhat reluctantly. "We definitely heard footsteps on the third floor when no one was up there. No doubt about that. Two of my sisters are convinced they heard a woman weeping a couple of times." He gazed at me and then at Bob. "I don't usually tell people this, but my mom and I think we saw Natalia floating down the stairs. She was as real as you are now but dressed in a ball gown with her hair up. I was only nine years old and it scared the life out of me. I slept with a baseball bat by my bed for years."

"Oh no!" He was a little boy at the time. I could imagine his terror. "Well, since I don't live there, I thoroughly enjoyed your mom's stories."

"I'm sorry Brannigan thinks you're mixed up with me. He's convinced that I murdered Manny. The truth is that I'm sorry he was murdered. What an awful way to die. We Throckmortons don't have killer in our genes. I'm afraid we generally back away from confrontations."

"But you're into judo," I said.

He smiled at me. "Judo teaches respect for oneself and others."

I reminded myself that as nice and attractive as Hayes was, Manny had been killed by some kind of judo move and Hayes was deeply into Judo. "Do you think any of your friends were sufficiently angry with Manny to do him in?"

"I don't know. A lot of the guys were mad that he got away with cheating. But mad enough to murder? I doubt it."

Bob eagerly interjected, "They're saying you choked him from behind."

Hayes sighed. "The rear naked choke. You don't have to know judo to pull that off. My lawyer is waiting for the release of the autopsy results. The cops seem to want it to be a specialty move taught in judo because it fits the narrative they want to develop. Namely that *I* murdered him, which is baloney. I would never have harmed a braggart and show-off like Manny. He was a bonehead. Whoever murdered him must not have realized how harmless he was. I hope they resolve this soon. My poor mom is distraught. She thinks it's all her fault for setting up her decorations the way she did."

"I hope it won't stop her enjoyment of Halloween. She and her next-door neighbor Gene appear to have a contest going."

"Gene," he muttered with disdain. "He yelled at us if we so much as stepped on a blade of his grass when we were kids. We lived with ghosts, but we were more scared of Gene when a ball accidentally landed in his yard. No one wanted to be the one who risked his ire by collecting the ball. And now, of all the weird things, he appears to be attracted to Mom. He keeps going over to her house to give her legal advice about Manny. My sister jokingly suggested that he's the one who planted Manny there so he would have an excuse to visit Mom and be helpful."

He meant it as a joke but it raised red flags for me. What if there was some truth to it? "Do you know of any reason Gene might want to murder Manny?" I asked.

Hayes's eyebrows jumped up in surprise. "Gene? I'll have to give that some thought. I've got to get back to work. Give me a call if Brannigan annoys you."

Hayes handed me a business card before he walked out the door. I gazed at it. *Hayes Throckmorton, Chiropractor.*

"That doesn't bode well for him," Bob opined.

"Why not?"

"A chiropractor would know where to apply pressure to knock a guy off."

Bob smiled at a lady who was looking for a children's book and showed her to the children's section.

Hayes seemed like a smart guy. Surely he wouldn't try to make Manny's death look like it had been some kind of judo move. That would point directly at him. Or was that instinctive in people who trained in judo? Was it possible that someone else used a judo technique on Manny so that Hayes would be the prime suspect? It would have to be someone who knew about the issue Hayes had with Manny. That could be anyone.

At eleven o'clock, Professors Maxwell and Goldblum arrived, bubbling over with excitement.

"He did it!" said Goldblum.

I tilted my head. "Did what?"

"Maxwell had Harry tested."

Professor Maxwell removed Harry from a box he carried and set the skull on the checkout desk.

"So that's where he's been!" I exclaimed.

"We know for sure that he's from the early 1800s," said the professor.

Goldblum could barely control himself. "They're going to submit his DNA to some of the ancestry-type places to see if they can find any living descendants. How cool is that?"

"It's a shame Ellis isn't alive to hear all about Harry. I wonder where he got Harry in the first place," I mused.

Bob eyed Harry. "You do realize that there was no wailing while Harry was gone."

Professor Maxwell snorted and walked up the stairs, carrying Harry.

But Goldblum gushed, "You see? That's actual proof that Harry is a screaming skull!"

In the afternoon, I found Roxie downstairs at the checkout desk.

"I want to apologize for the fuss I made the other night. Finley says I was being ridiculous to even imagine that he was with someone else."

"What about the woman who has been following him?" I asked.

"Oh, Florrie. He claims he doesn't know who I'm talking about." Roxie winced. She whispered when she asked, "But you saw her, too. Right? I'm not imagining things."

My heart went out to her. She wasn't usually so insecure. "No, Roxie," I said firmly, "you aren't imagining anything."

I desperately wanted to shake some sense into her. To tell her he was lying. To wake her to reality. But I knew better. It was Roxie's life. Roxie's marriage. I had no reason to suggest that Finley was seeing another woman. It took all the restraint I could muster to winnow my thoughts down to something simple that might not sound accusatory. "Did he win at the poker game?"

She flipped her hand as though it were insignificant. She rolled her lips inward and glanced around before murmuring, "I went through Finley's pockets while he was in the shower. I'm allowed to do that, you know. It's not snooping. I'm the one who takes care of his laundry. I wouldn't want to throw something in the wash with a tissue in the pocket. I've done that before, and believe me when I say it's a dreadful mess."

Her defensiveness reassured me. She hadn't believed him. She hadn't swallowed his story at all.

"Did you find anything interesting?"

"Cash. No receipts. I want to think he was actually out playing poker." She heaved a big sigh. "He has a business trip coming up. It's about a first edition of *Alice's Adventures in Wonderland*. A man has been looking for a first edition to give to his wife for Christmas. Isn't that romantic? Imagine a husband being so thoughtful."

More thoughtful than *her* husband. That was for sure. "I'm always here for you, Roxie," I said.

She shot me a grateful smile. I was glad I hadn't released a storm of doubt on her as I had wanted to. Roxie might not be ready to admit to the rest of us that she had a problem with Finley, but she was perfectly aware of it herself. I changed the subject. "Roxie, what do you know about Balthus?"

Roxie's face flooded with a creeping scarlet tinge. She smiled softly. "He's so kind. Truly a good and gentle person. I've known him for a long time. We dated before I met Finley."

"Have you seen his new apartment?" I asked tentatively.

"He says it's not ready yet. He's waiting for furniture deliveries and the walls have to be painted."

Well, that was a lie. I knew people could transform spaces, but I didn't think fresh paint and new furniture would make that little dungeon habitable. I didn't blame Balthus for lying to her. I would be horrified to live in that dingy place.

"I don't even know where it is. I've been texting him but he hasn't responded today. I hope he's all right." She pulled out her phone and looked at it. "Still nothing. He's been so thoughtful, bringing dad books to read in the hospital and checking in with me to see if I need anything." She poked at her phone and frowned. "There he is!"

I circled around the end of the checkout desk and peered over her shoulder at a map with a circle over the dingy apartment. "How did you do that?"

"I turned on the Find My app. He must have forgotten to turn it off on his phone. We use it sometimes when we're going to meet up." She sagged with exaggerated relief. "I feel so much better. I'll swing by there to make sure he's all right."

"I'm headed in that direction with a book delivery. Give me a minute and I'll walk with you."

After letting Bob know where I was going and grabbing the delivery for Mrs. Hammond, I accompanied Roxie out the door. We strolled amiably in the direction of Balthus's new digs. While we chatted, I was glad that I hadn't spilled the beans about Balthus's new home. Roxie had located him on her own.

While I trotted up the steps to Mrs. Hammond's house, Roxie crossed the street toward Balthus's place.

Mrs. Hammond opened the door. "Thank you for bringing these by, Florrie. One of them is for my reading group. I'm woefully behind because it meets tomorrow evening."

"I guess I know what you'll be doing tonight," I said.

"I look forward to it. Honestly, some of the women in the group can be quite—"

A shrill scream interrupted her.

"What was that?" asked Mrs. Hammond, peering up and down the street.

Fear welled in me. A second scream confirmed my worst suspicion. I turned and rushed down the steps, ignoring Mrs. Hammond's questions. I darted across the street, watching a young guy in a maroon-and-gold jacket emerge from the stairwell that led to Balthus's apartment.

He ran toward me as if the devil were chasing him. I certainly couldn't tackle him, but I could slow him down. I stopped running and waited for him to near me. Just as he was about to pass by, I slung my purse down on the sidewalk in his path and not-so-accidentally rammed my left shoulder into him.

My plan worked. He fell headlong onto the sidewalk. The only problem was that I hadn't planned on just how sore my shoulder would be.

Passersby stopped and gathered around him.

I called 911. To no one in particular, I said, "I'm calling an ambulance. Don't let him get up. Keep him here."

People murmured to him, telling him to lie still and assuring him that he would be fine.

I dared to run to Balthus's apartment.

I could hear Roxie's voice. She was saying, "Balthus, no. Please, no."

I peered down the stairs at the door to the apartment. It hung ajar. I dashed down the steps.

Pushing the door open just a little bit more with my toe, I peeked inside. Balthus lay on the floor with Roxie kneeling next to him. Blood matted his hair. "Balthus!"

His eyes were open but glazed. If he could see us or knew we were there, he gave no sign of it.

I pulled out my cell phone and called 911 for another ambulance.

"Is he breathing?" I asked Roxie.

"Yes. But he's not responding."

Nevertheless, I took that as a very good sign. I sat next to him and promised him that help was on the way, though I didn't think he could hear me.

The little apartment was as depressing as it had been when I saw it. The walls were a drab gray. The furniture consisted of heaps of boxes. One was being used as a nightstand and table. Candles had dripped wax onto it. A tiny object gleamed under the cot. While Roxie tended to Balthus, I crawled over for a better look. It was a shard of glass. I used a paper napkin to scoot it closer. I didn't pick it up but could see that it was triangular with a smooth point. It had broken at the wide side. The glass contained tiny flecks of gold, sort of like Venetian blown glass I had seen.

I bent again and used the flashlight on my phone to peer under the cot. A small bottle glimmered in the light along with more shards of glass. And suddenly, I knew who had attacked Balthus. I had suspected her all along. That little bottle was definitely the same one Hilda Rattenhorst had passed around at her ill-fated reading.

I didn't believe for a minute that Balthus was bunking

with a friend. Balthus, the wealthy pharmaceutical heir, had absconded without paying his rent at his last apartment. This is what he was reduced to. I wondered what had happened to his money. Could that have something to do with Hilda's attack on him?

For no apparent reason, I felt slightly woozy. I ran up the stairs, called 911 again, and took some deep breaths.

The emergency medical technicians arrived promptly and split up between Balthus and the guy who had run out of the apartment.

I moved Roxie out of their way so they could evaluate him. She seemed to be in a daze. "You need some air." I forced her up the stairs and was telling her to take deep breaths when a policeman approached me.

"Are you the one who clobbered this guy?" He pointed to the man on the sidewalk.

"I didn't 'clobber' him. I tripped him. Roxie, can you tell the officer what happened?"

"My friend hadn't responded to my texts, so I came to check on him. The door was open and a man in a red-and-gold jacket was standing there and Balthus was on the floor, his head bloody."

"Do either of you know his assailant?"

We shook our heads.

"Okay. That pretty much matches what other people said who saw what happened. I'll need your names and addresses, please."

When he went back to Balthus's intruder, Roxie wasted no time in dashing down the stairs. I was right behind her.

"Is he okay?" Roxie asked. "Has he come around?"

"Not yet," said one of the EMTs.

As I looked on, my gaze wandered to his feet. Balthus wore athletic shoes with deep grooves in the treads.

While they prepared to load him on a gurney and take him out to the ambulance, I realized there were pumpkin seeds in the treads. In fact, as I looked closer, it seemed to me that he even had dried pumpkin guts stuck in them.

Could that place him at the scene of Manny's death? Had the police been able to discern treads in the pumpkin guts on the grass? But why would Balthus murder Manny?

We watched as Balthus was loaded into the ambulance. Roxie sobbed. "Balthus! I'll be there as soon as I can!"

She swayed and I caught her. "Do you need to sit down?"

"No. I can't believe this. Not another one. I don't understand. Do you think this is related to the attack on my dad? Florrie! What's happening?"

"Roxie, do you know of any connection between Balthus and Manny?"

She blinked at me. "What do you mean?"

"Are they friends? Archenemies? Did Manny do something that might have angered Balthus?"

Her face screwed up with confusion and anger. "No! I don't understand what you're getting at but I resent where I think you're going with this."

"The night Manny was killed, someone smashed a pumpkin at Coralue's Halloween display. I think Balthus may have stepped in it."

Roxie covered her face with both hands. "If you knew Balthus, you would realize how absurd that is. He's a pacifist. Besides," she argued, "it's not like Manny came back to life and attacked Balthus today. Somebody else did this." She gazed at me. "Has anyone verified Hilda's whereabouts during all these attacks?"

"She was at the bookstore with you and Jacquie when your dad was injured. We can count her out there."

In an indignant tone, Roxie asked, "Did you check Hilda's shoes? Or Coralue's? Or what about Hayes's shoes? He has always been a loose cannon."

I knew she was only trying to make a point, and a good one at that. "I wouldn't have thought of checking anyone's shoes, but I happened to see Balthus's shoes when they loaded him on the gurney. Roxie, I found Hilda's little bottle under the cot in Balthus's room."

"Hilda!" she said in a loud voice. "So it *was* her! I'm sorry, Florrie. I feel like my world has been turned upside down. Everything was going along so well. Right until that woman showed up and started following Finley."

At least she wasn't blaming it on Harry. I seriously doubted that the woman obsessed with Finley had anything to do with the murders and attacks. But Roxie gave me something new to consider. Did the victims all have something in common? Could one person be methodically avenging something?

Roxie accompanied me down the stairs to lock up. She gazed around Balthus's gloomy dwelling. "Oh my gosh. This must be where he lives. My dad mentioned something about his family having financial problems. I had no idea it had come to this. Why didn't he tell me? I saw him the other night and he never mentioned a word. Finley and I would gladly have put him up at our house."

"It can be hard to ask for help. Especially when you're used to being self-sufficient," I said.

"Of course. We have to find a way to help him that allows him to retain his dignity. He's going to need a job."

"Has he ever had one?"

She picked up a stack of napkins with a fast-food logo on them. "Maybe he's already slinging hamburgers. He's a year away from a doctorate in pharmacology. I tried to be sympathetic when he dropped out of the program. He wasn't interested in it and was tired of school."

Roxie squared her shoulders. "First things first. He has to get well and"—she pointed her finger at me—"*you* have to figure out who did this to him." She wavered again, grabbing at me for balance.

I rushed her outside and pressed the button on the inside of the doorknob that locked the door. When we were on the sidewalk, we both took deep breaths.

"Roxie, do you think there was something in that bottle that created fumes when it broke? Something noxious?"

"No one who smelled it at the bookstore became sick." She winced. "The EMTs took it with them. I guess we'll know soon."

Roxie hailed a cab to take her to the hospital. On my way back to the bookstore, I phoned Eric and told him about the bottle, the suspected fumes, and the pumpkin seeds and guts.

I barely knew Balthus, but it made me sad to imagine that he had killed Manny. If Balthus was hard up for money, was he associating with a rough crowd? Was the attack on Balthus related to his killing Manny? Had Manny's tough friends taken revenge? That made much more sense than Hilda. Why would Hilda want to kill Balthus?

I called Bob to see what was going on at the store. He said it was dull and boring so I dared to take an extra half hour. I strolled over to the cemetery and looked at the spot where we had found Ellis.

It was the first time I had seen it in daylight. I turned around in a circle. No streetlights, no houses, no roads or cars. Whoever brought Ellis out here had scoped out one of the few places in Georgetown where he could toss a body without being seen.

In daylight, the place where Ellis had lain was unremarkable. Leaves littered the ground as though his body had never been there.

On my way out of the cemetery, I paused at the spot where I had seen the headless ghost. I cut across neatly mowed grass and walked between headstones to the mausoleum. The name carved into the top stone on the front of the mausoleum read *BOSWORTH*. I smiled. Surely this couldn't be the mausoleum of the man who dueled with O'Malley? I stepped around the locked entrance and gazed at the wall the ghost had allegedly walked through. I knocked on it but the wall seemed quite solid. It was built of large cubes, possibly limestone.

I turned around and looked at the surrounding structures. The cemetery's office was about thirty feet away. I sidestepped tombstones and made my way to the office.

A woman with vivid green streaks in her hair smiled at me. "May I help you?"

"The Bosworth mausoleum." I turned to point out a window and spied a small box mounted on it. I walked over and looked at it. "Is this some kind of projector?"

"It's a security alarm. Are you casing the joint?" she joked.

I looked at it more carefully. It didn't seem like a security device to me. It appeared to be a small projector. "This is how you make the headless ghost walk into the Bosworth mausoleum."

"You did not hear that from me," she protested.

I didn't need to. "Why would you do that?"

"It's only at Halloween," she said with a shrug. "People love it. And it's based on a ghost we see all the time."

"Uh-huh, sure you do."

"Really. We have no idea who he is but almost everyone who works here has seen him. I find him sort of reassuring. He comes here looking for somebody, I guess." She tilted her

head at me. "I can tell you don't believe me. Other than suggesting you hang out here, there's not much I can say to a
nonbeliever."

That was probably true, especially now that I knew they
had tricked us. "The mausoleum has the name Bosworth on
it. Do you know if that's the Bosworth killed in a duel with a
Mr. O'Malley?"

"We have a couple hundred Bosworths interred here."
She flicked on her computer. "I don't know anything about a
duel. Do you know his first name?"

"Henry."

"Here he is. Henry Bosworth died in 1820. His wife,
Clara, was later interred in the family mausoleum, as well as a
whole bunch of their children."

I thanked her and left. But I stared at the mausoleum for
a few minutes. Natalia, O'Malley, and Bosworth hadn't seemed
like real people to me. Even though this structure didn't
prove the story had happened, I had to guess there was some
truth to it.

When I returned to the store, I found that Bob had as-
sessed the situation correctly. It was dead quiet. Bob was giddy
about being off the next day and, even more exciting, he had
plans with Julie.

"Get a load of Peaches," he said.

She sat on a bookshelf, twitching her tail and acting as if
she were watching someone walk through the room.

"Think she sees someone we can't see?" asked Bob.

I had to admit that it was odd, but after my visit to the
cemetery, I was more creeped out than normal. "Maybe she's
watching a moth or a fly."

Bob shook his head. "I don't think so."

I didn't, either. I let Bob take off early, since business was
slow. I made sure the back door was locked and strolled

through each of the other rooms, tidying up. It was beyond me why people picked up a book on one floor and left it on another floor.

I was reaching for a magazine someone had left on a chair in the nook by the stairs when Professor Goldblum raced down the steps and said, "Stop!"

"Is something wrong?" I asked.

He picked up the magazine about traveling. "I was browsing through this article on Rome and then I saw this photo of Georgetown." He held it out to me.

"I've been to Georgetown," I teased.

He lifted an eyebrow. "Just have a look."

It was a charming photo. The kind that usually made me wonder if only that spot was stunning or whether it really represented the entire town. It was of a popular restaurant in a corner location. People dined at outdoor tables and a waiter in an apron leaned over, speaking to a gentleman seated at a table. I looked more closely. "Is that Finley?"

"That's exactly what I thought!" Goldblum chuckled. "We have to show him. I bet he doesn't know about it."

I agreed to leave the magazine open where Goldblum could find it and made my way up the stairs.

The professor was in his office uncharacteristically late.

"What are you doing here?" I asked. "Something wrong?"

Peaches sat on his desk, knocking a pen around with her paw.

"Do you know why Jacquie was so eager to book Hilda Rattenhorst?" he asked.

Of course I knew the reason. We all knew why. "Because she is hoping to get information about Caroline from Hilda."

I watched as Peaches tapped the pen ever closer to the edge of the desk. It wouldn't be long before she performed the cat ritual of knocking it off the desk and peering at it from above with aloof detachment. I picked it up and placed it on a high shelf that I hoped would be too difficult for Peaches to reach.

"It's supposedly cursed, you know."

"What?"

"The pen."

I gasped. "And you let Peaches play with it?"

"Oh please, Florrie. You're smarter than that. Don't tell me you believe in ancient curses."

"Let's just say that I don't believe in tempting fate. What's the curse?"

"The death of your firstborn."

"An odious curse!" On the one hand, Peaches had already been spayed, so she had nothing to fear. On the other hand, it brought us right back to Caroline, the professor's young daughter who had been kidnapped and never heard from again. I sat down opposite him. "I wouldn't be too hard on Jacquie. If I were in her shoes, I would probably try everything I could in the hope of getting a lead about Caroline."

The professor leaned toward me. "Charlatans, Florrie. There are wicked people everywhere who are willing to take your money in exchange for false hope."

"I'm sure that's true. But hope is all she has." The words slipped out of my mouth before I realized that that was true for him, too. I hadn't meant to sound unkind.

The professor's head jerked up and he looked straight into my eyes. My heart beat a little bit harder. I hadn't meant to cause him more pain. It must be horrible not knowing if their little girl was dead or alive.

"Almost two thousand children go missing each day in the United States. Can you imagine that? About eight hundred thousand a year. In the beginning, each time a child was located, Jacquie and I held out hope that it was our child who was found. If she were alive, our Caroline would be an adult today, but chances are that she didn't live long after she was kidnapped. Her bones are probably out there somewhere. I thought as time passed that we would grow numb to those announcements. That we would know it couldn't possibly be our Caroline when unidentified bones are found, but that feeling never dies. You never forget. Not a day goes by that we don't wonder what happened to her or think about what she might be doing today. The trouble, I fear, is that when Jacquie and I are together, our pain doubles."

At that moment, the bell on the door downstairs tinkled, indicating that someone had entered the store.

"You'd better get that," said the professor.

I rose from the chair and started for the stairs, but in the hallway, I turned and looked back at him. He had picked up Peaches and held her tight.

Grief about Caroline had led to divorce for the professor and Jacquie. Mr. DuBois had been dead-on. I still didn't think we should try to manipulate them or cause jealousy, but I hoped they wouldn't split up again.

If I was right, and Hilda was behind the murders, then poor Jacquie would have to eat crow, but the professor would feel vindicated.

I found a lady downstairs browsing through new releases.

When she left, I did a little sleuthing online in regard to Finley but didn't see any mention of a first edition of *Alice's Adventures in Wonderland* for sale. Of course, it might be a private offering known only to certain people in rare book circles.

The store was quiet, except for the classical music playing in the background. While I was online, I looked up de Gama Pharmaceuticals. They had falsified test results on a drug that was released. It was thought to have sickened thousands of people but not all the claims were in yet. Heads were going to roll and the company had shut down all its plants. That explained a lot. The world that Balthus knew was drying up around him. Was that why he had been attacked? It could be that the assault on Balthus had nothing to do with the murders. An irate person who was angry with de Gama Pharmaceuticals could have taken their anger out on him. Was that the real reason he had moved? I didn't think so. If he still had money and was trying to avoid the public, he would probably have moved to a building with security. Besides, what was Hilda's bottle doing in his apartment?

Chapter 29

I locked the front door of Color Me Read and went upstairs to retrieve Peaches. She was still in the professor's office. But now my sweet cat was hissing at Harry. Her back was arched and she danced away from him sideways.

"Why would Peaches bother to hiss at Harry?" the professor asked me.

"Who knows?" I asked. "Cats do mysterious things."

"Goldblum and DuBois would say that an inanimate object, something as commonplace as a walking stick or a necklace, can be imbued with a spirit."

"Is that what you think?" I asked. "That Harry's skull has some sort of spirit attached to it that Peaches can see but we can't?"

The professor smiled and burst into laughter. "Of course not. But it is odd."

"It's even more peculiar that Frodo was afraid of Harry."

Professor Maxwell's eyebrows rose and he peered at Harry anew as though he thought he might have missed something before.

"Professor Maxwell, if someone is a trust-fund baby, can the trust go bankrupt if the underlying business fails?"

"What an odd question. No, Florrie. The trust would remain intact because it would be separate from the business.
Are you thinking of someone in particular?"

"Balthus de Gama. He appears to have fallen on hard
times. I suppose you could run through a trust?"

The professor nodded. "It all depends on how it's set up.
Some trusts provide that a lump sum be given to the child
when he reaches a certain adult age. It's not uncommon for
young adults to plow through their money quickly and have
nothing left."

"That makes sense. Maybe that's what happened."

He grimaced. "The de Gamas are facing a very big battle.
I fear that your Mr. de Gama may have a hard road ahead
of him."

"You mean the lawsuit?"

"Quite so. What they did was horrible. I suppose the
question that remains is how much the de Gamas were actually involved in the decision making and whether they knew
what was going on." He glanced up at me. "But I can tell you
the scuttlebutt on that front doesn't bode well for them."

I said good night, collected Peaches, and headed for home,
thinking about Balthus. I didn't really feel very sorry for him
because if the worst happened, as it appeared to have, then he
would have to work for a living just like the rest of us. That
wasn't the most terrible thing that could happen to a person.
But it would be a big adjustment for someone who had expected to spend his life lounging about.

I lay in bed that night, restless and unable to sleep. I was
missing something. There had to be a piece of the puzzle that
made it all fit together.

Dawn hadn't broken when I showered. I threw on a black
dress and wrapped a giant floral print scarf around my neck
twice, slid into short boots, and ran down the stairs. I popped

open a can of chicken liver for Peaches, apologized to her for leaving her at home, and rushed out the door.

Twenty minutes later, I strode into the hospital and asked for Balthus's room. I found it right away and tiptoed inside. Balthus lay still as death. He was pale and on oxygen. His vital signs were being monitored on a screen above him and slightly behind him.

I placed my hand over one of his. "Balthus, can you hear me? It's Florrie Fox. We don't really know each other well, but I'm Veronica's sister and a friend of Roxie's."

A nurse whipped in and made an adjustment on his IV. She smiled at me. "Keep talking to him, honey. Maybe he'll come around."

I stayed with him for a few minutes, making small talk and squeezing his hand from time to time. "Balthus, do you know who did this to you? Can you give me any signs?"

There was no reaction.

"Balthus," I said, intending to appeal to his emotional attachment to Roxie, "I'm worried about Roxie. Someone attacked her dad and now you." I squeezed his hand. "Can't you tell me who it was? For Roxie's sake?"

If he could hear me, he absolutely did not respond.

I looked around the room. Friends must have visited him last night. Cards, flowers, and even a small stuffed elephant crowded the room.

After telling him he had to get better because Roxie needed him, I left his room and headed down the hall to check on Cyril.

He was awake. "Florrie! Great news. I'm going home today!"

"That's fabulous." I gave him a peck on his cheek. "Will Roxie be staying with you?"

Cyril took a deep breath. "I have hired a company that provides guards. They wanted me to have a nurse, but frankly,

I've had enough of them. I don't expect to need any nurses, but I'll sleep better with a guard until they catch my assailant."

I looked up at the monitor and wished I knew how his heart was. I was about to ask him if he had contacted Ellis Willoughby before his death when a familiar voice behind me said, "Good morning."

I knew who it was without looking, but I swung around anyway and smiled at Eric, who wrapped his arm around my waist and gave me a squeeze.

"Cyril," he said, "we'll be keeping an eye on your house. I know you'll have a guard there, but we'll be checking in with him or her regularly."

"Haven't you found any leads?" asked Cyril. "Fingerprints, DNA, anything at all?"

"Nothing helpful yet," said Eric. "But there is no perfect crime. Your assailant must have left something behind."

Cyril did not look happy. "How about all those unsolved crimes?" he muttered.

"Cyril, are you certain you hadn't hired Ellis Willoughby to do any work for you?" I asked.

"Absolutely. I hadn't spoken with Ellis in months. I wish I had been in touch with him. If he had told me what was going on, maybe I could have helped him. Maybe he would be alive today. I have spent far too many hours lying in this bed considering all the things I should have done but didn't."

I tried to comfort him. "You can't blame yourself, Cyril. You wouldn't have been with Ellis twenty-four hours a day. And whoever killed him might have done you in, too."

Roxie practically danced into the room. She looked happy again, and a cheerful Finley followed right behind her. "Dad, I just spoke with the doctor. They're getting everything ready for your release right now!"

Cyril's room was becoming crowded. Roxie and Finley needed to be there, but I didn't. I slipped out and took the elevator down to Glen's room. A lady in a hospital gown looked up at me from the bed where he had been.

"Excuse me! I was looking for someone else." I hoped he was all right and hurried to the nurses' station, where they told me he had been released the day before.

I checked the time. I had expected my hospital visits to take longer. Walking briskly, I stopped by Color Me Read and dashed upstairs. I crossed my fingers that Ellis Willoughby had included his address on the note he enclosed with Harry. He had. It was beautifully embossed across the bottom of his stationery.

Armed with his address, I locked up and hoofed it over there. I was worried that I might be too early. That neighbors who might know something wouldn't be out and about, but I went anyway.

On my arrival, a woman in her thirties opened the door and stepped outside with an Irish setter.

I took a chance. "Ms. Willoughby?"

Her short bob was a perfect match with the Irish setter's shining rich red coat. Her skin was flaxen, almost as pale as Roxie's. "Yes?" she said.

I walked toward her and extended my hand. "Florrie Fox. I'm so terribly sorry for your loss. I didn't know your father but he was a dear friend of my boss, Professor Maxwell."

She allowed herself a faint smile. "Uncle Maxwell. I presume I'll see him at the funeral, assuming they ever release Dad's body to me."

"It must be so hard for you."

She nodded. "It was such a shock. My brother says it was bound to happen, given Dad's line of work. Let's face it. If you need a private detective, something perilous is probably going on in your life."

"Is that what you think? That he was killed because of a job he was involved with?"

"It makes sense. I don't know what kind of shady characters he might have used as sources of information. And the
police clearly thought the same. They stripped the place of
everything electronic, his computer, his phone, his tablet."

"I suspect that's pretty standard. Did he ever mention a
skull named Harry to you?"

A gentle smile wavered briefly on her lips. "No. But that
sounds like my dad. He never should have gone into private
investigations. He wasn't tough enough. He was a softie who
wanted to help everyone with a missing loved one. I don't
know who he ran up against."

"Don't PIs hunt down people who jump bail? They can
be very dangerous."

"I guess a lot of them do. Dad's interest was in reuniting
families. He was adopted and spent his life searching for his
birth family. Don't get me wrong, the family that adopted him
is fabulous. He was very lucky. But his desire to know his
own background drove him to focus on that. I know he
searched for Uncle Maxwell's little girl, Caroline. He thrived
on adoptions and missing people."

"Do you have any idea what he was working on?" I asked.

She ran her hand over her forehead. "When I wasn't able
to reach my dad, I came to check on him. Nothing was out of
order in the house. But his bags were packed and standing by
the door, as though he was planning to leave. I checked his
computer history for flight or train information. The only
thing I found that was of interest was searches regarding the
Order of the Moon."

I frowned at her. "Never heard of it."

"I hadn't, either. According to their website, they're a
mystical group who sound rather unwelcoming. According to
the police, they support themselves through crimes, like conning people and taking their money, welfare fraud, and blackmail."

"Ugh. Do you think he joined them to investigate?" I asked.

"I suspect he would have taken his luggage if that had been the case. More likely he was one of their victims."

At that moment, the door on the adjoining town house burst open. A beefy woman with an expression of displeasure barked, "Lydia Willoughby! Have you seen my broom?"

Lydia's pale face flushed as though she had done something wrong. In a calm voice she said, "No, Mrs. McNeel."

The irate woman's nostrils flared. "I don't believe you. That dog of yours probably picked it up and carried it off somewhere."

"Rudy is a very good boy and he hasn't been out here off leash since I arrived."

Mrs. McNeel let out a screech. "Liar! You're every bit as hateful as you were as a child." She leaned into boxwoods that separated their walkways and pulled out two branches. One had twigs tied onto the end of it. "Why would you do this? I made it myself with branches and twigs I found in Rock Creek Park. How dare you!"

Mrs. McNeel held the two branches together, and I could see they had once been one long piece. Together they formed a rustic witch's broom. "Someone did this on purpose," she snarled. Banging one part of the branch against her brick walkway, she said, "This was good and sturdy. I made sure of it. And now someone has gone and ruined it." Her puffy eyes narrowed. "And I think it was you."

Lydia closed her eyes as though she couldn't handle the ridiculous accusations and wished Mrs. McNeel would go away. When she opened them and the grumpy woman was still there, Lydia said, "Perhaps it was the same person who damaged Dad's wind chimes." She pointed upward.

All that remained was the circle that had once held chimes.

It hung from a hook, with loose threads dangling where chimes had once been.

"You probably beat it with my broom." Mrs. McNeel waggled her forefinger at Lydia. "You watch yourself, missy. I will not tolerate this kind of behavior." She threw the broom pieces back into the bushes, entered the house, and slammed the door behind her.

Lydia looked at me, her face pained. "I'm sorry. I'd like to make an excuse for her but I have none. She's been like that since I was a little girl. I can't imagine going through life being so unhappy about everything. It's a stick, for heaven's sake."

"How long have the chimes been broken?" I asked.

"Hmm? I don't really know. They were like that when I arrived in town."

I scribbled my name and number on a piece of paper. "Cyril Oldfield, a friend of your father and Professor Maxwell, was attacked in his home shortly before your father was killed. I'm trying to figure out if there was any connection. If you think of anything, would you let me know?"

She glanced at the paper I had handed her. "Florrie Fox. Well, Florrie, my first suspect would be Mrs. McNeel."

I smiled. I knew she was joking but probably wished the obnoxious woman would be whisked away to prison. I waved at her and walked back to the bookstore.

On the way, I passed Cyril's house and heard hammering. The front door stood open. I poked my head in, calling, "Cyril?"

He didn't respond, but I spied Roxie at a desk in a luxurious home office with a fireplace and walls full of books.

"Roxie?" I said gently.

She jumped and turned around in her chair. "Florrie! What are you doing here?"

I wondered the same thing about her. Was she here alone with the workmen? "Is Cyril here with you?"

"Finley is driving him home from the hospital." She appeared upset but forced a wan smile that wouldn't have fooled anyone. She stood up but quickly wafted some papers on top of others on the desk as though she meant to hide them from me.

Chapter 30

"The window has to be fixed, so one of us had to be here."

"Of course. I forgot all about that. I'm so sorry. I broke the glass, Roxie. I should be the one who pays for the damage and repair."

"Nonsense." This time her smile was genuine. "I won't hear of it. The police say dad might be dead if you hadn't created that distraction and alarmed the intruder. We will be forever grateful."

"Don't be silly. Anyone would have done the same. It was just happenstance that I was there at the right time."

One of the window installers passed the doorway. "Roxie, we've run into a small snag. Would you come look at this?"

"Of course." Roxie bustled out the door.

I stayed behind for just a moment and quickly flicked the papers on the desk to see what she had covered up. It was Cyril's hefty credit card bill. The kind I couldn't afford to pay. I couldn't help wondering if she had seen something on it that troubled her. But there was no time for that. And it certainly wasn't any of my business anyway. I hurried after her and found her in front of the window discussing a two-inch piece of wood frame that would have to be replaced.

I still felt a bit guilty for throwing the brick. And I hadn't kept a close eye on Roxie at all. As far as I knew, no one had threatened her. She was doing okay, though, in spite of whatever had upset her about her father's credit card bill.

I waved to her and rushed toward the bookstore. I rounded the corner and sped up. A customer was already waiting at the door.

"Good morning," I said, hoping she was early and that I wasn't late. I unlocked the door and held it for her, then dashed past her to turn off the alarm behind the checkout desk. "How can I help you?"

She was probably in her late sixties. White streaks ran through her blond hair, which had been cut short in a sleek, modern style. Deep wrinkles edged cold, faded blue eyes. She wore a bold red knit jacket with so many double buttons marching down the front, it looked like a military uniform. The handles of a satchel-style purse hung on a painfully thin arm. A bony wrist protruded from her sleeve, and a hefty gold bracelet dangled from it. In a breathy, carefully stilted voice, she announced, "Mags Delany to see Professor Maxwell."

In my years at Color Me Read, I had seen a lot of different types of people and had learned not to jump to conclusions. But this woman sent shivers up my spine. "I don't know if he's here. Would you like me to check first or would you rather follow me up to the third floor?"

There was something coldly arrogant about her. Possibly the way she held her head as though she was literally looking down on me. I swear her chin was parallel to the floor.

"He may come to me."

Ouch! I tried to smile. "Perhaps you would like to take a seat in the parlor."

She wrinkled her nose. "How quaint. Calling it a parlor does not make it so."

I reminded myself that her arrogance had nothing to do

with me. I didn't have to like her. Without another word, I hurried up the stairs to the third floor. Thankfully, the professor was in his office.

"A Mags Delany is here to see you."

He leaned and peered behind me.

"She declined to come up."

He raised his eyebrows. "Very well. That speaks volumes, doesn't it?"

"Do you know her?" I whispered.

"She's one of our neighbors, but we've never met. DuBois tells me she moved into her house two years ago. He's chummy with her housekeeper."

I trailed behind him down the stairs. As I stepped off the landing, chimes pealed gently in response to the movement of air. I paused briefly and glanced at the chimes that hung near the chair where Goldblum and I had left the magazine. And in that moment, I thought of Lydia and her chimes. Something clicked rather neatly in my mind.

That would have to wait. I followed the professor.

When he walked into the parlor, Mags slowly uncrossed her long, scrawny legs like a seductress in a bad movie and stood up to offer him her right hand, poised like a swan's neck.

I was glad *I* didn't have to deal with her.

"I've seen your picture, of course, but I had no idea you were so stunningly handsome," she purred.

I wanted to retch.

"Perhaps we could discuss our plans over a cup of coffee?" she asked. "Where little ears aren't listening?"

I darted out of sight and waited behind the checkout desk. *Their plans?* It had to be something for a charity.

As they walked by me, she slid her hand under the professor's elbow and glanced back at me. "Don't wait up."

I hated her. I had known her for all of five minutes and I

already hated her. I sucked in a deep breath. They were gone and Mags Delany was not my problem.

I had bigger things to worry about than a haughty, rude, self-impressed woman. I rushed back up the stairs, just high enough to get a good look at the chimes.

They were exactly as I'd thought. I called Eric, who answered immediately.

"I think I know what the cylinder is. It's a wind chime tube. The part that makes it ring. The two holes are threaded and attached to the top in some fashion so that it hangs."

"That sounds plausible. But why would a chime be out in the leaves like that? Could the wind have blown it?"

"How about if the wind chime was broken in a scuffle when the victim was being murdered? It was knocked aside or pulled on, and a chime somehow lodged in something and made the trip to the cemetery with him. There is exactly such a wind chime at Willoughby's house. I bet it will be a match."

"An interesting observation. Thanks, Florrie."

"One other thing. Was there wood on Willoughby's throat?"

"How could you know that?" Eric asked.

"You might look in the bushes for a stick. The neighbor was complaining about the dog carrying it around and tossed it in the bushes. But it wouldn't surprise me if someone used it on Willoughby to choke him."

"I'm heading there now." He hung up.

Veronica walked in at that moment. I described the entire scene with Mags Delany to her while I started the coffee.

"Mags Delany," she murmured. "That name sounds familiar."

"You would remember her if you had met."

Minutes later, Veronica's under-five storytelling group began to arrive. I stayed by the checkout desk while Veronica and the moms wrangled the children.

In a lull between customers, I located a pencil with a deep, rich plum color. I snagged a sheet of paper from the printer stash and drew four faces, each one in the corner of an imaginary square. The first was Cyril with his glasses and kind eyes. Opposite him, I sketched Manny's sullen, attitude-laden expression. Below Manny, I added Ellis Willoughby. I quickly looked up his obituary. I was struck right away by his easy smile and prominent cheeks that created angled brackets on either side of his mouth. He had a broad forehead and a full head of neatly trimmed hair.

I couldn't help comparing him to Mags Delany. Maybe Veronica was right, I was a snob who leaped to conclusions about people based on their appearance. It was wrong of me to think that I would have liked Ellis. Of course, my feelings about Mags weren't based only on how she looked. It was mostly her rude pomposity that turned me off.

I drew Ellis's cheerful face in the corner below Manny, thinking all the while that I was even more sad he had been murdered because he seemed so friendly in his photo.

Balthus went in the final corner.

I studied the four men, trying to figure out if there was any connection between them. Cyril and Ellis were definitely acquainted. But as far as I knew, they didn't share any current activities. And Ellis was clearly afraid of someone, while Cyril had no idea why anyone would attack him. I added a line between them.

Balthus had dated Roxie, so chances were good that he knew Cyril. And he needed money, which might have been an incentive for him to steal a valuable clock from Cyril. But murder him? I didn't see how that would benefit Balthus. Besides, Balthus himself had been attacked. Still, I drew a line between Balthus and Cyril, which didn't really help. I wasn't making much progress.

On the side of the paper, I sketched potential suspects, beginning with Hayes. Had they been his patients? Originally, I only associated him with Manny. But what if the other three had gone to him for treatment?

Next to Hayes, I drew the sweet face of his mother, Coralue. I couldn't see her being physically violent. Not that it was out of the question. Maybe she was in cahoots with Hayes. I drew a little line between Coralue and Hayes.

I couldn't omit Hilda. I had been suspicious of her from the beginning. Maybe that wasn't fair, but she was the only person who stood to gain from the murders.

A woman walked into the store and asked if we sold cookbooks. I led her to a room in the rear, which had been the kitchen when the building was a home. We had left the charming farmhouse sink and turquoise refrigerator. Our modern coffee and tea servers looked right at home on the counter. In addition to cookbooks, the open shelves were full of collectible teapots and cups, as well as assorted kitchen equipment perfect for gift baskets.

When I returned, Eric was standing behind the checkout counter, studying my sketches.

"Are you helping customers?" I asked jokingly.

"If any had come in, I'd have gladly assisted them. But mostly I don't like standing with my back to the door these days."

I took a deep breath. "Are you worried that someone is after you?"

He grinned and tapped his finger on my sketches. "It's a cop thing. Back to the wall for safety. I see you've noticed that a killer is on the loose. Maybe two."

"Two?"

"As you can see from your clever sketch, we haven't been able to link the attacks. For instance, Cyril's throat was slit with a knife from his own kitchen. Manny was choked from behind. Ellis Willoughby was also choked. But Balthus was hit on the head and chloroformed."

"I see what you're saying. The person who harmed Cyril didn't come prepared. But the person who killed Manny and Ellis used the same basic technique, so those attacks could be related. And the chloroform was new? Not used on the others?"

"Exactly. We do think that you interrupted the perpetrator in Cyril's case. Otherwise we might be looking at three deaths. But everything seems different with Balthus."

Eric pointed at Hilda, Coralue, and Hayes. "Are these your suspects?"

"So far. I'm considering who might have known all four victims."

"If that's your criteria, you'd better add Roxie and a fellow named Gene Germain."

I eyed him. "They knew Ellis?"

"Roxie called Willoughby 'Uncle Ellis,' though I don't believe there is actually any blood relation. And Gene Germain had used Ellis's services. It's even possible that Jacquie and Professor Maxwell would have to be in that group of suspects, though I'm not certain they knew Balthus."

I assumed that Eric had information that he could not share with me. Nevertheless, I asked ever so innocently, "What do you know about the Order of the Moon?"

Eric looked at me with serious eyes. "Promise me that you will not have anything to do with them. They're fanatics about guarding their compound. And they are malevolent people who think nothing of committing crimes."

"Do you think they murdered Ellis?"

"It's possible, except for one thing. If they were responsible for his death, we would still be looking for him. The people they kill go missing, never to be seen again. Promise me you will not get involved."

"Where are they located?" I asked.

"I'm not going to tell you." He turned and had his hand

on the door handle when he looked back me. "You're going to look them up."

I grinned. "Of course."

"They're in an isolated location in West Virginia. Leave them alone. I don't want anything to happen to you."

They sounded like bad news. But if the police were already investigating their possible involvement in Ellis's murder, then there really wasn't anything I could do anyway. I smiled and nodded at him. "I promise."

He left and I turned my attention to unpacking new books.

I carried several historical books upstairs to shelve them and was stepping off a footstool when Finley entered the room.

"Hi, Florrie. Have you got a minute?"

"Of course."

He leaned against a chair. "I'm worried about Roxie."

Chapter 31

I was concerned about Roxie, too. But I decided to listen to Finley first.

"She used to be so easygoing. The smallest thing made her smile. But lately she's gloomy and cross with me. I don't know what to do. Has she said anything to you?"

Had she ever! But I wasn't about to divulge her confidences. "She's been under a lot of stress, what with Cyril being attacked and nearly murdered."

"That's understandable. But he's home now. It all turned out fine. I expected her to be happy today."

"She's not?" I didn't mention the papers I had seen.

"She's still cranky. Cyril and I are walking on eggshells lest we do something wrong."

I couldn't bring up the other woman. Could I? I wondered if he would. I kept mum.

"The other night, for instance. She never made a fuss about my playing poker before. And that nonsense about another woman!" He threw his hands in the air.

"Maybe she's afraid." I chose my words carefully. "Someone did try to kill her dad. Maybe she's afraid of losing you or Cyril."

"But that's ridiculous. No one is after me. And you thwarted the attack on Cyril. That guy won't be back." He gazed at me hopefully. "Or do you know something we haven't been told?"

"The only family Roxie has is you and her dad." That was blunt. And then I was sorry I had said it. Poor Finley had no other family, either.

"Quite right. Cyril claims the police haven't got a thing on his intruder. Have you heard differently from Eric?"

"He's keeping me in the dark." I wrinkled my nose. "He's not really able to share much with me, but I know they're working on it."

"Good to hear. Keep me posted, will you? I need to cheer up my wife!"

Poor Roxie. I watched him leave and moved the footstool back into place. I looked out the French doors for a moment. As my gaze drifted, I noticed the attractive woman who had been following Finley.

She was standing on the opposite side of the street, looking at the bookstore. Was she waiting for him? Did he know that? Had they planned to meet while Roxie was tied up with her father?

I scurried out of the room and stopped dead on the stair landing.

A thirty-second glimpse of Finley changed my opinion of him. I observed his profile at a moment when he must have thought no one was watching. Somehow, I had never noticed his sharp nose, as pointed as a witch's. But it was his eyes that sent a shiver through me. He had glanced to the left surreptitiously, in a cold and sneaky manner like a weasel. At that moment, I suspected that Finley had another side to him.

His face changed abruptly as Veronica greeted him.

Suddenly, he was again the handsome man to whom women

were attracted. But all I could see was a worm whose mistress was waiting for him outside.

For the next hour, I pondered whether or not to tell Roxie.

At one o'clock, Professor Maxwell returned to the bookstore.

"Did you have a nice lunch?" I asked innocently.

He stopped at the checkout desk and rested his arm on it. "Should Mags Delany call or drop by, I am not in. And should any circumstance arise in which Mags Delany would be involved, kindly count me out." With that, he marched up the stairs to his office.

"You're awfully grumpy," I remarked.

Professor Maxwell paused on the first landing of the stairs to shout at me, "No exceptions!"

To my surprise, Ellis's daughter, Lydia Willoughby, showed up in the afternoon. "Is Uncle Maxwell around?"

"He's upstairs in his office on the third floor."

She held out a handwritten note to me. "I found this in a soup pot, of all the strange things."

> *Dear Mr. Ellis,*
>
> *Thank you for your kindness to my father. He mentioned you often and I was pleased to finally meet you at his funeral. Everyone always offers to help after a loved one dies, but there's really little they can do. Except perhaps in this situation.*
>
> *My father was born in the home where he died, something that probably doesn't happen often anymore. The house has been in my family since 1802. Alas, there must be a hoarding gene in our line because it appears no one threw anything out. Happily, some items are rather valuable today, though the vast majority have gone into the trash.*

*I must admit it was a huge shock to find a human
skull in a box labeled Harry. It was in the attic along
with this strange mirror. I have no idea how long they
have been there, and shudder to imagine why anyone
in my family came to possess the skull. I fear there
may have been foul play, though I expect all involved
have probably long since gone to their own graves.
Naturally I reported it to the police in our small town,
but after a cursory examination and a meeting with a
local historian, they agreed that this is beyond their
scope and resources. Perhaps you know how to identify
the person or at least can pass Harry on to someone
better equipped to find out where he belongs.*

*With sincerest gratitude,
Molly Butler*

"You'll be happy to know that the professor already took
Harry someplace to see if they can learn anything about him
through DNA. It will be interesting to hear what they dis-
cover."

"Fabulous!" She headed up the stairs at a brisk pace.

"Lydia," I called after her.

"Yes?"

"Just a word of warning. Some people think that Harry
screams."

"This just gets better and better!" She continued walking
upstairs.

I was up early the next morning. I had wangled two days
off, a deal made with Veronica when she took a long weekend
to the beach over Labor Day. After a shower, I wrapped myself in a towel and stood in my closet, considering the power
of clothes. I was no fashionista. For years my instinct had been
to wear clothes that I hoped allowed me to recede into the

background. The less obvious, the better. But now I had become an introvert with loud clothes. I considered my goals for
the day. A visit to Hilda and maybe to Manny's family, if I
could find them. I didn't know what these people were like.
But perhaps I would appear more sympathetic in traditional
black. After all, they had lost a cherished member of their family and probably weren't feeling very cheerful. I pulled on a
black turtleneck and a pleated skirt that fell below my knees.
The abstract leopard-print pattern gave it a boost without
being flashy.

Peaches seemed to approve, although I suspected she
would have liked anything in her zeal to get to breakfast. She
scampered down the stairs ahead of me.

While the kettle heated for tea, I spooned an egg-and-
cheese cat meal into her dish. She settled down and devoured
it as fast as she could.

The refrigerator looked woefully empty. I opted for yogurt again, making a mental note that a trip to the grocery
store was an absolute necessity.

The fall sun was already shining through the French doors,
and Peaches had wasted no time in taking a bath in the warm
rays of the sun. I left her to her grooming, took care to lock
the door, and was on my way. I stopped by the bookstore and
grabbed a copy of Hilda's book in case I needed to follow her
and she caught me in the act. I could always claim a customer
had asked for a signed copy. I slid it into my bag and walked toward her house. My path, not uncoincidentally, led me by
Balthus's previous rental. I paused for a moment and studied the
recessed area around the front door where Hilda claimed she had
seen a rug with a foot sticking out of it. Anyone going in would
have noticed a rug. But would the neighbors have seen it?

An elderly woman toting a foldable shopping trolley on
wheels stopped and eyed me. "There's no one there. Are you
looking for a rental?"

"No. I heard the story about a rug in the doorway."

She edged closer to me. "It's true."

"Did you see it?" I asked.

"Me? No, I was away visiting my daughter, but Maury saw it."

"Maury who?"

She pointed across the street. "I bet he's home."

I followed her to his front door. She rapped and shouted, "Maury! It's Linda." She turned to me and said, "He's a little hard of hearing."

Maury opened the door. I guessed he was in his eighties. Loud enough for everyone on the block to hear, she shouted, "Maury, this young lady would like to hear about the rug you saw across the way."

"Beautiful day!" he shouted back.

"The rug. You saw the rug!" she yelled.

"The rug? Yes, it was right across the street."

Raising my voice and enunciating as clearly as I could, I asked, "Did you see it?"

"Not me." He pointed toward heaven. "It was Frieda."

"Has Frieda passed?" I asked Linda.

"No. She lives in the apartment upstairs."

A lady about their age wearing blush-pink eyeglasses slowly made her way down the steps behind Maury. "I thought I heard someone down here."

The slender woman gazed at me. "Are you with the police? It's about time."

"No. I work at Color Me Read. The bookstore?"

She smiled. "What a lovely job."

"So you saw the rug?" I asked.

"It was Hilda who saw it first." She smiled at me.

I winced at what I suspected was coming. "Do you know Hilda's last name?"

"Ratter-something."

"Ratterburst," corrected the man.

"Rattenhorst, maybe?" I asked.

"That's it! She's the one who saw the rug," said Frieda. "Come, we'll take you to Hilda."

"That's really not necessary," I protested.

"Nonsense, it's a beautiful day. It will do us good to get out," Frieda insisted.

I stopped them. "I have heard all about the rug from Hilda. I just hoped one of you might have seen it as well."

Frieda appeared distressed. "That's what I called the police about. You see, we all heard about the rug. But none of us had seen it. That's what we told the nice policeman who came around that evening. But that night, around two in the morning, I got up and went in the kitchen for some valerian tea to help me sleep. My kitchen window looks out that way and I thought I saw a rug."

I looked back at the house where the rug had supposedly been. "Were the lights on? Inside or outside of the house?"

"No. You see, I had the same thought. It didn't make sense that someone would put the rug there again. Then my cat, Astrid, very thoughtfully presented me with a mouse by dropping it on my foot."

"A dead mouse?" screeched Linda.

"No. Quite a live one. I shrieked, and the mouse scampered down the hallway with Astrid in hot pursuit. When I returned to the kitchen, it was gone."

"The mouse or the rug?" I asked.

"Both. I expect the mouse will make another appearance, but I don't think the rug will."

"Then you're not sure if you saw the rug?" I asked.

"I felt I should report it to the police the next morning anyway. I *thought* I saw it."

"Are you certain that it was after you heard about the rug?" I asked.

"Yes! That's why it was so confusing to me. After that, I looked for it before bed and every time I got up during the night. I haven't seen the mouse or the rug again."

Linda's brow furrowed. "Dear, Hilda is remarkable. You shouldn't doubt her. I always carry a hankie with me when I'm going to see her because she makes me cry. It's amazing how she can contact our loved ones who have crossed over. If she says she saw a rug, then there was a rug."

Before I could explain how I had met Hilda, Maury said emphatically, "He did not die. He was murdered."

I turned to look at him. "Do you mean Manny? Did you know him?"

"We all did," Linda said sadly. "Alas, he wasn't very tolerant of anyone over thirty."

"Thought we weren't worth his time," said Frieda. "He could be quite ugly. I imagine that's partly why Hilda despised him."

"She's probably happy now that he's dead," announced Maury.

I wasn't sure how reliable their gossip was, but sometimes there was a nugget of truth. "Hilda knew Manny?" It was a simple question but I hoped to get some useful responses.

"Definitely," said Linda. "He was leading Hilda's niece down the wrong path. We all knew about it. Kaya was such a lovely little girl. Frieda gave her piano lessons."

"Did something happen to her?" I asked.

"Kaya thought the sun revolved around Manny. Suddenly out came the heavy black eyeliner and the low-cut blouses," said Linda. "She wore her skirts far too short."

"Like a tramp," Frieda said in a half-whisper of disapproval. "This beautiful, smart girl looked like a streetwalker. She was planning to be a nurse. But when she got involved with Manny it was as though her life plans didn't matter anymore."

Kaya might know about the big break Manny had spoken about. "Do you know how to reach Kaya?" I asked.

Linda and Frieda exchanged sour glances.

"What did I do now?" asked Maury.

Frieda leaned over and spoke into his ear. "We're talking about Kaya."

He nodded his head. "Nice girl. Pity she got involved with Manny."

Frieda said, "She works at that odd store on M Street. Mostly they sell mystical stuff and junk that someone else wanted to get rid of. The one on the second floor over top of that fancy hairdressing salon that no one can afford. You have to go up narrow stairs to get there." She shuddered. "I can't stand that place. It's so cluttered that I want to throw everything out and clean it up."

Her description wouldn't have meant a thing to a tourist, but I knew exactly the store she meant, Curiosities. The door to the stairs was so uninteresting that it almost blended into obscurity. But the locals knew it was the place to find oddities. Veronica had gone there looking for Halloween decorations.

I thanked them all for their help and left my name and number with Frieda, in case they determined that someone else had seen the rug. I walked away realizing they had never inquired why I was interested in finding someone who had seen it.

I abandoned my plans to snoop on Hilda and walked straight down to M Street. Stores had opened but it was still relatively quiet. I found the glass door that led to the store. The name *Curiosities* was adhered in an arc.

The walls on both sides of the stairs were lined with old posters in frames. At the top, I walked through a hefty carved wooden arch. I spotted Kaya immediately. Dressed all in black with heavy makeup on her eyes, she held a crystal ball in her hand.

"Kaya?" I asked.

"Yes. May I help you?"

I smiled at her sweetly. "Florrie Fox. I'm so sorry about Manny."

She blinked at me for long seconds. "Thank you." She tilted her head and studied me. "Are you Veronica's sister?"

Everyone knew Veronica. "Yes! She bought some Halloween items here."

"We've been swamped. Mrs. Boyle loves creepy things. She haunts flea markets and yard sales for them. And she has friends all around the world who send her the weirdest stuff. How did you know Manny?"

I explained about buying pastries from the bakery but omitted his attempted theft of Harry. In fact, as I gazed around at several skulls, which I hoped were faux, I wondered if he had intended to bring Harry to her to sell.

"I still can't believe he's gone. The Boyles were very nice and said I didn't have to come to work, but I don't know what else to do. At least it distracts me for a bit. Manny was very special. I don't know how I can go on without him."

"I heard he had gotten a new job."

"Yeah. He was real amped about it. He was gonna get me a black diamond engagement ring with his first paycheck."

"I'd have liked to see that. Do you know who he was working for?"

"He was hiring himself out, you know, like a bodyguard. He won all kinds of stuff in judo. A lot of people didn't know that. He wasn't a big guy, but he knew how to fight."

I was thinking that he hadn't won the fight for his life, but that would be unspeakably rude to point out. "Do you know who he was a bodyguard for?"

"Some rich dude."

I tried not to groan. There were plenty of rich guys in Washington, not to mention Cyril and Ellis. Balthus probably didn't fit in that category any longer. And wouldn't Cyril or Roxie have said something if Cyril had hired Manny and he was murdered?

"Are you the one who solved that case of the dead guy in the bookstore?" asked Kaya.

"I can't really take credit for that. But as it happens, a friend of mine was attacked very much like Manny was."

Her dark eyes widened. "You think there could be a connection?"

"Maybe. That's why I wanted to know more about his new job."

"Yeah. Yeah." She seemed to be thinking.

"Would his parents know more?"

Kaya snorted. "Not likely. Manny was a talker, but he talked in circles. Know what I mean? My dad called him a windbag and didn't believe a word he said. But then no one in my family liked him."

"Not even Hilda?" I prompted.

"Especially not Hilda."

Why, then, would he have attended her reading?

"He called her the woo-woo lady. Sometimes I thought maybe he was afraid of Aunt Hilda. He asked me once if she could read people's minds."

"Can she?"

"It runs in my dad's family. Aunt Hilda is kind of funny that way. If something is bothering you, she can usually figure it out. I'm not sure if that's actually reading minds or just being super-perceptive. But it's not the first time she locked in on the thoughts of a living person."

"At her reading the other night, she collapsed and said she was reading someone's thoughts."

Kaya nodded. "My dad is trying to get her to go to a doctor."

"A shrink?" I asked softly.

"No. For a regular checkup. You know, to do blood work and see if something's off that might have made her faint." She smiled. "For a long time, my mom was afraid I might have inherited the family trait of being able to read thoughts. Aunt Hilda says I haven't nurtured the ability. That I've tried to block it instead. But I don't think I have it. My family wasn't fond of Manny because they didn't understand him. He had ambitions. He was going to do things. Important things. This was his first big deal." She set the crystal ball on the table and pulled a tissue out of her pocket. As she dabbed at her eyes, she sniffled. "I went through his apartment but the cops had taken everything important, like his tablet."

"Did he ever mention someone named Cyril Oldfield?"

"No."

"How about Ellis Willoughby?"

"That's the other guy who was murdered recently."

"Yes. He was a private detective. Is there any chance that Manny was working for him?"

She said very loudly, "If we get any of those in, I'd be glad to call you."

Nola Boyle walked toward us.

I followed Kaya's lead. "Thank you. I appreciate that." I wasn't certain what was going on but quickly took my leave.

I browsed through a couple of specialty shops, buying Havarti, Parmigiano-Reggiano, and a wedge of totally indulgent triple cream Brie.

The pumpkin chocolate-chip cookies looked delicious. I had some pumpkin at home but bought an extra bag of chocolate chips to bake them myself.

I added a dozen eggs, a loaf of crusty bread, four apples, luscious grapes, and a living head of lettuce to my cart. As I shopped, I found beautiful pork chops and chicken breasts. Armed with my purchases, I headed home before anything spoiled.

When I reached the carriage house, I found Kaya and Roxie standing at my door.

Kaya greeted me with enthusiasm.

I unlocked the door and we stepped inside. Peaches ambled over to check out our guests.

"I hope you'll forgive me. I just need to put some things in the fridge so they won't spoil." I put on the kettle for tea and stashed away everything, except the bread, Havarti, grapes, and an apple.

"I'm sorry to bother you. Veronica told me where you live," said Kaya.

I poured tea for us all, and Roxie took our mugs over to the sofa. Meanwhile, I shook fishy kitty kibble into a bowl for Peaches, then sliced crusty bread and set it on a large cutting board along with napkins, the buttery Havarti, the wedge of Brie, grapes, and crisp fall Fuji apple slices.

I set the cutting board on the big ottoman I used as a coffee table. "It's not much, but perhaps you'd like to join me in a midday nosh."

Roxie perked up. "It's lovely!" She helped herself to bread and Brie right away.

Either Kaya wasn't a cheese person or she was too anxious to eat. She sighed. "There were a couple of things I couldn't tell you at the store today. The Boyles would be very angry with me if they knew I was talking about their personal lives. They're very private. They know how to put spells on people who cross them. I've been careful not to upset them. I mean, what they do is none of my business, right?"

Chapter 32

Kaya took a deep breath. "But Manny is dead and this might be important. So the thing is that Mr. Willoughby came by the store, only he called himself Jeff Green. He said he'd received some things from the estate of a friend and would the Boyles tell him if they had any value. They were really excited about the skull."

"Harry!" Roxie and I chimed.

"Yeah. You know about Harry?" asked Kaya.

I flashed Roxie a look, hoping she would follow my example and wouldn't blab about him. "We've heard about him."

"Before Mr. Willoughby met the Boyles, he told me he might like to run a shop like that. And he asked me how many employees there were. I said it was just me and the owners. And then he asked if the owners' children helped out."

Kaya looked down at her fingers intertwining on her lap. "It's a natural question. I get that having your kids help is a great idea. But . . . I'm not supposed to know this, but really, if people want to keep things secret, they shouldn't talk about them in front of other people. You know what I mean? I just picked up bits and pieces, but as I understand it, Mr. Boyle has a son who is about twelve. He lives with his mom in Florida but he ran away. His mom has called the store and begged me to tell her if I've seen him. I haven't! Honestly, I have never seen that child. You asked me if Manny was working for Mr. Willoughby. I think he would have told me that and he would have asked if I had seen the boy. You know? That's not the kind of thing a person keeps secret unless there's a really good reason, like maybe if the child was being abused at home and you need to protect him when he runs away. Manny would have come right out and asked me." She paused and sipped her tea.

"Did the Boyles realize who Willoughby was?" I asked.

"I don't think so. Neither did I. Not at that point, anyway. The Boyles were very intrigued by the skull. But what I noticed was while they were looking at the stuff he brought, he was, like, scoping out the place. You know what I mean? He wasn't browsing like a buyer. He asked where the bathroom was, but he didn't use it. He turned on the water in the sink so it sounded like he was in there, but I saw him peeking into the storeroom in back. Don't you think that's weird?"

"You think he was looking for Mr. Boyle's son," I said.

"Yeah. So did Manny. That's another reason why I don't think Manny was working for him. If he had been, then Willoughby wouldn't have had to come over to snoop. Manny could have asked me if there was a kid playing in the storeroom."

I had to agree with her. "When was this?"

"Maybe three weeks ago?"

"I guess he didn't sell Harry to them," said Roxie.

"No, he didn't. But I was alarmed by his visit because it was so odd. I would have noticed if he came in again while I was there. I had pretty much decided it was just a fluke. Then I saw his picture in the newspaper after he was murdered. I was at the shop at the time, and Mrs. Boyle said to her husband right in front of me, "Well, well. If it's not our Mr. Green. I expect he got what he deserved."

Roxie and I exchanged glances.

"That scared me. I stayed home for a couple of days but it was driving me crazy being there with my folks. I had to get out. So I went back to work. Do you think Manny could have been a police informant?"

I seriously doubted it. "Why would you think that?"

"He had mentioned it in the past. I thought maybe he was telling the truth."

I was getting a bad feeling. Even his girlfriend didn't believe the things he'd said. "You didn't trust him."

"It wasn't like that. Manny liked movie and TV talk. 'If I told you, I'd have to kill you.' And 'It's safer for you if you don't know about it.' Stuff like that."

I tried to phrase my next question carefully. "Did he tell you about his conflict with Hayes Throckmorton?"

"Conflict?" She snorted. "That's a pretty way of putting it. Hayes accused him of using illegal moves in a competition. It was a scummy thing to do and Hayes knew it. Some people will do anything if they lose."

I wasn't particularly surprised to hear her defend Manny. Every argument had two sides. "Do you suppose the two of them got into an argument?"

"The police asked me all kinds of questions about Hayes. Manny despised him. I don't know what might have happened if the two of them ran into each other on the street. I do find it highly suspicious that Manny was found on Hayes's mom's property. That *can't* be a coincidence."

"Did you come to Hilda's reading at the bookstore?" Roxie asked.

"I wanted to, but I had to work. I didn't know Manny

was going, to tell you the truth. He said he had a job to do that night and I figured that meant he was working. But then he was killed. The police came to my parents' house to talk with me about Manny." She shook her head. "And a couple of days ago, they came to the store asking about Willoughby. I really wanted to quit. I keep thinking I'll be next because I know too much."

"You believe there's a connection," said Roxie.

"There almost has to be. Don't you think?" Kaya gulped hard and drank her tea.

I didn't know what to make of her. She wanted to be engaged to Manny, but she didn't believe what he told her, and she was willing to accept that he had some kind of mysterious job. Who would do that? My sister, Veronica, that was who.

"You're looking at me like my mom does." Kaya groaned.

"I'm sorry. I didn't mean to." I sought something nice to say so I wouldn't sound like a bossy big sister. "You seem pretty smart. Why are you still working there?"

"Because I owe it to Manny. If the Boyles had something to do with his death, I would be devastated. It would be my fault." She winced. "You see, I don't know what I know. I mean I haven't seen the kid who is missing, and I don't know of anything else that the Boyles might be involved with. I've thought about it a lot. I haven't seen any drugs or anything that I think is illegal. And if Manny wasn't working for Willoughby or the police, why would the Boyles kill him?"

Roxie's eyes grew large and round. "Kaya, you need to quit that job today. I don't know how you've been brave enough to stay there."

Kaya gazed at me. "What do you think?"

"If you're afraid, you should definitely leave your job."

"You don't think I would be helpful to the police?" asked Kaya.

"Are you kidding?" Roxie clapped her hands to the sides of her face. "Get out of there!"

When Kaya was ready to leave, I said, "If you think of anything you might have overheard or something Manny said that seems odd now that he's been killed, I hope you'll let me know. Most days I'm right up the street at the bookstore."

"I get what you're saying. I've thought it myself. You'd think someone who talked all the time would have let something important slip. I guess Manny didn't have loose lips, after all."

Roxie lingered after Kaya was gone. I heated more tea and the two of us nibbled on cheese.

"I know the Boyles," she said. "Socially, that is. I'm as plump as Nola Boyle so I thoroughly understand her obsession with wearing black. Anything to slenderize our curves. But there was always something a little bit creepy about her. She was polite and nice enough, but I knew she was into paranormal stuff. Their house gives that away, I suppose."

"Their house?" I bit into the deliciously soft Brie on the fresh bread.

"It's near my dad's house. The one with the gargoyles."

I nearly choked. "I think I saw Willoughby watching their house!"

"You should tell Eric."

"I have. I just didn't know who lived in that house."

"So Mr. Boyle's ex-wife thinks their little boy ran away to be with him. Or for all we know, maybe Mr. Boyle snatched him. Then the ex-wife hires a local PI, Ellis Willoughby, who spies on their house, looking for any sign of the boy."

"And then they murdered him," I said dully.

"Which must mean they have the kid. Why else murder Ellis?" asked Roxie.

"Do you think Manny could have been onto them?

Maybe his big new job was blackmailing people?" I speculated aloud.

But if the Boyles murdered Manny, why did Balthus have pumpkin guts in his shoes? I didn't dare say it aloud, given Roxie's fondness for him. "How are things with Finley?" I asked.

Roxie's expression changed. "Exhausting." She averted her eyes and massaged her fingers. "Sometimes I wonder if my expectations are too high. I realize that the stories Jacquie writes about romance are fiction, but sometimes I wish real life were more like them."

"Do you think he's still seeing that woman?" I asked cautiously. Depending on how she responded, maybe I could tell her about seeing the woman lingering outside the store.

"I haven't seen her in the last couple of days. I don't know if she's better at hiding from me or if she gave up on him. Balthus thinks they're playing me."

"Roxie!"

"I hate being the feather-brained fool. Thanks for lunch, Florrie. It was delish! I need to check in on my dad. Jacquie is out having lunch with Gene Germain so she won't be back for a while."

"Gene? Coralue's neighbor?"

"That's the one. I expect it has something to do with Halloween. Have you seen his house? If I were a little kid out trick-or-treating, I would be afraid to enter his yard."

I locked the door behind her just to be on the safe side. I should probably drop by and welcome Cyril home, but first I wanted to sketch. I cleaned up our lunch dishes and stored the leftovers. Then I settled on the sofa with my sketchbook. I kept coming back to the carpet with the foot, drawing the rolled-up carpet from different angles.

My morning hadn't gone as I'd expected. I had meant to find out more about Hilda and instead, I learned about definite links between the Boyles, Manny, and Ellis Willoughby. I drew a couple of gargoyles perching atop a brownstone house. Next to it, I sketched the Boyles in their dark attire. Mrs. Boyle held a skull, and a scrying mirror was behind Mr. Boyle.

I flipped the page and went back to my rectangle concept, sketching the victims—Cyril, Manny, Willoughby, and Balthus in the corners.

Using a red pencil, I drew lines from Willoughby to Manny and Cyril. Using a blue pencil, I drew lines from Cyril to Willoughby and Balthus. Using green and purple pencils, I repeated the process, connecting Balthus and Manny to the people they knew. And I had nothing but a colorful mess. Something was still missing.

Hilda had reason to dislike Manny. But in similar instances, didn't most families just hope their daughter would come to her senses and break up with the troublesome boyfriend? People didn't actually kill the undesired mate who was courting their child.

Of course, that didn't put Hilda in the clear. She was the one who started the rumor about the rug. Had Frieda really seen it, too? She seemed so unsure. It was dark at the time. And the timeline was off.

Hilda claimed she saw the rug the night of her reading. But Eric and I confirmed that it wasn't there. If I understood Frieda correctly, she had seen it later that night. Had it been a prognostication? Or had someone been watching Manny at Hilda's reading, waiting for him to leave? The mere thought chilled me to the core.

I wished I knew the exact times. But did it matter? Could Hilda's collapse have been a sign for someone present to go after Manny? No, that didn't make sense. When Hilda collected herself and went to sign books, Manny was still in the store. And Hilda had gone home with Jacquie when she left. Could she have slipped out in the night? But how would she have found Manny to kill him? And she would have had to find a carpet somewhere.

I gasped. How could I be so obtuse? The carpet! Whoever killed Manny had wrapped him in a rug. But where did he get it?

I phoned Eric and to my surprise, he answered his phone. "Hi!" he said. "I feel like I never see you anymore."

"Same here. It's my day off. Could you come for dinner?"

"I can't make any promises right now but I'll try to stop by."

"Great! Eric, I was wondering about the rug Manny was wrapped in. What kind of rug was it?"

"It was an indoor rug. Like you put in your living room."

In my mind's eye, I could see him shrugging.

"Okay, so an indoor rug. Was it a throw rug or an old shag rug?"

There was a long moment of silence. "It was an Oriental rug. The guy who sells them over on Wisconsin Avenue says if it hadn't had a body wrapped in it, he could get about ten thousand dollars for it."

I was stunned. "Coralue says it's not hers?"

"Correct. Florrie, I've got to go. I'll call you later about tonight."

He hung up abruptly. The fact that it was an expensive rug fit with Manny's claim that he was working for someone with money. Could his new boss have wrapped him in that rug? I wondered if any rugs had been reported stolen. Then again, if I had murdered someone and wrapped him in a rug that belonged to me, I certainly wouldn't report it stolen.

I spent the next hour baking pumpkin cookies with chocolate chips in them. I had more than enough as dessert for dinner if Eric stopped by. When they cooled, I packed them up and used them as an excuse to be nosy.

Coralue was out in her yard, adjusting the plaid scarf on her faux butler's neck while two preschoolers danced around her Halloween decorations.

"You put your Mr. DuBois back out!" I said.

"My daughter thought I was being ridiculous. And she rather liked him. The police still have my coffin, though. I expect I'll never see that again. We thought it would be cute if vampires had a butler. Most nights there will be two faux vampires standing out here, but for Halloween night, I've hired a young couple to dress as vampires and hand out hot cider and candy to children who pass this way." She cackled and leaned toward me. "That'll beat Gene Germain's decorations!"

"I hear he's been very helpful to you."

"He's been surprisingly kind, which I cannot say for the police. My, but they're persistent. Honestly, they've treated me like a criminal. And Hayes, too. I'm as troubled as everyone else about the recent murders, but I don't know anything about them! I wish . . ." Her voice broke. "I wish Manny hadn't been buried in my yard. I wish he hadn't been murdered to begin with. He was a horrid person. He did things he knew he shouldn't. But none of that matters. He was a living being and no one deserves to be treated that way." Coralue breathed in so deeply that her chest rose.

"On a brighter note, I received a call from an organization searching for people of a certain lineage. I was a match and I'm going over to see what we can piece together about my ancestry to find out who this person was. Maybe I'm related to Natalia!"

As though Gene had sensed that his name was mentioned, he ambled over as his bulldog, Liberty, romped toward the children.

I greeted him and held a platter of cookies out to Coralue. "Thank you for being so kind to me."

"How lovely! Thank you. We'll have these with our afternoon tea."

"I'm glad you're both here. Do you know anything about Mags Delany?" I asked.

They exchanged a glance.

Chapter 33

"Mags is always impeccably dressed," said Coralue stiffly.

Gene guffawed. "If we're making an effort to say nice things about her, I shall second that."

"I take it you two don't like her."

"She's a dreadful woman," said Coralue. "She asked Gene to accompany her to a party before she had even split with her husband."

"And what a split that was," added Gene. "When he left on a business trip, Mags hired a couple of handymen to remove all her husband's possessions from the house and then she changed the locks. Everything was piled in the driveway for two days like trash. I wouldn't be at all surprised if some items had gone missing before he found out."

"Can you imagine coming home to that?" asked Coralue. "At the very least she could have put it in storage for him or given him some notice. He's lucky it didn't rain. His furniture would have been ruined."

"I'm almost afraid to ask why they separated," I said.

"I don't like to gossip, but—

"For pity's sake, Coralue," Gene interrupted. "It's not idle gossip. It's fact. He works for de Gama Pharmaceuticals. It's spiraling downward and everyone is fleeing like rats on a foundering ship. No one is going to hire him. He's done."

"What Gene is trying to say is that Mags likes money. And her husband will not likely have any in the foreseeable future."

"She's husband hunting," explained Gene.

Coralue moaned. "I really don't like to speak ill of people, but Gene is right. She hasn't even bothered to make a secret of it. She's coarse and rude, and just plain hateful."

Gene tried to suppress a smile. "That pretty much sums her up."

It dawned on me that the professor's lunch with Mags and Jacquie's lunch with Gene probably weren't coincidences. I had a sneaking suspicion that Mr. DuBois had a hand in those arrangements.

"How is Hayes doing?" I asked.

"Fortunately, his practice hasn't suffered from all this nonsense."

"I heard Balthus was one of his patients," I said casually.

Gene raised his eyebrows.

"Now, how could you know that?" asked Coralue. "Hayes wouldn't even tell *me* if Balthus went to him."

"If I were Balthus, I think I would change my last name," muttered Gene. "That case will take years to settle and he'll be haunted by the de Gama name."

I checked my watch. "I need to bring these cookies over to Cyril. Will you call me if you hear anything about Manny?"

They assured me they would, and I walked briskly in the other direction. When I approached Cyril's house, I focused on the window I had broken. The repair job was perfect. No one would have known anything untoward had happened there. It was open, which wasn't particularly surprising, given the lovely autumn weather. The sun shone high in the sky and the temperature was heavenly with no humidity. I suspected a lot of people were enjoying open windows to let fresh air into their houses.

But when I raised my hand to grasp the knocker, I heard voices. Or one very loud voice.

Roxie was saying, "I won't have it. Do you understand?"

Someone, probably Cyril, responded in a muted tone. I couldn't make out what he said.

"I don't care what your intentions were," shouted Roxie. "Don't you *ever* do that again."

More murmuring from Cyril.

"No! No, no, no. What a mess. I'm so ashamed. I have to straighten this out. Ugh! Now I feel like I have to spy on you. How could you do that to me?"

I could hear Cyril's soft tone and then a door slamming.

Maybe it wasn't the best time to pop in on them. I scurried out to the sidewalk and walked away as rapidly as I could. Given that Cyril had once hired a PI to follow Roxie, I wondered if he had made such arrangements again following the attack on him.

I stared at the cookies I held. Once again I changed directions and walked a few more blocks to the building where Frieda and Maury lived. I knocked on the door.

This time it was Frieda who opened the main door.

"I brought some home-baked cookies. I hope you'll share them with Maury and Linda."

Frieda acted as if I had brought them a four-course dinner. "What a lovely gesture." She lifted the wrap on them. "And they smell so good! I'm glad you stopped by. We said such ugly things about Manny. Of course, they were all true. But when we heard what happened to Balthus, it dawned on me that we didn't tell you anything about *him*. I want you to know how kind he was to us. When Maury sprained his ankle, Balthus came by every day. He picked up groceries and wouldn't even let us pay for them! I've read about his family's corruption. But Balthus isn't like that."

"Thank you, Frieda." I walked home thinking about the fact that Roxie, Frieda and her friends, and Veronica liked Balthus. But the pumpkin seeds and guts in his shoes still troubled me. When he recovered, maybe I should just come right out and ask him about that.

My phone rang. It was Eric confirming dinner. I strode faster. As soon as I entered the house, I set the table and preheated the oven. I had a little extra time to make French apple cake for dessert.

At six, there was a knock on the door and it opened. "Am I too late for dinner?" asked Eric.

"Perfect timing."

After a lovely romantic kiss, I offered to make him a drink.

He picked up Peaches and snuggled with her. "No alcohol for me, thanks. Water or iced tea would be fine."

"Are you planning to go back to work tonight?" I asked, pouring iced tea into tall glasses.

He set Peaches on the floor. "No, but I'm standing by in case I get a call. Cyril and Balthus are both out of the hospital."

I gasped and nearly dropped the iced tea I held. "You think someone is going to try to finish them off?"

"I don't know what to think. There's a good chance that the attack on Cyril was just a burglary gone very wrong. But Balthus is terrified."

"I'm surprised they released him. He wasn't conscious this morning."

Eric gulped iced tea. "Apparently he was trying to fool everyone because he didn't want to go home."

I didn't blame him. "Have you seen his new apartment?"

"Yes. I swung by when they were collecting evidence. It's

pretty sad. I've lived in some holes-in-the-wall myself, but at least they had decent windows. Somehow, though, I don't think it's the architecture that worries Balthus."

"Then you think the murders and the attacks on Cyril and Balthus are connected?" I chopped a red pepper and threw it into a bowl of fresh greens, followed by halved grape tomatoes.

Eric washed his hands. "Did you say pork chops?"

"I did."

The son of a chef, Eric always jumped in to help in the kitchen. He was, in fact, a far better cook than I was. While he sautéed the pork, I added crunchy pecans and sweet apple slices to our salad.

"The answer is that we don't know if all or any of the events are related. By the way, that was some fancy footwork on your part tripping the guy who came out of Balthus's place." He grinned at me. "You okay?"

"My shoulder is a little bit sore. Nothing I won't get over. Did you arrest him?"

"He claims Balthus listed a Bose music system for sale on Craigslist. He was going over to look at it. When he arrived, the door was unlocked and Balthus was lying on the floor. It spooked him because he thought it might be some kind of sicko setup to hurt him. Then Roxie arrived and he felt trapped, so he bolted up the stairs to get away and you tripped him."

"Do you believe him?" I asked.

"He had Balthus's contact information as well as the ad where Balthus had indeed listed a Bose for sale. When Balthus came around, he confirmed that he'd made an appointment with the guy. Everything fits in place."

I felt so guilty! "Is he okay?"

"Oh, sure. He didn't have anything worse than scraped hands and knees. He'll be fine."

I set the table and asked, "Do you think Balthus knows who attacked him?"

"If he does, he hasn't told us. But I can tell you this, he's scared of something."

"Or someone," I added.

"Did I mention that we found chloroform in the broken bottle?"

I gasped. "Are you going to arrest Hilda?"

"Not yet. There's no evidence she was ever in Balthus's apartment. The bottle belonged to her, but it's loaded with fingerprints."

Eric brought the pork chops to the table. During dinner our conversation drifted to more palatable subjects. But when I brought after-dinner decaf coffee and French apple cake topped with sweetened whipped cream to the sofa, I found Eric looking through my sketchbook.

I settled next to him.

"Aside from admiring your art, I always find it interesting to follow your sketches. They're like a story in pictures. Something tells me you're not fond of Hilda."

"It's not that I dislike her. I don't trust her. You would have to agree that her vision of a murder and a foot in a rug is a little bizarre. Right?"

"It's certainly unusual, especially since it happened. But almost everyone has some uncanny moments. Haven't you ever thought of someone and later learned that they were in surgery at the time? Or maybe you dreamed about a dear friend and when you woke, you learned that he had died?"

"Kind of like déjà vu?" I murmured.

"Not exactly, but I suppose it might fall into the same category simply by being inexplicable. I don't know quite what to make of Hilda, either. In any event, Manny wasn't dead at the time and she has an airtight alibi for his murder."

"Could someone else have done it for her?" I asked.

"It's possible. He was dating Hilda's niece, Kaya. Manny's family thinks Kaya's family knocked him off and Hilda was in on it."

"Is that what *you* think?" I asked.

"I think we have no evidence suggesting that's the case." Eric flipped the page. "Coralue Throckmorton," he said dully. "There's another one."

"What do you mean?"

He smiled and pointed at the image in the window that I thought I had seen. "I trust she told you in great detail about all the ghosts haunting her house?"

"I thought there was only one. The Russian ambassador's widow."

"What disturbs me about Coralue," said Eric, "is that she's smart. She knew Cyril, Manny, Ellis Willoughby, and Balthus. Every single one of them. Her attorney, Gene Germain, is quick to point out that she's quite petite, not young, not particularly athletic, and not likely to have been physically able to have inflicted the wounds they suffered."

"I'm sorry to disappoint you but I have to agree. *I* couldn't have slit Cyril's throat with a knife from behind. But Coralue does have a son."

"I presume he's in here." Eric paged forward. "Hayes Throckmorton. Local heartthrob, martial arts enthusiast, and beloved chiropractor—"

"Really?" I interrupted.

"So I'm told. But no matter how popular he might be with his patients, Hayes knows how to crack your spine and break your neck."

"Was someone's neck broken?" I asked, thinking I had missed something important.

"No. My point is that he knows how to kill someone. As a chiropractor, he's well informed on what *not* to do so he won't hurt you."

I sat back and stared at Eric. I was reading between the lines, of course, but the way he spoke led me to think Hayes was his top suspect.

Speaking as casually as I could, I asked, "What do you think of the Boyles?"

"You know there are things I can't tell you."

"Like the fact that Ellis Willoughby was hired by Mr. Boyle's ex-wife to find their missing son?"

Chapter 34

Eric froze. He glanced over at me. "Where did you hear that?"

"I have my sources."

Eric grinned and rubbed his forehead. "You never cease to amaze me, Miss Fox."

"So I'm right?"

"I can neither confirm nor deny that information."

"I shall take that as a yes. After all, I saw Ellis staking out the Boyles' house. Is it then possible that Manny was lying in wait for the Boyles and tried to blackmail them? I'd been thinking that someone was waiting for Manny, but perhaps it was the other way around and Manny was hanging out watching for the Boyles."

"And they turned on him?" he asked. "Does your source know if they have the boy?"

"No. I would have told you immediately if anyone had even a clue to where he might be. As far as I know, no one has seen him. But I'm wondering if that's the mess Willoughby referred to. Maybe he discovered something about the child's whereabouts?"

"It's an interesting theory. Worth consideration, I think. Is this the ghost in Coralue Throckmorton's window?" Eric pointed at my sketch.

"How did you know? Have you seen it?"

"She showed it to me. It's set up so that it only appears in the window every hour for thirty seconds. She thinks that makes it seem more real."

I sagged against the cushion. "I thought I was losing my mind. I have only seen two ghosts in my life, and both of them were of artificial construction. But you think you really saw one?"

"You'll think I'm crazy or a sap," he protested.

"You promised to tell me."

"When I was twenty, I woke very abruptly at two thirty-one in the morning. My mom's father was in my room. He looked very much like himself, but a little bit grayed out. He said, 'I'll be going now, but you'll be okay, kid. You'll be okay.' And then he was gone. In the morning my mom called to tell me he had died during the night."

"You're sure you didn't dream that?"

"Not a chance. He wasn't even sick. His death came as a big shock to everyone. For a long time, the only person I told was my mom. But one night after work, I was having a beer with some of my friends on the force and the subject of ghosts came up. You wouldn't believe the things they've seen. Like intruders who slam doors on their way out but there aren't any footprints in the snow. A couple of guys insist that they turned off the lights in an unoccupied building and left. But when they were outside, all the lights turned back on. Since then, I've been more open, and it turns out my experience isn't all that unique. Quite a few people have had a visit from someone they're close to."

I thought about it for a minute. "Clearly no one could have set up something like what you experienced. For starters, how would anyone know he was dying?"

"Exactly. It changed my opinion on ghosts entirely." He chuckled. "I've responded to a few calls from people who think there's a ghost in the house. There's not much I can do but sympathize." He turned to look at my clocks. "I hate to make it an early night but they've got us working overtime because of the murders, and I'm beat."

"I understand completely. Hey, was the metal cylinder a match with Ellis's wind chimes?"

"It was. And the wood from the broomstick is being analyzed, but I'd be very surprised if it wasn't used against Ellis."

I was pleased. "But it doesn't really matter. We already knew Ellis was dead. Those items just establish where he was killed. I guess Ellis's daughter told you his bags were packed and standing by the door like he planned to go somewhere?"

Eric opened my door and stopped. "I don't want to scare you, but Ellis may have been involved with some dangerous people. There's a very good chance that his death had nothing to do with the attack on Cyril or with Manny's murder. Can you do me a huge favor and let Ellis's situation go? I promise you, we're on top of it. But I don't want you walking into anything."

I nodded. "Of course. I don't want to get in your way."

"Thanks." He wrapped his arms around me. "Wish I could stay."

"Me, too."

He kissed me and fled, which was just as well. We could have stood in the doorway kissing for an hour.

I cleaned up a little and then threw on a black jacket, slightly fitted but sturdy enough to break the wind. It was dark outside. I had mixed feelings about that. It wasn't as safe as daylight, but Manny's murder had happened at night, so it was more realistic.

I walked over to Color Me Read and stood outside for a moment. The show windows and French doors glowed with light. The store looked great. I watched as Hilda walked up the stairs and entered the store. What was she doing there?

I had half a mind to go inside but then I heard Finley's voice. He was walking on the other side of the street with a woman who definitely was not Roxie. I darted behind a tree and watched them walk up the block. Trying to be unobtrusive, I followed them. They turned right and continued walking. I trailed behind them until they entered a Chinese restaurant.

Sticking to the other side of the street, I paused in front of the restaurant's huge window. A waiter showed them to a table. The woman was definitely the same one who had been stalking Finley.

My heart hammered in my chest. What was the right thing to do? Call Roxie and tell her? Mind my own business? Get my own table in the restaurant and insist Roxie join me? That was silly; they would leave if I entered.

What would I want Roxie to do if the tables were turned and Eric was in the restaurant with another woman? It seemed like there should be an easy answer to this question.

Uncertain, I pulled out my phone and called Roxie.

She answered right away. "Hi, Florrie."

"I thought I'd check to see how Cyril is doing."

She lowered her voice. "Well, all I can say is that it's a good thing I'm here. The guard turned out to be an old friend of Dad's, so now they're sitting by the fire, drinking spiked cider, and reliving old times. Can you believe that? Honestly, if he weren't an old chum, I would call the agency and have him fired!"

"Is, um, is Finley with you?" I asked.

"He's at a business dinner tonight. I think I'm going to stay over with Dad since no one else around here is on the alert."

I froze. I felt just awful. Roxie needed to know. But maybe not tonight. She'd had so much trauma in her life recently that this news might be too much. And she probably shouldn't leave Cyril right now anyway. All she could do was fret and get upset. I would tell her. But maybe at a better time, though heaven knew when that might be.

"I'm glad Cyril is feeling better. I'd be just as aggravated as you are, but maybe it's good for him to have an old friend there. It will take his mind off the night he was attacked."

I disconnected the call and felt like a complete crumb. It was done now. I took one last look at them. I was no expert in reading people, but if you asked me, it looked like they were arguing. Maybe that was a good thing.

I returned to Color Me Read and concentrated on what had happened the night Manny was murdered. He left the store and somehow landed in Coralue's yard. What had happened to him in between?

Obviously, he could have gone in any direction. I didn't think Kaya had seen him that night, so he probably didn't head down to M Street. He might have waited for the Boyles outside of the bookstore. They probably would have gone home, so I began to walk in that direction. There were half a dozen paths they could have taken, turning up one block or down another block. For my purposes, I took the most direct route. It took me past Cyril's house, which appeared quite tranquil. Much as Ellis had done, I stood across the street from the Boyles' house with the gargoyles looking down at me. Lights were on. I presumed they were home.

Had they noticed Manny? Had he followed them all the way home and accosted them as they entered their house? Had Ellis seen him? Had the Boyles rolled him up in a rug and deposited him at Balthus's old home? Why would they do that? They probably needed a car to transport him there. But then why not drive him out of town? Or had they driven him to Coralue's and the entire, foot-in-a-rug thing at Balthus's was simply fiction?

I walked on to Balthus's previous home, which wasn't that far away. Still, it would have been difficult with a corpse. I had to expand my theories because the one with the Boyles was leaving a lot of questions.

Standing in the alcove at Balthus's former residence, I looked around. I could see the light coming from Maury's television across the street. Maybe it was my imagination, but I felt as though I could hear it a little bit, too.

A strong light blazed upstairs in what must be Frieda's kitchen. Naturally, I was looking up and she would have been looking down, but I wondered how much she could see. There were streetlights, and the light of the moon might have helped. Or maybe a car was parked on the street with headlights on and pointing in that general direction.

If Manny had been deposited here, then he had most certainly been murdered somewhere between the bookstore and here. So far, my tracing of the possible path had yielded no insight whatsoever.

I was inclined to believe that Hilda had gotten the location wrong. And that Frieda was only imagining that she saw the rug late at night.

In any event, whoever murdered Manny had taken him to Coralue's house. I walked back thinking the only clue I really had pointed to Balthus. Could the pumpkin in his shoes be a coincidence?

As I neared my own neighborhood, the homes grew bigger. A car driving far too fast turned into a driveway right in front of me as though the driver hadn't noticed me. I stopped and watched to see who had been driving.

The car stopped near the front door. The engine was still running and the headlights were on. A man I didn't recognize got out of the driver's side and walked around the car to open the door for his passenger.

Mags Delany stepped out. She was speaking too loudly, as

if she'd had too much to drink. The driver must have had enough of her because he ran back to the driver's side, slammed his door shut, and pulled out of the driveway in reckless haste.

Mags had had enough sense to leave the lights by the front door on. She yelled, "And the same to you, buddy!" Swaying, she began to sing a show tune very badly and off key.

She stumbled and fell, laughing hysterically.

I loathed her. She wasn't a nice person at all.

But I was. Or I liked to think I was.

Chapter 35

I walked over to Mags and held out my hands to help her up.

She batted at me. "Get away from me!"

"Ms. Delany, I work for Professor Maxwell. You need help. Now give me your hands. Okay?"

"Ugh. I'm surprised Maxwell tolerates someone like you." She tried to stand without my help and promptly fell again.

I was through trying to be polite. "Take off your shoes."

"Never!"

"You won't be able to make it up the steps in those pointy high heels."

"How dare you criticize me. They *are* from last season, but I wouldn't expect the likes of you to know *that*."

"Take them off."

Reluctantly she kicked them off her feet.

I picked them up.

"Be careful with those. They're Louboutins."

I set them by the door and returned to her. I'd have held on to the shoes but I was afraid I might stab her with a heel— by mistake, of course. "Now hold on to my hands."

She frowned but finally capitulated. I hoisted her to her

feet. With my arm around her waist, I assisted her up the stairs.

"Where is the key?" I asked, hoping she had it in a pocket.

"In my purse. But don't you go grabbing things!"

I eyed the empty driveway. "Where is your purse?"

For the first time she looked at me like a human being.

"He drove off with it. That creep!" Her entire body sagged.

"Do you have a spare key or a hidden key somewhere in case you get locked out?" I asked.

"Yes. But I don't want you to know where it is."

She was horrible. "That's fine. I understand completely. Good night!" She would probably fall down the steps, but I wasn't going to argue with her.

"All right!"

I thought she tried to frown but couldn't through the Botox.

"It's around back. Under the ceramic frog. You'll have to unlock the kitchen door and come through the house to let me in."

I walked down the steps and she yelled, "And don't steal anything!"

What a gracious woman. I followed the drive to the garage and opened a gate that led to darkness. Not a single outdoor light was on. I pulled out my phone and switched on the flashlight. The beam didn't go far but it was strong enough to find the frog and help me unlock the door.

I switched on a light and stepped into a sleek kitchen. It was surprisingly small. Everything from the floor to the countertops to the cabinets was high-gloss white. The only color in the room was a pale, barely there green backsplash of a solid glasslike material that appeared to glow.

There were two doors. I opened the one most likely to

lead to the front door and found a hallway to the foyer. I turned on lights as I went and opened the front door for her.

"Are you insane? Why have you turned on all the lights? And what took you so long? Were you snooping?"

I handed her the key. "Should I call someone for you?"

"No!" She stumbled into the house.

I set her shoes inside. "Don't forget to lock the back door."

In a much smaller voice, she said, "Don't go." And then she walked right into a wall.

I helped her into what appeared to be a living room. Giant windows looked out on darkness. I suspected a garden would be visible in daylight.

She sat on a stiff, uncomfortable chair. "There's not much left." She laughed without mirth. "Coralue Throckmorton murdered her lover and buried him in her yard and what's everyone talking about? That Mags Delany put her husband out of the house! How's that for ridiculous? At least I didn't murder him and bury him in the garden. Though that might have been the easier thing to do, now that I think about it."

"I would be very surprised if Manny were Coralue's lover."

Mags shrugged her thin shoulders. "Yard man, handyman, pool man. Whatever. She needed to get rid of him, but they're talking about me. Like it's a bigger sin than murder to put your husband's belongings on the driveway."

"Why did you do that?" I asked.

"I didn't *want* him in the house. Do you know that idiot is claiming I stole some of his things?" She snorted. "I'd like to see him prove that. I don't want anything that belongs to him. He accused me of selling his precious rug, as if I were some kind of merchant."

"Rug? Like an Oriental rug?"

"Don't pretend you know about rugs. It's not becoming when one speaks with authority on subjects they know nothing about."

"Did you put this rug out with his other belongings?"

"Now *you* think I stole it, too? I must say you have a lot of gall. How dare you make that sort of accusation?"

I skipped over her insults. "When did you set the rug outside?"

"I didn't do it. My housekeeper did on her last day here."

"Would that have been the night that Manny was found at Coralue's house?"

"How would I know? Possibly."

"Would your husband be able to identify this rug?" I asked. "Do you know where he's staying?"

She stared at me before chuckling. "You needn't go after him. If he were worth anything, I wouldn't have put him out."

I resented her implication that I wanted to meet him because I was a money-grubber. But I had to overlook that. I had to bribe her with something she understood and appeared to need. Money. "Do you know where this rug is? The professor has been looking for one for his library."

She flicked a fingernail against her thumb and studied me. "Get out. I didn't want my husband in this house any more than I want you in my house. Maybe less, even."

"Then I'll be on my way."

She flicked a bony hand at me as if dismissing the hired help.

"Good night, then." I walked to the front door and let myself out.

Before I made it down the stairs, something caught my eye on the ground beside the stairs, as if wind had blown it there. I picked it up.

It was one of my adult Halloween coloring books!

I heard the lock turn and she shut off the lights. I stood in darkness. Nevertheless, I managed to make my way up the steps. I knocked on the door. "Ms. Delany!"

"Go away!"

"I have your coloring book."

"Go away or I shall call the authorities."

She was a shrew. Her husband was lucky to have gotten away from her.

I walked down the steps and across the driveway. I stood on the sidewalk outside of Mags Delany's house again, this time clutching my coloring book. Had Manny's murderer been here? Had he stolen her husband's rug from the driveway where Mags had left his belongings?

Had he rolled Manny in it and taken him to Balthus's prior residence? Or straight to Coralue's house? Had he stashed Manny and the rug in the bushes while he fetched a car to transport the body?

It was possible. Even among the meticulously groomed homes there were plenty of hedges that would have hidden something in the night.

Manny must have been killed somewhere around here. Manny and his murderer probably met on the street. But who was it that Manny met or followed?

As I ran through the names of possible suspects, Hayes stood out. He knew the area. He had a motive and no alibi that I knew of. My heart would break for Coralue if that was the case.

I walked home considering the possibilities. It wasn't far but I was worn out when I reached the carriage house. I had carried the coloring book all the way home but hadn't given it another thought until I was in my house and tossed it on the coffee table. Scratching behind Peaches's ears with one hand, I picked it up with the other.

The binding of the coloring book was still crisp and new. No one had used it or even looked through it much. I suspected it had been blown about by the wind but it didn't look worse for the wear. As I flipped the pages, a receipt fell out. It had been purchased at Color Me Read.

Chapter 36

I fed Peaches in a hurry the next morning. Dressed in jeans, an oversized dusty turquoise sweater, and a slightly darker vest, I locked the door and rushed to the bookstore.

It was quiet when I arrived. I doubted that even the Professor was there yet. I could feel my heart pounding, although the rational part of me knew that the coloring book probably didn't mean a thing. Some child had probably dropped it on the way home. If that were the case, I could return it.

On the other hand, what if a child hadn't dropped it?

I turned the alarm back on and ran upstairs to the office, where I did the bookkeeping. The receipt was dated the same day that Hilda had come to the bookstore. It wasn't difficult to track. Several copies had been sold that day. Coralue had paid cash. The receipt in the coloring book indicated payment by credit card. Three people had paid by credit card but only one matched that receipt exactly. It had been bought by Finley Brimble.

I sat back in my chair. What did it mean, if anything at all? Had Finley dropped it? Had he given it as a gift, maybe to his girlfriend, and she dropped it? Or had it somehow come to be in the possession of Mags Delany's husband and was unceremoniously thrown out on the driveway?

I didn't know when it came to be there. It could have been well after Manny's murder. Still, I called Eric to let him know.

He was sweet and not dismissive as any cop who didn't love me would have been.

I needed coffee.

I locked up and dodged across the street to my favorite coffee shop. I had just picked up my pumpkin spice latte and a pumpkin muffin when Finley's girlfriend walked in.

I hustled to a corner table and set my purchases down. Pretending to need more napkins, I sidled up near her. I had no idea what I was going to say and blurted, "Hi! You're Finley's friend, aren't you?"

She looked straight into my eyes. "I can't talk with you." She looked around, clearly fearful. "I've been to your bookstore. You seem like a nice person. I'm glad Roxie has a friend like you. But please. If you have an ounce of kindness in your heart, please go away."

She turned quickly and walked out of the store at a determined pace. The clerk behind the counter yelled, "Hey, lady! You forgot your coffee."

She didn't stop or look back. I wanted to catch up with her. That fear hadn't been an act.

I knew the clerk fairly well. As casually as possible, I asked, "Did she pay by cash or credit card?"

"Credit."

"Is her name on it?"

"Yeah. Rebecca Porter."

"Thanks." I sat down with my latte and looked up Rebecca Porter on my phone. Swell. There were over four hundred on LinkedIn and many more than that on Facebook.

Was she afraid of Finley? As I bit into the moist muffin, it dawned on me that she might be married, too. What a mess.

I sipped on my latte and sketched Rebecca's face on a napkin. Maybe I had been going about this all wrong. I had been trying to connect the murders and attacks. Could I be overlooking the obvious?

Cyril's throat had been slit. The assailant had removed a priceless clock from the house. Had he meant to steal the clock? Then why not grab it and run?

Manny had been rolled in a rug, possibly obtained from Mags's driveway. My coloring book, purchased by Finley, was also found there.

Manny had been sloppily buried in Coralue's yard. Why hadn't the foot been buried? Because it happened at night or because the killer was being hasty?

Manny had a new job working for someone wealthy. That might be true or it might not.

Ellis had been choked from behind, much like the two previous attacks. But it happened at his front door. He had been transported to an obscure location, callously dumped and covered with leaves. That was definitely different from the attempt to hide Manny's body.

Balthus had been attacked in his own home. I didn't recall anyone mentioning that the door had been forced open. Had Balthus opened the door to someone he knew and trusted? Or had he opened it expecting the man who was interested in buying his music system? It was also notable that he was chloroformed, not attacked from behind as the others. Why had the killer switched his method of killing?

I finished my muffin and doodled on the napkin where I had drawn the face of Finley's girlfriend. Next to her face I drew his, but not the handsome, dimpled face that I knew. The sneaky weasel face I had glimpsed. That brief moment had been etched in my head. It was as though I had caught a glimpse of a dark side that I didn't know he had.

And now I had to tell Roxie about seeing him with the other woman last night. I dreaded that.

I folded the napkin and stashed it in my pocket as I left. From the doorway I could see that Color Me Read was open for business and one of our regular customers was opening the door to go inside.

I walked home slowly, all kinds of absurd thoughts running through my head about the murders. At Coralue's house, the fall scarf on the butler waved in the wind, giving her display a somewhat comedic flair. As I gazed at it, Coralue emerged from her front door, pulling a grocery tote on wheels behind her.

"Florrie! Your pumpkin cookies were a big hit with my grandchildren."

"I'm glad to hear that. I was just admiring your Mr. DuBois. It was a stroke of genius to add the scarf. It gives him so much character."

"I think so, too. I'd like to take credit for it but it wasn't my idea. Someone else wrapped it around his neck. I came outside and there it was."

Chill bumps rose on my arms. "A stranger?"

"I really don't know. I just thought it was creative and amusing."

"Coralue, do you remember when it happened?"

She took a deep breath. "Does it matter?"

"I'm not sure."

"Let's see. When did I first notice it? Hmm. He had it on when we discovered Manny. So I think it was around then. Should I remove it?"

"No. In fact, I would appreciate it if you didn't touch it at all."

She frowned at me. "It couldn't have anything to do with the murder . . ."

"I'm not sure." I walked closer. It was tan and chocolate brown, with a fine line of cranberry running through it. I had sketched this scarf. But who had worn it? "Have a good time shopping. I'll see you later."

She watched as I abruptly left her and hurried home. I burst into the carriage house, alarming Peaches, who watched me run to my sketch pad. I flipped pages back quickly and promptly found the scarf. It was Finley's.

Chapter 37

I pulled the napkin out of my pocket and stared at the wickedness in Finley. I sat down, turned my sketch pad to a clean page, and focused on a close-up of his face in profile. As I sketched, I was again surprised by his sharp nose. It wasn't at all noticeable from the front or when one spoke with him. He had a prominent chin and high cheekbones, but it was the eyes that conveyed a mean spirit. I wasn't sure I could capture the evil in them, but when I was finished, the sneaky side glance from hooded eyes frightened me. His eyes were calculating.

I put down my sketch pad and went to the computer. *Finley Brimble* popped up immediately in a number of places where he was promoting his business as an antiques and rare book dealer. His website was professionally done and quite impressive, citing a few amazing sales he had made and offering quotes from delighted customers.

There were plenty of stories on the net about the Brimble family in England. Sadly, the part about the plane crash was true. The Brimbles were a wealthy family involved in banking and real estate in London. Their private plane crashed on the way to Salamanca, Spain, killing Finley's parents and their other two children. Anyone doing a superficial search would readily find that information to be true. But when I dug a little deeper, I ran across a sentence that sent chills up my back. *One child survived because she had chicken pox and was left at home.*

She? That child wasn't a boy? It couldn't be Finley. Or had it been a typo? I continued to read about them, in the hope that another article would mention the baby left at home.

Although the Brimbles perished, their business continued and flourished. I located a number for the main office and dared to call it.

I explained to the woman who answered that I was interested in finding living members of the original Brimble family. She put me through to someone else, who put me through to a woman who was painfully polite.

"As you might expect, the Brimbles are exceedingly private people. You understand that I cannot give out any personal information. However, if you would care to leave your name and phone number with me, I can pass it on to them."

My breath caught in my throat. What if Finley was one of "them"? Would he be upset if he discovered that I was asking about his background? Probably.

But I had come this far. I gave her my name and phone number, thinking it would very likely be a dead end. Chances were good that I would never hear from "them," whoever they were.

I sat back on the sofa and considered calling Eric when Peaches jumped into my lap. In spite of the sketchbook in front of me showing me Finley's evil gaze, I realized I had overreacted. What would I tell him? What would I tell Finley's relative if one called? That he was having an affair? That I caught him at a bad moment when he looked devious? That he lost my coloring book? That he had the good sense of humor to tie his scarf around a faux butler's neck?

How stupid could I be? I chalked it up to being obsessed with Manny's murder. I had no leads and in my desperation, I was trying to link everyone to it. Finley might be a philanderer, but I had nothing to tie him to Manny's murder. Besides, he had an alibi. He had been with Roxie and Cyril at the hospital.

I was mortified. I would have to think of something to say just in case one of his relatives phoned. Chiding myself, I straightened up around the house. If, heaven forbid, a Brimble called me from England, I would invent a celebration for Finley and invite them.

Oh, what a muddle I had created. I had always thought of myself as a fairly level-headed person. But I had made a mess of things now.

When my phone rang, I jumped, fearing it would be someone calling from England. But it was Eric. I sighed with relief.

"I just wanted you to know that we did a quick check on the credit card. I'm sorry about your book, but I don't see anything criminal happening here. The only hiccup is that it was charged to Cyril's credit card."

"But I'm sure Finley bought it."

"Maybe Finley and Roxie can charge to Cyril's account. I had a card like that when I was in college. It bore my name but was billed to my dad's credit card account."

"I guess that's a family matter. I sort of saw Cyril's credit card statement the other day. Roxie seemed upset about it. And yesterday afternoon, I went over there but didn't knock because I could hear Roxie and Cyril having an argument. I don't know what it was about, but it would not surprise me if it had something to do with the credit card."

"*Sort of saw?* Really, Florrie?"

I was appropriately ashamed. "It doesn't matter. I thought it might lead to Cyril's attacker in some way. I still don't understand how the coloring book made its way to Mags's house, but I guess that doesn't really matter, either."

"I don't want to sound like a jerk, but you do know that we're working on Cyril's case. And the attack on Balthus and the murders."

"You're telling me very nicely that I don't have to call you every five minutes to tell you about charge slips and coloring books that have been lost." I could hardly tell him about the scarf. I had pestered him enough.

Eric laughed. A nice hearty laugh that let me know he wasn't upset with me. "I'll talk to you soon."

It was almost noon when I hung up. Peaches was playing with her favorite toy, a green cricket nearly the size of my hand that made absolutely authentic and very loud cricket chirps. She tossed it in the air, and when it fell and chirped, she attacked it again.

I put on the kettle for tea, determined to concentrate on my next coloring book. But, try as I might, my thoughts wandered back to Manny, Coralue, and Kaya. I took my tea out in the garden and had just settled in a chair when someone knocked on my door.

Out of an abundance of unnecessary caution, I peered out the small window first. Roxie was standing outside.

I swung the door open. "Hi. I didn't expect to see you. How's Cyril doing?" In the back of my mind, I thought this might be the right time to tell her about Finley and the other woman. I hoped I would be brave enough. "Could I make you a cup of tea?"

Roxie looked pained. "No, thank you. I won't be here long." She took a deep breath. "I feel like there's something I have to address." She shot me a feeble smile. "The looming elephant in the room. I know how handsome and charming Finley is. Obviously, or I wouldn't have married him. So, the thing is that Finley told me about you following him around. I can't blame you for having a crush on him. I would, too. This is so awkward. Anyway—"

"Excuse me?" Surely I had misunderstood her. "You think I have a thing for Finley?"

"It's so obvious, Florrie." She hustled to my coffee table and picked up my sketchbook. Flipping it to the first drawing of him, she held it out to me and made a sad face.

"Do I also have a crush on you, and Cyril, and Manny? Because there are sketches of all of you in there." I snatched my sketchbook out of her hands. "Did he tell you that he had dinner with the woman who has been following him?"

"Oh my gosh! He said you would say that! Are you trying to break up my marriage?"

"Of course not. I want you to be happy."

"For your information, he went to dinner last night with a woman who represents a collector of rare books. She could give him a lot of business."

"Oh, Roxie! I flipped over to the page where I had drawn her picture. "Her name is Rebecca Porter. Don't you recognize her as the woman who's been stalking him?"

Roxie's face flamed. "Have you been following her, too?"

"No. Look, I'm really sorry about this. But you're my friend, Roxie. And Finley is jerking you around."

"I have to say that I'm surprised, Florrie. I never expected you to go after Finley."

I took a chance. "Why is Finley charging things on Cyril's credit card?"

She gasped. "How could you know that? That's private information between my dad and us."

"I run a store, Roxie. Finley buys things." I hoped that in the heat of the moment she wouldn't realize Finley's name was on the credit card.

Roxie looked away from me. "Finley and I have been living beyond our means. I should have known but I don't keep track of Finley's income. I thought he was doing well. But apparently he has been going to my dad for money and suggested this horrible credit card arrangement."

"And Cyril agreed to that?"

"You know Dad. He wants us to be happy. But I'm not having it anymore. I had no idea that Finley was siphoning money from Dad. I'm so embarrassed."

"What happened to Finley's money? I thought he had a huge trust fund or something."

"Apparently there are issues with cousins who have instituted litigation in England."

This many years after the plane crash? It was cruel but I had to say it. "And you believe that?"

Roxie's nostrils flared in anger. "You saved my father's life. I will always be grateful for that, but from here on out, I would appreciate it if you left my family alone."

She stormed out the door.

I watched her run along the driveway. I'd handled that poorly and managed to lose a friend in the process. I needed chocolate. And not just chocolate chips.

The back door of the mansion opened and Mr. DuBois stepped out. "Was that Miss Roxie?"

"It was." I made sure the door wouldn't lock behind me and closed it before Peaches came to investigate. "Finley is seeing a woman named Rebecca Porter. I caught them in a restaurant last night. But he promptly made up a story about her and has told Roxie that I am infatuated with him."

"I thought you were involved with Sergeant Jonquille."

"I am. But Roxie is drinking it up, eager to find excuses for Finley."

"What a pity. I'm quite fond of Miss Roxie."

"You've stopped coming over to my house," I observed.

"Miss Jacqueline has been staying home to finish her

book. She works in the library and I bring her coffee and sustenance."

"And the ghosts?" I asked.

"Behaving remarkably well. Miss Hilda says they were looking for each other and may leave altogether. You needn't give me that look. I get enough of that from Maxwell."

"Speaking of Maxwell—"

Mr. DuBois sighed. "You were right."

I tried to hide my smile. "You set them up? The professor with the odious Mags Delany and Jacquie with Gene Germain?"

"It might well have worked had I chosen better. Who knew Mags was such an old biddy? Actually, that term is too kind for her. I hear she has some choice things to say about you."

Now I grinned. "I imagine she does."

"I had better get back to Miss Jacqueline."

"No more matchmaking?"

He flapped his hand at me and disappeared into the mansion.

I checked on Peaches. She sprawled in a ray of sunlight that flooded through the French doors. I popped a plaid scarf, a paper bag, and my wallet in a tote, and went to get chocolate.

First, though, I walked directly to Coralue's house, intending to swap my scarf for the one on her faux butler. But from the sidewalk, I could see that the plaid scarf was gone.

Chapter 38

I wanted to think that Eric had sent someone over to pick it up but I hadn't mentioned it to him. I approached the butler slowly, hoping the scarf had blown off and fallen to the ground.

I gazed around, feeling quite nervous. Maybe someone stole the scarf, I reasoned. There wasn't a soul to be seen. But on the ground, in the grass, lay a leaf.

It stood out among the other leaves. The golden and red oak leaves were longer. It was similar in shape to the sugar maples that I liked so much, but it was rounder. The edges were flaming red, but the center was a stunning cool green. The stem matched the edges and sent fine threads of red through the leaf.

I had seen one before. I didn't move. I studied the trees on Coralue's lot. Many of them were large and old. But I didn't see even one with leaves that matched the one that lay before me.

I snapped a photograph of it with my phone before picking it up. There was no point in calling Eric about a leaf. He would think I had lost my mind.

Using another leaf, I scooched the vibrant one into the

paper bag I had brought along. Walking fast, I got out of there and made a beeline for Rose and Violet.

Rose set aside the arrangement she was composing. "Hi, Florrie. What can I do for you?"

I pulled the leaf out of the bag. "I know this isn't really up your alley . . ."

Rose gasped. "It's a full-moon maple leaf!"

"Really? You recognize it?"

"They're very desirable. You can see why. The trees can be a little bit fussy. They like the sun but can burn easily if it's too hot. Isn't it beautiful?"

"Is it common? Are there a lot of them around?" I asked.

"I wouldn't go so far as to call them rare. I don't think any nurseries in our area carry them, but you could probably order one online."

"Have you noticed any in yards around here?"

"Old Mr. Glasson is quite the horticulturist. Most people know him for his amazing lilies, but it wouldn't surprise me if he had a full-moon maple."

"Where is he located?" I asked.

"He's up in Cleveland Park."

"So it's unlikely that a leaf would have fluttered its way down here?"

"Probably. Oh! Roxie Brimble has one in front of her house. It's a wonderful specimen. They tend to be a little smaller than other maples."

"I've seen her tree. Thank you, Rose." I tucked the leaf in my bag and left, deep in thought. So deep that I slammed right into Rebecca Porter.

"I'm so sorry," we chimed simultaneously as we squatted to pick up the items that spilled from her purse.

"Are you afraid your husband will find out?" I asked, reaching for a business card that had fluttered away.

Her hand stopped moving. "It's not what you think."
I glanced at the business card.

Ellis Willoughby IV
Private Investigations
Specializing in Locating Loved Ones

Rebecca snatched it out of my hand and ran before I could get to my feet. I didn't know what to make of that. I glanced around. There was no sign of Finley, but Rebecca was charging down the sidewalk as fast as a woman in three-inch heels could go.

I followed her all the way to a nice hotel. She dashed inside and took the elevator up. I supposed she could be visiting someone but chances were she was staying there.

I ambled back. If it wasn't what I thought, then what was it? Had she hired Ellis? Had she met with him? Who was she looking for? Finley, obviously. She had followed him and checked out his house. Was he an old boyfriend she wanted to find? Or a long-lost relative?

If that was the case, I owed Finley and Roxie an apology. But if she was family, why hadn't she met Roxie? Why did Finley say it was a business dinner? Who *was* Rebecca Porter? And what was she afraid of?

I didn't like the way Finley seemed to be cropping up everywhere. Of course, there could be very reasonable explanations for the leaf in Coralue's yard. It wasn't inconceivable that someone in our neighborhood had a full-moon maple and a leaf had blown away. We *had* been having some powerful winds. Or the person who stole the scarf might have happened to have the leaf clinging to his clothes. Maybe Finley or Roxie recognized the scarf and nabbed it. They had every right to do that since it probably belonged to Finley, anyway.

All quite innocent explanations. I walked into The Sweet Life, where the walls were lined with all manner of chocolate and hard-to-find candies. The display case in the rear was packed with French pastries that were baked on the premises.

I picked out a bar of my favorite Swiss chocolate and gazed at the pastries. The cream-filled profiteroles were Roxie's favorites. The least I could do was bring a box of them to Cyril's house as an apology. It might not do any good, but as my mother would say, a nice gesture never hurt anyone.

I added a huge bag of individually wrapped chocolates and candies for us to hand out at Color Me Read on Halloween. Children usually trick-or-treated at local stores in the afternoon.

Carrying a pastry box tied with a gold ribbon, I headed for Cyril's house. At the front door, I squared my shoulders and knocked.

A man in a guard uniform answered the door.

"I brought a treat for Cyril and Roxie," I explained.

Cyril must have been listening because he promptly appeared and told the guard I was okay.

"I hear you and Roxie had a falling-out."

"It's really more of a misunderstanding."

"I expected as much. You seem quite happy with your Sergeant Jonquille. I can't imagine why you would chase after Finley. And, frankly, chasing a man doesn't really sound like the Florrie I know. She would suffer in agonized silence."

I chuckled. "Thank you, Cyril. You are exactly right."

"Give her a couple of days. She'll come around. My Roxie can never hold a grudge."

I handed him the package. "Maybe this will help. Does the name Rebecca Porter mean anything to you?"

"I may have had a student by that name. It sounds vaguely familiar."

"Could be. Apparently, there are a lot of Rebecca Porters."

He thanked me and closed the door.

I walked home wondering if Rebecca was adopted and searching for her birth family. That would explain Ellis's card. Could she be related to Finley?

I could hear my phone ringing inside the carriage house. I scrambled to unlock the door and rushed to the phone.

"Hello?" I said breathlessly.

"I should like to speak with a Florrie Fox, please." The voice was male with a gorgeous British lilt. I immediately imagined a breathtakingly handsome man on the other end of the call. Someone who was undoubtedly holding a martini as he spoke. Stirred, not shaken.

"Speaking," I croaked.

"Rupert Brimble calling. The office gave me your number."

"Mr. Brimble!" I gushed. "How nice of you to return my call. I am doing some research on Finley Brimble and I'm looking for a relative who knows him."

I was totally unsettled by the long pause that followed. Was that because of the overseas connection? Or because Rupert was thinking about hanging up on me?

Finally he asked, "How can I help you?"

"Do you know Finley Brimble?"

"Indeed. I do know Finley. He is the son of my brother."

"That's wonderful! So Finley is definitely a boy. I read an article that said a girl had remained at home and survived the crash."

"Mmm. That's the trouble these days. Someone makes an error, does nothing to correct it, and suddenly everyone thinks it's true. No, Miss Fox, Finley is most definitely male."

"Would you be the uncle who took him in and raised him?" I asked.

"I would. He had no other uncles. My sister and I have no children of our own. Naturally we took in the only living child of our brother after that horrible accident. We may seem a bit of an odd family but this was apparently what life and fate held in store for us."

I paused, unsure what he meant by that.

"May I ask the nature of your interest in Finley? Are you a researcher?"

Researcher? Suddenly I felt a bit queasy, as though I had stumbled into something quite different from what I'd expected. "I'm a friend of Finley's," I said, which was true.

Another long silence followed. Rupert's tone changed. "In that case, you have the wrong Finley Brimble."

He was going to hang up! I spoke hurriedly. "You see, my friend married Finley. She is very sad about your estrangement from Finley and would like to know more about his family. That's why I'm calling." It was partly a lie, but not completely.

"You reached out to me through the company. Has Finley represented himself to be the surviving child of my brother?"

"Yes."

"Then, Miss Fox, I am sorry to inform you that he is an impostor."

Chapter 39

A chill ran through me. "How . . . how can you know that?"

"Because this is not the first time I have received such an inquiry. The real Finley is directly outside my window watching his little terrier bark at ducks on the pond. After my brother's death, while in the care of a nanny, Finley climbed upon a rather large wardrobe which fell over. He suffered a traumatic brain injury. While he is a delightful fellow, he is unable to care for himself, much less travel to America and marry."

"I'm so sorry," I said. And I truly was.

"Every now and then a researcher tackles just this kind of injury. They're making such strides in many fields that we remain ever hopeful that one day it will be Finley's turn."

"I very much hope that will happen for him."

"Thank you, Miss Fox. In the meantime, Finley lives in a world of dogs and ducks and chocolate-marshmallow ice cream. Because we live quietly and largely off the Internet, I'm afraid Finley is a favorite target of swindlers. It's all too easy to concoct a story about the cruel relatives from whom the impostor is estranged. I wish your friend the best, Miss Fox. I don't know whom she married, but I can assure you that it is not the Finley Brimble who was the sole survivor of the Brimble family that died in a horrific plane crash."

I thanked him profusely and hung up the phone. His number showed on my caller ID and I quickly entered it on my phone as a contact. I had no intention of calling him again, but I felt compelled to make a note of it.

Poor Roxie. I would have to tell Cyril. He should be the one to break it to her. But was his heart strong enough for this kind of news?

Every fiber of my being wanted to alert Roxie immediately. But how could I do that? She wouldn't believe it if the news came from me.

Of course, it explained why he didn't have the real Finley's vast wealth. How many other lies had he told her?

If he wasn't Finley, then who was he? Did Rebecca know his true identity? Was he the person she hired Ellis to find?

I shivered. Had Finley murdered Ellis because he knew the truth?

I jumped up and checked to be sure all the doors were locked. Cold to the bone, I heated water for a cup of hot, bracing tea and sat down at the table with my sketch pad. I had overlooked something so important. I had focused on the expensive clock that had been removed from the house. But the real question was: if Cyril was dead, who would benefit? I had to assume that Roxie, as his only child, would inherit his estate. How long would it be before Finley did away with her and claimed the money for himself?

I drew a rough map. From east to west, Color Me Read was farthest east. Then came Coralue's home; the professor's mansion, where I currently sat in the carriage house; Mags's home; and then Balthus's previous rental; and, beyond that, the hospital.

Finley had a great alibi for Manny's murder because he

had gone to the hospital to be with Roxie, but I didn't ask what time he got there. Did he have an alibi for the attack on Cyril?

I texted Cyril. *Can you find out from Roxie what time Finley arrived at the hospital the night you were attacked?*

It was a long shot at best. But it served two purposes. It would alert Cyril to possible danger from Finley and it just might change everything that I had been thinking.

I gazed at my map and inserted events. They made absolutely no sense. The rug had allegedly been seen at Balthus's former place, yet Manny's body had been found at Coralue's. And what was I to make of the coloring book at Mags's house?

If Finley had arrived at the hospital late, then that changed everything. But why had he murdered Manny? Had Manny caught him fleeing Cyril's house?

And why try to kill Balthus? Maybe Eric was right and there was more than one killer.

Balthus had been afraid of someone all along. What I didn't understand was why he didn't tell the police who had attacked him. That's what I would have done. I had to find him and coax him into telling me who had tried to murder him. I still had some of the pumpkin cookies. I could stop at the coffee shop and buy a couple of pumpkin lattes. Okay, it would be my second one of the day, but desperate times called for desperate measures.

I packed up the cookies, locked the door, and headed for the coffee shop.

While I walked, Cyril responded to my text. *It took him hours. Apparently he had car trouble.*

Unless Finley could turn up a mechanic to verify that, he didn't have an alibi! Armed with two steaming-hot lattes, I headed for Balthus's drab little apartment. When I rapped on his door, I heard voices. Rats! He wasn't likely to confide in me if someone else was present. Even worse, it was Roxie who swung the door open.

I forced a brave smile. "If I had known you would be here, I would have brought three lattes!"

In a dull tone she asked, "What do you want, Florrie?"

I stepped forward, forcing her to move back, out of the doorway so I could enter. "How are you feeling, Balthus?"

"Still a little shaky."

"I brought you some home-baked pumpkin chocolate-chip cookies and a latte. Everyone has been worried about you. It must have been terribly scary for you."

Balthus graciously accepted the cookies. "As you can see, Roxie brought me an espresso, one of my favorite indulgences."

As he spoke, I saw a movement in the tiny high window with bars in it. In fact, it looked like men's shoes. Was someone standing there listening?

Balthus continued speaking, unaware of the motion in the window behind him. "Espresso used to be the way I started every day." He gestured around his cramped room. "I'm afraid things have changed for me."

"Maybe you can get a job working as a chemist," said Roxie. "You do have a master's degree."

Balthus looked exhausted. He had drained his espresso, but certainly didn't appear alert. "It would beat working in fast food."

"I can help you spruce up your résumé," offered Roxie.

Balthus weaved and plopped down on his bed.

"Balthus!" screamed Roxie.

"Are you okay?" I asked.

He fell over on his side. "Don't . . . know . . . what's . . . wrong . . ."

I pulled out my phone and pressed 911. I looked at Roxie. I thought she liked Balthus. Had she been playing me for a fool? "What did you give him?"

"Me? Nothing. It's espresso!" She was wide-eyed.

I told the dispatcher where we were. "Are you sure?" I asked Roxie. "Maybe it was too strong for him?" I picked up the cup he drank from and sniffed it. It smelled like coffee but there was an acrid scent, too. "Did you also drink an espresso?"

Roxie gave me a cold look. "You know me better than that. I can't stand the stuff."

I studied her. She knelt on the floor and stroked Balthus's arm, telling him he would be okay. Was it remotely possible that I had misjudged her? But why would she want to kill Balthus? Was her horror an act when she had discovered him earlier? Had she expected him to be dead from the chloroform?

I knew that they had dated. Was he so in love with her that he refused to tell the police? But why would he accept and eat any food or drink from her if that was the case? Had she sweet-talked him into thinking she loved him, too? But why? Why would she want to kill him?

Tears ran down her cheeks.

I looked up at the window. The shoes were gone.

Chapter 40

Finley burst into the apartment. He flew to the bathroom and returned immediately.

"Roxie," he said gently but with undeniable urgency, "we have to go. The Uber is waiting for us. The ambulance will be here to help Balthus any minute." He tugged at her.

Roxie reluctantly got to her feet.

"What did you put in his espresso?" I demanded.

Finley strode to Balthus and patted his pockets. He grabbed Balthus's cell phone and hurriedly pushed Roxie out the door.

I followed them. "Finley!"

He turned to look at me. "I didn't expect you to be here. But I'm not sorry. You've been nothing but trouble."

I tried to dodge past him. He manhandled me and wrenched my purse off my shoulder.

He used both his hands to thrust me backward with such force that I landed on my back. I heard the door click shut and a key turn in the lock.

I jumped to my feet and grabbed the door handle. It didn't move. There was no knob to flick. I needed a key to open it from the inside. I jiggled it as hard as I could and glanced around in desperation for a key. "Balthus!" I screamed. "Where's the key? And then I smelled it.

The sour, rotten-egg smell of gas. Balthus and I were stuck. And Finley had our cell phones. I kicked at the door. It didn't budge. I tried running and hitting it with my shoulder like they do in the movies. Man, that hurt. My shoulder was still sore from running into the man who came to look at Balthus's Bose. Nevertheless, I tried again, but the door stayed solid.

I dashed back to the bathroom and found the culprit. Finley had cut a gas line feeding the hot water heater. Gas was pouring into the apartment.

I returned to Balthus, who moaned. "Balthus! Where's your key?" I patted his pockets but found nothing.

There was only one window. It was small, had bars on it, and it was high. Way higher than I could reach.

I gazed around for anything long. A broom handle? I rapidly looked through the room, desperate for anything that might be long enough to break the window.

The bathroom didn't yield anything helpful, either. And the gas was way too strong in there to stay long.

And then I saw it. Possibly my only hope. The shower curtain rod. It was old and metal, screwed in on both ends. Holding my breath, I jumped up to grab it and swung from it, raising my knees to let it hold my full weight.

I swung my body the best I could. I heard something crack, and the next thing I knew I was lying on my back, still holding on to the shower curtain rod. I rolled over on my belly. Did gas rise or fall? Stay low in a fire. But gas? I wasn't sure. I crawled out of the bathroom on my hands and knees, jerking the curtain rod along with me.

When I reached the bedroom, I tied a T-shirt over Balthus's nose very lightly, hoping that would filter the gas. Probably not. I tied a similar one over my nose anyway. Why hadn't the ambulance arrived?

I stepped onto the bed and over Balthus's body. The shower curtain rod almost reached the window. I would have to jump. Holding one end of the rod, I jumped and banged it at the pane.

I couldn't believe it. The stupid window held tight.

Hoping I wouldn't fall on Balthus, I tried again. I took a great leap, thrusting the shower curtain rod upward and at the window. It didn't budge. But I landed squarely on Balthus's torso.

There was no choice but to keep trying. I was beginning to feel very tired, no doubt the effects of the gas. I jumped again, doing my best to shatter the window.

The last thing I heard was the sound of glass breaking.

Chapter 41

Someone was carrying me. We were going up stairs. I could hear voices all around. I had to be dreaming.

"Florrie? Florrie? Can you hear me?"

It was the worst nightmare ever. I had no strength. All I could do was move the fingers on my right hand. The arms let go of me and something landed on my face. I tried to bat it away. Not Finley! I wasn't going to let him suffocate me. No!

I opened my mouth to scream but nothing came out. Dream paralysis? Was that what they called it?

"Come on, Florrie. Don't leave me." It was Eric's voice. Dreams were weird things. I desperately wanted this one to end.

I opened my eyes and looked around. Sirens blared and I realized I was in an ambulance.

Everything came flooding back. The gas. The espresso. The poison. Finley and Roxie. "Balthus," I uttered.

They rolled me into the emergency room and left me on a gurney in the hallway while nurses jumped to work. When someone removed the oxygen mask and tried to put something in my nose, I sat up and yanked it out.

A nurse objected but I saw Eric's face and he grinned.

"No, thank you," I said politely to the nurse.

She glanced at Eric. "Try to get her to wear the cannula."

"Fat chance," he said.

The nurse sighed and moved away just as Balthus was rushed by me on a gurney.

Eric took my hand into his. "Are you okay?"

"Will Balthus live?" I croaked.

Eric's smile vanished. "Hard to tell."

"Finley poisoned his espresso."

Eric's eyes widened. "Are you sure?"

"Get the cup."

Eric pulled out his cell phone and made a call instructing someone to collect the cups as evidence and bring them to the lab to be tested. While he was talking, he adjusted the back of the bed for me.

I waited until he hung up. "Could I have something to drink?"

Eric smiled at me as if I had done something brilliant. "Don't go anywhere."

I looked around for Balthus. They must have taken him into a room. I hoped he would make it.

Eric returned with ginger ale. "Little sips, okay?"

I nodded and gulped the cool liquid. "How come you were there?"

"I heard the call for an ambulance to Balthus's address. Lucky thing I went. Someone canceled the ambulance. When I pulled up, I heard the glass break in the window and could smell gas. I called for the ambulance. Luckily, they hadn't gone back yet. It took a few minutes to bust down the door, but we did it."

I didn't have to ask if he had carried me out. I just knew it. "Thank you. I hate that apartment. It's a firetrap."

While someone took my blood, I looked away and said to Eric, "Finley must have killed Manny. He wrapped him in a rug from Mags Delany's house and carried him to Balthus's place. But Balthus wasn't living there anymore. That was when Frieda saw the rug. I guess he went back in the night and moved it to Coralue's house."

"Mags Delany?"

"She lives near me. She put all her husband's stuff out on the driveway when he was out of town. He's missing a rug."

"And you think that's the rug Manny was rolled up in?"

"Don't you? Plus, I found a coloring book at Mags's house that Finley bought. Finley probably left it behind in his haste."

I gasped as another thought came to me.

"Are you all right? Should I call a nurse?" asked Eric.

"No, no, no. The night I found Manny's foot, someone had called 911 and said they were locked in the bookstore."

"Right . . ."

"Don't you see? All those cops responded. It was the middle of the night and they all came to the store instead of cruising, thus giving Finley time to bury Manny."

"Except he was in a hurry and didn't realize the foot was exposed."

"It must have been Finley who wrapped his scarf around the faux butler's neck. Do you think that was some kind of message?"

"What kind of message?" asked Eric.

"Don't mess with me? Or maybe it was some weird way of staking his claim. Oh, and there's a chance that Finley also murdered Ellis Willoughby. I thought the woman following Finley was having an affair with him, but when I ran into her, she had one of Ellis's business cards. Did I mention that Finley isn't who he claims to be?"

Eric stared at me like I had fallen from outer space. "I think we'd better pick up Finley and have a chat with him." Eric pulled out his phone again and made a call. When he was through, he asked, "So what's this about Finley not being who he claims?"

When I finished telling him about my discussion with Rupert Brimble, Eric received a call. He walked away from me, which I found highly annoying. I wanted to know what was going on.

He returned and said, "Roxie is fine. She's at home with Cyril and the guard. But no one knows where Finley is."

Chapter 42

"It's interesting," I said, "that Finley took Roxie to her dad's house but left me to die."

"He needs her," said Eric.

"That's a strong emotional attachment for someone who murders so casually."

"It's not an emotional attachment, Florrie. He wanted Cyril to die so Roxie would inherit Cyril's money."

"How long have you suspected Finley?" I asked.

"Technically since day one. The first thing I did was examine who would inherit upon Cyril's death. But then, when the other murders occurred, it seemed less likely that Finley was involved."

"You never said a word to me!" I protested.

"I didn't have anything on him, except a motive for Cyril's death."

At that moment, Veronica charged into the emergency room and headed for us. "Florrie!" she shrieked, drawing everyone's attention and some shushing from nurses.

She hugged me and wiped tears away. "I thought you were dying."

"She could have," muttered Eric.

"Who's minding the store?" I asked.

"Really? That's what worries you? Bob is there. Zsazsa and Goldblum are pitching in."

The doors blasted open again as Professor Maxwell and Jacquie strode in. Jacquie pointed at me and hurried over.

More hugs and questions.

"Where is her doctor?" Professor Maxwell asked Eric.

The two of them wandered off just as my parents arrived. I was thrilled to see everyone, but we were clogging the hallway.

"Mr. DuBois wanted to come with us, but I told him he'd better check on Peaches," said Jacquie.

"Poor Mr. DuBois, faced with the decision of actually having to leave the house or care for a cat!" I joked. "I'm not surprised that he chose Peaches. I believe he might be re-thinking his abhorrence of felines."

A nurse threw them all out into the waiting room, except for my mom.

I thought the chaos we caused probably helped them decide that I could go home. It was ten o'clock at night when Eric, Veronica, and I descended upon the carriage house with the two of them arguing about who would stay over.

Mr. DuBois opened the door, holding Peaches in his arm.

I tried not to grin but snickered a little inside.

"Straight to bed with you, young lady," he said sternly. "May I bring you a tray? I made chicken soup."

The truth was that I wanted to stay up and talk but I was exhausted. "Maybe a little bit of soup."

As I walked up the stairs, I could hear Mr. DuBois asking about my condition in a subdued voice.

I ate more soup than I expected but fell asleep before Mr. DuBois came to collect the tray.

★ ★ ★

The sun streamed through my windows on Halloween morning.

Veronica stretched in the daybed and complained, "Why don't you close those drapes at night?"

I hopped out of bed and closed the curtains for her. After a long, hot shower, I reconsidered the ghost costume I had intended to wear. Maybe not this year. Yesterday had been a close call. I dressed in a leopard-print dress, slid on a leopard-kitty ear hairband, and made up my face to look like a cat's. Carrying Peaches's costume, I went downstairs, where Mr. DuBois was serving mushroom-and–goat cheese omelets to the professor, Jacquie, and Eric.

They all spoke at once.

I assured everyone that I felt just fine and had every intention of working. After all, it was Halloween and a lot would be going on at the store.

"We'll all be there, then," said Jacquie. "Safety in numbers."

"What about Mr. DuBois?" I whispered.

"Thank you for considering my welfare, Miss Florrie, but the yard man will be coming today to rake and winterize the outdoor facilities."

"Finley knows I live in the carriage house," I said.

"I'm sure he also knows that it will be watched. Just like Cyril's house. Coffee or tea?"

"Tea, please. Any leads on Finley?" I asked.

Eric shook his head. "After he dropped Roxie off at her father's house, he took an Uber to the bus station, where he bought a ticket to Miami. Then he walked over to the train station and bought a ticket to Newark, New Jersey. We were able to check the bus but he wasn't on it. We weren't fast enough to catch the train before it arrived in New Jersey," said Eric.

"Is there any news on Balthus?" I asked.

"He's not out of the woods yet," said Eric. "As near as we can tell, Finley picked up the espresso for Roxie and doctored it with Cyril's Coumadin."

"Did you find Rebecca Porter?" I asked. "What's her deal?"

"There was no Rebecca Porter staying in that hotel. Either she checked in under a different name or she was there for another reason, visiting a friend, maybe."

"I can't believe that. Did you find her name among Ellis's records?"

"They're looking into it," said Eric.

"What's taking them so long?" asked Jacquie.

"Ellis was looking for a missing kid. That takes priority."

Jacquie blinked hard. "Of course. I pray they find the child."

I noticed that Maxwell didn't say anything but reached for Jacquie's hand and squeezed it.

"While you were incapacitated, we got some news on Harry," said Professor Maxwell.

"No kidding?"

"It seems that in the early 1800s two gentlemen dueled and one shot the other. But before he died, he placed a curse on the family of the other man."

"O'Malley and Bosworth!" I exclaimed. "Goldblum and Coralue told me about them."

"It seems that the survivor, O'Malley, ran into quite a bit of bad luck, which he attributed to the curse. So he paid a grave robber to detach Bosworth's head and take it where it would never find its way back, in the belief that would remove the curse."

"So Harry is Bosworth?" I frowned at him. "I thought Bosworth's name was Henry."

Jacquie smiled at me. "Harry is a nickname for Henry. You've heard of Prince Harry. His given name is actually Henry."

"I had no idea."

"Molly Butler, who found Harry in her uncle's attic, wasn't too happy to learn that a couple of her ancestors were grave robbers," said the professor. "But she was relieved to know that they didn't kill Harry."

"How did you figure all that out?" I asked.

"Goldblum and Coralue searched through old documents and archived letters and were able to piece it together."

"Eww. The grave robbers took his head home and just put it in the attic?" I was thoroughly grossed out. "What about the scrying mirror? Why was that there?"

"No one has figured that out for sure. There's speculation that it might have been on top of Harry's skull so that anyone opening the box would be horrified and close it. You have to remember, people were extremely superstitious. You never know what you might find in some of these old houses," he said.

"Kind of like Coralue's casket," I mused. "There's something spooky about opening a box and seeing yourself."

Jacquie shot me a look. "Remember the headless ghost we saw?"

"That was a fake. I saw the projector," I told her.

"But they based it on a ghost they regularly see there," she insisted.

I looked at Professor Maxwell, expecting him to say something snarky about ghosts. "We have applied to open Bosworth's casket and place Harry in it. And you'll never guess who happens to be a direct descendant."

"You?"

"Coralue Throckmorton!"

"As I recall," I said, "Bosworth had a bunch of kids. That will keep her busy for a while. She must have dozens of cousins."

"So, Maxwell, what do you think of Hilda's abilities and

life after death now?" Jacquie asked with an amused smile. "After all, there's no way she could have known about the foot in the rug or Ellis's death."

Maxwell grinned. "I believe I may have to do more research on the subject."

Jacquie snorted. "Maxwell, you can never give in. Oh wait!" She dramatically flung the back of her right hand against her forehead. "I'm having a vision. I see myself . . . in white . . ." Jacquie held out her left hand to show off an incredible diamond ring. "We're getting married!"

Chapter 43

The professor swept the towel off a bottle of champagne and Mr. DuBois hurried to my kitchen for glasses.

The sound of the champagne cork popping brought Veronica running down the stairs. "Was someone shot?"

We all laughed. In spite of all the murders, it was a celebratory, happy breakfast.

Afterward, I slid a lion's mane onto Peaches and we struck out for Color Me Read on foot, surrounded by a posse.

Eric had to go to work but promised he would be close to the bookstore most of the day.

Zsazsa and Goldblum were waiting outside the bookstore, applauding as we walked up. It was like a party. The bookstore would be full of friends.

A local newspaper had run the story with Finley's photo in the morning edition. That brought an avalanche of customers. For the most part, I didn't worry about Finley. I had to admit, though, that when someone in a mask entered the store, my breath caught in my throat.

Hilda Rattenhorst dropped by in the afternoon. She entered with a flourish, wearing a deep purple dress and a black cape. "Florrie!" she cried. "I'm so relieved to see you well. I am truly sorry, my dear."

"You have nothing to be sorry about," I assured her.

"But I do. I knew about the rug. I knew about the second body. But I wasn't able to piece anything together to protect you."

"I guess you can't foresee everything," I said cheerily.

She leaned toward me. "My phone has been ringing off the hook. Police are calling me. People are phoning to see if I can help them find someone. Other people want me to connect with their loved ones who have passed. It's crazy! This afternoon, I'm being flown to New York City, all expenses paid, to be on a TV show tonight!"

"That's exciting!"

"I'm so nervous that I'm a wreck!"

People had begun to cluster around her, peppering her with requests. She shuffled off to hold court in the parlor. Word spread quickly by social media, especially now that the police were on the trail of the prime suspect in the murder of the man in the rug.

While Hilda was there, her niece, Kaya, came to the store. "I read about what happened. I'm glad you're okay. I wanted you to know that I'm going back to nursing school. I lost my path for a little while, but that's what I was meant to do."

"Any word on the Boyles' missing son?" I asked.

"Not that I've heard. Of course, now that I don't work there anymore, I don't hear the scuttlebutt." She smiled at me and joined Hilda's admirers in the parlor.

I was astonished to see Cyril show up just as the professor ambled down the stairs.

"You look great!" I said to Cyril.

"I'm feeling like my old self again. Very foolish, of course. I should have known something wasn't right with Finley."

"He fooled a lot of people. But didn't it worry you that he

was coming to you for money? Why didn't you tell Roxie? I would want to know information like that about my husband."

His eyes met mine. "I was afraid of losing her. All I ever wanted was for her to be happy."

"You're everything to her, Cyril. There's nothing you could do to lose Roxie. She might be upset initially—"

Cyril's laugh sounded like a bark. "I thought you knew Roxie. In a contest between Finley and me, he would have won every time." He closed his eyes for a moment. "I'm just so grateful that you survived. I would never have forgiven myself for closing my eyes to Finley's shortcomings. Though nothing like this ever crossed my mind."

"Really? You didn't call Ellis to investigate Finley?"

"No. I honestly did not. I gather Finley must have come to his attention in some way, but I had nothing to do with it."

"Where's your guard? Finley's still out there, you know."

"He's watching the house. I'm not too worried. If Finley has any sense, he has left town. Besides, killing me won't help him anymore. Roxie is at the lawyer's office right now changing her will and filing for divorce." He waved and leaped up the stairs as though he had never suffered a vicious attack.

During my lunch break, I walked over to the hospital to see Balthus. Roxie was in his room when I entered.

I was pleased to see him sitting up and lucid. "How do you feel?"

"A little rough, but I'm doing much better. They're running some tests. I'm hoping to go home this afternoon."

My breath caught in my throat. Not to that horrible apartment!

Roxie smiled at him. "He's going to stay in my guest room until he's back up on his feet. It's small, but—"

"It's a vast improvement," said Balthus. "I could never stay in that other place again."

I didn't blame him one bit.

"You look pretty good, Florrie," said Balthus.

"I didn't swallow an overdose of Coumadin. We were both lucky that we didn't inhale the gas for long."

"Long enough," said Balthus.

"Let me guess," I said. "You were afraid of Finley all along."

Balthus paled and sank back against his pillow. He whispered, "I still am."

Roxie motioned to me to follow her out of the room. "I owe you an apology."

"No, you don't."

"But I do. I was so blind when it came to Finley. He's a psychopath and I believed everything he said."

"Don't be too hard on yourself. He fooled a lot of people. At least he took you home and didn't leave you there to die with Balthus and me."

"That doesn't make up for anything. Ugh." She covered her eyes with her hands. "I slept in the same bed with that man and I don't even know who he is!"

She was going to have a hard time working through this.

"I was so misguided. I was angry with all the wrong people. With you and my dad, especially. I should have realized that you would never let me down. Can you ever forgive me?"

"Don't be silly. There's nothing to forgive." I gave her a big hug and left, stopping by a café to buy a take-out sandwich for lunch.

I had my back to the street when someone came up beside me and said, "I'm so sorry."

"Rebecca Porter!"

"Call me Becky." She tilted her head a little and looked me in the eyes. "I read about what happened to you and I feel just awful."

"Were you having an affair with Finley?" I asked.

"You thought I had a thing for him? That's a hoot! I guess it's not surprising. A lot of women chase him." She shook her head. "I'm his sister."

Initially, I didn't believe her. But as I took in her features, I realized that she had the same chin and sharp nose I had drawn on Finley. Her eyes were different from his, though. "But you were following him. Stalking him."

She raised one eyebrow but nodded in agreement. "I guess you could say that."

"Why? Why wouldn't you hug him and say hi?"

She snorted. "I haven't hugged Tommy in ten years, probably more. Most of the time we don't know where he is. Now and again, my mom or I get a call from someone Tommy has swindled."

"What?"

"We try to ignore those calls. We live in dread of them. And then for a period of years, no one called. We began to wonder if he had died, but I happened to see a picture in a magazine that was clearly Tommy."

"The travel magazine with the photo of him outside a restaurant."

"Exactly. I called a private investigator in Washington—"

"Ellis Willoughby the Fourth."

"Right. He told me Tommy was going by the name Finley Brimble. I flew out here and hung around Georgetown, hoping to see Tommy. The next thing I knew, I couldn't reach Ellis, and then it was all over the newspapers that his body had been found. Mom and I were afraid of the worst, but Tommy is a con artist, not a killer. And with a private investigator, it could be any of his clients who murdered him."

"But you're afraid of Tommy," I said.

"I am. In a normal situation, I would have been invited to

the wedding. I would have met Roxie, who seems really nice. But that would have blown his cover. I had to be careful. I didn't know how he would respond to my presence here."

"You went to dinner with him," I pointed out.

"And was promptly told to leave town. I lied and said I was here on business. My mom and I own a store and we travel occasionally on buying trips."

"Is your dad alive?"

Becky took a deep breath. "We don't know. My mom says Tommy got his dishonest ways from our dad. But I'm not so sure that can be passed down genetically. We kids were better off when Dad left. He drank the grocery money and couldn't hold a job. We tiptoed around, trying not to set off his anger. Still, I Google him sometimes. Porter's a pretty common name. But I figure he'll pop up if he died or did something that landed him in jail."

"I'm sorry," I said softly.

"Don't be. Mom and I have a good life now. Deep down, though, we're always waiting for the next phone call about a disaster Tommy has caused for someone."

I looked at the huge window in the front of the shop. "You know he's out there. They didn't catch him."

"My best guess is that he's already on a train or a flight, planning his next evil game."

I had to get back to the store. "They're blocking off our street for a Halloween party tonight. I hope you'll come. I'm sure Roxie will be there. You two have a lot to talk about."

Becky smiled. "I'd like that. Thanks."

When I walked into Color Me Read, Hilda had left. Goldblum, Veronica, and Jacquie were chatting at the check-out desk.

"I'm glad to catch you all together," I said. "No matter whether we believe in ghosts or not, I think we can all agree that Harry cannot move himself."

I saw some smirks and grins. "Okay, which one of you was moving him?"

Jacquie confessed, "I was trying to spook Maxwell. It drives me crazy that he's so adamant that ghosts can't exist. So when I saw Harry in his office, I would move him."

Goldblum guffawed. "I was moving Harry for the same reason!"

Veronica avoided my eyes. "I might have moved him a few times to spook Bob."

We all laughed. No harm done. It was all in good Halloween fun.

Chapter 44

By eight o'clock that evening, not a single piece of chocolate or candy remained at the store. Veronica dressed as Lady Gaga; Bob dressed as Frodo from *The Hobbit*; and I did our usual walk-through to be sure no customers remained. I gently plucked Peaches out of her perch in the display window and put on her harness. We turned on the alarm, locked up, and walked toward the mansion. Enterprising food trucks lined the street, selling everything from sodas to tacos. Barricades blocked off traffic.

Julie, Bob's new girlfriend, met us there, wearing a gauzy blue dress and pointed elf ears like those of the elves in *The Hobbit*. They paired up and went their own way.

As Coralue had promised, vampires roamed on her lawn, handing out hot apple cider and candy. Spooky music drifted from her house. Excited children squealed but dared to get close to the live vampires in their quest for candy.

Coralue watched from her front porch in an 1800s-style, mauvy-pink ballgown adorned with ivory lace. She wore what I assumed was a white wig and had applied some kind of white makeup to her face and hands. "Florrie!" she called.

I carried Peaches lest someone in the crazy crowd accidentally step on her. "Natalia?" I guessed.

"Exactly! That poor girl. Did you hear that I'm related to Bosworth? I feel a bit like the enemy living in this house."

"At least you don't have to fear the curse," I joked.

"I always thought Natalia's story was an intriguing tale. But now so much of it is turning out to be true. It's rather disturbing."

I steered her away from the sad story. "You make a fine Natalia. Are some of these little goblins your grandchildren?"

"Yes! They're having a grand time. Even Hayes is here somewhere enjoying himself." She leaned toward me and petted Peaches. "Have they caught Finley yet?"

"Not that I'm aware of."

"To think you and Balthus could have been his victims, too. It shakes me to the core. And what on earth possessed Finley to bury Manny in my yard?"

"I don't know. I think he probably killed Manny up the street at or near Mags's house."

"I'm glad it's over," she said.

I walked away wondering if Finley had fled, as Cyril and Becky seemed to think. There was nothing for him here anymore. He couldn't go home. By now his friends must have heard the truth and wouldn't allow him to bunk with them. Maybe he *had* left to start anew elsewhere.

As I gazed around for Veronica, my phone rang.

It was Eric. "Just checking on you. How are you feeling?"

"I'm great. Our street is wild."

"So I've heard. I'll be out there in a few hours. I wanted you to know that the Boyles are in custody."

"For Ellis's murder?" I gasped.

"For kidnapping and hiding Mr. Boyle's kid. The boy has been with Boyle's sister at the Order of the Moon."

"So Ellis was onto them."

"That's who he feared. They have a reputation for being violent. The boy is fine physically. His mom is already here with him. Remember the weird cylinder that you identified as a chime?"

"Sure."

"We found an identical one in Finley's car. It had rolled under a seat. Great evidence that Finley transported Ellis's body out to Rock Creek in his car after killing him. Good sleuthing, Florrie!"

I was laughing and said good-bye in a hurry when I saw Finley's sister, Becky. Waving to her, I called. "Have you seen Roxie yet?"

"I don't think so. Is she wearing a costume?"

"Not the last time I saw her. But she could have changed clothes since then."

We walked for a bit, passing creatures of every imaginable variety among the witches and ghosts. A lion was holding hands with Dorothy from *The Wizard of Oz*, and as they came closer, it dawned on me that they were Balthus and Roxie. I introduced them to Becky, and both women began to cry.

I excused myself because I really had to get Peaches home. A cat could take only so much partying!

Along the driveway to the carriage house, it was still and quiet, but I could hear the merriment going on in the street. I let myself in and opened a can of salmon cat food for Peaches. She snarfed it like she was starved, then went off to groom herself.

I checked upstairs, just to be sure I wasn't leaving her there with Finley. But all was well.

After double-checking that the door was properly locked, I made my way around the Maxwell mansion to the front. Mr. DuBois was handing out candy to children, while the professor and Jacquie, dressed as Gomez and Morticia Addams, chatted with Becky, Roxie, and Balthus.

"Love the costumes!" I said to the professor and Jacquie.

Jacquie shook her head. "I tried and tried to get Mr. DuBois to wear a costume but he wasn't having it."

"I wasn't sure I wanted to wear one," Roxie said. "Life has been sufficiently horrific without having to pretend."

"I'm glad to see you up and about, Balthus." I smiled at him.

"Thanks, Florrie. I'm feeling much better now."

"How's Mr. DuBois doing with your resident ghosts?" I asked Jacquie.

Mr. DuBois must have overheard me. "I have informed Maxwell that I will resign my post if he does not tell me who the ghosts are."

"Say what you will about Hilda's prognostications. I can't account for them. But ghosts do not exist," Maxwell protested. "They're nothing more than a story. For all we know, these people might not have existed at all. Someone along the line made up that ridiculous story. I, for one, shall not continue it."

"Maxwell," said Jacquie in a most reproving tone.

The professor raised her hand and kissed it Gomez Addams style. "Fine. A butler by the name of Grover Throop worked here for the Maxwells and fell in love with a society lady named Natalia O'Malley."

Mr. DuBois's eyes widened. He appeared aghast, as if someone had slapped him. "That's improper on so many levels," he sputtered. "And I had thought him a decent ghost."

"He's not telling you everything," said Jacquie. "Natalia's husband was a dreadful man who had lost all his money. To provide for his daughter, Natalia's father gave her gold coins. But she knew her brother or husband would find them if they were in her house, so she entrusted them to her beloved Mr. Throop.

But Natalia's brother and husband got wind of her love for Mr. Throop"—she glanced at Maxwell—"and they shot Mr. Throop dead right here where we are standing."

Mr. DuBois stepped back, horrified.

"Don't look so troubled, DuBois," said Maxwell. "It's a fable. Nothing more. Just a tale woven and embellished over two hundred years. The whole point is that they shot and killed the only person who knew where the gold was. It's simply a tale of caution."

Jacquie looked up at the mansion. "If there were gold coins, they would have to be here. Mr. Throop would have hidden them somewhere in this house."

"Which only proves that it's all nonsense," said Professor Maxwell. "If they were hidden here, someone would have found them by now. The kitchen has been renovated several times, as have the baths."

"Maxwell," said Jacquie, "it's a good thing you weren't the one hiding them. Have you no imagination? They wouldn't be in the kitchen. You're a fan of history. You must be aware that people have stashed coins in clothing and belts so they could flee with them. In one of my books, the heroine sewed coins into the hem of her skirt."

Mr. DuBois listened silently. He swallowed hard and said, "It's true. It's all true."

Chapter 45

"Nonsense," said the Professor most emphatically.

"Maxwell," said Mr. DuBois, "if a butler was discovered with gold coins stashed in his quarters, say under a floorboard or in a box, he would have been sacked immediately. I seriously doubt that the Maxwells who were alive at that time would have permitted those idiots, O'Malley and Ivan, to search his quarters, but if you or Miss Jacqueline thought I might have hidden gold somewhere, wouldn't you look for it?"

"Jacquie would," he said, giving her a squeeze.

"You make it sound like I'm greedy." She chewed her upper lip. "But I admit I would have searched for it. I want to search for it now!"

Mr. DuBois smiled. "There is a dress in the attic that I have wondered about. Maxwell, your mother told me to ask your sister if she wanted it. I believe her exact words were, 'Are you serious? You think I would wear something like *that*?' It was very old. So I wrapped it in muslin, placed it in a preservation box, and stashed it in a trunk upstairs. I remember thinking how difficult it must have been for women to wear such heavy dresses."

Jacquie's eyes widened.

Professor Maxwell sighed. "I won't get any peace around here until you find that dress."

Mr. DuBois handed him the bowl of candy and marched into the mansion.

The rest of us followed him up the stairs. Jacquie had a little trouble with her tight Morticia gown. Nevertheless, we followed him up to another floor, where Balthus gave up. The rest of us trooped higher and into an attic.

It was unfinished and chock-full of antiques. Three sizable windows across the front of the house would have let in daylight had it not been night. There were cupboards and filing cabinets and chairs that had gone out of vogue. And at one end were stacks of ancient trunks. On top of them were leather suitcases, hatboxes, and one giant birdcage.

Mr. DuBois methodically removed an ancient picnic basket, two hatboxes, and four suitcases from the top of a trunk. He eagerly opened it. Inside was a sealed box. "I never understood why this was so heavy." He gingerly lifted out a fragile dress of robin's-egg blue. It was covered with a long vest of sorts in Prussian blue. The short sleeves were made of a gold lace, which also adorned the bustline and the hemline.

Jacquie whispered, "It's beautiful!" While Mr. DuBois held it up, Jacquie ran her fingers over the neckline and sleeves.

"Nothing," she said. "I was so hopeful." But then she knelt and touched the hemline. "I can feel coins!" She gently lifted it to show the reverse side.

I leaned over her shoulder to see. The stitching was perfect.

Balthus entered the attic and cleared his throat. He looked terrified.

Someone in a Darth Vader mask stood behind him.

Jacquie quickly dropped the hem and motioned to

Mr. DuBois to close the trunk. I was fairly sure that, under normal circumstances, he would have sealed the box again but there was something about the man in the mask . . .

He didn't wear a cape like Darth Vader. In fact, he wore a scarf draped over his sweater. It was tan-and-chocolate-brown plaid with a fine line of cranberry mixed in. My heart skipped a beat.

"Too bad Mr. DuBois was wrong," Jacquie said way too cheerfully. "Let's return to the fun!"

"He's not the only one who was wrong." Darth Vader removed his mask. It was Finley.

Roxie screamed.

I reached into my pocket and held down the side buttons on my cell phone. I didn't dare take it out. I could only hope it would alert someone.

"Becky. I warned you about interfering in my life," said Finley.

"You can drop the British accent, Tommy," she said. "They know."

"Tell her, Balthus," said Finley. "Tell her what you did to Cyril."

"I'm in love with you, Roxie," said Balthus. "I always have been."

Roxie flushed and Finley jabbed Balthus in the back. "Tell her the truth! They have it all wrong. It was Balthus who tried to murder Cyril."

"What?" cried Roxie. "Is that true?"

"That wasn't me," moaned Balthus. "I'm very fond of Cyril. I would never harm him." He gazed at her. "I couldn't stand how Finley treated you. Everyone thought he was such a great guy. He's a psychopath, Roxie. He doesn't care about you."

Roxie seemed confused. "Finley! Tell me the truth. Who slit my father's throat?"

"It was Balthus. He also killed Manny."

"That's not true!" yelled Balthus. "You left his body rolled in a rug at my old house to make it look like I murdered him. You idiot! Didn't you know that I had moved?"

In the most chilling voice I had ever heard, Finley said, "You know I love you, Roxie. We've had a few bumps in the road, but now they're trying to blame everything on me when it was Balthus. It was all Balthus."

"Don't believe him, Roxie. He left a coloring book at Mags Delaney's house when he stole a rug from her driveway," I said.

Roxie spoke in a heart-broken voice, "That's why it took you so long to get to the hospital. You told me the car wouldn't start and you had to wait for someone to come and jump it." She shook her head at him. "Our entire marriage was a lie. How could you do that to me?"

Not counting Roxie, who might not be dependable in this situation, there were five of us. We ought to be able to subdue Finley. But how?

I tried to buy time. "Why did you have the coloring book with you anyway?"

"Roxie asked me to bring some things to the hospital. I thought it might give her something to do. But the wind caught it and blew it away. See, Roxie? I love you. You're always on my mind. You can't believe their lies."

Balthus spoke softly. "I was horrified when Hilda said she saw a foot in a rug in my old doorway. I knew that couldn't be true. But it made me nervous, so I drove over in the middle of the night. Manny was rolled up in a rug in my old doorway, just like Hilda said. I panicked. I knew they would blame it on me. I placed him in the trunk of my car, planning to take him down to the canal and throw him in, but when I arrived, a bunch of kids were hanging around down there." His voice grew shrill. "I was driving around with a corpse in the car! What if a cop stopped me? What if someone ran into me from behind and called the cops? I left him in the trunk overnight. I was in a complete meltdown. I had to get rid of the body. The next night, I was driving around, thinking I would just ditch him in some bushes when I saw the perfect thing. A coffin. Even better, the soil underneath it was soft, so I buried him and took off as fast as I could."

"Did you fake a call to the police?" I asked.

"Yes. I wanted to distract them. But I didn't murder anyone. You have to believe me. Finley's scarf was tangled in the rug, so I hung it on the fake butler as a message to Finley that I knew what he had done."

That rang true to me.

"You are not an accomplished liar, Balthus," said Finley.

Did he have a gun? He still stood behind Balthus, who appeared to be afraid to move. I couldn't see if Finley had a weapon. Trying not to be obvious, I scanned the attic for anything that might work as a weapon.

Mr. DuBois motioned behind me ever so slightly with his head. I inched backward toward the wall and groped it.

I touched cold metal. It curved like a sickle. Hoping I wouldn't give myself away, I attempted to remove it from the wall. It came off easier than I would have expected. I held a two-foot-long curved blade mounted on a wooden handle that was probably meant for farming a century ago. Was DuBois kidding? My heart beat far too rapidly. I had no choice. There wasn't anything else. I held it by my side, hoping Finley would not notice and that an opportunity might arise for me to launch myself at him.

"Roxie," said Finley, "can't you see that I need your help? Everyone is against me. You're the only person who believed in me. It was Balthus who did these terrible things."

Roxie stepped toward the windows and away from me. I was shocked by her courage. "Why did you take me home yesterday?"

"Because I love you. You know that's true. I couldn't leave you there to die. That should prove my love for you."

Finley left a quivering Balthus and slowly walked toward Roxie. The gun he held flashed under the light. "If you will help me, together we can straighten all this out and be happy again."

Mr. DuBois grabbed the sickle from me and flung it like a boomerang. The point on the end hit Finley squarely in the abdomen. It hung for a moment where it had pierced him.

The gun fell out of his hand. I ran for it and kicked it out of Finley's reach. Blood had begun to seep through his clothing and he fell to the floor.

I picked up the gun and called 911 with trembling fingers.

Roxie didn't go to comfort Finley. She stood over him, watching him bleed out.

Only Becky knelt by him and held his hand. "Tommy. What have you done?" she moaned.

But Balthus had found his moxie. "Looks like it's your turn to tell the truth, Finley. You're the one who murdered Manny and stuck him in my doorway."

Finley gave him a dark look. "Manny would be alive today if you hadn't sent him to kill me."

I had never been so glad to see November first. No more costumes. No more being on the lookout for Finley.

I was horrified for Roxie. The two men she thought had loved her only loved her father's money. She almost lost the only close relative she had on earth, all because she married the wrong man.

I left Peaches at home that day. If experience was a guide,

people would pile into the bookstore just to look around. Nothing had happened there, but murder seemed to attract attention like a wreck on the highway.

Eric was waiting at the front door to Color Me Read. I didn't have to ask if he had been up all night. As adorable as he was, he looked like he was about to keel over from exhaustion.

"Are you going home to sleep?" I asked, unlocking the door.

He followed me inside. "Yeah, I'm beat."

"Then I won't offer you any coffee."

He nodded. "I thought you'd like to know about Finley. They operated on him last night. The next forty-eight hours are crucial, but the doctors are optimistic. His sister, Becky, has been by his side since the surgery. Pretty amazing, given what he has put her through over the years. She tells me she's going to try to get him to take a plea deal. Privately, she said she was actually relieved because he wasn't dead, but he wouldn't be running around conning and terrorizing people anymore if he is in prison."

"It must be awful to know a relative is doing that. What about Balthus?"

"That's going to be interesting. It appears that Balthus hired Manny to kill Finley. With Finley out of the way, Balthus could marry Roxie, the woman he loves, and have access to her daddy's wallet."

"Basically stepping into Finley's shoes."

"Except that he's not a psychopath. But we found some interesting paraphernalia in his apartment. Specifically, the material needed to make chloroform. He has confessed that no one attacked him the first time he went to the hospital. He passed out from the chloroform he was trying to make. You were right about the bottle belonging to Hilda. He was planning to fill it with chloroform and use it to murder Finley, thus pinning the blame on Hilda. But chloroform is notoriously unstable stuff, and he knocked himself out. His head hit the bed frame as he fell, hence the bleeding. And he dropped the bottle, which shattered on the concrete floor."

"If Balthus made the chloroform . . . are you saying he accidentally made himself sick?"

"Exactly. Of course, we have your testimony about the gas. There's no question that Finley attempted to kill him, but it appears Balthus nearly did himself in with the chloroform he was making."

"That's why he was so afraid. He hired Manny to kill Finley, but it didn't work because Finley killed Manny instead. Balthus isn't a hands-on kind of guy. He feared Finley. After all, now Finley knew that Balthus had tried to have him murdered! Balthus needed to get rid of Finley, so he made his own chloroform, intending to use it on Finley! It all fits together."

Eric took a deep breath. "Hard to believe all that was happening under our noses. But here's the thing. Even though the de Gama business is in big trouble, his family isn't broke. They made enough investments to keep themselves nicely afloat. Mommy and Daddy are flying in to hire a fancy attorney."

"Then why was Balthus living like that?"

"He didn't want them to know he had wasted his entire trust fund."

I saw what Eric was getting at. "A good lawyer could get him off of a murder-for-hire charge because the only real witness, Manny, is gone. Finley is an unreliable witness because he'll say anything to make himself look good. So there's really no proof that's what happened?"

"Our buddy, Balthus, may walk."

"What about Ellis? Did Finley murder him, too? Or was that the Boyles?"

"Finley murdered Ellis. His sister, Becky, had hired Ellis to find him. Finley had to get rid of Ellis, who would have revealed his true identity to Cyril and Roxie. The jig would be up! And now I'm going home to fall into bed." He leaned over to give me a kiss and left immediately.

I was still reeling from that news when I took down the scrying mirror and carried it up to the professor's office. He could decide what to do with it.

When I returned to the checkout desk, Glen, our delivery guy, was carrying in eight boxes.

"It's good to see you around again. Are you back at work full time?" I asked.

"That was something, huh? I was bitten by a cobra. Can you believe that? A cobra! Some idiot kid shipped it to another idiot kid and it managed to wiggle out of the box while it was in my delivery van. I'm lucky I lived to tell about it."

"Unbelievable. Is it legal to ship a dangerous snake like that?"

"There are some special companies that ship them in accordance with a specific protocol. They're usually drugged so they'll sleep through the trip. But these two wise guys thought it was okay to stick a snake in a box and ship it!" He leaned toward me. "Still got that skull?"

"Actually, it was identified and is being returned to the mausoleum where it belongs."

"I hope I never have another shipment like that one!"

I hoped not, either. Glen left and I walked outside for a breath of fresh air. It was nippy but the sun was shining. Best of all, now that it was November, the ghost craze in town would fade away.

A large van blocked my view. On the side was written *Harry's Plumbing*. A man opened both doors in the back. He grabbed some equipment and saw me when he turned around. "Good morning! I hope the noise hasn't been bothering you."

"Noise?"

"Those old plumbing systems can be cranky. Sometimes it sounds like somebody's dying in there. But I'll have it all fixed by the end of the day." He nodded at me and entered the building next door.

So Harry hadn't been screaming, after all. I wasn't going to tell. After all, maybe it wasn't the plumbing that howled!

RECIPES

Russian Tea

If you are a fan of tea but don't care for cinnamon or cloves, it's very refreshing just to combine the tea with sugar, orange juice, and lemon.

4 cups water
3 tea bags, black tea
½ cup granulated sugar
1 cup orange juice
3 tablespoons fresh lemon juice
2 cinnamon sticks
2 cloves
1 orange

Pour the water into a medium pot. Add the tea bags, sugar, orange juice, lemon juice, cinnamon sticks, and cloves. Bring to a boil, then lower the heat and simmer for ten minutes. Slice the orange and use as a garnish.

Mr. DuBois's Cinnamon-Apple Pancakes

Makes about 7 to 10 five-inch pancakes. I made these by mistake once and they were so good I had to re-create them. I have tried grating the apples, as well as slicing them, but they're not the same. Too thin and they disappear, too thick and they don't cook through. You can probably achieve the same effect by adding apples as described here to your own favorite pancake batter. You can also make these the day before. Just wrap aluminum foil over the top of the bowl and refrigerate until you're ready to use the batter. Or make half one day and the other half the next morning!

3 tablespoons melted butter
1 cup milk
1 cup flour
2 tablespoons granulated sugar
½ teaspoon ground cinnamon
¾ teaspoon baking powder
½ teaspoon salt
1 egg
1 teaspoon vanilla
1 apple
Oil for pan (canola or corn oil)

Melt the butter. In a large bowl, mix together the milk, flour, sugar, cinnamon, baking powder, salt, egg, and vanilla. Add the melted butter and stir. Lumps are okay. Peel the apple and use the vegetable peeler to slice it very thin. Do not include the core. Add the apple slices directly to the batter and turn to coat them. Heat a large pan or griddle. Add oil. Using a large cooking spoon, ladle the pancake batter onto the pan. When the bottom side is light brown, flip and cook the top side. Add more oil and adjust the heat as necessary. Serve with maple syrup.

Pumpkin Cupcakes

Makes 12 regular-size cupcakes.

2 eggs
½ cup sugar
½ cup dark brown sugar
1½ cups flour
1 teaspoon baking powder
1 teaspoon baking soda
½ teaspoon pink sea salt
1 teaspoon ground cinnamon
¼ teaspoon nutmeg
Pinch of cloves
½ cup vegetable oil
1 cup mashed pumpkin
¾ teaspoon vanilla

Preheat oven to 350° F. Place cupcake liners in wells of cupcake pan.

Crack the eggs into the bowl of a mixer. Add sugar and dark brown sugar. Beat on slow for several minutes, until thick. In the meantime, place the flour, baking powder, baking soda, sea salt, cinnamon, nutmeg, and cloves in a bowl and stir well with a fork to combine.

While the mixer is running, slowly add the oil. When it is incorporated, on low speed, slowly spoon in the flour mixture. Add the pumpkin and vanilla and mix to combine. Divide among the cupcake liners, filling each cup three-quarters full.

Bake 20 minutes or until a cake tester comes out clean. Test two cupcakes to be sure they are done. The cupcake papers should be pulling away from pan.

For the Cream Cheese Frosting
12 tablespoons unsalted butter, softened
8 ounces cream cheese, softened
2 teaspoons vanilla
4 cups powdered sugar (more if needed)

Place the butter, cream cheese, and vanilla in a mixer and set on high speed. Lower the speed and gradually add the powdered sugar. Return to the high setting and beat for 10 minutes. (You can beat it for a shorter time, but it's creamier if you let it beat longer.)

French Apple Cake

I love this cake! It's not overly sweet but so delicious. If you don't have a springform pan, you can make it with a cake pan. No apple cider? Use apple juice. Or you can omit the 1 cup of liquid and just use the 3 tablespoons. It won't be as moist, but it will still be delightful. Instead of apple cider, I have also used raspberry and peach liqueur, which was very good.

9-inch springform pan or 9-inch cake pan
1 cup plus 3 tablespoons apple cider
1 stick (8 tablespoons) unsalted butter
2 eggs
2 firm apples (I use Fuji)
1 cup flour
1 teaspoon baking powder
¼ teaspoon pink salt
⅔ cup sugar + 1 tablespoon
1 teaspoon vanilla

Bring butter and eggs to room temperature. Pour 1 cup apple cider into a small pot and simmer uncovered until it reduces to about ½ cup. Set aside to cool.

Preheat oven to 350 and grease a 9-inch springform pan. If using a cake pan, place parchment paper on the bottom and grease the sides well with butter.

Peel, core, and chop the apples. Place flour, baking powder, and salt in a bowl and mix well with a fork or small whisk. In mixing bowl, beat the butter with the ⅔ cup sugar until well blended, about 3 minutes. Add the eggs one at a time and beat. Add the flour mixture slowly, mixing until the batter is nicely smooth. Add the vanilla and 3 tablespoons apple cider and mix in. The batter will be quite thick. Pour the chopped apples into the batter and fold until the apples are coated. Pour into the baking pan and spread. Sprinkle 1 tablespoon of sugar over the top. Bake for 38–40 minutes.

If using a springform pan, unlatch and remove the outer band. If using a cake pan, turn it out onto a plate and then turn it over onto a rack to cool.

When cool, slowly pour the reduced apple cider over it. Serve with sweetened whipped cream.

For the Sweetened Whipped Cream
1 cup heavy cream
⅓ cup powdered sugar
1 teaspoon vanilla

Beat the heavy cream until it begins to take shape. Add the powdered sugar and vanilla and continue to beat until the cream holds a firm shape.

Read on for a special sneak preview of the next Pen & Ink mystery from Krista Davis . . .

A Colorful Scheme

Forthcoming from Kensington Publishing Corp. in Fall 2022

Chapter 1

I thought someone had been following me so when Mr. DuBois shouted and banged on the door of the carriage house, I was momentarily alarmed. I peeked out the window to be certain it was him. When I opened the door, he barged in and demanded, "Is Miss Jacqueline here?" He panted as if he couldn't catch his breath.

It was most uncharacteristic of him. Mr. DuBois had been trained as a proper butler. Pounding on doors and shouting ranked right up there with the most egregious sins in his mind. But that only made his question and behavior more worrisome.

My sister, Veronica, who was acting as a wedding coordinator of sorts, leaped out of her chair, spilling coffee on her bathrobe. She reminded me of our mother when she took a moment to catch her breath and then with forced composure asked sweetly, "Did you lose our bride?"

Mr. DuBois, who watched far too much true crime TV and was prone to seeing murder everywhere, closed the door behind him. "She is not in the mansion. I have searched from the basement to the attic. She is simply gone."

I froze for a moment. Was she being followed, too? "When is the last time anyone saw her?" I asked.

Veronica nodded at me, her head bobbing with too much vigor thus exposing her true level of anxiety. "Excellent, Florrie!"

"I last saw her yesterday evening around nine, I believe. I asked if they wanted anything before I retired for the night."

Elderly Mr. Dubois was a petite man, always impeccable. He had worked as the butler for the Maxwell family for decades. John Maxwell, adventurer, professor, and heir to the Maxwell fortune happened to be my boss, which was how I came to reside in the small carriage house behind the mansion. He owned the Color Me Read bookstore but had neither the time nor the inclination to manage it and relied on me to do it all from payroll, to selecting stock, hiring, and paying the bills. At night and on my days off, I indulged my artistic side by drawing adult coloring books.

"I trust you have seen the professor this morning?" I asked.

At that moment, there was a brisk knock at the door. Mr. DuBois opened it and John Maxwell strode in. Tall and dignified, he was the type of man who commanded attention. Despite his age, he remained decidedly handsome. His well-trimmed beard was black at the bottom but curiously changed to snow white along his jaw line and sideburns, then back to black at the top of his head. He glanced around the open room. "She's not here?"

"I'm afraid not," I said. "Are you sure Jacquie didn't have plans? Breakfast with a friend? Some kind of spa treatment?"

Veronica frowned at me. "I would have known about anything like that."

Somewhat bashfully, Professor Maxwell asked, "You're not hiding her here? That silly thing about not seeing the bride on the wedding day?"

"I'm afraid not," I said. "Have you notified the police?"

"No!" cried Veronica.

We all looked at her.

"Not yet. It's her wedding day. I'll admit that it's usually the groom who takes a runner, but maybe she has cold feet. Maybe she just needs a breather before everything gets underway."

Professor Maxwell gazed at her silently. "Perhaps you're right. DuBois, did you hear anything in the night?"

"No. But someone had turned off the alarm system before I rose this morning," said Mr. DuBois.

"Must have been Jacquie." Professor Maxwell turned to look at my clock collection. "We'll give her two hours. If she hasn't called or turned up, then we'll go to the police."

I wondered if he was thinking about Jacquie's previous disappearance. Jacquie was Jacqueline Liebhaber, the well-known romance and women's fiction author. Ultimately, her previous disappearance had been the event that brought Jacquie and John together again. That time she had been missing for days. Her agent had been so worried that she hired a private detective to find Jacquie. The fact that she had vanished before was concerning yet something of a relief as well. It worried me because I hated to imagine that she had a change of heart about the professor and was now an aging runaway bride. He would be devastated. On the other hand, I was comforted by the notion that she had most likely left on her own and hadn't been kidnapped. She could have at least told one of us so we wouldn't worry all day, wondering if we should cancel the wedding.

I nodded and hoped I sounded reassuring when I said, "I bet she turns up."

Professor Maxwell stiffened. "I'm going out to look for her."

"I shall stay by the phone in case she calls," said Mr. DuBois, holding up a wireless landline phone as though it were proof of his intentions.

The minute the professor was gone, Mr. DuBois said, "I'll bring coffee over.

Half an hour later, he rolled a serving cart into the carriage house. *Coffee* turned out to include croissants and eggs Benedict, and a fruit salad in jewel tones. The reds, oranges, and greens glistened under a sauce.

Veronica vaulted toward the table and picked up a croissant. "Oh my! Does the professor eat like this every day?"

Mr. DuBois tsked at her. "Did you think I serve him boxed cereal in cold milk?" He busied himself, placing a covered plate in my oven.

For a moment she appeared chastened, but her humor returned quickly. "How the other half live, eh?"

The three of us sat down to eat. Even though I was busy being indulged, I noticed that Mr. DuBois wasn't eating.

"I, um, may have notified the police," he said quietly. "Sort of. Not really. Not officially, you understand."

Veronica choked on her breakfast. In between coughs, she croaked, "You didn't! You know how they feel about the press. If they get wind of this . . ."

Mr. DuBois poured more coffee for her.

Normally a missed bride wouldn't be of much interest to anyone outside of the families and friends involved. But Jacquie's books sold worldwide. In addition to that, she had been Professor Maxwell's second wife.

They had one child, a girl named Caroline, who had been kidnapped at a young age and never found. The loss of Caroline had worked its way between them with Jacquie pursuing psychics and the professor partaking in wild adventures, all of which eventually led to divorce. It wasn't surprising that the remarriage of two such high profile figures had generated interest in them and their missing daughter once again.

"How would one unofficially notify the police?" I asked.

"One might have phoned a friend on the police force," he said.

Veronica's eyes grew large. "Florrie and I aren't properly dressed yet!" She jumped to her feet, but it was too late. Someone rapped on the door.

I tightened the sash on my own bathrobe of flowing silk the rich color of red plums, a gift from my parents. I peered out the window in the door. "I believe your police contact has arrived, Mr. DuBois. Relax, Veronica. It's Eric."

I opened the door and smiled at him. He planted a quick kiss on my lips, the polite sort employed in the presence of others. But the grin on his face told me how happy he was to see me.

I could feel a flush rising up my cheeks. I was a bookish type, perfectly content to stay home with my tabby cat, Peaches. All I needed was a good mystery or my sketchpad where I drew pictures for my coloring books. I loathed bars, dance clubs, and other noisy places packed with writhing people trying to meet Mr. or Ms. Right.

Growing up I'd been called names like squirt, brains, and goody-two-shoes. I was the big sister, yet the smaller one. Veronica and I were only a couple of years apart in age, but we couldn't have been more different. Veronica had long slender legs, the kind short woman envied, and blond hair that she wore in a sassy cut. She was athletic and loved nothing more than a great party. She knew the trends, had always been popular everywhere she went, and frequented local bars and events.

The day I met Eric, I only dreamed that he might be interested in someone like me. His eyes were a bright cornflower blue, and his sandy hair fell in loose curls. He looked like the sun had kissed him, though I would never tell him that. It was an unbelievable stroke of good fortune that he had responded to my 911 call, and even more miraculous that he was as drawn to me as I was to him.

"I knocked at the kitchen door of the mansion," he said. "No one answered. I thought I might find Mr. DuBois over here."

Mr. Dubois rose to his feet. "Thank you for coming. I knew I could count on you."

Mr. DuBois fetched the covered plate from my oven and lifted the top. "Won't you join us?" He deftly set a fourth place at the table with the additional plate of eggs Benedict.

He had clearly been prepared for Eric's visit.

Eric greeted Veronica, and asked, "Has Jacquie turned up yet?"

"Not a sign of her."

We settled at the table again and Veronica whined in a stressed tone, "The professor said we should give her a couple of hours, but people will be arriving soon to set up."

"Do you have any reason to think she didn't go of her own free will?" asked Eric.

Mr. DuBois shook his head. "No. I suppose we should be thankful for that."

"Does she still have an apartment somewhere? Maybe she went there for some reason," suggested Eric.

Mr. DuBois sighed. "She moved into the mansion months ago. I believe she still owns her condo but has rented it to someone, so it's unlikely that she would have gone there."

"What about the underground passage between the carriage house and the mansion?" I asked.

"Maxwell checked it this morning," said Mr. DuBois. "She's not hiding there, either."

Veronica's phone rang. She almost dropped it in her haste to answer the call. The rest of us watched her expectantly.